Heysel

Other Stories

– a collection of short stories, articles and poems

by

Steve Wilson

CONTENTS

Senseless

It is the smell that alerts me, the aroma of apples reawakening those long-forgotten images of my youth. I can't, of course, say where the smell actually comes from, but it is an unmistakeable odour all the same.

In my mind, I am back in Preston, standing outside the little sandwich shop in the main street. I tried to go there as often as possible for my lunch, not for the sandwiches (good as they were) but for a slice of their home-baked apple pie. I still can't really say what it was about it that so attracted me – possibly the combination of the wafer thin melt-in-your-mouth pastry and the unsweetened tang of the natural apple, so unlike the mass-produced ones that were so sickly-sweet once you bit into them.

I lick my lips at the memory, but as I do so, I recall again the cat. I never can think of that apple pie smell without the image of the cat popping into my mind as well.

It had been a normal lunchtime, I was leaving the shop with my packed lunch when I heard a screeching of brakes on the main road directly behind me. I whirled round to see a car skidding to a halt, but, too late; the driver had been unable to avoid the cat that had run out into the road, and had driven right over the poor beast's head. I expected that to be the end of the matter, but suddenly, the cat leapt up, ran round and round two or three times in a very tight circle before dropping dead to the floor. I often wondered whether or not the cat had been dead all along, and if it had just been nerve responses that had caused its bizarre death dance.

The apple pie and the cat, the smell and the sight inextricably linked for me forever afterwards. Every time I see a cat, I remember the pie, and vice versa. It's strange how the mind works, and I start to think of how we all react to sensory inputs, often in the strangest manner.

The sound of music is one of the most evocative as far as I'm concerned. It takes me back to places I haven't visited for years – whenever I hear "America's" 'Horse with no Name' play, I'm back in my flat in Stafford, soaking in the bath while the radio in my room blares out the Sunday night top ten. Every loving couple is supposed to have 'their song', and I'm no exception, even though only the song remains now. The sound of Olivia Newton John singing "I Honestly Love You" brings the images of my true love before my eyes once again, along with tears of both joy and sadness. I hadn't heard that song in years until that party on my first night here, and as I heard the words I saw a vision of loveliness across the room and I knew that the song was telling my story.

A tear forms but I leave it there. Some people will misunderstand, of course, but I know that the tear is for her, not for me. I try to take my mind elsewhere, but it is difficult. The five senses dominate my thoughts, and I can't control the memories that each one imparts.

When I think of taste, it's a little different. This time, apple pie doesn't invoke any particular feelings, as I hadn't actually eaten the pie when the cat was killed. But thinking of sounds has set my mind working in its own special way, and another taste does bring to mind a vivid memory. It is the taste of fresh strawberries, eaten directly from the plant. Again, it is a bittersweet taste, and a bittersweet memory.

It had been such a glorious day, ten long years ago, with my newfound love, on our first date after the party. We had seen a sign for 'Pick Your Own Fruit' and thought it might be a fun thing to do. And it had been, under the hot sun, popping one strawberry in the mouth for every two we put in the basket, the sticky juices running down our chins as we laughed out loud. Such simple pleasures, priceless memories. It was there that I claimed my first kiss, tasting at second hand those self-same strawberry flavours. How sweet it was, as our lips met, and how bitter it felt as I was pushed away when I tried to slide my tongue between those luscious lips.

The touch of her hand on my chest, the memory still sends a shiver down my spine.

After the initial surprise and shock, the pressure that forced me back on my heels in the strawberry fields felt delicious, because I realised what it was leading to. It was a game, of course, for she never really meant to stop me, and I knew it was so. Even her pretend struggles when I pushed her to the ground and 'forced' myself onto her were a part of it. I hadn't dared hope that she, like me, would relish rough love. It made me so happy.

A sound interrupts my reverie – an unwelcome one this time. It is the buzzer to indicate it is time, and it brings me back to my present predicament and full remembrance of why I am here, strapped to this table. Ironic, in view of what I've just been thinking about, but this is all down to a kind of sense as well – common sense, or rather a lack of it. I had, of course, strangled her in the fields, because it was how the game always ended, but I had been so caught up in the passion of the moment that I hadn't the sense to remember that we were in full view of everybody; carried away by my passion, I hadn't thought to wait until we were alone.

Of course, if I'd chosen a state that didn't still execute its criminals, I would soon be eligible for parole – though after what had been said about me, I would stand little chance of release, so would a ninety-nine year jail sentence have been any the better?

I've already served ten waiting for this day. But now the sound of the buzzer reminds me that my long wait is over, and suddenly ninety-nine years begins to look very tempting. I wonder whether there will be any pain or will it just be like falling asleep. Instead, I feel another sensation, perhaps the last of all. It is the touch of the needles entering my body at various points, one of them containing the lethal cocktail of drugs that will make me, forever, senseless.

Web of Deceit

Roger Hewson sat at his desk, pondering what to do next as he looked at the screen of his laptop. In his early thirties, he lived alone in his tiny flat. There were no bright decorations to illuminate his room, which consisted of four yellowing woodchip walls and a brown stained rug covering two thirds of the floor.

That he lived alone was hardly a surprise, as he had spent much of his adult life as a guest "At Her Majesty's Pleasure", and the few friends that he did once endure the company of had long since abandoned him. Prison hadn't reformed him – rather, it had served to harden his hatred of those more fortunate than he - and in the long years inside, rather than use his above-average intelligence to prepare for a better life once released, he devoted his thoughts to developing the 'perfect' crime.

As a child he had learned at an early stage that it was more fun to pick on the weaker elements of the class than to study, and as a consequence he had failed to make anything of his years at school, as well as soon finding he was loathed by his classmates. While his single-sex senior school colleagues departed for further education, he used his brains to develop scams whereby he could separate the many older people who lived in his town from their pensions. Unfortunately for Hewson, he always made at least one mistake that led the police to his doorstep. Instead of acknowledging that he was to blame for his current situation, he chose to blame others for his problems, always coming back to his unhappy schooldays. He considered elaborate ways of getting revenge, always discarding each idea as cowardice was one of the more dominant of his traits. But now, as he sat staring at the screen, a dark, damp stain spreading from his armpits, a sly smile touched his lips.

#

Although not computer literate, he had learnt the basics whilst serving his latest stretch. Overhearing two people discussing a website that allowed people to contact their former school friends, he had seen his opportunity. There was one girl in particular, a mousy little thing, but he had quite liked her. She had rebuffed him though, a cruel blow to his young and fragile self-esteem, one that had probably set him on the track to where he now was, for he still recalled the laughter of his classmates when he was turned down, and the anger that he felt as a result.

The only problem was – he couldn't remember her name. If only he could, perhaps he could contact her and try and form a friendship and arrange a meeting – and then, when she trusted him completely and least expected it, he would exert the ultimate control as he throttled the life from her. He grinned as he imagined leaning over while she gasped her final breath. And this time he wouldn't be caught, he would plan the event, take his time and ensure that he had removed anything that could be traced back to him before he committed the act.

He began by visiting his local computer store, where he purchased a very basic laptop, and once back home he quickly located the website. "It will be a case of 'Fiends Reunited' if I have my way," he chuckled to himself, pleased at his ability to pun with such ease.

He typed in the name of his old junior school, and was amazed to see a list of more than a dozen pupils with whom he had shared his formative years. Some names were instantly recognisable, others only vaguely so, a few he didn't remember at all, but one caught his attention immediately – Issy Venables.

His next step took him some time, though, for he was reluctant at first to register on the site under his own name – that could immediately lead the police back to him. His first thought was to use a false name, but he realised that nobody would recognise it, and consequently nobody would be likely to respond to any contact that he made. There were one or two names from his schooldays that he did remember and that *weren't* on the list, but he knew nothing about them now. He considered pretending to be one of them, but then thought that it would only take the slightest of errors on his part to unmask him – his chosen alter-ego might even be dead by now, after all. Despite wracking his brain, he was unable to think of a way round his dilemma, and finally he took the plunge and made the registration as himself, knowing he would have to extend his plan to include removal of all traces that could lead back to him.

But, registration made, he was once again viewing the list of names on his screen.

#

"So Miss Venables," he muttered to himself, mimicking the tone that the teacher always used when addressing the girls, "I think it's about time we got in touch again, don't you?"

He thought once more about the young Issy. He remembered her as being a very slight girl, friendless like himself, and with an obsessive interest in the television soap "Coronation Street" – that, allied to her initials, probably led to her derisive nickname of 'Ivy', who he remembered as one of the less pleasant cast members of the programme. The thought sparked a new memory, of constant tears as he led the rest of the class in chanting, "Ivy, Ivy" at her each and every playtime while her television character was involved in a key storyline concerning a love triangle. That was after she'd rejected him, of course. Nobody stood up for her at all, and he smiled at the recollection. He wanted an easy victim, one who wouldn't put up much of a struggle, one with no friends to come to her aid.

Just for a second, he frowned – something didn't seem quite right somehow. From what he had just remembered, he found it hard to imagine *that girl* ever wanting to have a reunion and joining such a site, but he quickly shrugged the feeling off. People changed, and this was all a long time ago. Of course, for all he knew, Issy could have *really* changed – perhaps grown into a formidable woman, or become the life and soul of the town's social life. If so, he was quite prepared – leave well alone, and bide his time while he conceived another plan. He was in no hurry; the anticipation was possibly more delightful than the actual execution ever would be.

He clicked the button that allowed him to compose an email to his former classmate and began to type the introduction that he hoped would lead to the fulfilment of his aims:

Hi Issy,

I don't know if you'll still remember me after all of these years, but we were at junior school together – in fact I think we might have sat together. I was the one who was always getting into trouble for talking in Miss Watson's class – wasn't she strict!

I'm trying to get in touch again with all of my old schoolmates to see how they are doing, as I have a colleague in the media business who has suggested making a television programme about a school reunion, to relive the old times and to see how everyone has progressed. Talking of television, what about Corrie recently eh? Still as gripping as ever!

Would you be interested in getting in touch so we could discuss this? Even if not, I'd still love to know how you're keeping.

Hope to hear from you soon,

Your old classmate

Roger

He checked over what he had typed, hoping that it would be just enough to snare her interest, and that she wouldn't remember that he *never* sat with her at school. He couldn't think of anything more to add that would help, so he clicked the *Send* button, and the communication was on its way.

He could hardly wait for the next evening so that he could check his responses, but when he connected to the Internet, there were no messages for him. "Perhaps she only uses her computer at weekends," he thought, trying to keep his hopes alive, but when he had still received nothing three nights later, he had to accept that he wasn't going to succeed after all.

He went on to the site to look for another victim, but none of the names stood out in the way Issy's had. He was about to give up when his pc 'beeped' to indicate the arrival of a new message, and he rushed to check his emails. It was from the website, to let him know that he had received a reply to his original message!

He found it hard to describe the feeling of elation as he clicked on the *Messages* button and saw Issy's reply:

Hello Roger,

How lovely to hear from you after all these years. Of <u>course</u> I remember you – better than you remember me it seems! We didn't sit together, by the way, but I used to wish that we did. In fact, I've thought about you many times over the years. I'm not sure I want to get involved in any television programme, though – but I'd love to catch up with you to see what you've done with yourself. I hope that's okay with you?

Love Issy

xxx

"Of course it's okay with me – it's *exactly* what I want," he muttered to himself as he began to compose his reply.

Emails passed between Roger and Issy on a regular basis over the next few days. Roger sent her his private email address, and they gradually began communicating without their messages going via the website – ostensibly, according to Roger, "to avoid some problems that I'm having logging on to the site" but actually to try and ensure that there would be little linking the two of them together once he had accomplished his deed.

From his questioning, he managed to find out that Issy was still single and lived alone. She had only worked at irregular periods since leaving school, and she didn't keep in touch with anybody from her past. She had no job currently, and kept herself to herself.

Roger's elation grew with each response that he received from her – it couldn't have been more perfect if he had written the specification for his 'ideal victim' himself. Although they didn't divulge their addresses, they told each other the general districts where they lived, and found that they were just a few miles apart.

She sent him a recent photograph, a mousy, thin bespectacled girl who looked as if a summer's breeze would knock her to the ground. For a moment, just a slight instant, he felt those stirrings of old once again – although only seven years old, he really *had* liked her. But he forced those thoughts into the deep recesses of his mind.

After some thought, he sent her a photograph of himself, knowing he needed to be as open as he possibly could at this stage if he were to gain her trust. He thought he was reasonably attractive for his age, and hoped that the picture hadn't put her off, but he still felt uncomfortable until he saw a new mail message from her waiting for him.

One lie that he did tell concerned his marital status. He told her that he was married, but unhappily. He begged her to keep their communications a secret, as he dreaded what would happen if his vindictive wife found out what he was doing. Again, he agonised over whether or not to go down this course, as she could drop all contact if she thought he was married, but once again, she continued to reply to him, offering great sympathy for his situation and agreeing immediately to his request for secrecy. Once again, Roger could hardly believe how easy it was all turning out to be.

He did become a little frustrated at how much time it was taking to make any real progress towards his eventual aim, with the norm being just one email a day passing between them. It was Issy herself who provided the solution to this, as she, too, was apparently anxious to proceed to the next level. She suggested they use one of the messenger services, and after explaining to Roger how to go about downloading a suitable provider, he registered himself on the site under the nickname of 'TheDodger' and logged on to wait for her alias 'Hollyanthe' – a nice joke at her own expense, he thought - to come on-line.

He didn't have to wait more than a few minutes before his computer beeped to let him know that he had received a message:

Hollyanthe: Hi – at last we can talk to each other - it's almost as good as meeting up.

An evil grin lit up Roger's face – the stupid girl had already brought the idea of an actual meeting into play, making it so much easier for him. He typed in his reply and began a conversation that he felt could have been taking place face to face – although she would only see the image he was presenting via his keyboard.

The Dodger: Yes, it's great to be able to communicate quickly. Email is ok, but when it takes two days to get a reply, you lose the thread a little.

Hollyanthe: I know – it's frustrating. There are loads of things I want to ask you, and I haven't felt able to – before now, that is.

As they 'spoke' Roger pretended an interest in everything that Issy talked about, hoping that it would lead towards his next goal. He wasn't to be disappointed. Issy was an avid fan of several American television series, keeping up-to-date with the plotline by downloading new episodes off the Internet the day after they were aired in America. As he questioned her about this process, he saw that the chance he had been looking for had opened up. All he needed was to make the correct responses, and he'd be home and dry.

TheDodger: Can anyone download these episodes?

Hollyanthe: Yes, any1. I can tell you how to do it in moments. But, you should only try it if you have a fast connection – you do have broadband, don't you?

He thought for a moment before replying, deciding to lie as he saw a way of moving quickly towards his ultimate goal.

TheDodger: No, I've only got dial-up – I need to change ISPs!

He wasn't to be disappointed, as his computer displayed her latest missive:

Hollyanthe: I could copy the files onto a CD and post it to you, but my CD writer isn't working properly. Do you mind if I make a suggestion?

TheDodger: No, of course not.

Hollyanthe: I've got a memory stick and can copy the files on to it. I can't send it to you through the post, but if you've got a laptop I could put it directly on there.

Roger paused for a moment before sending his reply, his hands shaking as he touched the keys.

TheDodger: Yes, I do have a laptop, but wouldn't we have to meet to do that?

Hollyanthe: Yes, but I want to meet you anyway if that's okay?

He couldn't believe how easy it had been – and *she* had been the one to make the suggestion. The only problem he now had was that he didn't want to be seen in the vicinity of her house, but she even supplied the answer to this dilemma for him.

Hollyanthe: We could meet tonight if you like. I'm checking in on a former workmate's house while she's away in London for a few days sorting things out for her new job. I can give you the address if you want and then see you there around 7? Don't forget to bring your laptop!

Just for a moment, he felt uneasy – had she told her workmate about him? He thought for a moment before composing his response:

TheDodger: So you've been telling your friends all about us have you?

Hollyanthe: No – course not! This is private – besides, I don't know her that well, I just happen to live fairly close to her.

Satisfied, he leaned back in his chair, a look of contentment on his face. Everything was all set now.

#

Three hours later, dressed in his best suit, he stood outside the front door of the address that she had given him – the house had been easy to find, as she'd told him to look for the only one with a 'For Sale' notice in the garden. He looked all around the quiet streets to ensure that nobody was watching before ringing the doorbell with his gloved hand. He knew that he would have to take his gloves off inside, but he would take care about what he touched and wipe any prints away afterwards.

Issy opened the door, looking if anything even more wretched than she had in her photograph as she wore a shapeless dress that totally hid any semblance of womanhood, but she became instantly attractive as she greeted him with a smile.

"You look even better than in your photograph," she said, and he muttered something similar in response, caught off guard by her comment. Just for a moment, he wondered if there could possibly be *something* between them, but only for a moment – the anticipation of what he would do to this mousy girl outweighed any thoughts of a romantic liaison with her. Besides, she was so pathetic looking – he wouldn't want to be seen dead with her. He chuckled, though, at the thought that she would soon be seen dead *by* him!

"What's so funny?" she asked, a slight look of concern on her face.

"Oh, nothing, nothing – I was just surprised at what you said. Nobody has ever complimented my looks before, and I didn't quite know what to do," he spluttered in reply, chiding himself for letting his control slip and perhaps putting her on alert. But the smile she gave him in return was enough to reassure him.

She took his laptop away so she could copy the files from her memory stick, which Roger noticed protruding from the back of her machine, and the last piece fell into place as far as he was concerned. After she was dead, he would take her laptop away and not have to worry about anybody ever finding his emails and linking the two of them together.

"It'll take a few minutes to do the copy," she said as she came back into the room, "I'll just put the kettle on and make a drink while we wait. Tea or coffee?"

"Tea, please," he replied, enjoying the ordinariness of it all. The knowledge of what he was about to do to disrupt the normality only served to add to his sense of anticipation. While she was in the kitchen, he chatted a little and managed to confirm that she had kept their entire relationship a secret.

"Anyway, there isn't anybody I could tell about it even if I wanted to," she said. Before he could reply, she put her hand to her head and uttered an exclamation of annoyance with herself. "Oh, what an idiot – I didn't bring any milk. Perhaps there's some left here." She went to the fridge and checked, bringing out a bottle. She raised it to take a sniff, and then said, "I think it's fresh enough – I thought it might have been off as they've been away a few days."

She brought his tea over and sat down opposite him. For a few moments, there was an uneasy quiet between the two of them, and Roger was transported back to his schooldays, and how he had felt about her. But now it was different – this time she was smiling coyly back at him, and he wondered again whether he could really go through with his diabolical plan. Perhaps there could be a romantic future for him after all? He allowed himself to daydream of how their life together could be as he raised the cup to his lips.

He took a sip of the tea, and screwed his face up at the sour taste. He put the cup down, trying not to let her see that he found it tasted awful. The incident served to harden his resolve, and finally drive away any thoughts of mercy that he'd been entertaining. No wonder she lived alone – what man would ever want her if she couldn't even make a cup of tea without noticing that the milk was off?

He realised that she was talking, and he turned to look at her to catch what she was saying.

"..always secretly liked you. I just never thought you'd ever noticed me – most boys didn't."

"Oh yes," he responded, taking his cue, "I always noticed you. I was just too shy to do anything about it, though." Funny, though, he thought, she doesn't even remember *she* rejected *me* – or she hopes I've forgotten!

The television was on in the background, and the familiar music from "Coronation Street" began to play. With a "tut", Issy stood up and walked to the set, turning it off. "I can't stand that programme," she said to explain her actions.

"You've changed your tune – you used to be obsessed with it." Roger was beginning to feel a little unwell. It was very hot in the room, although he couldn't see a fire, and he loosened his collar. Issy was staring at him with a strange look on her face – she was smiling, but it was no longer the coy grin she had greeted him with earlier. This time, the smile was filled with satisfaction.

"No I didn't – I hated it. I said right at the start that you didn't remember me that well at all! You're thinking of Deirdre Vernon – now she really was obsessed. Don't you remember – we called her 'Dreary Deirdre' and used to chase her at playtime when the *Deirdre – Ken – Mike* love triangle was being shown. You used to fancy her but she turned you down – I nearly peed myself laughing at your face *that* afternoon"

And suddenly he did remember. How could he have got it wrong? *Deirdre* was the weak little crybaby, not Issy. So why had he thought it was 'Ivy' – and the memory returned in full, but too late. Vernon and Venables – the girls had sat next to each other at school. Ivy *was* taunted at playtime, but because of some incident in cooking class – one of the boys had been very ill after eating some bread that she'd baked and he had led the rest of the class in the taunts as they called her "Poison Ivy".

He looked at her, unable to hide the horror and revulsion in his eyes, but he found it difficult to focus. She seemed blurred and far away as she spoke to him again.

"Yes," she said, "I can see you remember me now. You made my life hell, and yet I did nothing wrong. It *was* an accident, but I've never been able to live it down. I couldn't believe my good luck when you contacted me. I took a few days to check you out before replying, and I've planned this very carefully. I've been watchful about what to touch so I can remove any prints afterwards, and nobody knows I'm here tonight – I stole the key from an estate agent, while I was looking around flats, and they never even noticed. In fact, I think I'll leave it with you as I leave."

Roger tried to rise but he couldn't make his limbs move. With an effort, he was able to turn his head to watch Issy as she walked around the room with a cloth in her hand, wiping all of the surfaces that had been touched.

"It was so good of you to keep our little affair secret. Especially from that non-existent wife of yours – I told you I've been checking. You don't *really* think I could ever fancy a loser like you, do you? I was just keeping you interested while the poison in the tea got to work – I checked on the Internet, and one sip is enough, so it doesn't matter about the taste. And thanks for bringing the laptop round, so I can delete all evidence of our correspondence. It's been a long wait, but revenge *does* taste sweet. Don't you think I've been very clever?"

But Roger never uttered a word in reply. He was dead.

What If?

Rachel Aarons left her lab at the TTA (Time Travel Authority Ltd) buildings, eager to get to her grandparents' home. She hadn't seen them since their return from Central Europe, where they had been researching the family's ancestry. When her grandfather had telephoned her that morning, all he'd said was that he wanted to see her. He had sounded a little withdrawn – strained, even - and consequently, she had found it difficult to concentrate on her roll with the time portal all day. As her navigation system guided her auto through the busy suburban streets, her mind replayed the unpleasant episode with Senior Technician Matthews earlier that afternoon:

"Aarons, what do you think you are doing?" he had yelled as she had been about to close the contact and activate the portal while fellow technician Bob Simmonds was still in the process of affixing his harness. "Are you trying to kill him - and the project as well?"

"Sorry sir, of course not" she had stammered, not knowing what more she could say. The problems currently encountered by the TTA were well known to all. Senior politicians were constantly asking why such huge resources were being ploughed into the venture, especially when nothing concrete had yet been seen from the billions of dollars invested over the past decade. And when you took into account the fatalities from earlier attempts, it was no surprise that all the polls showed that the public, too, were beginning to question the wisdom of such an undertaking.

Rachel cursed herself silently for her stupid mistake. They were so close to unveiling a working model, one that would allow a traveller to view any time period in history. The current tests were expected to eliminate the last remaining problem, the ghosting effect, and then the huge investments made would be seen to be well spent. And she had nearly ruined it all by failing to concentrate on her task. "Damn you, grandpa Danielson," she muttered under her breath, "why did you have to be so enigmatic this morning? If you'd told me what you'd found, bad news or not, I would have been able to accept it and move on." But he hadn't, and she hadn't.

The subject of time travel had been at the forefront of public interest for more than a century, with endless books and videos on the topic. In her opinion, none could better the nineteenth century Wells' story "The Time Machine", as it at least tried to apply *some* scientific principles to the journey, even though the spatial rules that affected the movement of the Universe were more-or-less ignored.

Wells' offering appeared half a dozen years after Twain had written "A Connecticut Yankee in King Arthur's Court", a good story in her opinion, but bereft of scientific fact and relying on the fantastic method of a hammer blow sending the hero backwards through time.! But Twain's story showed how history could be altered by somebody travelling into the past, and had set scientists arguing incessantly ever after about whether or not the past could be changed.

Of course, if it ever *were* to be changed, nobody would ever know, as every point of time forward would also have changed to fit with the new reality, and that, too, had set the scientists into endless discussions - not least in the conclusion that the past might well have been changed, but the 'now' that would have resulted from the change would bear no witness to the pre-change history. Just one of the many paradoxes surrounding time travel.

The so-called *grandfather paradox*, as described in Barjavel's "Le Voyageur Imprudent", suggested a person could theoretically travel back in time and kill their own grandfather before he had met their grandmother, thus preventing the time traveller's future birth – and therefore preventing the time traveller from growing up to become the time traveller who travelled back to commit the deed! Even now, after all that she had learnt, Rachel's head ached as she tried to come to terms with *that* paradox.

The concept of future time travel had been accepted ever since Einstein's relativity theory gave it credence. The example most often used was of a journey at almost the speed of light to a distant star, with the spaceship slowing down, turning around and returning to Earth, again at velocities approaching light-speed. The traveller would arrive back on Earth after a journey – to the astronaut – of just a few years, yet thousands of years would have passed on Earth, so in effect, the astronaut would have travelled into their own future.

But to travel into the past – great scientists such as Hawking had 'proved' that it was impossible. Rachel smiled to herself as her motor navigated a particularly congested junction, wondering what they would be saying if they were alive now that time travel to the past *was* available. Einstein's equations allowed for warps in space and time commonly known as wormholes, and the basic reasoning behind a traversable wormhole involved one end of the wormhole, or portal, being accelerated to light speed before being brought back to its original point – similar to the scenario for travel to the future. The difference now was that the end of the wormhole that had been accelerated would have aged with respect to the stationary end, and somebody entering at the accelerated end could – in theory – exit at the static end in the past.

This had remained theoretical, with the added disadvantage that it was believed that the date of initial creation of such a device was the furthest back in time that could be reached, as this would be the date of the static end of the wormhole, meaning that time travel to view the dinosaurs or the life of Jesus would only ever be a fantasy.

The auto pulled to a stop and Rachel saw that she had arrived at her destination. "You were so nearly there, Mr Hawking," she thought to herself as she walked up the pebbled drive, "but you hadn't counted on twenty-first century technology, and Arnold's discovery that if a traveller was inside the wormhole when the acceleration process began, they would move in line with the wormhole, resulting in the accelerated end becoming static and the original static end now flowing back in time with no limits whatsoever. All it took was a technician to operate the portal and the process could commence – and that, of course, had been where she'd made her mistake hours earlier, when she hadn't checked that Simmonds was secured inside the wormhole before she pressed the button. She'd been lucky that sickness had decimated the team, otherwise she'd have been thrown off the project for such an error.

As it was, she was still in there – "by the skin of her teeth" as Matthews put it, though she always wondered *exactly* what that was supposed to mean. She was on the schedule still for her own exploratory trip into the distant past – a time before man walked the earth - in one of the final tests before the portal was announced to a public unaware of what they were about to receive. She had been fully briefed on her role – time travel to the past was as an observer only, as Arnold's discovery hadn't extended as far as allowing a physical presence into the past. But that was good anyway, for it instantly put an end to all of the paradoxes that the news headline writers would have concentrated on. All they needed to do now was to eliminate the ghostly echo that allowed sounds from inside the portal to reach through to the past and they could begin to visit populated time zones.

#

Rachel's grandfather, Joseph, opened the door, and as soon as she saw the look of grief on his face, all thoughts about her work were driven from her mind. "Grandfather, what's wrong?" she cried.

"Hush, dear, calm yourself. Come inside and we'll tell you all about it." He took her hand and led her into the small front room where her grandmother Rebecca sat, a look of despair on her wrinkled face. Rachel took the chair that was offered and awaited the explanation.

"As you know," began her grandfather, "we have been researching the Danielson family bloodline while we've been away. Unfortunately, what we have discovered made us wish we had never embarked on this quest. Did you know that your – our – ancestors originated from a country called Poland, now part of Central Europe?"

"No, I didn't - all I know that we have been here in the States for the last hundred years or so."

"Yes, we've been here for a long time – this used to be called the USA, though I forget what that stood for. But my grandparents arrived here from Poland at the end of a very dark time for our people. And that is what we went to research, to find out what forced them to leave, and what happened to the rest of the family. It makes for a terrible tale, and I don't think I could bear to repeat it all, but I will tell you the basic details. You've heard, of course, of Hitler and the Nazis?"

"Yes, of course, we covered that era in our studies. But that was a century ago, what has it to do with us?"

"Because Hitler led an invasion of Poland, and his people had one mission – to exterminate every last member of the Jewish faith. And our ancestors were of that faith. They were indiscriminately killed by Hitler's followers, and only a few escaped. My grandparents were amongst those few, but they were the lucky ones. Their parents and seven brothers and sisters, as well as uncles, aunts and cousins, they all perished in Auschwitz."

Rachel went cold. She remembered being told about Auschwitz, even though it had been many years since she had heard the name. It had been a place where terrible things had happened, even though she didn't know exactly what. She knew she had to ask the question, difficult as it was. "I know of Auschwitz, but not what happened there. How did our family die?"

Joseph shuddered as he recalled the investigations Rebecca and he had so recently undertaken. "We still don't know the full story – probably never will now, as some things weren't recorded. The Nazis kept records, but they weren't always complete. They had two types of camp – concentration camps and extermination camps. Those sent to concentration or labour camps were recorded, unless they were killed on arrival. Those sent to extermination camps weren't – they were just killed immediately. The Nazis wouldn't bother making records of those they were going to exterminate, they just noted those who were going to be forced to work for them, their 'inventory'. Searching those records we managed to find some members of the Danielson family – there could be no mistake, because they included detailed information about addresses, occupations, parents, spouses – anything that would help to identify their 'stock'."

He paused, and Rachel stood to help him as he appeared to be on the verge of collapse. "It's alright, I'm just a little tired," he said to both Rachel and Rebecca, who had paused from her silent weeping to look up at him. "I can continue now.

"We couldn't find all the records, as I said. Many Jews who didn't survive the selection process were exterminated on the spot, in huge gas chambers. That usually meant those over fifty, or under fourteen, or mothers of young children, because they weren't capable of slave labour. But we did find some records, and we were able to verify the names from the inventoried information. But that wasn't the worst of it, it was the other details that were so horrific."

"What details, grandpa", she asked, torn between not wanting to know and a desperation to find out. "What was so awful, I, I can't remember what they told us at school," she said in a stuttering, guilt-ridden voice. It had all seemed such a long time in the past, an event that didn't concern her, when she'd been taught about it. She wasn't interested in history then just science – how ironic, then, that now she was involved in history *because* of her science.

"It's just base details, dear", he said, trying to soothe her, "but it was the cold way that they were itemised, just like packets of tea in a store, that was the most hurtful. They were *people*, but not to the Nazis." Again, he paused, struggling to compose himself for a moment. "I'll just give you the figures, from the official archives of Auschwitz. They came from the original Glücks records, and we were able to view them on our travels. They show that more than 173,000 of our people were interred in Auschwitz between 1941 and 1944. More than 58,000 of them died of typhus. Many were executed – 'administrative executions' as they called them, mainly Polish Jews, but those from other nations as well. And that was just one of the camps. We didn't have the heart to research others, such as Belsen." He stopped, unable to carry on, and there was an uneasy silence for a few minutes."

"So why did you ring me grandpa?" Rachel asked, half anticipating the answer.

"Because I want you to stop it. We know you are in a position to make sure it never happened. I want you to go back in time and kill Hitler."

"But you know I can't, grandpa."

"Can't? Won't, you mean," Rebecca shouted, anger in her eyes. Rachel gasped – she had never seen this gentle woman agitated like this before.

"No, I mean *can't* – we can travel back in time, but we can't change events." But even as she said the words, she was wondering if perhaps she could?

Seeing the pensive look on her face, Joseph's hopes rose. "I know you'll do whatever you can. It's strange, really, during our research we came across an article from somebody called R.P. Nettlehorst. I'll read you the relevant passages:

> *'Many times I questioned the choices that lead to today; thankfully, questioning the choices of my life does not give me any chance to change them. Without a time machine, I am not granted the opportunity for making a different decision, and playing it out, and seeing whether it leads to a better outcome. ….*

> *'Here are some interesting what ifs. What if Hitler had died in the first attempt on his life, when in 1938 he missed being blown to bits by ten minutes, because he ended his speech uncharacteristically early? What was God thinking? Would the world wind up a better place, if Hitler died then? Or maybe if he had died of his childhood illnesses?'*

"When I read it, I felt sure we were being told what to do. *Without a time machine* it says – but we *do* have a time machine, and somebody who has access to it. Because of historical records, we know exactly where Hitler was at one particular time. I want you to go back and make sure he dies in that explosion".

He passed the article to Rachel, who read it with a growing interest. There was an extra paragraph that Joseph hadn't read out to her – *'But if we assume that this really is the best of all possible worlds, we have to assume any alternate scenario is actually worse than what happened.'* Rachel didn't believe the author was correct in his final assumption – how could the evils that Hitler was responsible for be better than any other scenario? Looking across at Joseph and Rebecca, still sobbing silently, she asked herself how their grief could possibly be any worse.

The big question remained, though - how could she make use of the portal when she knew that time travellers couldn't change events in the past? What was the idea that entered her mind seconds earlier, giving her a glimpse of an opportunity? She decided to articulate her thoughts in case the act of speaking the words would give substance to the thought.

"Changing the past by time travel isn't as simple as it might seem. Yes, we can travel to any point in the past, but all we are able to do is observe – nobody could step out and do anything to change events. So, for example, it wouldn't be possible to somehow make Hitler overrun by those ten minutes, causing him to be inside the building when the bomb went off. And even if it were possible to somehow influence those events, would it make much difference? At that point, his ideas were already well established. If he'd died, how could anybody be certain that Nazism would die with him?

"No, Hitler needs to die before he has the chance to become a leader and influence people. We are still working on some elements of time travel, which is why we can't visit any populated era. Our tests show that an impression of our visit is left behind – a sound, but not a physical presence – and I wonder if we can make use of that? It would have to be soon, though, because the technicians have found the cause and are confident of removing this discrepancy very shortly.

"The article gave me the idea - *if he had died of his childhood illnesses*. What If? Do we know enough about that period of his life to be able to identify a potential fatal illness? And if so, could I somehow ensure he *isn't* cured? I don't know how, yet, but let me think about it. Besides, after the numbers of our people who died of disease in those camps, it would be poetic justice. Let me go away and research."

She rose to leave, aware that in a matter of seconds she had changed completely from a loving granddaughter to a woman contemplating killing a child. For a second she hesitated – could she justify such an action, whatever the circumstances? But just one look at the hope-filled eyes of her grandmother sealed her resolve, and she was now totally committed to her act of murder.

#

She could hardly wait for her motor to return her to her apartment, where she straightaway switched her terminal on and set it the task of accessing the archives. It only took a matter of moments, for Hitler's life was one of those subjects that obsessed numerous writers, and details of his early life were plentiful. She scanned the reports, looking for something she could make use of. Hitler suffered from acute pulmonary tuberculosis in his mid-teens, but the articles couldn't agree whether or not this was fact or just an embellishment of a lesser illness. She couldn't risk the latter – she would only get one chance to deliver her death warrant, for the authorities would see that she had visited a time where people existed, and she would never be able to use the portal again. She looked at the articles again, and saw what she'd been looking for – Hitler had suffered from scarlet fever when he was about eight years old. She knew of this disease, and although it had now been eradicated, it wasn't that long ago that it was still a potential fatal disease.

She set her terminal on another task, researching scarlet fever, wondering what – if any - use she could make of this information. She saw that scarlet fever, or Scarlatina, was a deadly bacterial infection of childhood, symptoms being a very high fever and a unique red rash. Severe cases of the disease could result in kidney disease, pneumonia or meningitis – all potential killers. However, by the late nineteenth century, antibiotic treatment meant that the disease was rarely fatal. Then she saw the sentence that gave her a solution to her problem - *Scarlet fever used to be confused with the appropriately-named German Measles, rubella (Röteln / Rötheln in German) – the disease showing the same redness, but the disease being of lesser severity.* If she could somehow manage to effect a mis-diagnosis of rubella instead of scarlatina, it might result in the death of the child Hitler. It wasn't certain by any means, but unless she could think of a way of causing the wrong diagnosis, it was all academic anyway. She fell asleep at her desk, her mind wrestling with the problem.

#

She awoke with a start – and with a possible solution. The field dampener that was expected to stop the sound leakage was in the final stages of testing. Once proven, it would be installed as a permanent immovable part of the portal, but whilst still in test mode, it was a temporary implementation. This meant that if she were in control of the portal, she could disable the dampener and have one attempt at influencing the mis-diagnosis. She didn't know if that would work or not, but she hoped that the superstitions of the time could work in her favour, and her supernatural prompting would be interpreted as a message from the gods.

Rachel was scheduled to use the portal that afternoon, along with Simmonds. She needed to prevent his travelling with her if she were to remove the dampener *and* reset the destination to 1897. Normally, two technicians were in the portal, but it wasn't unknown for single occupancy – yesterday, Simmonds had been on his own. She needed to get him out of the way, and she had a plan to prevent his joining her.

She was still refining the details as she made her way to the TTA lab. Her trip was scheduled for three hours' time, at noon. As with most workers, they would have a mid-morning drink breaks, and that was when she would empty a small phial of powder into Simmonds' mug of coffee.

#

Coffee break over, the final preparations for the next test of the portal were under way. Simmonds put his hand to his mouth and stifled a yawn, and Rachel seized her opportunity.

"Feeling tired, Bob?"

"Yes, I am rather – it's just come on in the last few minutes."

"What were you up to last night, you old rascal?" she asked with a laugh, and Bob smiled back in response.

"Nothing like *that*, you know I'm a boring married man! I don't know why I should feel so tired, but …". He couldn't finish, as this time his yawn refused to be stifled.

"Look, why don't you stay behind this time? After all, you went by yourself yesterday – and it will give you a chance to get your own back on me for almost sending you back before you were harnessed in."

Simmonds smiled back at her. "Yes, perhaps you're right. You'd better watch your back!"

Rachel smiled wistfully. She enjoyed the banter in the lab, and she'd miss it, but it didn't sway her from her intent at sabotaging the project. She climbed into the portal, and with another smile at Bob, she fastened her harness.

#

Travelling through time was a strange experience. For a few moments after the journey began, Rachel was caught up in the euphoria of the feeling before she remembered her purpose and unbuckled her harness. Although she was taking a risk by being unfettered, it was mainly at the initial and final stages of the journey that there was most danger. Disconnecting the dampener was a simple task, although it immediately set off a warning 'bleep' that Rachel knew would also be flashing back in the laboratory. Perhaps they would think this was just a malfunction, but once she altered the time co-ordinates, they would know she was sabotaging the mission.

As her fingers worked away at the console, she pictured Bob calling the rest of the team over, and their futile attempts to abort her mission. That was one of the possible problems with time travel, one of the objections that had been put forward – if something happened to the person controlling the portal, there was currently no means of bringing it back automatically. Developments to have an auto-return after a specified time were at the design stage, but the push to make this a commercial venture meant that the portal would likely be made available initially without that safeguard. Or perhaps it never would become available, thought Rachel guiltily, as she realised the probable repercussions of her actions.

She set the location co-ordinates for Lambach, Austria, which she believed to be the home of Hitler in 1897. This, of course, was where her task could fail before it began, as her limited research hadn't been able to identify the exact date at which Hitler suffered his illness. Fortunately, and perhaps ironically, she had as much time as she needed, so she had decided to target the Hitler household at the beginning of the year and move gradually forward looking for signs of infant illness.

All she had to do now was wait and see, and after a period of 'fast forwarding' through time in the bedroom, she saw what she took to be Hitler's parents arguing in front of a child – the young Adolf Hitler? – who was lying in bed. The boy had the typical symptoms of scarlet fever, with the reddish tinge to his features, but from the heated discussions, she could tell that there was dissent between the parents.

The woman (surely Hitler's mother?) was almost pleading with the man (his father?) and there was a hint of desperation in her voice.

"Alois - Er, ist krank, ich will nicht ein anderes Kind verlieren. Nennen Sie den Arzt". Rachel roughly translated what she had heard – it was something like *"He is ill, Alois, I don't want to lose another child. Call the physician".*

"Wir brauchen nicht einen Arzt. Klara, das ist nicht Ernst". Again, Rachel approximated the translation to *"We don't need a doctor. It isn't serious, Klara."*

Rachel knew for certain now that the couple were his parents, Alois and Klara. She sympathised with Klara, who lost four of her six children in childhood. Klara was talking again,

"Ich denke, dass es sein könnte, nennen Sie ihn bitte" - *"I think it might be, please call him."*

Alois looked at the young Adolf, then across at Klara, and appeared to be on the point of conceding the argument. Rachel knew that if she was going to act, she had to do it now, so she whispered the single word *Rötheln* in a low voice, hoping the whisper would carry to Alois alone. Alois had opened his mouth to speak, but then he stopped. "Tat Sie hören das, Klara" he asked - *"Did you hear that, Klara".*

"Nein, ich hörte nichts" - *"No, I heard nothing."*

For a moment, Alois seemed undecided, then he spoke with authority. "Es ist Röteln, es gibt kein Bedürfnis nach einem Arzt" - *"It is Röteln, there is no need for a doctor"* - and having spoken, he turned on his heels and left the room.

Was this the key point in time, or – if not - would she have a chance to try again? She adjusted the controls of the portal and moved forward in time, constantly watching the boy in the bed. She saw no sign of any doctor at first, just the mother by the bedside, but after a few days, a third person entered the room, carrying a black bag. She had failed, the doctor had come after all. But then she saw him turn to Klara and Rachel almost screamed with joy as she translated his words - "It is too late, you should have called me earlier". She had succeeded. At the same moment, Klara broke down, wailing hysterically, and Rachel was filled with extreme remorse – for all of the evils that Hitler would later perpetrate, his mother had done nothing to deserve the loss of yet another of her children. But at least it meant her own family, the Danielsons, would have a chance of life.

She didn't want to watch any more, so she adjusted the settings to return to the present time, prepared to face the consequences of her actions and content in the knowledge that she had done all she could to prevent the holocaust from occurring. But the controls wouldn't respond to her manipulations, and instead the days trickled slowly forward in the dying Adolf's bedroom.

She saw the same doctor visiting the young Adolf again, only this time as he left he covered the face with a sheet. Rachel tried again to make the controls work, but with no success. She looked up, and saw that she was still looking at the same room, yet it was very much changed. In the corner was an old fashioned television set, and above it was a calendar – it was showing 1942. She listened to the voice on the television, translating what she heard as best as she could: *'nations across Europe are beginning to question the influence of the Jewish community. If only there was somebody strong enough to stand against them'*. "No" she shouted, "you've got it all wrong. You have to live and work alongside each other, that's the only way. Intolerance leads to genocide." But there was nobody in the room to hear her echoed words.

Before her eyes, the scene changed, with much of the interior of the room altering. The television set in the corner was a larger version, and the calendar above it now read 1967. Again, the set was on, even though there was nobody present in the room – it was almost as if it were there for her benefit alone. The newscaster was reporting on *'clashes across many of the major cities of Europe, with soldiers of the National United European forces implementing martial law in London, Paris, Berlin, Warsaw and Budapest'*. Harrowing pictures accompanied the commentary, entire communities of people being forced into trucks by heavily armed soldiers sporting a cross with its arms bent emblazoned on their tunics. Rachel felt that she'd seen the symbol before, but couldn't remember where. "This isn't right at all", she said, "why is nobody opposing them? That isn't what happened." But she couldn't remember what *did* happen and why it felt so wrong.

She wasn't able to move any more, all she could do was look ahead as the scene changed once again. The calendar had gone now, but the television was a huge coloured screen. The pictures, though, didn't seem to have changed much, as thousands of people were being herded onto trains by soldiers wearing the exact same uniforms, although the newscast was now in a form of English. The people in custody now included many different groupings – black, white, and yellow, tall and short, young and old, with nobody seeming to be exempt from this treatment. The news bulletin moved on to show what appeared to be a coal mountain in the distance, but as the camera closed in, Rachel's eyes widened in horror as she realised it was a mountain of bodies.

The camera panned over the broken naked corpses piled high on each other, thousands on thousands of them, stopping here and there to linger on a particularly horror-stricken face as its owner realised their final moment of life had arrived. Rachel looked at one face in particular, as it seemed familiar to her – despite the look of anguish in the eyes, she thought she recognised it from an old photograph. A name seemed to go with the face, Joseph Danielson. But then the scene in front of her contracted, so that all she could see was the centre of the television screen. She was losing her hold on life, she knew, and the last thing she saw was an evil face on the screen, an ugly man with dark hair that slanted across his brow from right to left and with an almost comical toothbrush moustache below his nose. She felt great fear as everything went black, and she just heard one final phrase from the television before she ceased to exist – the newscaster was asking *What If?*

Unchangeable

It started about four months ago, late at night after a ve-e-ry long day at work. I put it down to tiredness then, and forgot about it. But when it happened again in the middle of the day, and then early in the morning, I knew I couldn't ignore it any more. Since then, it's happened so often that I think there's something wrong if I *don't* see the visions any more, and today....

But I'm getting ahead of myself. Perhaps you don't all know the full story? I know Doctor Wilkins has only just returned from astronomical 'research' in Hawaii – I'd love to know how you swung that one, Jennifer! And Professor Rogers, you are always so intent on research, Greg, I'm not sure you're aware of anything outside of that field. Anyway, you *might* not have heard the gossip. So humour me, let me tell you three something about myself – who knows, perhaps it might even help someone understand what's happened.

As you know, I'm Jack Trenton, and I used to be a software developer at the University. I was pretty good at my job, even if I have to say it myself, and I rose from a trainee to senior developer in less than ten years. I'm the guy who made the Virtual Reality – VR - breakthrough last year, bringing anyone's wildest dreams to life at practically zero cost thanks to a single implanted chip. Because of me, every household in the country can now live out their fantasies whenever and wherever they wish – though not everybody seems to want to thank me for it, but that's their problem. I developed it, I can't be held responsible for how people use it, can I? Is Henry Ford to blame every time some drunk gets behind the wheel and mows a bus queue down?

But that's just background, setting the scene if you like. After the big breakthrough, or VR Day as it's become known, my life changed, and instead of software development, I spent my time at meeting after interminable meeting, going to countless functions and openings to talk about – or defend - my discovery. Hell, I'm a coder, not a talker, this isn't me – you should have done that, Adams, but you left me to flounder. And the working days became endless. You know, it's strange in a way, because when I was writing the system, I'd be working all night without ever once feeling tired. Now, though, after a couple of hours of meetings I'm comatose.

It was after one of those day-long meetings that it first happened. Like I said, it had been *the* longest day, and I just wanted to get home to bed. I was walking back to my flat – I live in one of those roads with the garages round the back, to stop people parking in front of the houses and blocking the street. Only it doesn't work, because the residents dutifully park in the garages, but the uncaring public leave their cars in front of our houses while they do whatever it is they do. But that's a different battle, perhaps I'll be able to tell you how that goes someday, if only...

So, there I was, twenty yards from the flat, feeling in my pocket for the keys, when the door opened and somebody came out. No, not somebody – it was me. At least, it sure as damn looked like me, and if anybody knows what I look like, I think I do! And it wasn't night where the other 'me' was – it looked like morning. This 'me' was in some sort of a hurry, 'cos he rushed down the path and ran right past where I stood gawping at him as he booted an old tin-can out of the way.

I rubbed my eyes, and when I looked again everything was normal again, black as it should be at that hour. I was shocked, I'll admit, and after I managed to hold the keys steady enough to open the door to the flat, I poured myself a drink – okay, *several* drinks – before going to bed. And, of course, I overslept, so it was mid-morning by the time I woke up, and I'd missed the faculty morning meeting - so something good came out of it then. I washed, dressed and breakfasted in a hurry, and I ran down the street to the garage, booting an old tin-can out of the way as I went. Yes, Jennifer, I know it's obvious now, but be honest, would you have made anything of that without benefit of hindsight?

So I thought about what I'd 'seen' on the drive to work, and smiled at my stupidity. If anyone should know how VR can affect the mind, well I'd be the one, wouldn't I? Especially when you're tired. I convinced myself that was what happened and proceeded to forget all about it. And I managed to, at least for a few days.

Things returned to normal, attending meetings or running the gauntlet through demonstrations where VR was constantly being lambasted by the 'moral conscience' of our society – the sad busybodies. I became more and more frustrated by the role I had to fulfil – I kept telling you, Adams, but you took no notice.

It was at a meeting a week or so later, to discuss ways of making VR a more attractive proposition, that it happened again. For hours we'd been arguing about the public protests and I remember thinking that it was time to break, and hoping that you'd give it a rest for once so I could go for a much-needed liquid lunch.

But you went on and on, Adams, about who was to blame, so I leaned back and stared wistfully out of the window at those fortunate enough to be outside and free, when I saw an argument taking place by the front doors. And it was dark there, as if the sun had been obscured. But the sky was clear, not even a hint of wispy white cloud up above. I took another look at the front door, at the two people who seemed to be having a heated row, and – sorry to use this old cliché, but I can't think of a more appropriate description of the feeling – my blood froze in my veins. Even at a distance of fifty yards, there was no mistaking that the two combatants were myself and you, Adams!

I must have shouted out or something, because next thing I knew, everyone was gathered round me, seeing if I was alright. And when I looked back outside again, 'I' was no longer there, so I could tell them nothing, but I didn't half get some funny looks from my colleagues. One good thing did come out of it though, because the consensus was we needed a break for lunch. But that was only a temporary relief, for it wasn't long before we were back in the room again, continuing the meeting, and by the time we'd finished it was around midnight. Somebody once remarked how academics have an easy life, doing their ten hours a week and playing golf the rest of the time. I wish!

I was in a terrible mood as I hurried to leave, and I brushed past somebody without even noticing they were there. It was only as I pushed the door open that I felt a grab on my jacket, and I turned to see it was you, Adams, haranguing me for my failure to support you at the meeting. Now you know me, normally I'd have let it wash over me, but I'd had more than I could take that day, and so I let rip a tirade back at you.

And so it went on, for a couple of minutes, until I suddenly stopped in mid-sentence – I was doing what I'd seen myself do twelve hours earlier. And as I realised that, I remembered kicking the can in the street, and that, too, had happened twelve hours after I'd 'seen' it. Yes, Greg, I can see you'd have come to this conclusion much sooner, but I accept that your thought processes are swifter than mine.

You, Adams, must have thought I'd capitulated to your arguments, for you strode off with a look of triumph in your eyes, but I had far more important things to think about now. I've always had a scientific mind, so I tried to make rational sense of what had occurred, but I have to admit, this one had me beaten. But at least now I knew something about what was happening, and so I could be prepared the next time.

Unchangeable   23

I didn't have long to wait. A couple of mornings later, at the weekend, I had just showered and was towelling dry my hair when I saw 'myself' answering the phone. This time, I could listen in as well as view, and I heard myself arguing vehemently before yelling "Go to hell" and slamming the phone down agitatedly. Once again, I missed what happened next – some water trickled from my hair into my eyes, and instinctively I shut them as I dried my face. When I opened them again, there was nobody in the room but me – the 'now' me, not the future me.

I was edgy all day, waiting for the phone call that I knew would come about 7 pm. Sure enough, the phone rang and I replayed the scene I had witnessed that morning. It was you on the phone, Adams, telling me how you'd given my contact details to the press so they could talk to me directly about the harm VR was causing.

I was so angry that I forgot the scientific purpose of the moment. It was only when I'd shouted "Go to hell" and banged the phone down that I realised I had responded *exactly* as the 'other' me had that morning.

Since that day, the premonitions have come with increasing regularity. At first, I thought I'd been given a chance to change things, but it didn't take me long to realise that no matter how hard I tried, I couldn't alter what was going to happen. I know, Greg, it sounds ridiculous – surely if I saw myself turning left and saying 'black', I could turn right and say 'white', but believe me, I tried and I failed. What I'd seen in my premonition was what I did at the prescribed time, what I'd said then I uttered without being able to change even the inflection of a single syllable. Everything was unchangeable. Perhaps you can research this phenomenon? Maybe Jennifer could take you with her to Hawaii next time she goes? But I'm being facetious, I apologise, neither of *you* deserves this.

However ... my private life was no longer private, thanks to you Adams. Are you really so naïve that you believed the press when they said they wouldn't publish my address? I've had to face protestors outside my home every day since then, and my life has become unbearable. At the same time, more and more of these Future Reality visions occurred.

And so we come to today's FR vision – or two visions, actually. This morning, I saw myself in this room, with you three, telling you what I've just told you. This was the longest vision I've ever had – or will have, come to that - but it's nearly complete now. All that remains now is for me to put my hand in my pocket – like this – and take out the revolver I bought for protection after the protestors descended on my flat. Yes, you all gasped when I viewed this moment this morning.

Especially you, Adams, for you knew then, as you know now, that I'm going to kill you with one of my two bullets. The second bullet? Well that's the strange thing. My final vision, not half an hour ago, didn't include me. It was just a newspaper headline – "VR inventor kills himself after murdering colleague". A great loss, but as I said, it's unchangeable.

#

Two shots ring out, two seconds apart. After a moment's silence, a woman screams.

Christmas Time

"*Christmas Time, Mistletoe and Wine...*" With an angry flick of his wrist, Arnold Ledger turned the radio off. "I'm sick of hearing these damned Christmas songs day after day, it's still three weeks off and I've had enough of it already."

His wife, Sue, and the children Louise and Rachel in the backseat of the family Audi, said nothing – they knew better than to contradict their father when he was having one of his rants. He didn't like Christmas, he didn't like the numbers of cars on the roads, or the numbers of people in the shops. Truth was, it was hard to find something he did like. The three females in the car cast a quick glance at each other. Without saying a word, the message was clearly conveyed – it was going to be a miserable Christmas time again.

Sue couldn't, in fact, think of a time when Christmas *had* been fun – at least not since she had met Arnold, twenty-five years ago as a fifteen-year old. She'd hoped that once the children were born, fifteen and thirteen years ago respectively, things might change, but she'd soon found that to be a false hope. "*At least,*" she thought, "*while he's ranting about Christmas, he lets up on everything else*". Behind that thought was the knowledge that once the New Year came in, and until he could turn his attentions to Valentine's Day, Sue knew that she and the girls would once again become the subject of his bullying – both verbal and physical. She sighed deeply – life wasn't supposed to be like this. In fact, it was hardly worth living, and if it hadn't been for the girls, she might have considered ending it. She sighed again, her misery almost overwhelming her.

"What you sighing about woman? It's your bloody fault that we're stuck in this traffic. I don't know why you want to buy presents for that family of yours. Bunch of wasters, the lot of 'em. I blame that Dickens fella for all this rubbish – you're not telling me that Scrooge would have done a complete about turn just because he had a bad dream one night? But people are stupid, they believe it and so they think that Christmas is magical. Absolute twaddle – it's just an excuse to make people spend what they haven't got."

He carried on mumbling under his breath, but Sue wasn't listening. "*If only,*" she thought, "*if only something would shut him up. I can't put up with this much longer.*"

No sooner had she had the thought than he turned to her again. "And where do they think the money comes from, these no-good layabout relatives of yours? I graft all year to earn my money, and I don't do it just so you can squander it on that lot."

Sue had to clench her jaws closed to stop herself replying. '*Graft all year*' – he spent most of the year on the sick with his supposed bad back, and the money he 'earnt' usually found its way into the till of one or other of the local hostelries (although as he'd been barred from most of them for fighting, at the rate he was going he wouldn't find anywhere he could buy a drink by next Christmas). He only came with her on this shopping trip so he could exert his control over her spending. Even the girls couldn't look forwards to anything special on the big day - he was of the belief that children nowadays were spoilt, and as he'd got by with a colouring book, apple and orange without it affecting him, they would do the same.

The traffic was moving again now, and Arnold put his foot down to overtake a line of cars that wasn't travelling fast enough for him. He was about to launch another tirade at his wife when the steering wheel suddenly spun in his hands, and the car sped on in a direction other than the one he intended. His last view was of the lorry speeding towards him in the other lane, then there was an explosion of noise and blackness.

#

Sue opened her eyes and wondered what the bright lights were. She was lying down, but couldn't remember why. Then it all came back to her – the terror as she saw the lorry approaching, the screeching of tyres, rending of metal and breaking of glass. She vaguely recalled her forwards motion being stopped by the passenger-side airbag, and then, in a panic, she thought of Louise and Rachel. "My children," she cried, "my children."

"It's alright Mrs Ledger, they're fine – just a few cuts and bruises, nothing more. Now just rest." Sue turned her head to see a white-uniformed nurse smiling down at her, but she had a look of sadness in her eyes. Sue knew instantly from that look that Arnold was dead – she remembered seeing the steering column impaling itself in his chest as the vehicles impacted, and wondered why the airbag on his side hadn't inflated to save him. But she didn't feel sad – there was just a huge sense of relief. Her children were well and her life was her own again. She closed her eyes and drifted back to sleep.

#

She woke again and it was dark. Louise and Rachel were sat by the bed, looking fine apart from each having a plaster over their eyebrows. "Hi mum, how are you feeling?" asked Louise.

"The doctors say you'll be home for Christmas – there's nothing broken, the airbag prevented any serious damage," said Rachel. "Dad's dead, though," she added, quietly.

Sue closed her eyes again. She knew she should feel sad, but she didn't – what a terrible woman she must be. She could hear the sound of Christmas songs in the background, and felt an element of surprise that nobody was turning the radio off. She smiled as she thought that Christmas might be a pleasant one for once.

Louise and Rachel looked at each other, no words needing to be said. It had been an enormous gamble, loosening the steering wheel and disabling the driver's side airbag, but it had been worthwhile. Even if they'd been killed, at least the abuse would have ceased. Both girls smiled, as in the background the music played. "*Christmas Time, Mistletoe and Wine, Children Singing Christian Rhyme...*"

Time to Reflect

It had been a tiring day, and Kurt Hauptmann was ready for home. He glanced out of the open office window at the heavy black clouds and wondered if he'd be able to make it back to Angie before the storm broke. *Most certainly not,* he thought, *I'm going to be caught up in the worst of it.*

The journey from the Embassy HQ at Ferdowsi Avenue to the Tajrish district in the north of the city always took an age at this time of evening, and as the first rumblings of thunder sounded, Kurt resigned himself to a slow unpleasant journey home. *I hope I'm in before she puts the twins to bed,* he thought, leaning forward to switch off the monitoring device on his desk. As his finger brushed the button, he heard a faint noise behind him, and instinctively half-turned in his chair to see what had caused it. At the same time, a bolt of lightning shot through the window and struck the monitor just as Kurt's finger touched it. There was a blinding flash of light, and Kurt was thrown backwards off his chair.

\#

Kurt found himself lying on the floor, but he couldn't make out the surroundings as bright flashes were dancing across his eyelids. *What on earth was that?* he wondered as he rubbed his eyes to try and refocus them. And it had suddenly become much cooler, had the storm broken that quickly?

A door burst open and Kurt heard many booted feet charging in. His eyesight finally returned just as several pairs of hands grabbed him, and he heard a rough voice shouting, "Here's another of the krauts – well this one will wish his mother had kept her legs shut." Before he had a chance to speak, his body shook with the blows from dozens of fists and boots, and as the pain became unbearable, the blessed relief of unconsciousness came to his rescue.

\#

When Kurt came round, he thought his eyesight had failed again, as all he could see was a blinding light. He tried to move, but couldn't, and for a moment he didn't know where he was or what had happened. But then the pain returned, all over his body, and he remembered the beating he'd received.

"He's coming round," said a voice somewhere to the left of him, and when he involuntarily turned his head in that direction, he realised that he could see after all, although his field of vision had narrowed, as if his eyes were only partially open. The blinding light was an electric lamp, as he found when his head was yanked harshly back to face the yellow heat.

"Who said you could move, scum? That was your one and only warning."

Kurt was panic-stricken. *What the hell is going on?* He asked himself. *Am I having a nightmare?* But he knew he wasn't – the pains racking his body were all too real for it to be a dream.

"Tell us who sent you and what your part in the plot was," shouted a different voice, which appeared to come from directly behind the lamp.

"I don't know what you mean – who sent me where? I work here, in the communications department, just over .." A backhanded swipe sent Kurt and the chair flying across the room.

"None of your lies, Nazi. I asked you a question, now tell me the truth, else you'll be sorry."

Nazi? What sort of nightmare was this? Had the racists infiltrated the British Embassy? Kurt didn't know what to say – a mistake, he realised, as a punch thumped into his lip, splitting it and knocking out one of his front teeth. He spat blood out, then realised he'd better try and explain himself – but what was there to explain? "No, you d-don't understand," he stammered, "I'm Kurt Hauptmann, and I've worked here for three years. I was posted to Tehran along with Mr Saunders – just ask him, he'll confirm what I'm telling you."

"Saunders? Who the hell is Saunders? There's nobody of that name here. And if there was, and he vouched for you, a jerry, he'd be facing the firing squad alongside you."

Sweat poured off Kurt's face. Firing squad? Madness – what was happening? "I don't understand," he pleaded, desperation in his voice. "I was talking with Mr Saunders just half an hour ago, he told me to go home before the storm hit. I don't know what you're talking about, what you want."

Another thump to the face dislodged a second tooth, and his head was yanked up so it was facing the light again. "Don't know what we're talking about? Do you think we're stupid or something? Well let me remind you, shall I? You're part of a group who were plotting to kill Churchill here this week. We thought we'd got everybody, but then you turned up – what happened, did you lose your nerve at the last minute? Your plot failed, you know, von Ortel couldn't keep his mouth shut over a brandy, and our Russkie comrades got the information out of him. We know all about operation Long Jump, and that thug Scorzeny's plans to eliminate Churchill, Stalin and Roosevelt while they met here.

"When your radio operators parachuted into Qum, we knew they were coming. Every message they sent to Berlin after they came to Tehran was intercepted, and we've arrested everybody involved now. I can assure you, Churchill had a very happy birthday."

Kurt couldn't take it all in. Churchill? Stalin? Roosevelt? Was he involved in a war-game reconstruction? But they were never brutal like this. He did remember hearing about this Long Jump plot, though he didn't know the names that had been put to him. Was that part of the test, to see if he recognised them and gave something away? But he didn't recognise them, so did that mean he'd failed? Or passed? Utter madness.

#

Kurt's ordeal continued as the days passed. Because he couldn't tell his interrogators anything, he was systematically tortured, both physically and mentally. He still understood nothing about what was happening to him, about why it was happening to him. These people were acting as if it were 1943, reliving events that had occurred more than sixty years earlier. It was as if Germans were not part of the European Union, and were still at war with the world. That was two generations ago, Kurt hadn't even been born in Germany, he was from Stockholm. Why was he being treated like this?

As time passed, though, he began to realise that this was far too elaborate to be a hoax. He thought back to the events just before the nightmare had begun, to when the storm had been raging. It had been a normal summer's day, slightly warmer than usual but that was due to the storm. Now, though, it was positively chilly – it was more like early winter than high summer. Kurt tried to remember everything he could about the 1943 assassination attempt. It had come in late November – they'd referred to Churchill's birthday, and he thought he remembered that as being on the 30th.

The interrogation continued unabated. Every time he was about to fall asleep, ice cold water was thrown at him and he was dragged back to the interrogation room. After a few days of this, Kurt was ready to admit to any and everything, only now even if he admitted his part in the plot, they didn't believe him. He learnt that many people had been arrested on suspicion of being involved in the plot, but once the visit was over and the leaders had returned to their respective countries, they were released if they were deemed not to be a threat. Unfortunately, such considerations weren't given to Kurt, and his confinement continued.

After several months, Kurt was finally taken out of the holding area. He thought that sanity had prevailed, but in truth, his ordeal was about to get much worse, as he was handed over to the Iranian authorities. Bundled into the back of a van, he was conveyed at high speed to Evin Prison in the north of the city. Kurt could see the outside through the dirty barred windows, and he recognised some of the buildings as the van sped past them. Hardest to take was when his transport took him past his own home Tajrish district, and he realised that he would probably never see his wife and family again. At that moment, life didn't seem to be worth living.

#

The prison at Evin was far worse than anything that he had ever imagined. Torture, beatings and rape were the norm, and any spirit that Kurt might still have harboured soon fled his body. Eventually, though, the guards tired of their sport, and sentenced him instead to a fate that was almost worse – total isolation. It was as if he had never existed, and as the months became years and the years decades, he became the forgotten man. Most people in his situation would have given in and expired, but some tiny spark within Kurt kept him alive.

More than sixty years had passed since Kurt had first been arrested, and he was now approaching his ninetieth year. Surprisingly, his cell was opened one day and he was taken outside the prison and left outside the gates. Finally, they'd had enough of continually feeding him, having expected him to have died years earlier. How he was expected to fend for himself with no money and just the tatters that he wore when arrested, in a world that was now foreign to him – well, that just wasn't their concern.

Kurt walked slowly through the streets not knowing what to do next. He shunned any human contact, having been alone for so many years, but as he walked, an idea began to form in his mind. He knew roughly *where* he was, but not *when* – if he'd been released *before* his young self had touched the button, he might yet be able to prevent his doing so, and thus secure his future. It was too late for the Kurt who had been sent to the past, but hopefully not too late for the young idealist scientist.

He walked very slowly, and passed within a mile of his former home, but he couldn't bear the thought of seeing his wife and children – or rather of them seeing what a pitiful creature he had become. And what if he saw himself – what sort of paradox might that result in?

#

It took him a week to reach the Embassy, days in which he scavenged for food from the bins and slept in the streets. At least it was the warmth of summer, and when he'd seen a newspaper shortly after his release from jail, he'd noted with his fading eyesight that he was only a few days shy of the fateful moment. Perhaps, after all those years, fate was being kind to him at last.

He reached the secured entrance to his office late in the afternoon. The clouds were gathering, a storm was on its way. If he'd had to remember a coded number to gain access to the building, all would have been lost, but access was biometric, via fingerprints and retinal scans, and – although much older - they still produced the same computerised patterns.

Dragging his weary body along the corridor, he opened the door to his former office. All plans fled his head, as he saw himself poised over the control panel, ready to switch off the monitor. He was too late! Despairingly, he shouted "No, don't do it," but his voice was so weakened by lack of human contact that barely a croak emanated.

He saw the young scientist half-turn in his chair towards the noise, but his eyes never met those of the older Kurt. With horror, Kurt saw his young self's finger slip from the off button to the 'standby' one alongside it, at the same time as lightning flashed. The strain was too much for his weakened heart, but as he slumped to the ground, he remembered the slight noise he had heard all those years earlier, and realised that it was his own weak shout that had caused him to press the wrong button, the button that the lightning bolt struck.

#

Kurt found himself lying on the floor, but he couldn't make out the surroundings as bright flashes were dancing across his eyelids. *What on earth was that?* he thought as he rubbed his eyes to try and refocus them. And it had suddenly become much cooler, had the storm broken that quickly? ...

Queueless

Amazing,
Brilliant,
Cosmic,
Delightful,
Elation,
Fantastic,
Great,
Hurray,
Ideal,
Jubilation,
Knockout,
Lovely,
Marvellous,
Nice,
Okay,
Perfect,
Rejoice,
Super,
Terrific,
Unbelievable,
Victory,
Wonderful,
Xanadu,
Yippee,
Zowie

Outmanoeuvred

He'd known for quite a while that there would be no glory at the end of this day, but he'd struggled on anyway. Now, though, everybody could see that his defeat was only minutes away. As he looked at the scene before him and surveyed his scattered forces, outnumbered and outflanked in all areas, he wondered how it had all gone so terribly wrong. It grieved him to see so many of his men prone at the side of the battleground.

To begin with, he'd appeared to have the upper hand, but he now saw how his perceived victories had just been sacrifices on his foe's behalf. They'd been designed to lull him into overconfidence and to draw him out, committing resources he could ill-afford to lose. Too late he saw his folly, and ever since then, despite valiant efforts, he'd been unable to repel the relentless advances of his adversary. After the foot soldiers had been picked off one-by-one with ease, and his limited mounted forces had succumbed with barely a whimper, it had always been just a matter of time before his inevitable defeat.

Now, the fortress had been breached, crumbling under the incessant barrage of attacks, and with the royal household in disarray, he considered the possibility of surrendering as a means of avoiding total annihilation. The thought brought with it the taste of bile; his humiliation would become legendary, but as he surveyed his beaten army, with only the Right Reverend remaining to protect his sovereign, he could see no other choice.

But as the attacking forces moved even closer, he looked into his opponent's face and realised that even that option was no longer open to him. Dejectedly, he only half-heard the single word that sealed his doom: checkmate.

Sins Of The Father

Peter Coventry frowned as he read the letter that had been tucked inside his copy of *The Financial Times*:

> *I encountered your father in Potocari when I was young. He escaped my vengeance but there is a tradition amongst my people: if the father can't pay for his sins, the son will. It's taken me years to find you, but now I have. You die on Friday.*

He was inclined to dismiss it as the ramblings of a lunatic, but he knew that his father had a brutal past. His mother Adrijana had left Belgrade with Peter years earlier, fleeing from her brutal husband. Once in England, she changed his name from Petar Kovak in an attempt to leave their past behind.

Peter did well at school, and his business acumen was to bring him considerable wealth. From small beginnings as a software developer, he founded *Coventry Software Consultants*, a thriving computer business that had managed to procure some significant government contracts in its first year of trading. Life was good; why was somebody trying to spoil it?

He took another look at the letter. The content didn't worry him, though he felt angry that he'd been tracked down. It appeared to have been printed on a home computer inkjet printer on standard A4 paper. The printed envelope bore no stamp; perhaps somebody had seen who left it? He asked around the other occupants of the luxury block of flats, but the only person they had seen that morning had been the woman delivering the morning papers. Whoever had brought the letter had managed to do it unseen.

He considered taking the letter to the police but decided it was just a sick hoax, and he wasn't going to let it ruin his week. After throwing it on the fire, he set off for work, a half hour drive to the city centre complex in the heart of the financial district. Arriving shortly after nine, he went straight to his office and motioned his PA to follow him in.

"What appointments do I have today, Maria?" He looked wistfully across at the slender young woman as she checked her Blackberry. With her straight, dark hair she looked like a film star; he wouldn't have been surprised if half his staff had lustful thoughts about her.

"You've the weekly project meeting at 10, a business lunch at 12:30 with Mr. Beddowes, and at 3 you're meeting the Heads of Finance and Recruitment."

Thanks, Maria, doesn't sound too onerous for a Monday. Can you send Anthony in please?" Just as she was about to close the door behind her, Peter called her back. "Wait a second Maria. Have I any appointments for Friday?"

She browsed through her organiser before replying, "You've a 9:30 meeting with Mr. Tuscan, that's all."

"Thanks again, Maria. I'll see Anthony now please."

As Maria opened the door, she came face to face with a tall immaculately-attired man. "Oh, Mr. Tuscan, you gave me quite a start! I was just about to call you - Mr. Coventry will see you now." And, holding the door open, she ushered Anthony Tuscan into the spacious office.

As he passed, Anthony turned to her and asked, "How many times do I have to tell you, Maria, it's Anthony, we're a very friendly firm? Or should I start calling you 'Miss Osman'?"

"Sorry, *Anthony*. I will try and remember," she replied as she shut the door.

"Hello, Anthony, did you have a good weekend?"

"Not too bad, Peter, a bit dull really, just the two of us. Mind you," he added, nodding towards the door, "it wouldn't be dull if I could spend the weekend with *her*."

"Hands off, Anthony, you're a married man! Look, joking aside, I want you to do something for me. Can you have a word with Johnson in security? Just ask him to keep his eyes open for anything suspicious this week."

"Why – is there a problem?"

"Not really, just a little..." At that moment, there was a knock on the door. "Come in."

Maria popped her head round the door. "Sorry to interrupt, Mr. Coventry, but you were asking about Friday. When I returned to my desk, I found a 'postit' note confirming an appointment for 4 o'clock with a Mr. Peterson. I've asked who left it, as I'd never agree to a meeting at that time on a Friday, but nobody seems to have seen. Are you alright, Mr. Coventry?"

"Errm, yes, Maria, yes, I'm okay. This Peterson – what company is he from?"

"I don't know, Mr. Coventry. I'll see if I can find out. Sorry for interrupting you"

Peterson – *Peter, son*. It no longer seemed like a harmless prank. He turned to Anthony, who was staring at him. "Can you speak to Johnson right away, ask him to be extra vigilant. And see if you can find out anything about Peterson. I've to make a phone call before our 10 o'clock."

As soon as Anthony left, Peter picked up the handset and called the local police station, asking to be put through to Inspector Reynolds. "Gordon? Hi, it's Peter Coventry here. Look, this might mean nothing, but I've had a threatening letter." After detailing the contents, he paused, awaiting his old friend's response.

"It's a pity you destroyed the letter, Peter, forensics could have been a great help there. What encounter is the writer referring to? Potocari sounds familiar somehow."

Peter waited a second before replying. He'd hoped never to have to speak of this again. "My father, Dimitar, was responsible for some of the atrocities in the Balkan conflict, when Serbian forces wiped out entire communities under the guise of ethnic cleansing. Following the genocide in Srebrenica in July 1995, he was caught and tried as a war criminal. I only know about it from the news coverage – I left Yugoslavia years before that. As he awaited sentence, he had a final trick to play on his victims, cheating them of their retribution when an associate bribed a guard to deliver a suicide pill into his detention cell. He was found the next morning dead in bed with his lip curled into one final contemptuous sneer.

"I know how bitterly peoples on both sides of the divide still feel about the war – remember the fighting at last month's Australian Open when Djokovic played Delic? The thing is, though, I no longer think of myself as anything other than a nationalised Briton. It's nothing to do with me."

"It begins to make more sense now, Peter. I can see why you're worried. The writer didn't specify home or work. How much do you know about your staff? Who can you trust apart from Anthony? Is this Johnson reliable?"

"We're a relatively new company, nobody has been here longer than a year. But I'm a good judge of people, I know who is trustworthy."

"If you say so, Peter, but meanwhile, I'll do some checking here. Don't worry, it probably is just somebody's sick sense of humour."

#

As the week progressed, Inspector Reynolds kept in constant contact with Peter, but had little progress to report, and neither Anthony nor Maria had been able to find anything out about the mysterious Mr. Peterson. Johnson in security kept a vigilant eye on proceedings, and had distinct instructions not to let anyone in on Friday without checking with Peter first. Inspector Reynolds sent one of his uniformed officers to work alongside Johnson, providing an obvious presence which might act as a deterrent.

Just before four o'clock on Friday, Johnson knocked on Peter's door and popped his head round.

"What are you doing here? Why aren't you keeping watch downstairs?"

"The officer suggested I come and check, he's keeping an eye on things down there. I'm checking the offices to make sure everybody has gone."

"Go on then, but be quick about it. I'll feel happier when you're back downstairs." Peter tried to concentrate on the contract on his desk; he'd been checking it while Johnson looked round, but the words just danced in the air in front of him. He didn't realise he'd been holding his breath until he heard his office door closing again.

Four o'clock came and went, with no sign of the elusive Peterson, and Peter began to relax for the first time in five days. Just then, the phone rang. It was the Inspector. "Peter, listen, this has just come through. It took some time, but we've found some links. Are you alone?"

"Yes, nearly everybody's gone for the weekend, but Anthony's coming to see me in a minute."

"Don't let him in – he isn't who he says he is. His real name is Antun Tuco. He's Bosnian. I think he might be planning to kill you."

Peter was silent for a second, then he roared with laughter.

"Peter? Are you alright Peter?"

"Yes, Gordon, sorry, but you really are on the wrong track there. Yes, I know Anthony – or Antun – is a Bosnian. I've known him for years – he's a Bosnian Serb. That's why I gave him the job. He came to England not long after my mother brought me here. I'd trust him with my life. Just a minute, there's somebody at the door. Yes, what is it?"

The door opened and Maria looked in. "Is everything alright Mr. Coventry."

"Yes, just something amusing, that's all. You can go now, I'll not need you again tonight. Can you just shut the window before you go, please, it's getting chilly." The voice in his earpiece was sounding insistent. "I've told you Gordon, Anthony is above suspicion. He's nothing to do with Potocari."

"Okay, perhaps you're right, but that's not all we found out. A family called Osmanovic was slaughtered by your father there. The only one to escape was a little girl called Marija, who your father left for dead after raping her. She might be..."

"Hello, Gordon, are you there?" But there was no answer; the line was dead. Puzzled, Peter looked at the severed cord on the hand piece as he heard a noise behind him. He'd forgotten that Maria was still there – *Marija*!

"Potocari was a long time ago," she said, wistfully. "I've had to rebuild my life, all alone in a strange country. People are nice, here, though – Mrs. Atkins at the newsagents has been good to me. Did you know I help her out by delivering morning newspapers when the girl doesn't turn up? That's how I first saw you two years ago – don't you remember, you looked at me when I screamed? I thought you were *him*. But of course you don't remember, otherwise you'd have said something at my interview. It's taken me a long time to make certain that you were his son. I'm no cold-hearted killer, I wouldn't eliminate the wrong person. But I have to admit I've enjoyed watching you squirm since Monday morning. I won't keep you any longer, as I've a plane to catch. Perhaps your friend the Inspector will be waiting for me at the airport, but that's a risk I'm prepared to take. Goodbye, Petar Kovacs."

Peter had been trying desperately to speak, but the blade that Maria had sliced across his throat had severed his vocal cords, and he was only able to emit a pitiful blood-engorged gurgle as she calmly tossed the knife into the bin and walked out of his office. He watched his lifeblood seeping through the fingers that had vainly been trying to stem the flow, and then everything went black.

Partners In Crime

Three masked men carrying holdalls burst through the bank doors, scattering in different directions as they made their pre-planned getaways. The first was three-quarters of the way to his car when a figure wearing an all-blue tight leotard and an eye mask dropped to the ground in front of him. He uttered the single word "Ice…" before her blast of breath froze him to the spot.

Wasting no more time on this miscreant – the police would arrive well before he thawed out – she deftly scaled the walls and skipped across the rooftops as she sought out the second thief. Moments later, he too was immobilised in ice and the final of the trio was in her sights. However, as she filled her lungs to deliver one final disabling blow, an ear-shattering screech from the other end of the dark alley knocked her from her feet. When her head stopped ringing, she saw that the villain was prone and standing over him was Night Owl.

"That was my catch," she shouted at him. "Why don't you go and haunt some other city?"

"Why do you get to say who saves Capital City, Ice Maiden? I've been tracking these felons for days. I knew what was happening tonight, I don't hang around on the off-chance. I say it's time for *you* to go and bother another city."

"I'm staying here. You know the press see me as a hero whereas they think you're more villain than saviour."

"You're wrong, Ice Maiden. Where there's crime, you'll find Night Owl." And, with a flourish of his cape, he vanished into the night.

#

Ice Maiden made her way across the rooftops towards her home in the suburbs. She'd lost her appetite for crime-fighting this evening; why did that misguided do-gooder always have to interfere, turning what should have been a straightforward capture into a near fiasco?

Once at home, she slipped out of her costume and become quiet housewife Alice Ronson once more. As she climbed into bed alongside her unsuspecting husband Kevin, she vowed to put an end to this; the city couldn't support two superheroes. *He* would have to go.

#

"I'm back," shouted Kevin, "you should have seen the queue at Sainscos! You'd think there was a world cornflakes shortage the way some of them were acting."

"Hmmph," replied Alice, mouth full of said cornflakes, "I don't know what they're fussed about."

"Hey," added Kevin, "I saw the new neighbours on the way back. Shall we pop over and welcome them to the area? I hope he's into darts – it's never been the same since Eric retired his arrers!"

Alice smiled at the banality of it all. If he knew that she went out *on the tiles* every night when he was asleep, he'd drop the darts he was so lovingly cradling. Placing her empty bowl in the sink, she replied, "Yes, lets, I'll just get my coat."

#

The pale-blue front door of number 7 opened to reveal a pleasantly-plump woman of a similar age to Alice. "Hello," said Kevin, "we're your next-door neighbours, the Ronsons. Welcome to the Crescent. I'm Kevin, this is Alice."

"How sweet," she answered. "I was just telling Victor that we really must introduce ourselves to the neighbours. I'm Betty by the way, Betty Gardener. Victor's finishing his breakfast, he works nights at the dairy. Victor, come and meet the next-doors."

As Betty moved to one side to allow Victor through, Alice all-but collapsed in shock. She'd never seen him like this before, of course, but a pair of spectacles couldn't disguise the fact that she was looking at the alter-ego of Night Owl. Fortunately, before anybody noticed her reaction, Victor's mug of tea crashed to the floor as he, too, recognised the vigilante who was his new neighbour.

"Tsk, clumsy!" scolded Betty, "I hope you're more careful at work. Still," she laughed, "no point crying over spilt milk, is there?"

#

Somehow, Alice found herself back at home, as Kevin whined on about what a good chap Victor was, though he thought Betty was a bit odd. Alice responded in autopilot monosyllables. Her mind was on the conversation she would be having with Night Owl that evening.

#

High on the rooftops, Ice Maiden and Night Owl were sparring verbally, whilst far below, for once the city's underbelly were able to carry out their activities unhindered. Neither would agree to leave the city to the other, and now that they were neighbours as well, there seemed no solution to their dilemma. Disgruntled, both superheroes relinquished their vigils and headed home.

As they entered the Crescent, both instinctively knew that something was wrong. The front doors of numbers 5 and 7 were wide open, and Ice Maiden and Night Owl ran into their respective homes without trying to hide their identities. Number 5 was empty – had the city's crime lords discovered who they were and exacted revenge? Ice Maiden raced next door, fearing the worst, but nothing could have prepared her for the sight facing her. The image of Betty's wobbling buttocks bouncing up and down on Kevin's skinny midriff would live with her forever.

"Hi, Alice, hello Victor," said Kevin conversationally, "we're just getting to know each other a bit better. In fact, we're thinking of making up a foursome. How about it, eh, we reckon you'd make a bonny couple?"

Reacting instinctively, Ice Maiden discharged a savage, icy blast, encasing the copulating couple, and at the same time, Night Owl emitted a screech of such force that it caused the newly-created ice sculpture to shatter into a million tiny pieces.

Taken?

<u>**Manchester, 14th March 1831**</u>

Antonio stepped into the open carriage at Edge Hill station, his eyes flitting nervously between the stern-looking features of the other passengers. He'd arrived in Liverpool the previous evening, after a long and tiring journey by land and sea from his home in Milan, and at just four feet in height, the eleven-year old felt dwarfed by his fellow travellers. Wearing cap, jacket and corduroy trousers, he clutched his only possession, a small box containing his beloved pets, two guinea pigs and five white mice. Everything else had been in the battered brown suitcase that had been stolen as he disembarked from the boat, leaving with him just the box, the clothes he was wearing and the letter that he'd received after the funeral. He took the tattered sheet from his pocket and read the tear-smudged words for one last time:

My precious Antonio,

I know you will be frightened at the thought of coming to live with us in England, but you must understand that there is nobody at home to look after you.

I have written to Father Paulo asking him to help you with your English and teach you the words you will need to survive in this cruel world. He will make sure you have the tickets...

Antonio turned the sheet of paper over to read the portion concerning this final stage of the journey:

You have to get to Edge Hill station, where the train starts, for seven in the morning, but you must let the first-class passengers take their seats before you will be allowed on. The time for you to board is a quarter after seven.

It will take about two hours to reach Liverpool Road station in Manchester. That is the last stop on the journey. I will meet you there and take you home.

Be careful, though, because the railway is dangerous. A famous man called Mr Huskisson died a few months ago after he stepped on to the track to talk to the Duke of Wellington.

But I know you are a sensible boy who will do as he's told,

Until we meet, Ciao, your brother Davis

He wondered why people used these mechanical monsters if they were such a danger, but he was a foreigner here; perhaps this was how things were done in England.

He jumped in shock as a shrill whistle sounded, and gazed in awe as huge clouds of white smoke billowed from the giraffe-like neck of the steam engine at the front of the train. He was so entranced by the sight that he didn't realise at first that the journey had commenced. It was cold in the March air, but he didn't feel it as the wonder of his first train journey overwhelmed all other feelings. He stared in awe at the huge rust-red rocks towering over them on both sides and stretching away in the distance. As he leant over the side of the carriage and looked ahead, the path through the rocks appeared to get narrower and narrower. Antonio felt that at any moment they would be crushed as the cutting seemed never-ending, but soon they were through it into the open sky again. Shortly afterwards, he was gazing at the ground far below as the train crossed a viaduct. A woman saw his open-mouthed look and smiled at him. "This the first time you've been on a train?"

Antonio nodded, not sure if he should talk to a stranger, but she didn't seem to notice as she continued. "We're crossing the Sankey Brook Valley right now, it's seventy foot high. This viaduct was built from sandstone slabs quarried from Olive Mount – remember the long cutting we went through?"

Antonio said nothing, and the woman smiled once more. "I expect it can be quite frightening being all alone at your age. And we're going so fast. The locomotive goes at *seventeen* miles an hour. I'm surprised our bodies can stand such speeds." Antonio looked down at his feet as the woman chattered on, and she soon stopped when she realised he wasn't going to engage in conversation with her.

The train stopped at several stations, and at each one Antonio remained huddled up in his seat while some people exited the train and yet more joined. As the journey continued, the initial awe and wonder faded a little, and to take his mind off the monotonous clink-clink of the wheels on the tracks, he carefully opened his box and lifted out his pets. He kissed them, one by one, before returning them, but kept his favourite, a guinea pig named *Gigio*, on his knee. Other passengers smiled as they saw him stroking it and whispering in its ear, but he was engrossed in his game and didn't notice them.

It was at the next halt that tragedy struck. The engine had been stationary for some time, and had just built up a head of steam in readiness for departure when the oversized man sat next to Antonio suddenly shouted out, "I can't stand it any more, it goes too fast," and barged into him in his haste to leave the carriage. Antonio was knocked over, and Gigio wriggled from his grasp as he fell.

Frantically, he looked around for his pet, but it was no longer in the carriage. As the train moved off, he caught a glimpse of it on the platform. The previous night, he had stood and watched as the thief ran off with his suitcase; bravely, the young boy decided he wasn't going to be inactive this time, and although the train was gathering speed, he didn't hesitate as he jumped onto the platform inches before it ended.

He didn't think about how he was going to get to the destination; a sign told him this was a place called *Newton Bridge*, but he had no idea where that was. The man who had caused the accident was in the distance, running from the train line as fast as he could. Antonio looked along the platform, trying to see his pet, but it didn't seem to be there any more. Panic-stricken, he ran up and down, yelling "Gigio, Gigio. Please come back Gigio." But to no avail. Disconsolate, he sat down on the floor and wept. He hadn't cried at all in the harrowing recent weeks, but this incident acted as a pressure release, and the tears flowed freely for half an hour.

Eventually, red-eyed and hoarse, his sobbing abated and, though his heart was still beating at double its usual pace, he stood up and wondered what he was going to do next. He had no idea if any other trains would come along this track, but he couldn't think of anything else to do other than wait and see. The station was deserted, and he didn't want to venture outside into a strange environment.

Out of the corner of his eye, he spotted a slight movement, and whirled round to see something small disappearing at the other end of the platform. "Gigio," he cried, half laughing, half shouting, and forgetting the warning he had been given about the danger of the train tracks, he jumped down and ran to catch up with the pet who was his best friend. He held the little animal close to his breast, tears flowing again, before dropping it carefully into the little box with the others. So intent was he on having found Gigio that he failed to notice the train that was bearing down on him until he was enveloped in black smoke. The air thickened around him as the engine chugged relentlessly on.

#

Davis Grafigna watched in vain as the last passenger left Liverpool Road station. Only a few people had alighted, and there wasn't a young boy amongst them. Neither was Antonio still in his seat, perhaps asleep; that was easy to tell by looking in the open carriages as he half-ran the length of the train. He decided to ask the engine driver if he'd seen Antonio, but by the time he reached the cab of the *Lancashire Witch*, it was empty. Beginning to panic, he ran back along the platform towards the last few passengers, three businessmen, shouting, "Wait, have you seen a young boy? He was supposed to be on that train, I'm his brother."

"A young boy, did you say?" asked a tall man wearing a top hat, "*I* saw no young boy."

He spoke with such authority that Davis didn't think to doubt him, but one of his colleagues interjected, "There *was* a boy. Surely you remember? He was playing with that rat."

"No, it wasn't a rat, it was a guinea pig," added the third passenger, "he had a couple of them, and four or five white mice."

"That sounds like Antonio," said Davis excitedly, "he's always loved his pets. But where is he now?"

"Oh yes, *now* I remember him," said the first man. "A small boy with chestnut hair, about ten years old? I'm sure I saw him leave the train, but I can't remember where."

"Did anyone else see him leave?" asked Davis, concerned that his brother had left the train when he'd been told to stay until the end of the journey.

The other two men shook their heads.

"Well can you tell me anything else about him?"

Eventually, Davis managed to elicit that Antonio had been wearing a hairy cap, Italian fustian jacket and drab corduroy trousers. Thanking the men for their help, but with a feeling of dread in his heart, he walked out of the station unsure what to do next. He couldn't imagine what Antonio must have been feeling; first losing his father, then his mother and sister, leaving him all alone; then having to come to a strange land to live with the only family that were left, but a family that would be like strangers to him. Davis had only seen Antonio once in the ten years since he had come to England to start a new life with his bride Maria, and that had been at the occasion of their father's funeral. He hadn't been able to return for the funerals of little Francesca or their mother.

He walked around Castlefield aimlessly, looking in every alley and field that he passed, but he didn't really know what he expected to find. The boy hadn't been on the train, he couldn't possibly be in any of the places that he looked. Although he searched for hours, time meant nothing to him. Before he knew it, he was back at his home, and he saw Maria running out of the door towards him, carrying their youngest child. "Where is he, Davis? Why isn't he with you? You should have been back hours ago."

"He wasn't there, Maria. Some men saw him on the train, but he must have left it at the wrong station. I don't know what to do," he continued, sobbing on his wife's shoulder.

"Now, now, Davis, not in front of the little one. It will be alright, you'll see. If he was on the train, he can't have gone far. Somebody will know where he is. We'll go to see the magistrate and ask him to put up a '*missing*' poster."

"What good will that do? Nobody takes any notice of them."

"They will if we offer a reward. We can say we'll give a whole pound if somebody can bring him back to us."

"We can't afford that much, woman! Are you crazy?"

"We don't have to pay it – if they find Antonio, they can hardly take him away again, can they? You hold the baby while I fetch the others."

Davis took little Luigi and watched Maria's retreating back. Perhaps she was right, and the reward money would jog somebody's memory. But, deep down, Davis knew that he would never see Antonio again.

#

Bolton, 4th August 1843

It was showing signs of being another hot August day as Alice quietly closed the door behind her, taking care not to wake the rest of the family. She'd read about the circus that was coming to Bolton, and she was determined to see it. She'd heard all about circus folk, and the exotic animals they kept in their cages, but she'd never been to one before. Since the posters had first appeared, two weeks earlier, she'd been desperate to see the Giant Horse centrepiece, but her parents had strictly forbidden her to go anywhere near the circus. But, being almost an adult herself, Alice had chosen to disobey them, hence her secretive early morning departure from the home.

The cobbled streets of the Lancashire town were bustling at this hour with people hurrying to work, and Alice would normally have been amongst them, making her way to the cotton mill to spend another long day working the mule to produce a variety of muslin, dimity and quilting for the rich Manchester merchants.

She regretted leaving home without her bonnet and shawl as she passed All Saints chapel, where she spent every Sunday, as she could have pulled them tight around her to hide her from prying eyes. But nobody called out after her and soon she was entering uncharted regions as she crossed the River Croal, the traditional boundary between Little Bolton and Great Bolton.

Alice knew that the main street led to the Market Place, where the circus was sited, so she walked in that general direction. She had to take care where she placed her clogs to avoid the ever-present horse droppings that made the surface hazardous at times.

It took her almost three hours, but eventually she saw it in the distance, a huge canvas tent dominating the skyline. When she reached it, the place was bustling with people, hurrying everywhere, and the smells and sounds almost made Alice squeal with happiness. *This* was where she wanted to be, not in that dingy mill.

She watched for some time, before a harsh voice jolted her back to the reality of the situation. "You! Yes, you girl. What do you think you're doing? We don't open until tonight. Come over here, now!"

With trepidation, she went up to the man she guessed to be the circus master and stood, head bowed, waiting for him to speak.

"Well, girl, what do you want? There's work to be done; we've a show to put on tonight. Who are you anyway?"

"Please, sir, why do you use a big tent like that?"

"All travelling circuses use canvas tents now. They've been using 'em in America for nearly twenty years. But why do you want to know that? What's it to do with you?"

"Because I want to join the circus. My name is Alice Boar... Alice Brimelow, sir."

"You want to join the circus?" he asked, mockingly. "What good would you be here? What can you do?"

She felt all her resolve disappearing as his harsh laughter rang out. Biting her lip to stop herself from crying, she forced herself to remain calm and answered, "I could help with the animals, I love animals and I want to work with them."

"Now listen, girl, and listen good. Our animals aren't your family pets, they are untamed, and don't take to just anybody. Our trainers have to be very experienced. Now go on, you've wasted enough of my time, get out before I set the dogs on you."

The severe look on his face showed that he meant what he said, and Alice backed away hurriedly. It was mid-morning now. She couldn't return home or go to work, not at this hour. She decided to look round the circus while she was here, despite what the circus master had said. Besides, she'd come this far expecting to see the Giant Horse and the other attractions, she'd never forgive herself if she left without seeing them.

She walked towards the exit, but once she was out of his sight, she headed towards the tent that was the centrepiece of the display. *Where else would the Giant Horse be?* she surmised. After her recent confrontation, she strode purposefully into the tent as if she belonged there. She entered with high expectations of seeing a horse that was as tall as the tent, but could barely hide her disappointment when she saw that it was empty, apart from a man who was sweeping up. He saw her and shouted over, "hey, gal, bring me that bucket will yer?"

She looked towards where he was pointing, saw a large metal bucket, and carried it over to him. He scooped up a pile of manure and dropped it in the bucket. Alice wrinkled her nose in distaste, and he laughed at her. "It's the most natural thing in the world, gal, if yer going to have horses galloping round and round this circle, yer going to have to deal with what they leave behind 'em."

"Do you mean the Giant Horse?"

"No," he chortled, "course not! It's the trick riding I'm talking about. Giant Horse! Get on with yer!" He turned and continued sweeping, laughing and muttering *Giant Horse? What next?* as he walked away.

If it wasn't here, then where could it be? Disconsolately, Alice trudged outside again, and wandered around aimlessly for a while. A snorting noise in the distance caught her attention and she walked over towards a row of small tents opposite a fenced-off area containing a number of large buildings. Outside one of them, separated from the rest, two horse-like animals with black stripes were grazing. Alice recognised them as zebras from pictures she'd seen in a book. Some of the other buildings looked large enough to contain her Giant Horse. But the fence was too high; she would surely never be able to climb it.

She decided to investigate the wonders in the tents; perhaps she'd find something she could use to climb over. She peered in the first, but was disappointed to see just a few clothes strewn across a small wooden chair. *Never mind*, she told herself, *one of them is certain to have something good behind it*. She never stopped to consider that the canvas might be concealing her worst nightmare, but when she opened the next flap, she came face-to-face with the most hideous creature she could imagine. If she hadn't known better, she would have sworn it was a repulsive pig, but this pig was standing upright, wearing a long green dress and white blouse, and was sipping genteelly from a cup of tea.

With a screech, Alice fled the tent and, fearing pursuit, she somehow managed to clamber over the railings into the adjoining enclosure, even though they were almost twice her height. She didn't stop running until she was concealed behind the door of a long barn. Peering out, she was surprised to see that nobody was looking for her. *Perhaps*, she thought, *in this place they're used to people screaming at all of the sights.*

Suddenly, the appeal of joining the circus had gone, and Alice very much wanted to be back home with her parents, however angry they might be with her. Before she could move, though, she heard a deep-throated growl, and, terrified, turned to see an enormous lion advancing on her. Alice could feel its hot breath on her, and the thickening air blackened as the roaring beast leapt at her with mouth wide open.

#

John and Esther Boardman walked up to the desk and asked to speak to the chief constable. Some minutes later, a tall man in his late fifties came over to them. "Now then, what's all this about? You asked to see me, I'm Chief Constable Harris."

Esther replied before John could speak. "It's our little girl, Alice. She went out yesterday morning and she aint come back. I told John summat was up, but he wouldn't let me come last night." Scowling at her husband, she continued, "He said she'd be back, but she aint! I want my baby back."

"Now, now, calm down luv," added her husband, "I'm sure there's a simple explanation. Here," he added to the constable, "we found this underneath her bed this morning." He handed over a torn handbill advertising the visit of the circus. "She's been going on about it for weeks, but we told her no, she couldn't go. We thought she'd gone t' the mill yesterday, but I checked up and they didn't see her at all, and she hasn't gone in today. Somebody said they saw her near the chapel, but that's in t'other direction from work. So we reckon she must have defied us and gone t' the circus after all."

"The Circus, eh?" mumbled the constable, "that left town after the show last night. If she's gone off with them, she'll be hard to find. Is she the circussy type, then?"

"No, nothing like. She kept going on about the animals, but she's never seen a real wild animal, she'd know nowt about 'em. And she can't do no tricks. She's just an ordinary lass who works at a cotton mill."

"Well that sounds like good news to me, sir. You see, circus folk are very particular about who they take on, they're a very close-knit breed. So, if she wouldn't be any use to them, they wouldn't let her join."

"Do you really think so?" asked Esther, desperately seeking reassurance.

"Oh yes, I'm sure of it. But, just to be thorough, tell me all about her and I'll put out a poster. I can find out where the circus is going next, and ask the local constable to check up."

"Her name is Alice Boardman," replied John, "she's fifteen…"

"No she aint!" interrupted Esther, "you don't even know your own daughter's age. Here, leave it to me. She's *fourteen*, a pretty lass with red hair and blue eyes."

"Pretty? She's a fat lass, I wouldn't say she was pretty."

"Shut up, John, that's my daughter you're talking about and I say she's pretty. She's a tiny mark above her cheek and another on her neck. She had an accident some months ago."

"Accident?" boomed John, "it weren't an accident, it were negligence, making her crawl under that machinery while it were still operating, just t' scavenge a few pieces of cotton."

"We've been through this, it has to be done and there weren't any of the smaller children that day. I used to do it, and it didn't do me any harm, besides…"

"So," interrupted the constable, "she has something distinguishing then. That should help. Anything more? Do you know what she was wearing?"

"I've checked her clothes," said Esther, "and all that she seems to have taken are her light drab Stuff dress and her white patched pinafore. She'll be wearing her black stockings and clogs."

"That doesn't sound like somebody who meant to leave for good, so I'm sure she'll be back home today. She probably felt bad about what she did and didn't want to come home and face you. She'll be waiting until you're both out before returning. I'll wager she's there now."

Reassured, Esther and John ran back home, expecting Alice to greet them sheepishly, only to find a funereal emptiness to the house. The constable contacted his equivalent in Salford, the next venue of the circus, but his investigations found no trace of Alice Boardman, and she joined the official list of missing people from the district.

#

Manchester, 17th June, 1857

Tom Connolly slipped his hand into the pocket of the snoring Mr Matcalfe, taking great care not to wake him, and smiled as he felt the hard coins there. As quietly as possible, he closed his fist over the money and pulled his hand away. Taking the time only to pick up his boots, he silently opened the door and ran on tiptoe down the cobbled street, waiting until he was out of earshot of the house before putting his clogs on.

He had been indentured to the firm of *Matcalfe and Lavendar, Lithographers* for two and a half years, ever since he'd been brought back home after running away as a mere fifteen year old. Indentured apprentice or slave, it was all the same to him, for from that day onwards, he'd sought every opportunity for escape before his six-year apprenticeship was complete.

Outwardly, the arrangement seemed a fair one, with *Matcalfe and Lavendar* providing board and lodging in return for training him in the art of lithography. The company produced many multi-coloured posters, and Tom became involved in the entire process. He began by learning how to copy designs and pictures onto the limestone, and about the chemical processes that were necessary before the posters could be produced. The oil-based image was first applied to the surface of the limestone, and a solution of gum arabic and weak nitric acid was added, with the gum sticking to the non-oily surface and penetrating the porous stone. When it came time to print the image, they wet the stone with water and printing ink and varnish were rolled over the surface. The water covering the layer of gum repelled the ink, but the oily surface used for the original drawing accepted it, and by passing the stone through a press, the image was transferred to the paper.

This process had to be repeated, as a separate stone had to be used for each colour and care had to be taken to keep the images aligned. It was a highly-skilled job, and a qualified lithographer would always be in demand. But Tom resented every moment of his apprenticeship. He felt little more than a prisoner, and was not allowed to spend time with girls, go to taverns, play cards or gamble on dice. He had no interest in the art of printing, and the chemicals used infiltrated every pore of his being. He was expected to be at his master's beck and call any time of the day or night, and to ensure he didn't get any ideas about absconding, he was secured by a chain to an iron post every night.

Except last night, when the drunken Matcalfe had fallen asleep at the table, forgetting all about the padlock. Tom had waited until the early hours of the new day, expecting Matcalfe to wake at any moment, but when it became clear that he was in a deep sleep, Tom took the opportunity to slip away, ensuring that he didn't leave empty-handed as he rifled his employer's pocket.

Now, in the remaining pre-dawn hours, he ran through the near-deserted streets of Manchester with no clear aim in mind. He didn't want to return to his home town of Rochdale; there was nothing there for him anyway, and it would be the first place the police would search when his disappearance was discovered.

He carried on running until he reached the aqueduct that carried the Hollinwood Branch Canal over the River Medlock. Seeing the river gave him an idea for his destination; if he followed it to its end, he would reach Salford, a place he'd heard some of the other apprentices talking about. It was far enough away to offer him some chance of making permanent his escape.

First, though, he needed to get there, and he realised he'd have a better chance if he could get out of his tell-tale clothes. An opportunity for this arose within the hour, as he saw a man walking towards him with his dog. The man nodded and said, "Morning, son", as he passed. Without hesitation, Tom whirled, kicked the dog down the bank and into the water, and, as his owner was torn between protesting and worrying about his pet, Tom struck him down, beating him repeatedly about the head and chests, first with his fists, then with a large stone. Turning the unconscious body over, he stripped it of its clothes and used them to replace his own tattered garments, marvelling at the feel of the cloth against his skin after the course materials he had been used to.

He felt a different man, now, as he pulled the black, glazed cap onto his head. As he put his arm into the black jacket, he saw the name *JT Spencer* etched into the sleeve, so now he knew the identity of his victim. It was a cold morning, and Tom was about to put his new top coat on when he saw Spencer's dog dragging itself back onto the shore.

He hadn't really noticed it when he'd kicked it aside. Now, though, he had time to see that it was a full-grown Irish Wolfhound, and it was growling at him as if he were its age-old lupine foe. He stepped backwards, only to find himself falling towards the water, and the dog leapt at him, hitting him in the chest with its front paws. The impact took them both beneath the water, and Tom gasped in shock as the cold chilled his bones.

He struggled to reach the side, but the dog was still attacking him, and as Tom tried to fight it off, he found himself sinking deeper and deeper with each passing second. His lungs were bursting for air, but all they received was the foul-tasting black water. Tom began to lose consciousness as the blackness spread and the water thickened around him.

#

Matcalfe reported the disappearance of his apprentice and the theft of the money as soon as he awoke from his drunken stupor. A full search was started, and the trail wasn't too difficult to find, although it stopped shortly after reaching the Bridgewater Canal. They did find, though, the naked body of a Mr James Thomas Spencer, and, after subsequently talking to the wife of the deceased, a *'Wanted'* poster was issued, based on the assumption that Connolly would now be attired as Mr Spencer and would probably attempt to steal his identity.

No trace was found of Spencer's prized dog Fergus.

#

Capitalia, 4th May, 117

Lars Geheran, President of New Earth, stood in front of the newly-completed *Planetary Archive Building* and addressed the crowds stretching into the distance to the outskirts of Capitalia. The multivision cameras trained on him were conveying this historic moment into every home on the planet; the entire global population of three thousand would be able to say to their descendents, *I was watching the day it opened*. Geheran knew that this was the most important moment of his political career, and he hoped the nervousness he felt would not be apparent as he spoke.

"Peoples of New Earth, as we now know, when the asteroid destroyed the home planet all those years ago, our ancestors were the only people who managed to escape the devastation. They had the foresight to predict the catastrophe and launch a spaceship carrying them in suspended animation to our new home, here, in the Canis Major Dwarf Galaxy, more than twenty-five thousand light years from home. The journey took thousands of years, and by the time it was complete, Earth was nothing more than a distant memory to the Universe.

"New Earth was a barren inhospitable rock, barely able to support life, and many died in the process of terraforming the world into its current state. Progress was slow, but in little more than a century, we have built a thriving community, with technology an equal of anything our forefathers had at their command. We are a young planet, but our race is steeped in history, and in honour of our forefathers and the home planet, this magnificent *Planetary Archive Building* has been painstakingly constructed over the past five years. The Archives contain a history of our past, using records of the time that our ancestors placed into the spaceship at the commencement of their journey. All of this is well known to you all, but what I have to say now is only known to a select few at the highest levels of government.

"Several months ago, our scientists sent out a series of radio beams to try and contact other lifeforms, in the hope that we were not the only ones to escape from the destruction of Earth. One of our transmissions intersected a solar flare of tremendous magnitude. Our scientists are convinced that this phenomena is unique, a result of more than a dozen suns simultaneously becoming supernovae.

"We received data from that beam that confirmed the existence of human lifeforms, and our scientists responded by sending a second, multivision beam along the exact same co-ordinates, enabling us to view these humans."

Geheran paused while the mutterings of the gathered crowd rose to a crescendo. Then, holding his hand up for quiet, he continued. "What we saw amazed us all. We had not made contact with another race of humans on another planet after all. Instead, we were viewing a small geographical area of our own prehistory, which was changing rapidly with time as if we were viewing a videocast on fast play."

The mutterings amongst the crowd began again, and Geheran had to wait several minutes for silence before he could conclude his introductory words.

"Our scientists proved that the link was stable, but had a finite existence, and all of our resources since then have been devoted to opening a gateway to our past, with the aim of preserving some historical artefacts for our future generations. As we all know, our history defines who we are.

"Ladies, gentlemen, the gateway has now closed, permanently. But, I can report that we were successful in our mission." Again, he had to raise his hands for quiet, and the president's armed guard had to fire a volley of bullets over the heads of the assembled throng before he could continue. "We now have in our archives exhibits from our own prehistory, and," pointing to the twelve honoured guests who were seated at the foot of the platform, "apart from myself, you will be the first people in countless millennia to view them. We were only able to make a limited number of visits to Earth, as we had to ensure that our presence did not lead to any ripple effects in time, or the 'grandfather paradox' that could have theoretically changed our past and destroyed our present. We had to be certain that every item we retrieved would play no further part in Earth's history to minimise those chances."

Geheran cut the ceremonial ribbon to formally open the building, and his guards raised their guns to make it clear to the assembly that only those selected few could proceed. Geheran led the dozen dignitaries towards a sealed iron door and paused before it. "Ladies, gentlemen, before we enter I must warn you that nothing – I repeat *nothing* – can be touched within this strongroom. The temperature and humidity are controlled, but such is the nature of our artefacts that if they were to be exposed to our atmosphere, they would age millennia instantaneously and crumble to dust. If any one of you tries to cross the threshold to reach them, you will be immediately incinerated. You will receive no further warning."

As the huge gate slid soundlessly open, the VIPs gasped as they saw the living exhibits of three human children, five white mice and two guinea pigs, floating on air currents on the other side of the static forcefield.

My Special Friend

Jack has always been there for me, ever since we met following the accident. He has been my constant companion and friend, and it doesn't worry me that it's just the two of us, because we have so much fun together. I saw him at the funeral, and he came and put his arm round me when I was crying. I told mum and dad how kind he had been, but they just told me not to be silly and went to talk to some of the others.

At first, I did try and introduce Jack to the others. It was Debbie who said what they all must have been thinking: "There's nobody there," and she sang, "Ann's got an imaginary friend, Ann's got an imaginary frie-ee-end," as she skipped round the tree. Once it had been said, George, Mikey, Carol and Freddy soon joined in, bringing me to tears. I wish that I was ten, or even nine, then I'd be bigger than them and they wouldn't dare.

Jack told me not to worry, he'd never make fun of me, and he never has. We've been inseparable, he's always there when I come out of school, and although the others still make fun of me, it doesn't hurt any more.

Jack has taught me how to climb a tree, and we've collected caterpillars and butterflies in the summer; I tried to make friends with George again, and I showed him my favourite furry caterpillar, but he just knocked it out of my hand and stamped on it. He's horrid, I never want to speak to him again. I cried for hours that night, but Jack was with me all the time, telling me not to worry.

Just lately, though, Jack hasn't come round as often, and I think he's tiring of me. He's been quiet when we're together, and I know something is wrong. I know I'm only eight, but I'm not stupid. And I think that's the trouble. We were both eight when we met, but Jack's older now. He'll be thirteen next week, and I think he's getting tired of me, because no matter how long he knows me, I'll always be eight, just as I was on the day of the accident.

Mind Games

Professor Summers droned on in his monotone voice, oblivious to the boredom he was generating amongst his captive audience. "Special relativity, a theory of the structure of spacetime, was introduced almost two centuries ago, in 1905, by Einstein's paper *On the Electrodynamics of Moving Bodies*, although the term dates back to the seventeenth century and Galileo's *Dialogue concerning the World's Two Chief Systems*."

Fidgeting from the back caused Summers to pause. He wasn't concerned about that; he knew that a class of twelve-year olds couldn't all be expected to show an interest in the material he was about to deliver. But he sensed someone was following him, and *that* was what mattered. He thought he might even have recognised him by sight, but they all looked similar, and it *had* been such a long time ago. He continued. "One rather surprising consequence of the theory is referred to as *Time Dilation*. Moving clocks have been measured and shown to tick more slowly than an observer's stationary clock."

One or two in the class were beginning to yawn, but he sensed concern. He sensed a concerned mind; it was somebody on one of the front tables on his left. He was getting close. Perhaps one more example might suffice. "Imagine you are a spectator at the Indianapolis 500." Wrong choice here; he detected interest from several minds this time. But he had started, he needed to complete the analogy, but discourage the others. He continued with his monotonous delivery: "Imagine one of the drivers has a new supercharged engine, and he can travel at the speed of light round the track. As the driver goes round and round and round, you, the spectator, will have aged faster, because for the driver, time has passed relatively slower." Good, the extra interest had gone now, it was back to just the one. He sensed fear, realisation, recognition. Summers looked to his left, but outwardly he saw nothing other than a class of Year 7 pupils. One more piece of information, one final push. Less monotone, more animated now.

"Or take another example. Let's say there are twins, Jonathan and James." A mental gasp. "Jonathan stays on Earth while James travels in space. When the spaceship lifts off, their watches show identical times; as it reaches the speed of light, time passes slower for James, relative to Jonathan. By the time James returns to Earth, Jonathan will have aged – he may even be a Professor by now – whereas James would still be a twelve-year old boy."

A boy at the front on the left shoved his chair away and made a run for the door, but despite his age, Summers was faster, and threw himself at the boy's legs, knocking him to the floor. The boy looked up and smiled as Summers said, "Good one, James, but now it's my turn. Tig. You're it." And Jonathan Summers ran out of the classroom en route to his own specially-selected hiding place.

Passionate

John Rushton was in a rut; he'd tried pretending that everything was fine, and occasionally had almost been able to convince himself that it was true, but in the quiet moments of the breaking autumnal dawn, he finally admitted that things were *not* fine. He looked over at Sandra, breathing noisily as she slept alongside him. It was hard to believe they'd been married for twenty years, and most of that time had been good. Now that their son Greg was away at University, John had hoped he and Sandra could recapture their passionate days of old, but he had finally come to accept that she was no longer interested in rekindling their lovemaking.

It wasn't solely in that department that things had changed. It hadn't seemed that long ago that they regularly went out for meals; after Greg was born they retained their social contacts, but gradually, they dwindled until now the only time they went out together was for a weekly drink with Barry and Elaine Donaldson. Even then, Sandra had to be persuaded to go at first as she worked with Elaine, but she said she didn't really like her; but John insisted, he wasn't going to forego their last remaining night out, and – to be fair – Sandra hadn't really objected. John thought about Elaine and a smile touched his lips. She wasn't the type who he was normally attracted to, perhaps a little too forceful in some ways, but over the last few weeks he'd noticed her glancing over in his direction more and more often, and wondered if there could be something between them. In a good mood now, he swung his legs out of bed and strode off to the bathroom, looking forward to their night out at the pub in twelve hours' time.

#

As the weeks passed, John became more and more enamoured with Elaine, and he could tell that his feelings were reciprocated. Elaine began to call round to the house, on the pretence of trying to clear a backlog of work with Sandra, but he knew it was only an excuse; Sandra had never been a work-motivated person and would gladly have left things until the next day without a second thought. John looked forward to these visits, which began to increase in frequency, although he rarely managed to get any time just alone with Elaine as Sandra was always around, but whenever Sandra was out of the room, he'd flirt outrageously and Elaine would always knowingly smile back at him.

His opportunity came one December evening when Elaine had come by bus as her car was in the garage, and Barry was 'too busy' to bring her himself. John offered to run Elaine home, and though Sandra said she'd do it – *perhaps she suspects*, he thought – John reminded her that she'd drunk half a bottle of wine and was in no state to be behind the wheel; John had taken great care to restrict his alcohol intake, and Elaine gratefully accepted his offer of a lift.

It was a good twenty-minute drive to the plush estate at the far side of town, and gave plenty of opportunity for conversation. Elaine had drunk a fair amount, and so was perhaps a little less reticent than she should have been.

"Do you realise," she said, "that this is the first time we've been alone together?"

"Oh yes, I realise it. I've been trying to get an opportunity to get you all to myself for ages now."

"Really? You should have said, then we could have done this sooner. You never say anything when we're all out together, and you don't say a lot at your house."

"I can't at home, not with Sandra there, and when we're out together, you're usually inseparable from Barry."

"Oh, *him*! That's not by my choice, I can assure you."

"You surprise me. I thought you were an ideal couple."

"Only on the surface, John. Underneath – well, it's a bit like him, I suppose, the bits you can see are full of life, but he's dead from the neck down, and don't I know it,"

John became fully alert. Was she telling him that she had no sex life with Barry? And from the tone of her voice, was she implying that she needed that fulfilment, even if not from her husband? He decided to see if his questions could elicit more answers. "You've been married as long as Sandra and I, haven't you? But you've never mentioned any children."

"That's because we never had them. I wanted to, of course, but ... well, you can't win the lottery if you don't buy a ticket, if you know what I mean."

John didn't know what to say. He knew what she meant, and he thought he knew what she was implying, but he didn't want to say the wrong thing and put an end to a promising situation. Elaine, though, answered his dilemma. "That's not a problem with you, though, from what Sandra tells me. She doesn't know how lucky she is!"

Lucky? Thought John. *I'll bet she doesn't see it that way – she just says I'm a sex-obsessed old man.* He looked across at Elaine as he was driving, and nervously asked, "Have you ever thought of leaving him then?"

"Thought of? I think of nothing else! There's just one problem – I like my standard of life, and don't want to give it up. But he controls all the money. If I left, I'd have nothing – I know, he's threatened me enough with it over the years."

They had reached Elaine's home now, and John saw it for the first time. He'd never been to this part of the town before, and gasped as he saw the luxurious mansions that formed 'The Avenue' as she termed it. Now he understood what she would have to give up, and his hopes left him as she opened the door to leave, only to return as she flashed him a wide smile and said, "But you never know, perhaps it would be worth it for the right man."

He didn't notice the drive home, it was as if the car floated gently along the streets until he was in his garage, and Elaine was in his dreams as he smiled through the night.

#

Over the next few months, Elaine's visits became the highlight of John's life. The four of them still went out together on a weekly basis, but Elaine paid less attention towards John on these nights out, as there wasn't the need to as their friendship was now well established. She still came round, supposedly to see Sandra, once or twice a week, but long gone was any pretence of work. Sandra confided to John in a quiet moment late in February that she didn't know why she still came round, and John wondered if she knew the real reason, but the look in her eye told him she didn't suspect a thing. Every so often Elaine came by bus, when Barry was working away, and on those occasions John ensured he remained sober and drove her home. On their journeys, they talked more and more, but nothing untoward happened – the closest to any intimacy came when Elaine gave him a peck on the cheek as a thank you for the lift; she saw the bewildered look in his eye once, when she pushed him away as he tried for a longer embrace, and she mouthed a silent *later* to him.

As the weeks passed, she began to elaborate on the *later* part. "I know this might seem odd to you, especially in light of what I'm going to suggest, but I made a vow of fidelity on my wedding day and I don't intend to break it. Much as I'd like to," she added, noting John's concerned look. "So I'll remain faithful to Barry as long as I'm married to him, or as long as he lives." She looked at John as she said this, and he knew what she was suggesting; she'd already told him that leaving him wasn't an option.

John realised that his reaction to this suggestion would shape the rest of his life. He thought long and hard as he drove before responding. "Is Barry not very well, then? He always looks a figure of health to me."

"Oh, he's well, too well. He has the constitution of an ox – he never even has a cold. No, he'll outlive us all, unless something happens to him."

"Does he play any dangerous sports?" he asked, knowing what the answer would be.

"No, he takes no risks at all. Nothing will ever happen to him that way. You know," she said, her tone suggesting a sudden thought she'd had, "wouldn't it be awful if we were to get home one night and find there'd been a robbery? There have been reports of break-ins in our area, and our house is as good a target as any. I'd hate to be in there if we ever were burgled," she said, with a shudder.

"But don't you have all the latest security gadgets?"

"Barry doesn't believe in them. He said he's got the only deterrent the thieves would fear." In a conspiratorial whisper, she added, "Don't tell anyone, but he's got a pair of handguns. The police don't know."

"Handguns? But the robbers won't have guns will they?"

"The police have said they are a professional gang – they've warned us to be careful as they'll likely be armed. Just think, if something were to happen to him, there'd be nothing to keep us apart."

John thought for a moment, and then remembered Sandra. "But what about my wife? I don't want anything bad to happen to her."

"Just leave her to me, dear. I'll look after her, but don't worry, I'll make sure nothing bad happens." She got out of the car and blew him a kiss before hurrying up the long drive to her home. John took a yearning look at her back, and wondered, just wondered, whether things might work out right for them.

#

They didn't discuss it again for some weeks, and it was early summer before the subject was next broached. Elaine unexpectedly rang the bell late one evening and as John answered the door, he could see that she was distraught. She had a bruise on her temple, and her eyes were red.

"What's wrong?" he asked, concern obvious in every word.

"He hit me. He accused me of seeing someone and he thumped me."

"Does he..."

"No, he doesn't know it's you, but he's not stupid, he'll find out."

"Who's that at the door?" shouted Sandra from the kitchen.

"We'll talk about it later," he whispered to Elaine, "when I drive you home," and then in a louder voice, "Elaine's here, she's had a bit of an accident."

Sandra came rushing through to see what was wrong, and was soon ministering to her work friend. "It's only bruising, no lasting damage there. I imagine you've got a bad headache, though, have you taken anything for it?"

"No, I just ran out, I didn't stop for anything."

"I'll get you something. Can you take aspirin?"

"No, sorry, I can only have paracetamol."

"Hmm, we don't have any of them. Look, just stay here, I'll go to Asda. I won't be long, John can look after you."

In moments, Elaine and John were alone together. "You can't drive me home tonight," she said, "I came in the car. But we can talk now. I didn't quite leave without anything – I bought this." And she pulled a small handgun out of her bag. "I've got the other one as well. If you went round tonight, you could do it. I'm sure he knows that you're the man I'm in love with."

In love with. John had longed for those words, but not under these circumstances. He looked at the gun she was holding, looked at the hurt in her eyes, and his mind was made up.

"You wait there," he said, "you can stay the night here, sleep in Greg's room, he's on holiday with his Uni mates. Go back home in the morning and you'll find Barry's body – that way you'll have an alibi for the time of the murder."

"And so will you," she replied, leaning over and pecking him on the cheek. "But what shall I tell Sandra?"

"I don't know, I hadn't thought of that. Perhaps it's not such a good idea after all, and I'd better..."

Passionate   **54**

"No, wait, I've thought of the perfect excuse for her. You go off now, quick, I put the back door key under a garden gnome, the safe is in the front room, here's the combination," she added, handing him a small piece of paper, "just make a noise and he'll come down, shoot him, then leave." She smiled at John. "I was anxious to leave," she said, "but still had time to prepare some things."

#

Before he knew it, John was pulling the car to a halt just around the corner from Barry's house. Elaine had told him of a route around the back of the houses, and a loosened fence panel leading to the back garden. As she said, the key was under the ornament, and he slipped it into his pocket after silently unlocking the back door. Everywhere was in darkness as he felt his way with gloved hands towards the front room and the safe. He tapped in the combination, but nothing happened. "Damn!" he exclaimed, "I thought I'd remembered it."

Just then, the room was flooded with light and he turned to see Barry standing at the foot of the stairs. As he saw John, he asked, "What are you doing here mate?"

But before he could utter another word, John pulled out the gun and shot him between the eyes. Almost like a scene played in slow motion, Barry tumbled to the floor and a red stain began to cover the white carpet. John was panting heavily. Nobody would have heard anything, as the gun had a silencer fitted, but his knees were shaking as he realised what he had done.

He was about to leave when he heard a noise from the backdoor. He raised the gun, but a familiar voice said, "It's okay, it's only me."

"Elaine? What are you doing here? You should be at home – what about your alibi?" He took another look at her face. "And what happened to the bruise on your head? It can't have gone that quickly."

"Oh, Sandra's seeing to the alibi. She's playing a recording we made of us talking and laughing loudly, so the neighbours will confirm that we've been in all evening. They're used to me being round there anywhere, including every Tuesday when you're out with the lads for a drink. Oh, and the bruise – why, just theatrical makeup dear."

"But I don't understand. What's going on?"

"Do I really have to spell it out for you? When I come back tomorrow, after my girly night with Sandra, I'll discover the scene of the crime. I'll tell the police you were always asking about my jewels, and you must have decided to steal them when I told you Barry was going to London. It was just a tragic mistake that he didn't go, and he caught you. Afterwards, nobody will think anything of two bereaved widows comforting each other, and after a decent time, Sandra will move in here. What a fool you are if you think I was coming round to see *you*." And with a disdainful look, she raised the second gun and pulled the trigger.

Alternativity

I'll never forget that moment. It was two o'clock on a Wednesday afternoon and we were midway through double-physics. As always, the class of fifteen-year olds was comatose during Professor Rylands' dreary delivery of an even drearier topic – about somebody called Tegmark and alternate universes - and I leant across to talk to Rachel. "This is even worse than usual, how can the school think that this geek is a teacher?"

"Yeah," she whispered, "but at least we finish after this lesson. So what time are you picking me up to go to Darren's party?"

I was in the middle of replying, and had said, "I thought about..." when there was a brilliant flash of light; my eyes began to burn, and I instinctively shut them for a second. When I opened them, muttering, "What the heck was that," Rachel wasn't at her desk any more. "What the..." I said, more audibly this time, and Professor Rylands turned slowly to me in his usual predatory manner.

"Perhaps you've something you'd like to share with the class, McAndrew? Some revelation that will extend the boundaries of science even further?" The one thing that was worse than having to listen to him droning on and on about physics was being the butt of his sarcastic remarks; the rest of the class sniggered, mainly out of relief that *they* weren't his chosen victim today. "I'm waiting," he said, and the laughter increased in intensity.

"Well, sir," I said softly, deciding to tell the truth as I was going to be in big trouble whatever I said, "I was talking to Rachel about tonight's party." Instantly, the room went silent; even Professor Rylands stopped, mouth half open. And then it suddenly hit me; how could she have left the room *and* cleared her desk in the short time my eyes were closed? "How did she do it?" I asked of nobody in particular, then stopped, waiting for the usual explosion from the professor.

But it didn't come. Instead – which was more frightening – he looked at me with concern on his face, and said, "You're looking a bit tired, Phil... I mean Peter. This is the last lesson of the day, why don't you go on home and get ready for Williamson's party tonight."

This was a first! The professor *never* called anyone by their first name – not even the girls received that courtesy. And to allow anybody to leave *before* the bell – well I wasn't going to miss that opportunity, so I grabbed my books and rushed out, turning just once to smirk at the rest of the class; but instead of envy, I saw a mixture of pity and anger on their faces.

Wondering how Rachel had managed to slip out without being seen, and guessing she'd gone straight home, I decided to call round for her. I knocked on the door, but was disappointed when her mother answered. "Oh," she gasped, "I wasn't expecting to see *you*." She looked a lot older than she'd appeared when I was round the previous night. *Make-up*, I thought, and an image of Rachel in thirty years' time invaded my thoughts.

"Hello, Mrs Thomas," I said, trying to be as polite as I could be; I knew she didn't like me, but under the circumstances, she couldn't very well keep me away from her daughter, could she? "I was wondering if Rachel was home? She left the class and I guess she came here..." Mrs Thomas went very pale, then slumped to the floor in a dead faint.

Mr Thomas came into the hall, saying, "Who's at the ..." then stopped when he saw his wife in a heap on the carpet. I was about to explain what had happened, but something about the look in his eye told me it was time to make myself scarce, and I turned and ran down the drive. Mr Thomas bellowed something unintelligible after me, and I wondered what had happened; we had always got on well together, and he'd approved of my seeing his daughter even *before* the incident.

I carried on home, and went up to my room. It was too early to get ready for Darren's party, so I lay on my bed and tried, unsuccessfully, to make sense of the events of the last hour or so. I must have dozed off, for it was getting dark when I heard noises, which appeared to be coming from the kitchen. Yawning, I walked downstairs, and saw mum putting the shopping away.

"Hello Peter love, what do you want for tea?"

"I'm not hungry mum. I'll leave it and eat at the party."

"The party? I didn't think you were going."

"Of course I'm going – we've been looking forwards to it for weeks."

"Oh *we* is it. Have you found yourself a young lady?"

"Stop messing about mum. I'm taking Rachel, as well you know."

Mum just stood there, and a small heart-shaped tear slipped from her eye and rolled slowly down her cheek. "Oh Peter, love..." she whispered.

"And you know what's strange, mum?" I continued, not wanting to get into the embarrassing areas of asking why my mother was crying, "she went out of school today, and she's not at home. I called round at her house and ..."

"You went round there? Oh Peter, you shouldn't have done that, you know they still blame you."

"Blame me? For what?"

"You know very well, Peter. Please don't make me say it out loud."

I was getting angry now. Something had happened that I was getting the blame for. "Say it out loud, mum. I don't like being blamed for things that aren't my fault and ..."

"I didn't say it was your fault, love. I know it was an accident, you didn't mean it. Many children experiment, some take drugs, others binge drink. You know you shouldn't have been smoking, but everybody does it."

"Look, mum, we're not going over that again are we? Yes, I smoked once at a party, and fell asleep and started a fire, but there was no real damage done. Anyway, that was six months ago."

"Yes," she answered softly, "but Rachel..."

"Yes," I interrupted, "and Rachel was there too, and I almost forgot about her, but I remembered in time and went back for her and brought her out. People see me as a hero. So why are you on my case?"

"Oh Peter," she said, deep sobs racking her body. Her face was wet now as a river of tears coursed over her cheeks. "You know that isn't what happened. You didn't remember about Rachel until you were outside, and by then it was too late."

I went cold. What was she talking about? "I went back in and carried her out," I shouted, rolling my sleeve up. "That's how my arm was burnt like this." I held my disfigured arm out to her, defiantly, then stopped, stunned; the skin was perfect, not a mark on it. What was happening to me? Mum just turned her face away, and I ran out of the door, back to Rachel's. This was a bad joke; somebody was going to pay for doing this to me.

An ambulance was outside Rachel's, and I could see her mother being carried out on a stretcher. Her father saw me and started cursing again; there was no sign of Rachel. I went to Darren's instead. His look of surprise as he opened the door told me I wasn't going to get any answers from him; at least not answers that I wanted to here. "I didn't think you were coming tonight, dude," he said, "besides, it doesn't start for a couple of hours. You know, after the old folks have gone out. Say, man, that wasn't right what you said in class this afternoon. It was very bad taste. We all loved Rachel, and you were right out of order. Some of the guys wanted to come after you, but I talked them out of it. But it might not be a good idea to come here tonight, if you know what I mean."

I walked away, stunned. Nothing made sense, but some of the evidence was irrefutable; my arm should have had severe burn marks all up the inside; nothing could have made those vanish while I slept. I played the last few hours over in my mind. It had all started in the physics lesson, and – without consciously realising it – I found myself outside the school gates. The lights were on inside, and I remembered it was an open night for the parents of the next intake into Year 7. I walked towards the physics lab, and saw that Professor Rylands was at his desk. There was nobody in the room, so I went in. He looked surprised to see me. "What are you doing here McAn... I mean Peter?"

"I don't know what's happening, sir," I answered. "Nothing makes sense. All I know is that you were talking about somebody called Tegman or something, and since then everything has been crazy."

"It was Tegmark, not Tegman, but I'm surprised you remembered that. I didn't think you were paying attention at all. And you should have been, because Tegmark – or 'Mad Max' Tegmark as he's sometimes known – claims that there are any number of universes, and each one is slightly different to the next. All utter bunkum, of course, but the sort of thing that Hollywood and trash sci-fi writers lap up. Any student of mine who submits a paper that includes anything like that will get an instant 'F'. But I'm sure you didn't come here to talk about that. What are you doing here?"

I didn't answer. It all suddenly made sense. I *had* been chatting with Rachel, of that I was certain. Then there had been the blinding flash of light, and afterwards – well, that's when everything changed. Bunkum or not, I *knew* I was now in an alternate Universe; a Universe where I *hadn't* saved her from the fire.

#

I still remember that moment, even though it was five years ago. It was two o'clock on a Wednesday afternoon when the only girl I'll ever love disappeared from my life. I've studied everything ever written about the multiverse and alternate realities, trying to find the catalyst that will initiate the transference back to my own world; people smile weakly at me, humouring my insanity. But I know I'm right, and one day I will return home to Rachel.

Inglorious Sunset

I stroll hand-in-hand with Angie along the sea-front as the setting sun produces a glorious panoramic view that most lovers would sell their souls for; an hour ago, I would have been at the head of the queue, but now...

#

I met Angie four weeks ago, and – clichéd though it may sound – fell in love with her at first sight. She came to the theatre group which I run, asking if she could join – she hadn't been involved with theatre before and didn't feel confident enough to go on stage, but wanted to help out in any other capacity if we needed her. *If we needed her!* We're overrun with *darlings* who think they'd betray the memory of Olivier and Gielgud if they did anything other than act, so how refreshing it was to get somebody who was happy to be *front of house* and didn't have any aspirations of being the next Dame Judi Dench.

We were busy rehearsing for our upcoming performance of *Billy Liar*, so I asked Angie if she wanted to watch and see what went on. My attentions for the next hour or so were torn between the Fisher family characters on stage and Angie, who sat watching in the wings. She was probably mid-thirties, about five years younger than me, with long brown hair flowing to the middle of her back. She was slightly Rubenesque, but I've always had a penchant for larger-sized females; I was warming to her already. Ever since Carol had suddenly decided to end our year-long relationship three weeks earlier, I had been stumbling through life aimlessly, but now I felt I had something to look forwards to once more. Every time I looked over at Angie, she glanced across at me, with a friendly – but knowing – smile touching her lips.

After the rehearsals were over, I introduced her to the rest of the group, and we chatted pleasantly over a pint in the local for an hour or so. It was raining when we were leaving, and I noticed she wasn't wearing a coat. "Have you far to go, Angie?" I asked.

"No, just a short bus ride, Chris. There should be one along in a few minutes."

"My car's just outside, can I give you a lift?"

"I don't want to put you to any trouble. Won't your wife be expecting you home?"

"It's no trouble, and I'm not married, so nobody is waiting up for me." Angie smiled as I said this, and flicked her fringe back with her left-hand, making it obvious that she wore no rings; for the first time, I was glad that I was no longer with Carol.

#

We chatted like old friends as I drove, and when I dropped her off, she gave me a lingering goodnight kiss. I gave her my mobile number, and she texted before I was halfway home.

As a school teacher, I was able to take full advantage of the six-week summer shutdown. We met every day, starting with a quiet drink in a local bar, but quickly progressing to more intimate nights in the confines of our own homes. I was falling deeper and deeper under her spell, and there was nothing I could do about it.

When I collected her tonight, she suggested we go for a stroll on the beach. The golden sun was setting as we set foot on the warm sands, and to all intents and purposes we were the only two beings in the whole of existence.

"Don't you wish it could be like this always, Angie? I mean, just the two of us, with nobody else around to spoil things."

"Oh, but it will be, Chris. Nothing can spoil things this time."

"I wish you could be right, but perfection such as this can't last. School starts again tomorrow, and I'm not going to have as much free time – you know, what with marking and all that. Anyway, what did you mean when you said *this time*?"

"I'm sure you'll soon see that I'm far more important than silly old marking." And she grabbed my hand and pulled me along with her as she walked towards the setting sun. I looked at the glare bouncing back off the gentle waves, and it took me a while to realise she hadn't answered my question. I put my hand on her shoulders and turned her to face me.

"Listen Angie, you know I love you, and I want us to be together as much as possible. We'll be able to meet every weekend, and on Wednesday nights, but I'm head of the sixth form, and for the next few weeks at least, I'm hardly going to have a moment for myself even, let alone anyone else. There's the new curriculum, the government requires that I fill in ream upon ream of paperwork, I've lesson plans to prepare, and with the cutbacks, I'm responsible for the football teams throughout the school. I'll spend most of my evenings driving a minibus full of sweaty teenagers the length and breadth of Lancashire."

"No, Chris, you'll not do any of that. Remember how Carol used to moan that you never spent enough time with her? You're not going to do the same with me."

"But Carol underst… wait a minute, I never told you that about Carol. How did you know?"

"Because she told me, dear."

"She told you? When did you meet her? You didn't tell me."

"Oh, we had a nice long chat about seven weeks ago. She wasn't too sure at first, but she soon got the message."

"You never said… Seven weeks – that was round about the time she finished with me."

"Yes, it was. In fact, it was *exactly* the time she finished with you. She didn't want to at first, but after I'd spoken with her, she was disgusted – I had a hard job stopping her going to the police."

"Police? What the hell are you talking about, Angie?" I was grabbing her shoulders tightly, now, and she winced a little in pain.

"Stop that, Chris. You're never to lay a finger on me again, unless you want a charge of assault on your record as well."

"As well as what?" I shouted, angrily.

"Calm down, Chris, that's no way to speak to your fiancée. The police don't look kindly on wife-beaters. Especially paedophile wife-beaters who are schoolteachers."

I was stunned, but her words also raised a defiance in me. "You're crazy," I yelled. "Go on, run to the police, I've never been with an underage girl in my life."

"Oh, but you have. Don't you remember, that girl you picked up in the Stable Bar that Christmas? I know it was a long time ago, but I thought you'd have remembered."

"What on earth are you..." Then I did remember. It was about twenty years ago, and I'd assumed she was of similar age to me as she was in the pub drinking Bacardi and coke. I'd taken her back to my student flat – my flatmates had all gone back home for the vacation – and it was the next morning before I realised she looked so much younger without her makeup. She'd admitted she was only fourteen, and I never saw her again after that. "Yes, Angie, I do remember. But she looked eighteen, she was in a pub, damn it, I never saw her again, nobody could blame me..."

"Oh, but they will, Chris. Ignorance is no excuse under the law. It's just your bad luck that poor little Angela kept a diary, and even now, twenty years later, if she were to take it to the police, they'd be interested. But I won't do that, not if you do what I tell you to. I was surprised you didn't recognise me. You've hardly changed, but I suppose a girl changes a lot – plus I've put quite a lot of weight on. Most men want nothing to do with me, but – well, I saw you coming out of school a couple of months ago, and that's not a problem I've to worry about any more, is it?" And she took my hand again and turned to face the setting sun.

#

And as I stare at its last rays as it sinks beneath the horizon, I look once more at the woman next to me. Before, I was happy. Now I'm terrified.

Mona Linda's Smile

Linda Sullivan exited Charles de Gaul airport and headed for the taxi rank. It was her first time in Paris, and she had a packed itinerary of places she wanted to visit, with today's list including Notre Dame Cathedral, the Eiffel Tower and her starting point, the Louvre. Newly divorced, she constantly ran her right index finger and thumb around the pale circle which denoted where her wedding band had owned her for the last ten years. Now, in her late twenties, she had the opportunity to restart her life, but before she embarked on any new romantic ventures, she wanted to see more of the world, having been restricted to fortnights in Benidorm by her controlling ex.

As the taxi moved into the city, she marvelled at places she had only previously seen in movies. After a short sightseeing tour, with the Arc de Triomphe her personal favourite, her carriage entered the 1ˢᵗ arrondissement on the Right Bank of the Seine and stopped outside the Musée du Louvre. Linda smiled as she took in the splendour of the Palais du Louvre, home to priceless collections for more than three hundred years.

She intended to see as many of the four hundred thousand exhibits as humanly possible during her week-long stay in the city, but on this initial visit, she ignored the lure of ancient Egypt, Greece and Rome and headed towards the High Renaissance collection of paintings. She took her time enjoying every feature of Caravaggio's *Death of the Virgin* and da Vinci's *Madonna of the Rocks*, but was slightly disappointed at the most famous work of all, *The Mona Lisa*. It was much smaller than she had expected, and although she had seen images of it on many previous occasions, only now, close up, did she realise how bland it was. Couldn't da Vinci have accentuated the bright colours of her clothing instead of portraying them so darkly?

#

She closed her eyes and tried to imagine how the real La Giocanda would have appeared as she sat for the painting five hundred years earlier. If she had been there herself, would the end result have been different? Granted, the lady's enigmatic smile would be impossible to better, but Linda believed her own golden-yellow hair would have softened the entire image. In her reverie, she looked at her clothing. Her dress was brown, her cloak green, but neither were the dark tones of the finished painting. Everything seemed so real. She envisaged da Vinci, brushes in hand, and tried to influence him to breathe more life into her image. Knowing only English and a smattering of tourist French, she held her conversation with the artist in her native language.

"Why do you make everything so dark, Leonardo?"

"My lady, I am not trying to copy your image, I intend to produce a work of art that will be admired for generations."

"But why does it have to be so dull?"

"Dull? You don't understand what I'm trying to achieve here. It is the aesthetic effect that I strive for. The contrast between light and dark is the key to everything. The glow of the light on your hands extends upwards to your breast, neck and face, a pyramid of focus in stark contrast to the shadowy elements of your hair and clothing." And then da Vinci paused, adding, "But your hair isn't dark, how could I have made that mistake?" And he shook his head, puzzled.

Linda took her opportunity while the artist was momentarily perplexed. "So you can't portray the contrast in that way. Why not give the painting colour and life? Everybody will love it for centuries to come, I assure you."

"Perhaps you are right, my lady, but I don't think my works will survive beyond my lifetime."

"Nonsense! Don't talk like that. *The Last Supper* is a masterpiece..."

"You've been to the Convent of Santa Maria delle Grazie, my lady?"

"No, I've never been to Milan, but I intend to go there one day. Believe me, your place in history is reserved, and not just for your art."

"What do you mean, *not just for your art*?"

"I mean your inventive mind will amaze people for centuries to come. Everyone will marvel at your conceptual designs of a helicopter, a tank, solar power, and a calculator."

"I'm sorry my lady, I don't know what you are referring to. What is a helicopter? Or a tank?"

"The helicopter is a flying machine, the tank is an armoured war vehicle. You have made sketches that will form the basis of the actual machines many years in the future."

"But they are just doodlings to while away the time, idle fantasies. There is nothing real about them."

"You're wrong, they *are* real. Your renown as an inventor will equal your fame as an artist. Your *Codex on the Flight of Birds* is the culmination of all your ideas on flight."

"But I haven't finished that yet! How do you know about it?" There was anger in da Vinci's voice, and Linda felt uncomfortable. She spoke rapidly in response.

"Everyone knows about your fascination with flight. It's fifteen years since your designs for a flying machine were first seen, so it's only natural that you'd investigate how birds fly." She didn't know if she'd said enough to defuse the situation, but da Vinci didn't pursue the matter. She took advantage of the pause to change the subject. "So are you going to breathe some light and life into this painting?"

"Mmm, what? Oh, the painting. Yes, I think you are correct, I will go away and produce a new batch of paints before resuming the portrait."

#

"Excuse me miss, could you just move aside for a moment."

Linda's eyes jerked wide open as she realised she was still in the Louvre. She turned towards the speaker, a uniformed tour guide, and behind him were a dozen Japanese tourists. Guide and group, all were staring open-mouthed at her, turning to look at the painting, then turning back to her. "It's you…" said the guide.

Linda turned, bewildered, to look at the painting again. But instead of the familiar enigmatic smile of La Giocanda, she saw a picture of a yellow-haired woman adorned with colourful browns and greens, carrying the inscription, in English, "The Mona Linda, Leonardo da Vinci, 1503 – his last work before dedicating his life to the study of birds in flight."

Countdown

Tick tock, tick tock. The ticking of the clock seems to be getting faster; I know it can't be, but however much I tell myself that, it doesn't alter my perception that time is running out with the rapidity of sand slipping through a child's fingers.

When I was a child, my mother used to *tut* at me as I lounged about, humming along with the ticking of the old grandfather clock. "You're sitting there while that clock ticks your life away," she would say, and I'd just laugh scornfully at her; but now I know she was right all the time.

#

It's my own fault, of course. The kids in the area used to call me a nosy neighbour, and they were right, I suppose. I've lived alone in this cul-de-sac all my adult life, and as I work from home, I don't get to see many people. Ours is a very quiet neighbourhood, to the extent that if a car drives down the road, it's a newsworthy item.

The new couple across the road moved in six months ago. I still don't know their names, but that isn't unusual around here – people keep themselves to themselves, and if I hadn't peered out of the windows on occasion, I wouldn't have seen any life at all. Nor would I be in my current predicament, if only I'd kept myself to myself.

The new family seemed perfectly normal, a man and woman of about forty years of age. He was tall, swarthy-looking, whereas she had more delicate, porcelain features. She seemed far too pretty to be with him, but I know it is a strange old world and physical attraction takes many forms. I rarely saw either of them leave the house, apart from when she went out to do the weekly shopping, and assumed that neither of them worked. Ours isn't a well-off neighbourhood, but neither is it a haven for down-and-outs, so I puzzled a little as to what their reasons for being here were. Of course, they could have thought the same about me, and I concluded that they, like myself, were part of the modern-day workforce-at-home.

I first became suspicious about four months ago. There seemed to be an unusual amount of activity, with four different cars pulling up outside their house in the same week. The visitors were all let in, and an hour or so later, came out again.

I thought nothing of it at first, but when the third new arrival came, I took a little more notice. All the visitors were males, probably in their mid to late thirties, and all hurried along the drive with coat collars pulled up to cover as much of their features as was possible; they obviously did not want to be recognised.

I considered what their reason for calling might be. Perhaps they were just legitimate business colleagues; but if that were the case, why the furtive approaches? I concluded that there could only be one reason why men of that age would be making house calls during the day; my new neighbours were operating a brothel out of their two-up two-down detached house. The front bedroom curtains were always closed, and although that in itself wasn't conclusive, I felt it was suspicious enough to add credence to my notion.

The very idea appalled me; I am not a prude, but there are places for this type of thing, and Acacia Drive is not one of them. I considered reporting them to the police, but realised they would take no notice of me; after all, I have on previous occasions been on the receiving end of the acid-tongue of the local constabulary when I've tried to perform my civic duty. No, I would need proof before I could involve the police, and as that was hardly likely to come my way, I resigned myself to living in an estate of debauchery.

Until this morning, that is, when fortune favoured me at last – or so I thought at the time. Mrs Porcelain went out for her normal weekly shop, but Mr Swarthy accompanied her this time. I knew that she was always out for at least an hour – after all, it's a fifteen-minute drive to the nearest large supermarket, and you can't buy a week's shopping in less than thirty minutes, can you? Before I even realised what I was about to do, I was across the road and opening the gate that led to their back garden.

I only intended taking a look outside, although what I expected to find, I don't know. But the French windows were ajar, and seconds later I found myself inside their home. I still didn't really know what I was looking for, but I headed upstairs to their bedroom. Perhaps there would be evidence of their salacious lifestyle – ceiling mirrors, fetish ware, possible handcuffs and whips. But no, their bedroom was just what it should have been – an ordinary room containing a bed, a chest of drawers, a medium-sized wardrobe and a table with sheets of computer paper all over the top of it.

I was about to close the door and return home, accepting that the only way I would be able to gain proof of their activities would be by becoming one of their clients myself – and that would never happen – when I noticed one of the sheets of paper on the bedside table. It was the headline that caught my attention, but at that moment, I heard a sound, and turned round to find Mr Swarthy and Mrs Porcelain blocking the doorway.

"I didn't see anything," I spluttered, desperately edging backwards, but it was no good. I could tell from the look in Mr Swarthy's eye that he didn't believe me for an instant, and I decided my only hope was to rely on the element of surprise. I swept all the papers off the table and, as his eyes followed the movement of the sheets, I ran for the door; I would have made it too, if I hadn't made the fatal mistake of forgetting about Mrs Porcelain. She may have looked as if a breath of wind might shatter her delicate features, but the punch she landed on my jaw was delivered like a rod of iron. I remember falling slowly backwards, then saw Mr Swarthy's boot heading for my face, and I blacked out amidst an explosion of stars.

When I regained consciousness it was dark, and it took me a few minutes to remember where I was. The curtains were, of course, closed, but I guessed that it was now night-time. I must have been out for several hours.

I tried to shout, even though I knew that it would likely do no good at all; as I've already said, ours is a *very* quiet neighbourhood. But I couldn't make a noise, even if there *had* been anybody around to hear it. Something was preventing me opening my mouth, but when I tried to check what it was, I found I couldn't move my arms. As my eyes grew accustomed to the light, I could make out the ropes binding me to the chair. I could move my head, but it seemed like gaffer tape had been stuck over my mouth to prevent me making any noise.

I looked around. Everything was as it was earlier, with the papers all over the floor. The one that had initially caught my attention was face up in front of me, and although it was too far away to read the details, I could still see the headline: *How to Make a Homemade bomb*. There was a picture of a crude explosive device on the front of the sheet, and I realised it must have been deliberately left there as a final, sick joke. Alongside it was the real thing, an alarm clock attached to a bundle of dynamite. If only I *had* stumbled on a brothel instead of a terrorist cell.

#

The ticking is so loud that I expect the whole world to hear it. The hour hand is almost at the twelve now, and I can see the second hand as it approaches the due North position. Thirteen ... twelve ... eleven ... ten ... nine more seconds until contact is made and the dynamite explodes, three ... two ... one ...

The Eye of the Beholder

"See you later mum," shouted Ryan, as he ran down the stairs,

"Where are you going? You've exams tomorrow."

"I know, but I'll not be long, I'm meeting Pippa and her friend. Must go, I'm late already," he said, slamming the front door shut behind him before his mother could object further. He had been dating Pippa throughout Year 13, as both were taking the same A Levels, but with the exams about to start, they had hardly seen each other recently. So, when Pippa suggested they meet up for an hour, Ryan accepted immediately, although he hated the idea of sharing their precious moments with somebody else.

He knew nothing about her friend Louise, as Pippa hadn't mentioned her before, but he hoped that they would soon be able to ditch her and spend some time together. As he rounded the final corner, he was disappointed when he saw that Pippa wasn't waiting at their appointed meeting place in front of the garage, but then he spotted her familiar strolling gait heading towards their rendezvous point.

He barely had time to give her a greeting hug when a shrill voice called out, "Hi Pippa, sorry I'm late," and Ryan looked towards the source of the noise, presumably Louise. She was almost the complete opposite of Pippa, whose neat, short styled brown hair contrasted totally with the new girl's long blond tresses, and where Pippa wore three-quarter length pants, Louise preferred a knee-length powder-blue skirt. *Presumably*, thought Ryan, *to mask her rather ample backside.*

"Not a prob, we've only just arrived ourselves. Louise - Ryan, Ryan - Louise. We were at primary school together until Louise moved away, and we lost touch until recently. She stole my boyfriend," Pippa added, half laughing.

"Hi," said Ryan, offering his hand, and feeling guilty for the sizeist thoughts he had been entertaining. *No*, he thought, *I was wrong. She isn't big at all, besides it's much healthier than the size zero models you see every day.*

"Hey, Ryan," said Louise, taking his hand and shaking it warmly. Ryan noticed a sharp glance from Pippa, and let go of her hand, perhaps a little too quickly.

Seeking to avoid an embarrassing moment, he asked, "Where do you want to go, then?" but had to repeat the question as neither girl was listening.

It was Louise who recovered first. "Can we just wait a couple of minutes? My boyfriend Thomas will be here soon."

Ryan noticed Pippa relaxing visibly at the mention of a boyfriend, and he sensed that the girls wanted to have some catch-up talk, so he stepped to one side to give them time and opportunity. He looked again at the dissimilarity between the two young women as they chatted animatedly, until he saw a youth walking towards them, wearing an *Indiana Jones*-style hat, light brown waistcoat and dark trousers. *He's as big a contrast to me as Louise is to Pippa,* he thought, glancing quickly down at his red shirt and white trousers. He saw Pippa staring at the newcomer and his own insecurities resurfaced; he hadn't really wanted to go on this double date, only agreeing as it gave him the chance to be with Pippa, but now he wondered if she was considering breaking up with him.

The new introductions were soon completed, and Ryan broached the subject again of what they should do. "Anyone fancy a drink? There's a decent pub across the way." He edged closer to Pippa, who linked arms with him before sending what Ryan took as a look of challenge towards Louise. *Great*, he thought, *Pippa fancies Thomas.*

Ryan turned towards Thomas, and saw – or thought he saw – something ephemeral out of the corner of his eye. He knew he must be imagining it, as it seemed to be floating in the air above them, but as he looked up to see what was really there, he glimpsed Pippa hurling herself at Louise, before a sharp pain in his back sent him flying forwards, crashing into Thomas as he landed on his hands and knees amongst the chippings. *Angela*, he muttered, as he lay on the ground in pain.

#

Pippa kept looking at her watch as she half-ran to meet Ryan. *Damn,* she thought, *the only chance I get to see him all week, and mum wouldn't let me go out until I've put these boring pants on. And I've to share him with Louise, but mum wouldn't have let me out at all if I wasn't meeting her.* "Not while you're doing your exams, dear!" She rounded the corner and saw Ryan looking forlornly at the empty garage forecourt, before smiling as he spotted her. She was looking forwards to a long, slow kiss, but no sooner had he held her close to him than she heard Louise's unusually high-pitched tones.

She made the introductions, but winced when she saw Louise hold Ryan's hand just an instant longer than was respectable. They had only been seven when Louise had *stolen* that boy from her; she couldn't even remember his name now. Surely she wasn't going to do it again?

Pippa was ashamed of her slim body, and constantly expected Ryan to leave her for a more voluptuous girlfriend. *After all,* she thought, *isn't that all that boys are bothered about?* But she didn't expect to be dumped for somebody she had introduced him to, and she was determined to do everything in her power to prevent that happening today.

Ryan said something in the background, but she didn't catch it, and he had to repeat his question about where they should go. It was Louise who answered, and Pippa relaxed as she mentioned a boyfriend. Perhaps there was nothing to worry about after all. Feeling ashamed of her thoughts, she turned to Louise and said, "Go on then, tell me all about him."

"There's not much to tell. I haven't known him long. I didn't want to be, well, you know, *two's company, three's a crowd*, so I asked him to come with me. Is that okay?"

"Of course it is, Louise, it'll be great as two couples."

"We're not really a couple. He's more a boy who is a friend than a boyfriend. I don't actually have a regular. Oh, here he comes now."

Pippa felt uneasy again. This wasn't turning out how she'd expected. All she'd wanted was to spend some time with Ryan before the exams. She looked at the strangely-garbed newcomer, Thomas, and understood why Louise had made it clear he was a friend rather than a date. Nobody could possibly fancy someone who looked like that. She'd have to make doubly sure she kept Louise well away from Ryan.

As Ryan walked towards Louise, Pippa intercepted and linked arms with him. She saw something strange, barely in her line of sight. When she looked towards it, she felt herself being pushed, and crashed into Louise, knocking her over. Out of the corner of her eye, she saw Ryan hurtling towards Thomas. Her first thought was *Angela*, but she didn't know why.

#

Louise had been surprised to meet Pippa again after so many years, and was delighted at the opportunity for a catch up with her. The only problem was, Pippa had wanted to bring her boyfriend along, and Louise felt she didn't want to be the gooseberry in this threesome.

She had fancied Thomas for weeks, and although they chatted regularly as friends, she hadn't the courage to ask him out. This, though, gave her the opportunity, and she was relieved when he accepted her explanation that she wanted a friend to accompany her. Truth was, she was ashamed of her body, and however much she tried to diet, she couldn't lose any weight. Tonight, she had tried to make herself look as enticing as possible, but when she looked at her image in the mirror before leaving, all she could see was an unattractive bleached blue whale.

It was too late to do anything about it, though, and she hurried off to the rendezvous point. Pippa was already there, presumably with her date. "Hi Pippa, sorry I'm late," she squeaked, instantly biting her tongue as her nerves had made her voice sound just like a blonde bimbo. Hardly a great first impression.

She barely heard as Pippa made the introductions, and realised to her horror that she hadn't let go of Ryan's hand. No wonder that Pippa was glaring at her. Ryan was asking a question, but it took her a couple of attempts before she realised what he had said. Seizing the opportunity to put Pippa at ease, she said the first thing that came into her head, and suddenly Thomas was introduced into the equation as her boyfriend.

She regretted her white lie, as Pippa immediately wanted to know all the details. This was going horribly wrong. Unless she told the truth, Pippa would ask Thomas leading questions and any hopes she might have of *ever* having a relationship with him would be dashed. She had to come clean. She could see Thomas walking towards them, and admitted to Pippa that Thomas was only a friend, but she knew instantly that was the wrong thing to say, as Pippa glared at her once more. She'd already made the comment about her stealing Pippa's boyfriend at primary school – they were only seven, and at that age a boyfriend was just somebody you looked at Pokémon cards with - and although she'd thought she was joking, perhaps Pippa really did still bear a grudge against her.

The atmosphere was strained as the final introductions were made, and Louise felt even more uneasy as she saw Thomas glancing perhaps a little too long in Pippa's direction. *I always knew he preferred catwalk models,* she thought, sadly. Ryan must have felt under threat, as he made sure that Pippa linked arms with him before they walked to the pub.

There was an odd look in Pippa's eye, and Louise noticed something strange, seemingly floating above the pair of them. Next thing, for some reason Pippa launched herself at Louise, who was caught unawares and knocked flying, while Ryan threw himself at Thomas. What was happening? The name *Angela* was on her lips; with certainty, she knew she was involved. But who *was* Angela?

#

When Louise asked Thomas to accompany her on a meeting with an old school-friend and her boyfriend, he couldn't believe his good fortune. He had been hanging out with her for a while now, but was too shy to ask her on a proper date. Besides, he knew he risked rejection, for although she didn't appear to have a boyfriend, a stunning blonde beauty like Louise must have had no end of admirers.

He knew she was only inviting him to make up the numbers, but that didn't matter; if he couldn't be her boyfriend, he was happy enough to have her in his life as a friend. One of his mates said she preferred the rugged adventurer type, and Thomas knew that he was far from that. He decided to wear an *Indiana Jones* style hat and hope that she might notice him a little more, but it was with little confidence that he approached the meeting-point.

As he rounded the corner, he saw Louise deep in conversation with another girl, with a lad standing just to the side. The girl wasn't his type in the slightest, far too skinny for his likes, and he imagined that her boyfriend might feel the same, especially as his eyes seemed to be focussed on Louise's bosom.

Louise noticed his imminent arrival, and all eyes turned in his direction. Pippa's glance became a stare, and he felt distinctly uneasy. This was turning out to be a bad mistake. Friendship or not, he wished he hadn't come. He wasn't sure whether he was glad or not when Ryan suggested they go for a drink, but at least it meant the others were no longer looking at him. Ryan linked arms with Pippa as they prepared to leave, and Louise didn't look happy.

Thomas saw Ryan staring at him, and he didn't like the expression on his face. There also seemed to be a strange disturbance in the air, but as Thomas tried to focus on it, he saw Pippa throw herself at Louise. Before he could go to her aid, Ryan charged into him, sending him flying. He whispered *Angela* as he fell, but he didn't know anybody with that name.

#

The four teenagers looked angrily at each other as they sprawled on the ground, encircling the area where seconds earlier they had been about to set off for the pub. But before they could stand, an explosion sent chunks of tarmac flying through the air in all directions. When the dust cleared, they saw that the forecourt had disappeared, leaving in its wake a huge crater. Shaken as they were, each realised that had they been on their feet when the explosion occurred, they would undoubtedly have suffered serious injuries at best.

#

Angela was in her early twenties when she died of cholera in the hospital in Scutari, Constantinople. She always felt it ironic that she had gone there to *help* people with the disease, not succumb to it herself, as one of thirty-eight nurses accompanying Florence Nightingale in November 1854. Fortunately, her departure from the earthly realm hadn't curtailed her ability to save people, though now her aid was for any need, not just medical.

When she had been told that the leaking fuel line running underneath the forecourt was about to ignite, she had to think quickly. Harnessing her ability to briefly control and direct the currents of air, she gave herself a metaphorical pat on the back for her solution, even though she accepted that nobody would ever know what she had done. But as she readied to leave for her next task, she could have sworn she heard four whispered *Angela's* carried on the remnants of the wind.

Amore Roma

Theme: palindromes.

#

I couldn't find my ticket, it was nearly time to leave, and I was starting to panic. Just in case it was still in the envelope, I opened it – it wasn't there, but I read the letter again:

> *Hi Anna,*
>
> *Only a few days till our hols. The tickets arrived today – I've enclosed yours - and I've told Elle when to meet us at Fiumicino. Pity we couldn't afford the Caribbean this year – rum, rum, I murmur wistfully!*
>
> *I'll have to meet you at Liverpool Airport, as the boat from Dublin docks too late for me to come to yours first, sis. Can't wait till we're out there – and all those sexy Italian guys! Amore Roma, I say!*
>
> *See you Saturday morning,*
>
> *Eve.*

I smiled as I read her words, a combination of looking forward to seeing Elle again after such a long time, and thinking of Eve leaving her home in Navan at some unearthly hour to catch the bus from County Meath to Dublin. When we first met Elle, she had been the voice of reason. Eve and I were arguing, as twin sisters do, but I tried to make a pact with her, as I felt we were making a scene. "My word is my bond, I'll not argue with you again," I said

"Don't talk rubbish," interjected Elle, "no word, no bond - row on. Don't hold it in and let it fester." And she was right, of course. Mind you, she enjoyed a good argument – but she always knew where the boundaries lay, and went never a foot too far, even though she sometimes took things to the absolute limit.

I looked at my watch. *Damn, I muttered, the taxi'll be here soon.* I still didn't know where I'd put my ticket, and I took my mobile out, ready to ring the taxi firm and ask them to delay a little. Then I suddenly remembered where it was - in my reward drawer, where I keep my stash of chocolate for when I've done something really good! Cursing my stupidity, I retrieved the ticket, grabbed my case, checked everything was switched off, felt in my handbag for my passport, and set off down the path. There was no way I was going to miss this holiday – why, with what it was costing me, I could have had the boob job that my last boyfriend suggested I needed! That was the last thing he had a chance to suggest to me! In the pre-dawn light, something scuttled in front of me. Was it a cat I saw? Or, more worrying, was it a rat I saw? I shuddered.

The taxi drew up, a brand new Honda Civic, and I climbed in. Wordlessly, the driver set off for the airport. On the radio, Abba were singing *SOS* – hardly the ideal song for somebody who is terrified of flying. What's it called, *aibohphobia* or something – no, *aerophobia*. I'm sure the first one means something though. The song went on, seemingly endlessly. *If I had a hi-fi*, I thought, *this song would never get a second's airtime.*

The journey to the airport seemed to take forever, and I began to fret as the minutes raced by. A memory forced its way into my head, of when Eve and I were children. Mum and dad took us on holiday every year to Butlins, and we'd set off at first light on the long drive to Bognor Regis or Filey. Funny, I know he drove a Toyota, but I can't remember what model. Anyway, we'd be arguing in the back, asking, "*are we nearly there yet*" before we'd even reached the motorway, and mum always used to give us a bottle of pop and play games with us to take our minds off the journey. One that I recall vividly was a nature spotting game in one of the puzzle books she always brought with her, and I still remember mum saying, "Did Anna see bees? Anna did." Eve, of course, sulked, until mum let her continue, and she said "Now I see bees. I won."

There was nothing to take my mind off the delays now, though. Eventually, the traffic began to move, but we came to a stop again within minutes. This time, though, the hold-up was caused by an old man trying to back his car into his drive. He went back a bit, then came forward again to straighten up, then drove a short way back before stopping and coming forward again. This went on for some time, and I was getting angrier and angrier. The taxi driver, though, didn't seem to care – well, the meter was running, wasn't it. "Can't you toot your horn and tell him to get a move on," I yelled, but he just shrugged his shoulders and continued to wait patiently. I wondered why Eve hadn't rung, asking where I was, and I decided to ring her to check she'd made it okay. I reached for my phone, then remembered – I'd left it on top of the drawer when I realised where I'd put my ticket!

Eventually, we reached the airport, and I ran to the departure terminal, fearful that I'd be too late. I looked out at the aircraft on the tarmac, through the heat haze, thinking how I'd be redder than a lobster if I was out there working on a day like this. However, when I went to check the flight details, I saw the one word *Delayed* alongside our flight number. As I stood there, suddenly deflated, Eve came alongside. "Yep, a great start to the hols, Anna. They reckon we won't be away till this afternoon. I've rung Elle to tell her - I tried to ring you, but you didn't pick up."

"That's because I forgot my phone," I growled. Eve knew me well enough not to say any more. As we had several hours to wait, she decided to try and get some rest on the uncomfortable airport bench seats. Despite being up early, I was no longer tired, so I took out the guide book I had brought for the holiday. But I couldn't concentrate, partly because of the heat, but mainly because of my mood, and I found myself reading the same passage over and over again. I think it said, *A new order began, a more Roman age bred Rowena*, but I had read Scott's *Ivanhoe* the previous day, and I might have been mixing the guidebook up with his Saxon heroine. I put the book down, resigned to a long, boring wait. I fiddled with the label on my handbag, which had come detached, and I was about to throw it away in disgust.

Alongside me, Eve was unable get comfortable and she sat up as she saw what I was doing. "No, tie it on," she said, "Hey, did I tell you about Elle? She was caught having it off in the photocopying room during the lunch break."

I laughed. I knew I was being drawn onward into one of Eve's stories, but I didn't care. Elle always was one avid diva. She had been in our year at school, but was always more into boys than books. Seemed like she hadn't changed. This holiday was going to be interesting. "During the lunch break?" I asked. "I'd rather have a sandwich, personally. Besides, sex at noon taxes the body, how could she expect to work afterwards?" I thought back to our last year at school, when Eve, Elle and I hung out together. We were studying Shakespeare's Henry V, and the Saint Crispen's Day speech. It was the one piece of literature that grabbed her attention, and she liked to refer to our trio as *we few, we happy sex-mad few*. "Last I heard of her," I said, "she was going on holiday to New Zealand."

"Oh yes," laughed Eve, "that was a hoot."

The word brought an image of a snowy-white owl into my mind, but this owl was wilting under the hot sun. "What was a hoot? Anyway, if it was as warm as this, it'd be too hot to hoot," I muttered.

"What was that?" asked Eve. I didn't answer, so she continued. "Didn't you hear the story about when Elle was in Auckland? She became involved with some native wiccans and was arrested after one of their festivities. Apparently it was late at night under the full moon."

Suddenly, I was interested. "Why, what had she done?"

"Well, you know all about wiccan gatherings, don't you? She was deported for it – she wrote to me, saying something like, 'It was a beautiful moon, fuller than any I ever saw in England, and I roamed under it as a tired, nude Maori.'"

"Surely nudity isn't something she'd get deported for?"

"Well, it seems it wasn't just nudity. You see, there was this huge sundial, the focal point of their gathering. And there was a male witch there too, a man called Dennis. Apparently, our Elle was deported for being laid at a dial!"

"You're making fun of me! That didn't happen!"

"Yes it did, Anna, I'm on the level, honest!"

"Well I hope she wasn't the only one deported – after all, Dennis sinned as well."

"I guess he did, eh? I didn't really think of it like that."

"Well, serves them both right. There's a time and place for these things, and it isn't under a full moon in front of a sundial!"

"Oh, I dunno, sis, with the right person, well…"

"Oh come on, Eve, just name now one man who you'd do it with."

"I can't," she replied, "I don't know *his* name," she added, nodding towards a good-looking guy standing a dozen or so yards away.

I couldn't stop myself from laughing. And it didn't surprise me one bit. I realised that – as always - Eve had lifted my spirits. Thinking of spirits gave me an idea. "Hey, let's have a drink while we're waiting."

"Yes, let's," she said. "And as we're on holiday, why not push the boat out. We'll pretend we're royalty. I'm glad to see you're happy again. You looked a right misery guts when I saw you at the departures board."

"I did, did I? Okay, you win, but steady on," I said, "I know we're on vacation, but the flight and the villa have taken all my savings. I'll have to stretch my spending money to last the fortnight – especially the way Elle likes to party."

"Yes, I know what you mean," said Eve, "okay, let's have a lager, a regal drink if ever there was one."

We walked to the bar, and out of the corner of my eye I noticed the usual airport religious fanatic, with a placard proclaiming *Live not on evil but on the good Lord* on the front and *Evil is a name of a foeman, as I live* on the other side. I quickly put him to the back of my mind as I walked past him. "See, I told you this was where us royals should be," Eve said, nodding towards the next table. I looked across, and saw a fabulously-dressed woman sipping a cocktail. But it was her engagement ring that caught my eye.

"Mega gem!" I exclaimed, "I'd sure like to borrow that!"

"Borrow or rob?" asked Eve in her most innocent voice. I laughed again.

One lager became two, and two became many more. I picked up an advertising leaflet off the counter. "Hey," I said, "there's a quiz here, let's give it a go."

"Okay, I'll ask the first question. It says 'The *Mille Miglia* starts and ends in Brescia with a turnaround in Rome. Which cities were included on the 2009 itinerary: (a) Rome and Venice, (b) Rome and Verona or (c) Rome and Vienna.'

"I know that one – it's Rome and Verona."

"Pfft," said Eve, "Anne, I vote more cars race Rome to Vienna," and she ticked box (c). I don't remember a great deal after that.

Before we knew it, our flight was being called, and it took all of our efforts to convince the airport staff that we were in a fit state to fly. "Anybody would think we were going to hijack the plane," I whispered to Eve as we were finally allowed to board.

I was tired, a combination of the early morning start, the heat and too much alcohol, and I dozed during the flight, missing my meal and only wakening when the steward leant across to hand Eve a cup of water and a carton of mixed fruit. "No lemon, no melon," she said quickly, and he took them away again. I glared at Eve, out of pique more than anything, as I grabbed a carton off the tray before the steward disappeared. It was a peach yoghurt, and I don't like peaches. But I was hungry, so I peeled the lid back.

Just as I was about to take a mouthful, there was a commotion behind me, and I turned round to see the man I had classified as a religious fanatic back at the airport. He was waving something long and metallic over his head, and shouting *retribution is here*. I immediately regretted my callous remark about hijacking.

Fortunately, one of the other passengers was alert, and he wrestled the fanatic to the floor, with other travellers quickly joining in to disarm him. I realised I'd been holding my breath while all this went on, and I gulped in a huge breath of air. I took a look at my yoghurt carton, and pushed it away. Talk about stressed desserts! The fanatic was led away, and I noticed the thick piece of metal as a steward picked it up.

"How could he get that on board?" I said to Eve. "Surely the radar thingy should have spotted it."

"Metal detector, idiot, radar is what the pilot uses. Anyway, I heard someone say it was in the overhead locker – a bit of airline carelessness, I think."

"Great, that really fills me with confidence!"

"Are you alright, madam?" asked the steward, but I waved him away with a forced smile.

Thankfully, there were no further incidents, and I relaxed as the plane landed and I was able to step onto solid ground. It had been an eventful beginning to our holiday, and I had a strange feeling that things would get even more chaotic over the next two weeks as we would inevitably engage in the usual battle of the sexes. I looked at Eve and smiled. Elle would be waiting inside for us, and in just a few more minutes, I would meet up again with my pal in Rome.

- *Aibohphobia – the irrational fear of palindromes*

Twenty-First Century Boy

"Hey, hang on Matt," shouted Josh, as he spotted his friend leaving the school entrance, "are you going to the library?"

Matt waited, schoolbag over his shoulder as Josh ran up. "Yea, first day back and old Stimpson has set us an English project. I'm going to read up on it."

"Me too," replied Josh, "only mine's for Bio. Still, we are doing A-Levels now, so I suppose it was bound to get tougher. How did you do in your GCSEs? You were on for As and A*s weren't you?"

"Oh, I did okay – 5 A*s, 4 As and 2 Bs. You?"

"I did better than I expected – 1 A*, 3 As, 4 Bs and 3 Cs. Mum was so chuffed she brought me a new *Parker* nib for the year," and Josh proudly showed Matt a hand-cut swan quill of exquisite manufacture.

"Nice," said Matt, admiringly, but with a little jealousy, considering the rather tattered goose quill that he was still using after two years; he had received nothing for his achievements and he felt a little resentment that somebody who hadn't performed as well should get such a reward. Changing the subject, he asked the first question that entered his head. "What did you do over the holidays? Go to Blackpool again?"

"Not this year. The parents took me to the Camelot theme park - it was ace."

As Matt moved out of the way of a bunch of youngsters who were kicking a ball about, his resentment intensified; his new choice of subject hadn't worked. Trying not to show how he felt – after all, it wasn't Josh's fault – he said, "That's out at Chorley, isn't it? It must have taken hours to walk that far."

"Oh, we didn't walk; dad hired a horse and carriage for the day."

"That must have cost a fortune. What, with your new quill as well, did you win the lottery?"

"Nah, but dad got a promotion at work; he's the factory foreman now. He's on forty grand a year. Not bad considering he…ouch…" Josh rubbed his face where he had been hit by the ball.

Matt had to cover his mouth to hide a snigger as he saw the cross-hatch imprint of the pig's bladder stitching on Josh's cheek; *serves him right,* he thought.

Josh looked round, then booted the bladder as hard as he could into a nearby field, ignoring the protests of the children. "I'm surprised they still want to be bothered with football, considering how rubbish England were in the World Cup."

"Yes, I saw the pictures, they were terrible, weren't they? And Capello said we'd win it. I hear the fans are going to protest when they get back."

"Yea, I heard that too. A load are supposed to be on their way to Southampton – the team boat is due back in a fortnight. I wouldn't like to be in their boots!"

"Just think, though, if they'd beaten Germany, it could have all been different."

"I know. That Lampard shot was a goal, everybody knew it but that stupid referee. You could tell from all the drawings - made from every angle - that the ball didn't go over."

"You can't blame the referee, Josh. It's Blatter's fault. He's the one who won't accept the need to move forward. They've been saying for years that there should be a proper crossbar *and* nets, not just two posts with a piece of rope dangling between them. Then everybody would have known that the shot wasn't too high."

They had been walking for some time now, and had reached the library. "Here's where we split up," said Matt, heading off towards the shelves where the

Shakespeare texts were kept. He had been set the task of studying *A Winter's Tale*, and he located the scroll and took it to one of the large tables. He spent the next couple of hours painstakingly making notes with his old quill on the scrap of parchment given him by the school, and it was almost dark by the time he'd finished. *Exit, pursued by a bear* he sniggered, *as if that would ever happen.* He looked across the library and saw that Josh was still there, scribbling away furiously. "I'm off now," said Matt, putting his notes in his pack.

"Hang on a second, nearly ready." Josh finished writing, took his scroll back to the shelf and followed Matt out. "Hey, do you fancy coming back to mine? I've got *Not Afraid* from *Eminem's* new album, *Recovery.*"

"Okay," said Matt, thinking, *I suppose this is another product of your dad's pay rise.* But he kept his thoughts to himself as they walked back to Josh's home.

"There it is," said Josh, pointing at the sheet music as they walked into the hall. "It's sold millions worldwide. Come on, let's sing it together."

And as Matt sung along, he realised how unreasonable he was being. It wasn't Josh's fault that he had rich parents, and he did share his good fortune with his friends. *No,* he thought, *he's not so bad, and this song is pretty good too. I'll bet not many kids my age have got their hands on the latest number one.* And he thought of how his parents had told him what things were like when they were children, and he smiled. So many advances had been made since then, to the extent that he couldn't imagine how technology could progress any further. *Yes,* he thought, *I'm glad I'm alive in this day and age. How great it is to be a twenty-first century boy.*

The Cow Jumped Over The Moons

Johnstone placed the cylinder in the machine, pressed play, and settled back to listen; perhaps this would provide the solution to the puzzle of the missing trio.

I don't know if anybody will ever hear this log, but I'll record it anyway. It's too late for us, but it might save others from suffering the same fate.

We arrived three days ago, on our exploratory mining mission. Captain Anders said that there would be rich pickings here, and Miller and I trusted him implicitly. The captain told us that the indigenous population were harmless despite their appearance, and we soon found he was right in his appraisal of the environment. We were ignored as we searched for the ores that would pay our expedition expenses many times over.

The first two days were lucrative, and we realised we were close to hitting our target. The prospect of an extra day at the pleasure domes on Arcturus made us decide to work on late into the third day. The three moons rose as we prepared to set off back to the ship with our packs laden with the ore that would make us rich; it was the first time we'd seen all three in the sky.

The captain was the first to go. He was gathering the final samples, and was about twenty yards away from one of the cattle-like creatures that he called leaks; when he told me about them, I though he meant the vegetable, and couldn't understand why. Then he explained that he called them that because of the small holes that were everywhere on their metallic hide, making them appear to be covered in an armoured coat that resembled a giant colander.

I glanced up just as the leak turned its single eye towards the captain. It would have been comical if it hadn't been real, as the leak sprang into the air, its shadow crossing the three moons just as ET had when he rode his bike. Only that was make-believe. In the time it took me to blink, the leak had closed the distance between them and all that was left of the captain was a bloodied array of dismembered flesh.

Miller had also seen it; he dropped his pack and ran back towards the ship, moving as fast as if the gravity was earth-normal. I was only inches behind him, but the ship was a couple of hundred yards away. The leak gained on us fast. Too fast. Miller leapt into a shallow ditch, turned and repeatedly fired his automatic straight at the monster. The bullets deflected off the metallic surface without leaving a scratch.

"There ain't no tin in him," said a frightened Miller, and a detached part of myself realised that the leak's metal skin was worth ten times as much as the rocks we had collected.

Here was a long pause, and Johnstone thought the recording had finished, but just as he was about to switch it off, he heard the narrator speak again.

It got Miller. It was terrible. But I managed to get away while it was gorging on his remains. I've taken cover, and the ship entrance is only a dozen yards away. There's nothing in sight, I'm going to make it. No. Not another of them. Please. No....

Johnstone retched at the sickening noises that completed the recording. When he'd wiped his mouth clean, he looked up. Three moons were in the sky. Then he saw the single eye, staring into his soul.

The Dream King

Ever had one of those experiences that defy logic? The sort that make you wonder whether there might be a higher power in control of our destinies? No, I don't believe in any of that tosh either. Or perhaps I should say *didn't believe*. This time last week, I was a sceptic. Now though – well, I'll let you judge for yourself.

It's difficult to believe how much has changed in just seven days. I'd gone to work on Wednesday, awaiting the long-heralded spending review, knowing that everybody would have to face difficulties once it was published; although, I suppose like most people, I thought *well, it won't really affect me*. After all, I was in charge of the departures section at the airport, and business had been booming, despite the recession. My boss discussed future plans with me as we left that Wednesday evening.

So I was totally unprepared when I turned up at work on the Thursday morning to be handed an envelope by the unspeaking MD. The way he refused to make eye contact almost made the act of opening the envelope as redundant as the information it contained. I forget the exact words, something to do with unsustainability following the decision of our major carrier to curtail their operations in Europe, but the three little words are indelibly imprinted on my memory: *You are fired*. To receive the dreaded pink slip after an impeccable employment record for twenty years was a bitter pill to take. To be forced to leave the premises under escort, without being given the opportunity to say farewell to my friends and colleagues, was unforgiveable.

As I drove home, I tried to work out how I could tell my wife, Kate. Relations were already strained between us, but I hoped she could put our recent differences behind us and offer the support I was very much in need of at the moment. I had to park several bungalows away, as our road was packed with cars belonging to staff from the nearby printing works. I walked in the front room, and saw the breakfast dishes still on the table. I picked them up as I walked into the kitchen, hoping that even a little gesture such as this might be seen as conciliatory, and collided with my wife, who was coming from our bedroom. She had been dressed in a t-shirt and jogging pants when I left for work; now all she had on was a microscopic pink slip. For a second, I thought my colleagues must have phoned home to tell her, and this was her way of showing me that everything would be alright. For a second. Then I saw my best friend, stood just behind her. He didn't even have a tiny pink slip to cover his – or my – embarrassment.

Everything began to make sense, the reason for the lovemaking rejections I had been the recipient of for the past several months, the furtive phone-calls that were always conducted in a tone too low for me to hear. I'll not dwell on the sordid details of the next few hours, save to say that they culminated in my being sacked for the second time in less than half a day. I left, only stopping to collect my collection of first edition novels. Kate had no objection; my books were of no interest to her, they were yet one more solitary passion for me.

For the next few nights, I slept on the sofa at a friend's house – a *true* friend this time – and on Monday I began job and home-hunting in earnest; I knew that in the current economic climate, lack of money would quickly become an issue, but I had no luck trying to find a new job. I had some success looking for somewhere more permanent to live, eventually finding a small flat, but even that made a huge hole in my dwindling resources. My spirits were raised, though, and despite my perilous financial situation, I gave the last of my change to an old man whose need appeared to be greater than mine. I smiled as I saw he had a small cat tucked inside his thin overcoat; his best friend was almost certainly truer than mine had proved to be.

I lay awake for hours that night, worrying about a future that only a few days earlier had seemed so secure. In the final in-between moments separating wakefulness from sleep, I saw two figures silhouetted by the window, one large, one small. Immediately, I was alert, but for some reason I didn't feel afraid. The taller figure, who I could now see was a male of indeterminate age, waved his hand in a simple, calming gesture. The smaller figure appeared to be an animal. As I watched, a soft, feminine voice whispered, "You helped us, now we're here to help you."

I rubbed my eyes, confused, as I was certain that it had been a man. As if reading my mind, the voice said, "You are right, he is male. But Daniel doesn't speak. I am Lucy, and I speak for him." The voice was coming from the smaller figure, which I could now tell was a cat, as my eyes became accustomed to the pre-dawn gloom. I realised then that I was dreaming about the man I had helped, but this was a strange dream, one that I couldn't wake from. The cat spoke once more. "Daniel is the Dream King. We have come to assist you." I rubbed my eyes again. The figures were fading from my sight, but just before they disappeared completely, Lucy, Daniel's cat companion, spoke one more time. "You will sleep now, but remember, your dreams will show you the way."

Harsh sunlight pouring through the thin curtains jerked me awake. I glanced at the clock and saw it was already after ten. Cursing, as I'd wanted to make an early start on the job hunting scene, I dressed as quickly as I could and headed out. Tuesday was no more fruitful than Monday had been in finding employment, and by early evening, I began to despair. I remembered that the local newspaper had its main job section on Tuesday evenings, so I headed for the nearest library to check out a copy. Hardly surprisingly, the job pages were as thin as my prospects appeared to be, and I began to think I needed to consider a change of career. But what could a forty-two year old retrain to do? I had always fantasised about opening my own antique book shop, as I knew I could make a success of it, but in this economic climate, no bank would lend me the money to get the business started.

I turned the pages of the newspaper over aimlessly, and came to the sports' section, with the racing cards for the following day listed. I shivered as I saw them, and suddenly remembered the events of the night before. I *had* dreamt again, of horse racing, a sport that didn't interest me in the slightest. I had been looking at a betting slip, with seven names written on it, and I could remember every one: *Magician's Apprentice, Pelican's Reach, Russian Ambassador, Maritime Visitor, Miss Universe, Harry the Hat* and *Night Starvation*. I took another look at the racing page. *Magician's Apprentice* was listed as one of the runners in the first race.

This was bizarre. I knew nothing about the sport, yet I had dreamt about one of the horses involved in the next day's racing. It must have been mentioned on the sport's news, and I'd subconsciously noted the name. I checked the rest of the races; the other six horses were all appearing at various meetings. I couldn't possibly have heard and remembered *all* of them.

I decided to go and see the friend whose sofa I had slept on, as I knew he took some interest in horse racing. I didn't tell him about the dream, of course, but looked at the paper with him and asked about some of the horses listed. He had never heard of *Maritime Visitor* or *Miss Universe*, and he knew of the others only vaguely.

I didn't sleep at all that night, but on the Wednesday morning, I wearily trudged into town, looking for the local bookmaker's. I didn't know what to do, and had to ask the clerk how to place a bet. He gave me a betting slip, and explained that I needed to write my selections on the top, white, copy, which I would keep, and hand him the bottom, pink, copy along with my stake. I wrote down the names of the seven horses, and passed it back to him, along with a five pound note. He took a look, and raised an eyebrow, before saying, "I'll have to check with the manager, just a minute sir." What had I done wrong?

Five minutes later, the manager appeared, holding the slip. "I'm sorry," I said, "I've never placed a bet before. I didn't know I'd got it wrong."

"There's nothing wrong with your bet, sir," he said. "You've bet on a seven-horse accumulator, which means that all seven have to win otherwise you lose the bet. The clerk was just checking with me first, as I have to authorise bets such as these. After all, if you were to win, it could cost us a lot of money."

Disappointed, I held my hand out for the return of the five pound note, but the manager just smiled. "It's alright, I've decided to accept your bet. If you do win, it will be good publicity for us if nothing else." But I could tell that he was taking the bet because he knew I *wouldn't* win.

I stayed in the bookies all afternoon. *Magician's Apprentice* romped home by five lengths, a 3-1-favourite victory that won me £15. With my stake rolling over, £20 was now going on the second horse. *Pelican's Reach* had a more difficult race, but came through on the run-in after the final fence, a 100-30 winner that raised my potential winnings to almost £87. I had to wait an hour before my next horse was in action. *Russian Ambassador* was an odds-on 4-7 favourite, and lived up to its billing by cantering home.

That meant £136 was riding on *Maritime Visitor*, but this was the first outsider of the day. I became as animated as all of the long-standing punters as I cheered it home, a 10-1 victor. I now had almost £1500 from my four winners, but it would mean nothing if the other three failed to win. I checked the board for the starting-odds for *Miss Universe*. 33-1. Even I knew that they were the odds you gave a no-hoper. I wanted to change my bet there and then, to quit while I was ahead. £1500 to an unemployed man was a fortune. But I knew that it was impossible. The bet was binding.

I didn't watch the next race, but I couldn't stop myself from listening to the result. There was a photo-finish, and I had to wait an agonising five minutes before *Miss Universe* was declared the victor. I mentally calculated my stake on horse 6, and almost fell when I realised the amount - £50,935. I was in a daze as I watched *Harry the Hat* cross the line first, a 7-2 victor. My stake had grown to more than £229,000.

I was sweating profusely, and my heart was beating at ten times the normal rate. I could barely make out through blurred eyes the race card for my seventh and final race. *Night Starvation* wasn't the favourite, but at 11-4 was one of the fancied runners. That should have made me feel better, but it didn't. The race seemed to take place in slow motion, but eventually, the final fence was in sight, with *Night Starvation* half a length ahead of *End of a Dream*. Then disaster struck, as *Night Starvation* almost fell. Although he recovered, he had lost too much ground and came in a distant second behind *End of a Dream*. What an appropriate name for the end of *my* dream. I did what I had seen dozens of other punters do during the afternoon, and tore my betting slip up in annoyance.

I was almost at the door when I heard the commentator mention a steward's inquiry was taking place. I turned back and watched, half in horror, half in anticipation. Was this a final cruel jest? And then came the announcement, *End of a Dream* had been placed second, after hampering *Night Starvation* at the last fence. The realisation hit me. *Night Starvation* had won. My bet had won. I raced to the betting window to collect my winnings, went to hand over my slip, then realised with horror what I'd done with it. I stood there, unable to say a word. The manager was behind the grille, and a smile was on his face. "I can tell you haven't bet before. You haven't got your slip, have you?"

I shook my head. "That's why there are two copies. I saw you tear it up, but this copy confirms you made the bet." And he held up the pink slip with the horse names neatly inscribed on it. "For a first timer, you've done marvellously. It's as if you had insider knowledge," he said, almost accusingly. I noted then that his smile failed to reach his eyes. He wouldn't have believed me if I'd told him the truth. He handed over a cheque, and I almost collapsed again when I saw the amount. *£859,529*. And a few pence.

I staggered out of the shop, receiving hearty backslaps from most of the other punters. Somehow, I made it back to my flat in one piece. Now I could afford to set up my book business. I could afford to do many things. As I put the key in the door, I heard a slight cough, and turned to see a woman standing in the hallway, looking at me. She was a few years younger than me, mid-thirties probably, and I took to her immediately. "I'm sorry," she said, "I know this is going to sound crazy, but I'm looking to go into business with somebody. You see, I need a partner to help me set up an antique book shop."

With everything else that had happened that day, this didn't surprise me at all. Her voice sounded familiar, yet I couldn't place it. "I was thinking about such a business not two minutes ago, but how could you know about that? My name is Graham, by the way, would you like to come in and discuss matters?"

I held the door open and as she followed me in, she said, "thank you, I'm Lucy. And, you see, I had a dream…"

Wishful Thinking

Gerald Cooper was an ordinary man, working in an ordinary job, living in an ordinary town. But one day, something extraordinary happened and life for Gerald was never the same again.

Throughout his forty-three years, he had gone unnoticed. To say he was a mild-mannered, inoffensive man would have made him more interesting than he really was. At work, he was largely ignored, and that suited him well, for he didn't find it easy to socialise. He had been employed as a computer programmer at a local textiles company for the past twenty-two years, a position that offered him the opportunity to immerse himself in his keyboard rather than having to interact with his fellow workers. He did enjoy being in the company of the predominately female staff, but found himself tongue-tied whenever anyone tried to engage him in conversation. When he noticed their poorly-disguised sniggers at his total lack of dress sense whenever he entered the room, he retreated even further into his solitude. So each day, after staying at the office as long as possible, he returned to his lonely home, where he sat night after night in the house he had been born in, all alone since the passing of his parents a year earlier.

One cold November evening, with nothing of even the remotest interest on the television, he decided to clear out the attic. He had been meaning to do this for many months, always finding excuses to prevaricate, but now, even this tedious task offered more interest than a night watching second-rate *celebrities* displaying their multiple left feet as they attempted to dance gracefully for the cameras.

Gerald was soon engrossed in old photograph albums and family memorabilia, but he paused, puzzled, as he spotted an old, dusty bottle. Why had his parents kept this? He wondered if it was perhaps a bottle of wine from their wedding reception, and used his sleeve to try and rub the grime away so he could read the label.

Suddenly, there was a flash of light, and he fell backwards on the floor. A smoky haze was forming around the mouth of the bottle, and as Gerald watched, it took the form of a young woman, with long black hair and wearing a white bikini top; below the waist, though, her form remained hazy, as if she were slowly emerging from the bottle. He gasped, unable to believe what was happening. Genies didn't exist in real life; had he fallen asleep whilst sorting through the items in the chest?

The apparition didn't appear to notice his unease, as she spoke, in a tinkling voice that evoked memories of a mountain stream making its way inexorably through a myriad of small stones. "So at last, you have decided on your third and final wish. I trust you have learnt from your previous foolish desires. Choose carefully, for this time you will *not* be able to wish any harm undone."

Gerald was perplexed, but gradually began to make sense of her words. His parents had never spoken about this, of course, but now he understood their troubled glances whenever he had asked to hear magical tales or fables. They must have used the first two wishes, and – from what the genie had just said – not too successfully.

"I'm waiting," she said, the tinkle in her voice now replaced with a harsher timbre. "You summoned me, you *must* tell me your desire. And remember, I warned you what would happen if you say *I wish for more wishes.* "

Gerald began to panic. He didn't like the sound of this at all. His first instinct had been to ask for riches, but he felt there would be a *Midas*-like catch if he did. He could see the genie was becoming impatient, and frightened of what would happen if he *didn't* make a wish, he blurted out, "I don't want to be the old me any more. I'm sick of feeling like this. I wish I had super powers."

The genie smiled, but Gerald saw no warmth in her look. "Wish granted," she said, and in a puff of smoke, both genie and bottle vanished from sight. Gerald spent the rest of the evening trying to find out what his power was, but with no success; he couldn't levitate, see through objects, melt substances with a ray from his eyes, turn into a human torch or do any of the other things he associated with a superhero. He went to bed convinced he had imagined the entire episode.

When he woke, it was almost nine, and as he rushed to get ready for work, he thought no more of the events of the previous evening. To save time, he dispensed with his morning shave, and whereas he normally strolled gently to the office, today he ran, hoping all the way that he'd be able to reach his office unseen; he wanted to avoid the sarcastic remarks his boss would make if he saw him arriving late. He was frustrated that people didn't get out of his way, as he was barged on several occasions; presumably they were all as late as he was, and were equally intent on getting to work before *their* bosses could make their lives miserable. He tried to keep a low profile as he ran to his corner office, and it seemed to work. *Good*, he thought, *they didn't see me*.

He logged on and started to work on his jobs' list. Nobody came in to see him, but that was as normal. It was only when his boss looked into the office as he walked past that Gerald began to think something was wrong; McGuire *never* missed the opportunity to make fun of Gerald and his quirky ways. Two minutes later, McGuire was back, this time with the head of security, Edmonds. "I tell you," said McGuire, "there's been a breach somewhere. Cooper hasn't turned in, yet the log clearly shows that his computer is being used."

"Don't be daft, man," said Edmonds, "there's nobody there. Are you telling me he's invisible or something?" And with that, Edmonds walked off, laughing as a red-faced McGuire watched his retreating back.

Gerald, though, wasn't interested in their petty spats. Everything began to make sense. The reason for all the bumping and barging on the way to work was because he *was* invisible. McGuire thought he hadn't turned in – well, he didn't need to come to work ever again now he had this power.

Quietly, he logged off and left the office. This time, he noticed there was no reflection as he passed the full-length mirror in reception. He walked home and thought about how to use this power. He could, of course, go into any shop and take anything he wanted. But he was an honest person, and even the *thought* of stealing made him break out into a sweat.

He spent the rest of the day at home, remembering the genie's warning. He had to be careful how he used his gift. He went to bed early, and awoke no closer to finding the answer. He didn't shave – not a wise thing to attempt with a cutthroat razor when he couldn't see his face – and grabbed some clothes. For once, his uncoordinated dress sense didn't matter; during his experimentations the previous evening, he had found that his *invisibility cloak,* as he termed it, extended a few inches from his body. Any clothing he wore automatically became invisible, but as soon as he removed an item and stepped away from it, anyone could see it.

After cleaning his teeth (a partial success), he left the house and walked towards the shopping precinct. As he walked past the swimming baths, he saw Marie, who lived across the road from him. She had moved in three weeks earlier, and had smiled at him whenever he saw her on his way home from work. She was in her late thirties, he estimated, and appeared to live alone. He blushed as he saw her, for he had taken an instant liking to her, but – as always – he had never plucked up the courage to do anything about it. She turned towards the entrance to the baths, and suddenly Gerald knew what he was going to do with his power. It was wrong, of course, but he couldn't stop himself. He changed direction and followed an elderly couple through the double doors, then headed towards the female changing rooms. He looked to make sure nobody was around – he didn't want anybody wondering why a door opened of its own accord – and walked in. Fortunately, she was the only person in the changing room; for all that he was doing wrong, Gerald was not interested in being just a common peeping tom. She took her towel and her costume out of her bag, and peeled her top off.

Gerald suddenly didn't want to be there. This wasn't how he wanted it to be. He turned to leave, disgusted at his weakness, wanting to be far away from the swimming baths as quickly as possible. And then Marie screamed. He whirled round, wondering what had startled her, and saw himself in the mirror. Or, at least, the bottom half of himself, but more of him was appearing every second. He *had* to get away. He turned and ran – and two seconds later, found himself up to his knees in bitterly cold seawater. He thought he must be going crazy, but he looked round, and saw he was wading in the foamy tide a dozen yards from the shoreline. *But the swimming baths were five miles away from the beach.*

It was at this point that he remembered the *exact* wording of his wish. He had wished for *super powers*, not a single super power. And, to make matters worse, the powers seemed to change according to his desires; he'd been invisible when he wanted nobody to see him, he'd acquired super speed when he wanted to get away from the locker room. He *hadn't* heeded the genie's warning. He began to shiver in the icy cold water and hurried back to the beach. Big mistake. He found himself in the middle of a dual carriageway, and had to run again to avoid being splattered by a Tesco delivery van.

It took him the rest of the day before he managed to navigate his way home, and he went, very carefully, straight to bed, terrified of making any further movement at all. Gerald's super speed disappeared the following lunchtime, to be replaced by the ability to freeze time; all he had done was express surprise at how fast the morning seemed to have gone. This was followed later the same day by the power to corrode metal by a simple touch - after merely seeing the rust spots on his relatively new and supposedly stainless steel window frames - and several hours later by the power to heal. This proved to be a very useful power, for his final inadvertent use of the corrosion power had resulted in him falling through the decayed girders of a footbridge, leading to multiple broken bones and abrasions.

Over the next few weeks, the powers came thick and fast, too numerous even for Gerald to remember. Despite making every attempt to control his thoughts, he found he always slipped up at least once a day. Once, when he had placed the TV remote just out of reach, he saw his arm lengthening as it stretched out to grasp the device. He was able to detect the tiny changes to his body that signified each change of power, but, despite that, it became almost impossible for him to keep his abilities a secret – the mere act of brushing away a strand of hair while he thought about the pleasant feeling of the breeze in his face caused him to fly twice round the world. He was exhausted and exasperated.

On Christmas Eve, Gerald cautiously left the house for the first time in a fortnight. He had little option, as he was out of food, but he dreaded what might happen whilst outside. His current power was magnetism, and he had to take great care to avoid passing close to any metallic objects in case they hurtled through the air to cling to him like armour. The power did seem to be weakening, though, as his own strength waned through lack of sustenance, and he managed to reach the corner shop without mishaps.

Marie was in the queue immediately in front of him. Gerald's heart fluttered in embarrassment as he saw her, and he was about to leave, when he stopped himself. *Enough* he thought, *after everything that has happened to me over the past few weeks, I'm not going to let my fears control me any more. But first, I need to start to put things right.* He leant forward and tapped Marie on the shoulder. "Excuse me," he said, "but I need to tell you something. A few weeks ago, in the swimming baths, when you were getting changed. Well, you spotted somebody spying on you. I've been carrying the guilt around ever since. It was me. I'm sorry."

Marie stared at Gerald, a strange look in her eye. "I *knew* it was you," she said, "after all, who else would wear green trousers, white socks and purple shoes? But where did you go?"

"Oh. Right. Well, I realised I shouldn't have been doing what I was doing, and I left as quickly as I could. I'm sorry," he said, head bowed.

"Apology accepted," she said, "and I'm glad it *was* you. Perhaps we can talk now? You always looked so frightened when you saw me. I didn't dare come over and chat. But you seem different now, somehow." And she smiled warmly at him.

And Gerald realised he *did* feel different, confident even. This was one power that he'd had within him all the time, and had finally come to the surface. The power of love. He thought he heard the genie, whispering *Lesson learnt*. He smiled back at Marie.

Listen to What the Man Says

My great grandfather told me about the old man when I was around eight years old. "Now listen, Eric," he said, "I'm going to tell you about a remarkable man who I've known since, well, since I was about your age, Eric. I'm very old now and won't see him again, so I think it's time I passed on the tale to you. Unlike grown-ups, I'm sure you'll believe me. Perhaps, one day, you can tell your own great grandson about him."

"What about him?" I asked, the impatience of childhood not wanting to wait another second to hear the tale.

My great grandfather laughed, a kind laugh, perhaps remembering the impatience he had felt at a similar age. "Alright young pup, I'll tell you. As I said, I was about your age, living in the village, though it was much smaller then. I remember I'd had a row with my mother – she died long before you were born – and I'd run away from home. Well, I'd run out of the house, I would never really have run away. I found myself walking down an overgrown path. I'd never been there before, and was on the verge of heading back home, when curiosity won over. I carried on, and the road became more impassable with every step; I suspected I was the first person to come this way for a long time.

"And then I saw a ramshackle cottage, in the middle of a field. Outside on the porch, sitting on a swinging chair, I saw a wizened old man. As I approached, I realised I was mistaken; he wasn't an *old* man, he was *ancient*. More wrinkle than skin. I should have been afraid, disgusted even, but for an eight-year old boy, this was an adventure, so I marched on up to the cottage, bold as brass, and said, 'Say mister, what are you doing all alone out here on your own?'

"The old man laughed, and said the strangest thing: '*He who pays the piper calls the tune.*' Then he just closed his eyes, and in minutes was snoring. I quickly lost interest, and, deciding I'd punished my mother enough, walked slowly back home. I didn't tell her about him, though, because I knew she'd be angry with me; she was always warning me about talking to strange men, but I knew there was no malice in that old man.

"I thought about him a lot, and about a fortnight later, when we broke up from school for summer, I walked down the path again, determined to find out all about him this time. Sure enough, there he was, sitting on the porch swing and gazing into the distance. As I looked at him, I thought he looked even older than I'd remembered him to be. 'You must be a *thousand*' I muttered under my breath, little realising the irony of my hyperbole.

"He looked up, as if my whisper had wafted through the air like a dandelion seed, and said '*A young idler, an old beggar.*' I just looked at him, feeling a little puzzled. Why did he say such strange things?

"'What's your name, mister?'

"'Ah, my name. It's been so long since I've used it, I've forgotten. You'd best just call me *Old Man*.'

"'Why? How old are you?' I asked, in the direct way used by young boys. But he just smiled, and said, 'You should be getting on home to your mammy.'

"That was one of the few times he said anything that made sense, at least in those early days. I saw the old man on many, many occasions after that day, often without really understanding what he was talking about. I did, though, begin to reassess my first impression of him. Yes, he was undoubtedly old, but he oozed a sense of health and wellbeing. Usually, he just uttered a single, incomprehensible, sentence. Occasionally, he'd say a little more, but more often than not, once he'd made his inane uttering, he closed his eyes and acted as if I wasn't there.

"As the years passed, the man looked older and more haggard every day, yet he was clearly in the prime of his health. I never once saw him ailing, and although I asked him time and again how old he was, he only ever spoke to me in riddles. I can't remember all the weird things he said to me, but a few of the stranger ones stick in my mind, such as 'A monkey in silk is a monkey, no less', 'Better lose the saddle than the horse', 'Dogs of the same street bark alike' and 'Fine words butter no parsnips'.

"Eventually, I realised that his strange words did make a sort of sense, in that they often were relevant to something that was on my mind. We became friends, although it was a strange friendship. I told my wife about him – your late great grandmother – but she never believed me. Nobody in the family did.

"I went to see him today, and told him this would be my final visit. I looked at him, barely able to believe that he was so fit and well, whereas I – a man at least eighty years his junior – was so infirm. But the man didn't seem to understand the import of my words, for he only said, 'Don't dig your grave with your own knife and fork'. I tried to get him to say more, but he wouldn't, and, sadly, I left, knowing I'll never see him again, and I'll die never knowing his secret."

The story seemed fantastic, but – to a young boy brought up on adventure stories – not quite the stuff that legends are made of. In fact, I was a little disappointed, and thought my great grandfather was – as mum had said – *going gaga*. I told her about our talk, but she just told scowled as she said, "I warned him not to go repeating that rubbish, especially to somebody as impressionable as you. The trouble that man has caused," she added, half under her breath, and then – in an even quieter voice – "perhaps it would have been better all round if we *had* signed the commitment papers."

Not long after that, great grandfather passed away, and I forgot about his tale until some four years later, when I had a row with my mother and stormed out of the house. As I stood, furious with her, but not knowing where to go, I remembered the story and looked for the track. It took me a while, but my great grandfather had described it so vividly, I recognised it the instant I saw it.

Intrigued, I set off along the path, and it was exactly as I had imagined from great grandfather's tale. The sun was warm, and I was sweating by the time I spotted the cottage. As I neared it, I saw an old figure swinging on the porch seat. He was even more ancient than the mental picture I had created of him. I stood, open-mouthed in astonishment. He looked at me, a piercing look that seemed to invade my soul. Then he said, 'Honey catches more flies than vinegar,' and closed his eyes, with a contented smile on his face.

I couldn't get any more out of him, so trudged home, a little angry at my great grandfather for telling me his ridiculous story. But I calmed down eventually, and next opportunity I had – about a week later – I went to see the old man again. This time he greeted me with, 'The mouse that has but one hole is quickly taken,' but this time I didn't leave, even when he shut his eyes and began to snore. I waited patiently for about ten minutes, then he opened one eye, saw I was still there and smiled. "You must be the lad Albert talked about," he said.

My great grandfather had been called Albert. "Yes," I said, "I'm Eric." And that was the beginning of a lifelong friendship. I tried to get him to say more, to tell me how an old man who met my great grandfather more than eighty years earlier could still be alive, but he would never answer direct questions along those lines. In fact, he rarely said much at all, but he was always there to listen and invariably when he did speak, his advice was sound.

When the Second World War ended, I was torn between continuing my studies and starting work on a local farm. I really wanted to get an education, I was eighteen years old and I felt I could contribute to the rebuilding of Britain. But my mother wanted me to bring some wages in, and pushed me towards the farm job even though, with my puny build, I was hardly cut out to be a farmhand. I poured my concerns out to the old man on my next visit – I had barely seen him during the war years – and this time, I had an inkling of what he meant when he said, *'Worry often gives a small thing a big shadow.'*

Sadly, I wasn't allowed to follow my heart, and I went to work on the farm. As I feared, I wasn't physically capable of doing some of the work, so I was moved indoors to work alongside the women. It was humiliating. It was there that I met the farmowner's daughter. She wasn't a very pleasant sort, neither in looks nor personality, but she took a fancy to me, and soon I found I was expected to marry her. I didn't want to, but neither did I want to lose my job. I went to see the old man to talk about my problem. "You see," I told him, "I don't get to meet many other women. The work on the farm is so tiring, and the days are so long, that by the time I get home, I just want to go to sleep. And you know," I added, "she isn't that bad once you get to know her."

He just looked at me, his penetrating stare slicing through the honeyed image I was trying to paint. *'Marry in haste, repent at leisure,'* was all he said that night. He didn't need say more. I should have listened to him, after all, I'd sought his advice. But I didn't. I married her, but nothing I did was good enough. I felt guilty about going to see the old man, after ignoring his advice, and I left it several months before next traversing the overgrown path to the cottage. When I poured out my troubles to him, a look of sadness crossed his face. *'The tongue wounds more than the lance,'* he said, and I could not dispute the truth of his words.

I made two resolutions that afternoon; to make the marriage work, and to visit the old man on a regular basis. No longer would I be hostage to my emotions. The second promise proved easier than the first. My wife and I did have a child, but I was kept away from his upbringing. I felt that the only reason for the wedding had been to produce offspring; now I had done that, I was no longer needed, and she made no secret of the fact. In fact, I was hardly required around the farm anymore, any pretence of my usefulness long having been dismissed. Despite everything, I loved my son, and waxed lyrical about him to my one friend on my daily visits to the old man.

And then, when my son was seven years old, my wife informed me that she was sending him to boarding school and I would only be able to see him during the holidays. It was a heartless thing to do; she knew I doted on him. But all my protestations were for naught and the move was arranged. "What am I going to do?" I asked my confidante, "little George is the only reason I have for staying at that farm. She says it is for his benefit, that he will receive the best education, but I feel that she is doing it deliberately to punish me."

His simple response, *'One father is more than a hundred schoolmasters,'* said it all.

Once George went away to boarding school, and I was no longer part of his everyday life, he began to forget the role I had played in his upbringing. When I saw him during the school holidays, I barely recognised him. Gone was the loving child I had raised, replaced by a miniature version of his mother, hard-faced, uncaring and unnecessarily cruel.

I poured out my latest woes on my next visit to the old man; I never doubted that he would be there; I had come to accept his incredible longevity as part of everyday normality. And with that agedness, came wisdom. *'The apple doesn't fall far from the tree,'* he said, and I knew he was right; my George was her child, and had inherited her traits.

Just when I thought things couldn't get any worse, my wife took a lover, one of the bulky farmhands, and I found myself out of a marriage, job and home in one afternoon. "I always saw her looking at the farmhands as they worked bare-chested in the sun," I told the old man, "I knew I could never compete with them. I guess I've always been a loser," I concluded, hoping, I suppose, for a sympathetic denial.

I didn't get one. Instead, I received yet more of his perception. *'Wisdom is better than strength,'* were the only words he spoke that day, yet they were enough. He had one more invaluable piece of advice for me, a few weeks later. I had let the ending of my marriage and loss of job and home get to me. I had been sleeping rough ever since, and bemoaned my misery. Again, instead of sympathy, I received commonsense. *'Poverty lies at the gate of idleness,'* he told me, and immediately I knew he was right.

That was more than half a century ago now, but since that day I have never looked back. I didn't remarry, but I did turn my life around, thanks to the old man's insightful advice. Although I had lost my wife and son, I had gained a father and friend.

#

Today is a sad day, though. Just as my great grandfather knew, almost eighty years ago when he told me about the old man, I know that this will be the last time I walk this pathway. As I see the cottage, for the last time, the old man is – as always – sat on the porch, swinging gently to and fro. "Hello," I say, "or really, I should say *goodbye.* The summer is nearing its end, and I have been finding it hard enough to get here in the pleasant weather. By the time the good days are here again, I fear I will no longer be able to make the journey, even if I am still alive. So I've come to bid you a fond farewell. My only regret is that I have no great grandson to pass the story down to, somebody who could continue our family tradition. I have no idea if my son has a family of his own, but even if he has, I would be a stranger to them."

"You have been like a son to me," the old man replies, "and I'm truly sorry that your own family haven't been as good to you as you have been towards me. When you first came to see me, you wanted to know the secret of my long life. You haven't asked me about it for a long time, though."

"That's because it no longer matters to me. You could be a hundred or a million, it wouldn't make any difference. Your kindness is what I value."

"I'm certainly not a million," he laughs, "but yes, I do have a secret, one I've never told in more than twelve hundred years. Yes, that's right, twelve hundred years. I'm actually one thousand, two hundred and seventy six years old. I was old –

or at least, what passed for old in the eighth century – when I discovered the magic. It's partly to do with this porch, and it's why I always sit here, watching the world go by. It might seem a lonely existence to you, but it hasn't been. Over the centuries, I've had a lot of visitors – you are but one of those who currently come to see me, sometimes as many as three or four a day. They never come at the same time, of course, that wouldn't do at all. The magic ensures that never occurs. But I'm getting tired now. I think it's time for me to move on. So, would you like to sit here, on my swing, and enjoy a long life?"

I think about it, initially rejecting the idea as the worst kind of existence. But then I think of the old man, and how serene he always appears. And I know he is happy. And I want to be happy too.

"Yes," I say, quietly, "I'd like that."

The old man stands, and beckons me to take his place on the porch. As he walks away, he visibly ages and stoops. No longer does he ooze wellness. Then he turns and says, "You, too, can choose to go at any time, but be patient. You will meet many a fine friend, just as I did when you came along. Just remember the two key ingredients. You can leave at any time, but must always return to the porch within twelve hours. I don't think I left it at all in the last hundred and fifty years. And secondly, and most importantly, choose your words carefully. It is imperative that you follow the sound advice of the sages: an adage a day keeps the doctor away."

The King's Speech

"I don't know why I bother listening to you, Sharon Docherty, you talk rubbish. He's never been to Britain and he's never going to come here, I just know it."

"Yes he is, Brenda, he's coming tonight. And I *did* see him before. He was in a car with Tommy Steele near Buckingham Palace. "

"I don't believe you. You just want to make yourself seem important. More fool me for agreeing to come with you. We're bound to get detention *at least* from Miss Watkins – she won't care why we've played truant, she hates his music anyway. And it will all be for nothing. "

"No it won't. I promise you, he'll be there, and we'll be there to see the return of the king."

The girls were fourth formers at the Notre Dame Catholic School in Cobham. Neither of them had been in trouble before, but when Sharon had received the letter from her brother in Friedberg, they both realised there might never be another opportunity like this; it was worth risking Miss Watkins' wrath. They had caught the early train from Euston to Glasgow and were now steaming through the countryside on the coastal route through Ayrshire.

Sharon fidgeted nervously; the train had been delayed, and it was getting close to five pm. She wasn't sure what time his plane was due to land, but she knew it wouldn't be too late, as it was only stopping to refuel before taking off for America later that evening. If they were going to get a good viewing spot, they would have to rush to cover the five or so miles from the railway station to Prestwick airport.

It was dark by the time they reached the airport, and cold; although spring was only a few weeks off, winter seemed intent on making one last attempt to chill the girls through their thin coats. At least there was no longer any doubt in Brenda's mind about the veracity of Sharon's story; hundreds of screaming teenage girls were packed, dozens deep, against the hastily-erected barricades. He *was* coming, but would they be able to see him through such a crowd?

"I can't see a thing," said Sharon, "I wish we were taller."

"We could do with one of those lanterns we saw at the Chinese New Year celebrations a couple of weeks ago. Isn't the red one supposed to be for growth?"

"Red? No, that stands for good fortune. We'll need that tomorrow with Miss Watkins. I think you mean the green lantern, that's the growth one."

"Yes, I remember now, it was light green like the shoots in the garden."

"It doesn't matter what colour it was, nothing is going to make us grow in time to see him when he lands."

The high-pitched screaming intensified, and the reason was immediately obvious; high in the sky, but coming closer every second, bright lights indicated the arrival of the flight from Germany.

"Come on," said Sharon, "we didn't come this far not to see him. Let's find another way." Brenda followed, whilst repeatedly looking back over her shoulder with misgiving in her heart as each step took them further away from the throng of teenage girls. "Here," said Sharon, "try this path." They crept along a grassy track for a few minutes until they found themselves up against barricades – but with horror Brenda realised they were at another set, way over to the left of the main ones. It was too late to go back, as the plane had landed and a few of the GIs were beginning to embark.

"He'll have gone by the time we get back there," spat Brenda, "why did you make me come all this way for *nothing*?"

But Sharon was trying too hard to prevent the tears from flowing to respond. The girls watched as one of the soldiers shook hands with some of the teenagers in the crowd, posed for pictures and signed autographs. "That should have been us," she whispered in a voice too low for even Brenda to notice. She saw him turn to an officer and say something, but he was too far away for her to hear him, even without the constant screaming from the young fans.

The party of soldiers then walked away from the crowd, and Brenda tugged Sharon's arm. "Come on," she said, "I'm cold. And I don't really blame you. I did get to see him, even though it was from a hundred yards away."

Sharon was about to leave, when she suddenly pulled Brenda back. "Look," she said, "they're coming this way." The soldiers walked over to where they were waiting, and a car drove up alongside the barricades. The lead soldier was about to get into the car when he saw the two open-mouthed girls. He walked towards them and said, in his Tennessee drawl, "How'd you get from there to here so quick?"

Sharon was struck dumb; he was talking to her, but her mouth wouldn't work. But just as he started to turn to leave, she heard Brenda's voice saving the situation. "We weren't there, Sergeant Presley sir. I mean, we were, but we were too far back, so we ran round here, but then we found we were too far away, and we could hardly see, and we were just going to leave, and then you came over, and Sharon said we should wait, and I'm Brenda, and I've always wanted to meet you, and, and..."

Elvis laughed, "Whoa, slow down a minute. Well, ah think ah understand all that. You sure are lucky, then, this is the car taking me to meet my buddies in the NCO club. You can take my picture if you like."

"We haven't got a camera," said Sharon, her muteness now at an end.

"Okay, well, ah've got to go now, it's been nice meeting you, ladies." He chomped once more on his gum and turned to leave.

"Can you take your hat off," babbled Brenda, "I mean so we can see you a bit more clearly and, well, you know..."

"Ah'm real sorry I cain't take it off, it kinda breaks the uniform if you know what I mean."

"What are you going to do when you're back home?" asked Sharon, saying the first thing that came to mind in a desperate attempt to keep him talking.

"Well, first ah'll get my feet up and have me a rest. Then ah'm booked to do a television show from Hollywood with Frank Sinatra."

"Are you ever going to sing over here?" asked Brenda.

"Ah kind of like the idea of Scotland. Ah'm going to do a European tour and Scotland will certainly be on my list. But ah've really got to go now. Here, ah've got something for you, till ah come back again." And Elvis took a photograph from an inside pocket, and wrote on it, "To Sharon and Brenda, Stuck on You, Elvis. Scotland, March 2nd 1960." He handed the signed picture to Brenda, saying "Get on home now girls, it's getting late," and then he was in the car and out of sight.

They stood there for several more minutes, watching as the car pulled away. Several other teenage girls reached their spot, but there was nothing for them to see, and they left, disappointed. Eventually, Sharon and Brenda left too, unable to wipe the silly grins from their faces. It was a few minutes before Sharon broke the silence. "See, I told you we'd get to see him, didn't I Brenda?"

"Yes, I'm sorry I didn't believe you. That was better even than hearing him sing."

"I know. We'll never *ever* see anybody like him over here. We only have people like Pearl Carr and that Johnstone bloke, Them who sang *Sing Little Birdie Sing* at last year's Eurovision Song Contest."

"Yeah, I know who you mean. Whatever happened to Teddy Johnson? He's the sort mum listens to. So dull. Why can't our singers be more like the Americans."

"Hey, this is the Chinese Year of the Rat, isn't it? You've heard of that *rat pack* in America, haven't you Brenda? You know, it had Humphrey Bogart at first, and Frank Sinatra, people like that? It was mainly film stars, but there was Judy Garland too. Perhaps as it's their year *The Rat Pack* might come over here and perform?"

"Sinatra's not Elvis, though, is he? *Love and marriage*? And anyway, who'd want to watch a group called *The Rat Pack*?" asked Brenda, scornfully.

"You're probably right, Brenda" laughed Sharon, "and it could be worse than that even. What if they named a group after an *insect*? Imagine, *The Earwigs* or *The Beetles*. Ugghhh. Nobody would *ever* buy any of *their* records?" And laughing, the girls ran back towards the railway station, no longer concerned about the problems they might face at school the next day; whatever happened, it had been worth it.

- Elvis never did tour the UK. His only official visit was that brief landing at Prestwick on a refuelling stop on the flight from Germany to America, although in 2008, Tommy Steele confirmed a report that the two of them had driven round London on a sightseeing visit in 1958; Elvis recorded and released *Stuck on You* on his return to the USA in March 1960.

Where's Sophie?

Charles Morris pulled the car onto the drive and sat quietly for a few minutes, letting the engine idle. It was Friday night, the end of a manic week at work, and he needed a drink. He was getting too old for this every day, but he was still more than a decade away from retirement, and that was before all the extensions in state pension age that the government were threatening. So he had no choice but to plod on, day after day. *"But it's weekend, now, a chance to relax. Perhaps we can go out for a meal tonight,"* he thought. He and Sophie had moved to the quiet Cotswolds town four months ago, but through pressures of work, they had yet to sample the fare at either the local restaurant or any of the pubs. In fact, such was the nature of their jobs that they rarely managed to eat together; Charles' travels to the office in Bristol meant an early start and a late finish, and Sophie's job as a supply teacher at the local primary school was necessitating a lot of time out of the house. Consequently, a night out was definitely high on Charles' agenda.

He switched off the engine and climbed out of the car. Even though it was well past 7 pm, it was still light; it was April, after all. As he opened the front door, he shouted, "I'm home, I hope you haven't prepared a meal as I really fancy eating out tonight. And a good few drinks wouldn't go amiss either." Charles hung his coat on the peg in the hall and paused, waiting for Sophie's response, but no sound came from either the kitchen or the living room. "Sophie?" he asked, hesitantly. Was she out again? He couldn't remember her mentioning anything that would keep her out on a Friday night, but he had been so tired recently, would he have noticed? Perhaps it was parents' evening? Thinking that was probably the case, he shrugged his shoulders and went upstairs to change. *"At least,"* he thought, *"she'll be ready for a night out as well when she gets home."*

It was almost 8 pm by the time Charles had showered and come downstairs again. He poured himself a whisky, and sat, waiting. When Sophie still hadn't come home after another hour, he realised that he would have to postpone the planned night out. He decided to make a start on the evening meal so it would be ready for when she eventually returned home; parents' evenings never normally went on beyond 8, and even if she went for a drink afterwards (and she'd probably need to after sitting through several hours with the parents of Year 6), she should still be home by 9:30 at the latest.

Charles didn't notice the time pass as he prepared his speciality, a grilled mushroom risotto, but he began to worry when there was still no sign of Sophie when it was ready. He looked at his watch; it was just coming up to 10 pm. Surely she would have rung if she was going to be this late?

Not wanting to waste the meal, he half-heartedly set about eating his portion. By the time he'd finished idly pushing the congealed rice around his plate, it was half ten. And still no sign of Sophie. Charles went to the phone book, and looked the number up for the school; he rang, but just heard an automated response detailing the school office opening hours. *"I know,"* he thought, *"I'll ring Andrew, I'm sure he'll know what's going on."* Andrew was one of the few friends Charles had made locally, and his wife, Jill, was a teacher at the school; he hadn't met her, but it was a small school so she'd undoubtedly know Sophie. In fact, the pair of them were probably out together right now, *discussing* problem parents over a much-needed glass or two of wine.

He dialled the number, and was surprised to hear a female voice answering. "Oh, hello, Jill," he said, "I wasn't expecting you to be in. It's Charles here."

There was a second's hesitation before Jill replied. "Oh, hello Charles, yes, Andrew mentioned you. Just wait, I'll go and get him for you."

"No, that's okay, Actually, I was going to ask him about you anyway, with you teaching at the local school. I just wondered what time the parents' evening finished tonight."

"What parents' evening? Have I missed something?"

"Wasn't there one then? It's just that Sophie hasn't come home, and I guessed that's where she'd been. She's not there with you is she?"

"Sophie? Who's Sophie?"

"You know Sophie. She's at the school with you."

"You mean one of the children? Why would a child be here?"

"No, she isn't a pupil, she works there."

"There isn't anybody called Sophie working there."

"Yes there is. She's a supply teacher, started after the Christmas holiday. You *must* know her."

"We don't have any supply teachers," replied Jill, her tone frosting over.

"Perhaps you haven't come across her yet," said Charles, beginning to feel uneasy.

"Look," snapped Jill, "I don't know what you're trying to do but I'm tired and not in the mood. Ours is a small school, with just six teachers, and all of them have been in every day since Christmas. Andrew told me that you were odd at times, I know what he meant now."

"Put Andrew on please," begged Charles. This was becoming bizarre. There was a pause of a few moments, and Charles could hear faint mutterings on the other end of the line.

"Here, what are you playing at, upsetting the wife?" asked Andrew, the usual bonhomie absent from his voice.

"Sorry, mate, I didn't mean to. I'm just worried about Sophie, and I was sure Jill would know her. I thought she worked at St Catherine's."

"She does work at St Catherine's, has done for ten years. She's never mentioned a Sophie, though. Who is she, your girlfriend?"

"Who is she? She's, well, she's Sophie. I'm always talking about her."

"Don't recall you ever mentioning *any* women, let alone one called Sophie. And I'd have remembered. I'm glad, though, 'cos I was beginning to wonder, well, you know... Look, Charles, it's getting late, and you sound like you've had a couple to drink. Let's not do anything stupid, here. Go to bed, and when you wake up in the morning, I'm sure you'll realise it was the drink talking. Night, see you soon." And Andrew put the phone down, not giving Charles a chance to tell him how wrong he was.

#

Charles was stunned. This was becoming a mirror image of the discussion he'd had at work at lunchtime, when his colleagues had tried to insist that the late 1970s remake of *The Lady Vanishes* was superior to Hitchcock's original. That argument seemed futile now, but it was the plotline of the film that was strikingly similar; in both versions, Miss Froy went missing, and in both versions, nobody admitted to ever seeing her. Now Sophie was missing. But why would Andrew and Jill deny Sophie's existence? In the film, there were a variety of reasons, from direct involvement in her kidnapping to self-interest. Could Andrew and Jill be involved in Sophie's disappearance? Or did they just not want to get involved?

Could Sophie still be in the house? He searched every room, although he knew there was little point; he'd have heard or seen her by now if she was anywhere. As he feared, there was no sign of Sophie. Worse, there was no indication that she'd ever been there; there wasn't a single photograph of her, her half of the wardrobe was empty, and despite looking in every cupboard and drawer, Charles failed to find a single sign that she had ever existed.

"This is ridiculous," he thought. *"How can anybody disappear so completely?"* He knew that this was way beyond anything he knew how to deal with; he would ring the police and let them find what had happened to Sophie.

He picked up the receiver on the 1960s-retro phone in the hall; Sophie had picked it out herself, being particularly impressed by its oversized nature in today's micro-world. A tear involuntarily ran down Charles' cheek at the memory. His fingers automatically located the slot, and were three quarters of the way towards completing the third '9' dial when he stopped and replaced the receiver. What could he tell the police? That Sophie was missing, yes, but he knew they would do nothing until she had been gone at least twenty-four hours. They would ask if he had contacted all of her friends, and he'd have to tell them he'd only spoken to one person – and she denied knowing her. No, there was no point involving the police until he had more to tell them.

Forcing himself to remain calm, or at least as calm as possible given the circumstances, Charles considered the options. He didn't believe that Andrew would have any part in Sophie's disappearance. Jill had denied knowing her, though, and that was inconceivable; Sophie had been at the school for four months now, and Jill had confirmed how small it was, so they *must* have met. Perhaps they didn't get on, and that was why Jill was so frosty with him? But why deny she existed? Just to be spiteful?

Neither he nor Sophie had any living relatives, so a visit to a sick elderly aunt wasn't a possibility. He didn't know any of Sophie's other friends, but assumed they would be listed in the address book. Surely one of them would be able to provide something, if only confirmation that they knew her.

Charles located their address book, but was disappointed to find Andrew and Jill's number as the only local entry. Many of the names and numbers had been heavily crossed out and were now illegible. The couple that he could still read were one each from their last two homes, as Charles' job had led to them moving regularly over the past few years. He rang both numbers, but there was no answer; hardly surprising at this late hour. Charles had no option but to go to bed, but he spent a sleepless night as his concern overwhelmed him.

As he tossed and turned in the bed, which seemed obscenely large for just himself, he ran over and over the possibilities in his mind. He couldn't get over Jill's reaction. Even if she didn't like her, why deny any knowledge of Sophie? And where *could* she be? He considered the options, and came to the conclusion that one of four things must have happened, each increasing in their level of absurdity.

At the simplest level, Sophie had been abducted. But if that were the case, why had there not been a ransom demand? And why had every sign of her at home disappeared?

Which led to the second hypothesis; she didn't want to be found, and Jill had denied knowing her because Sophie had asked her to. But that made no sense either; granted, they had been too busy to spend time together, but they had never had a cross word. Dense as he might be at times, he would surely have picked up on the subtle signs.

So if it wasn't either of those, the even more unlikely possibility was that *nobody* was lying because Sophie had never existed. But that would mean he was insane, when he had never felt saner in his life. But wouldn't an insane person believe they were perfectly normal?

He took a sip of water from the bedside glass before considering the final possibility, one which would only occur to a man desperately in need of sleep. Even to consider it meant that he could hardly call himself sane; he had read stories where a person had been deleted from time and memory, with only the main character recalling their existence. Even *Dr Who* had run such a story recently. Could it actually happen in reality? In the stories, there was always a happy ending, where the person was found and memories recovered. Perhaps that was what was going to happen here, and his life was becoming a mirror image of the stories he loved to read?

The possibilities sped round and round Charles' active mind throughout the longest night he had ever experienced, with each sounding increasingly bizarre with every new circuit.

#

Almost as soon as it was light, Charles took the address book over to the phone again. He dialled the number for the first name he could read. It was John, an associate of his from when he lived in Leek. The phone rang five times before he heard the vaguely familiar tones of his former colleague.

"Hello, John, it's Charles here. Charles Morris." There was a pause at the other end. "You remember, we worked together in Stoke towards the end of last year. We drew up the contract for the pharmaceutical merger."

"Oh, Charles Morris. Yes, now I remember. You went off to ..."

"To work in Bristol."

"Yes, that's right, Bristol. You left rather quickly, didn't you?"

"When the man comes calling, you've got to answer. Surely a good business man like yourself knows that, John?"

"Yes, of course. Of course. Well, it's been nice, but I have..."

"Sorry, John, I know it must come as a bit of a shock my ringing you up. Especially as we only ever knew each other through work. But I've got a bit of a problem, and I'm hoping you might be able to help."

"I'd like to but I don't really..." answered a hesitant John.

"It's not anything like that," Charles added quickly, realising John probably thought he was after money, "it's just Sophie's gone missing, and I can't think where she is. I thought she might perhaps have gone back to stay with friends in the area or something like that."

"Oh, I see. I'm sorry, Charles, but I don't see why she'd come here. I never met her, you see."

"I know you didn't, but I thought perhaps you might know of her."

"No, sorry, Charles. Like I said, I never met ... your wife, is she? I don't remember, sorry."

"Surely you remember me talking about her at work."

"Not really, Charles. In fact, we weren't that close. I'm surprised you've even got my number."

"But I told you, the contract. You gave it to me last autumn, when we were working together with Benson from the legal division."

"Oh yes, that's right. I've slept a bit since then, though," he added with a chuckle. "But sorry, Charles, I really can't help you I'm afraid. In fact, until you mentioned her, I wouldn't even have known your Sophie existed."

Charles put down the phone after saying goodbye. That hadn't produced much. Not that he really expected it to; it had been a long shot. As John had said, they barely knew each other, having worked together only briefly. Despite that, Charles was sure he would have mentioned Sophie. He *always* talked about her, to whoever he met. But perhaps John had genuinely forgotten.

He looked at his watch. Not yet eight a.m. Sophie had been missing for at least twelve hours. Was that long enough to inform the police? No, they would insist on waiting another day. If she wasn't back... No. He wasn't going to think back. She *would* be back. *Could* she have left him? He had seen no signs of her dissatisfaction with their life, but he had been working long hours. Perhaps he really hadn't noticed? It certainly made more sense than any of the other three options he had considered, even though it wrenched at him to even consider it.

He rang the second number in the book, but, as before, there was no answer. He had more hope for this one, as Eric had been a work friend rather than solely a colleague when they were in Cumbria. Granted, it was a couple of years ago now, but he would remember. And it would be just the sort of madcap place Sophie *would* disappear to, probably without even giving a thought to what Charles would be thinking. Not that she was thoughtless, far from it; perhaps just a little scatterbrained at times.

Charles felt a little better now he had resolved the puzzle as to her whereabouts, and he forced himself to eat breakfast; he would be no use to anybody if he was weak with hunger. But as he sipped his tea, he dismantled the happy place he had laboriously built, brick by brick. However scatterbrained she might be, she would never travel hundreds of miles without saying a word. She would at the very least have left a note.

As the thought entered his mind, the post arrived, and he almost tripped in his hurry to get to the front door. Three letters, all addressed to him. Two from the bank, one trying to get him sign up to Virgin broadband. Nothing from Sophie explaining where she'd gone. And no ransom note. He didn't know whether to feel relieved or disappointed. It meant little, of course; if she *had* been taken against her will, any posted ransom demand wouldn't arrive this soon. Unless the kidnappers hand delivered it, of course. Much more likely that he'd get a phone call, though. "*Stop it,*" he admonished himself. "*You're accepting the fact that she's been kidnapped. She hasn't. She's just gone off in a sulk somewhere.*"

Yes, that was it. They'd had a row, though, being a typical man, he hadn't noticed. And she'd gone off somewhere, leaving him to consider how he'd wronged her. Charles breathed deeply, and gradually the spots before his eyes disappeared. "*That'll be it,*" he muttered, "*she'll be somewhere near.*"

But where? She wasn't in the house and he didn't know any of her friends, so he couldn't cold call in the hope of finding her. He'd drawn a blank with their only mutual acquaintance. Perhaps she was somewhere in the town?

Convinced that this was the case, he spent the remainder of the day driving up and down the roads and calling in the shops, asking if anybody had seen her; nobody professed to even knowing her. This was getting more bizarre by the minute. *Somebody* had to know where she was. Where did the groceries come from if she didn't shop for them? He certainly didn't have the time. Perhaps she shopped online?

As he drove past the cut-price card shop, his stomach twisted in knots. It would be his birthday in a few weeks, and he always looked forward to the joke card that she would buy him. He was a typical Gemini, prone to moodiness, especially if things didn't go well at work, and she pulled his leg about his light and dark sides. Right now, he felt very dark indeed. He remembered her face when she had opened the card he had given her a month earlier. She had been surprised, thinking he had forgotten when her birthday was. "No," he'd said, "I know you aren't a Pisces, in fact you only ever think of others, never yourself. But we met, remember, in March, and so I always count it as the day *I* was reborn. It should be a card for me really." She had laughed, gently, and Charles had laughed too. Now, he had to stop the car as the tears blurred his vision.

It was dark by the time he returned to his empty house; without Sophie, it was just a shell. He didn't even go through the motions of forcing himself to eat, but retired for another sleepless night. *Tomorrow,* he muttered, *everything will be fine tomorrow.* But he didn't convince himself.

#

Sunday was little different to Saturday. Still no sign of Sophie, and everything was far from fine. Charles decided to go to the police once he'd called the final number in the book; he had a strange feeling about it, an inkling that this held the key to everything. But there was no answer all morning, and he was about to give up when, midway through the afternoon, somebody answered his call.

"Hello, what do you want?" asked a gruff voice. Charles barely recognised the speaker; he hadn't spoken to him for a year or so, ever since he had moved out of Carlisle.

"Eric? Eric Newton? It's Charles here, Charles Morris. From *Winslow and Peters.*"

There was a pause which threatened to stretch into the next millennium. Then, questioningly, "Charles Morris? Oh, hang on a minute. The name does ring a faint bell. *Winslow and Peters*? That must have been a year and a half ago now. You left rather hurriedly, didn't you? Wasn't there some sort of crisis? Somebody disappeared or something like that?"

"No, it was nothing like that," Charles hurriedly interjected. "I just got myself a new job down in Staffordshire, that's all. We did move rather quickly, but you know what it's like in this cut-throat business, any slight show of hesitancy and the job goes to someone else."

"Yes, I guess you're right," said Eric. "Anyway, that's all water under the bridge, as they say. What can I do you for?" He was beginning to sound jovial, and Charles remembered how much he had liked Eric during the months he worked near the Scottish border.

"I'm ringing on the off chance, really, though I doubt she'll be there. But I've tried everywhere else."

"Doubt *who'*ll be here?"

"Why Sophie, of course. She' went missing on Friday, and I've tried everywhere I can think of. You're my last hope."

There was a long silence at the other end of the line. Finally, Eric spoke. "It's coming back to me now. I'm sure that was her name. The woman who was reported missing, just around the time you left. I always wondered why you went so quickly. What did you do to her?"

"What did *I* do to her? I haven't done anything to her. She's gone missing, and I want to know where she is."

"Where are you calling from, Charles? I think the police would like to know about this."

"Yes, the police. She's been gone long enough now; I'm going to call them. Thanks for *nothing*."

Charles slammed the phone down. He was furious, and more than a little hurt. How could his former friend insinuate that *he* was responsible? And then threaten to call the police? "*Well I'm going to see them,*" he muttered.

He drove to the town centre police station and walked over to the desk sergeant. "Afternoon, sir," answered the bored-looking man, probably wishing he was at home enjoying a Sunday afternoon nap. "How can I help you?"

"It's Sophie. She's been missing since Friday evening. I don't know where she is."

"All right, let's take it slowly, shall we sir? Your name, please?"

"Morris, Charles Morris."

"Address?"

"15 Carver Heights."

"15 Carver Heights," the officer repeated very slowly, painstakingly writing each character on a sheet of paper. "Occupation sir?"

"Look, is all this necessary? I've been going out of my mind since Friday night. I knew there was no point coming to you until she'd been missing for at least a day, but I didn't expect to have to give you my life story before you'd do anything."

"Calm down, sir. It's just procedure. *God is in the detail*, as they say. Some people find it helpful to have some structure. Gives them focus, you see."

"I *am* focussed. I have been ever since she disappeared."

"Have you spoken to her family?"

"She has no relatives. It's just the two of us."

"Perhaps your family then?"

"I said, it's just the two of us. Our parents have died, neither of us had any siblings, and we've never been blessed with children."

"I see. Sorry to hear that, sir. What about friends, or work colleagues? She does work, does she?"

"Nobody I've rung has been able to help. And work is no good. It's weekend, nobody is about."

"Do you have a photograph of Sophie, Mr Morris?"

"I don't. They've all been taken."

"Taken? Has there been a burglary?"

"No. Yes. I don't know. All I know is that I've searched everywhere and I can't find anything of hers."

"What, nothing? Not a single photograph? What about her personal items?"

"I said I can't find anything of hers. I've looked everywhere, but there's nothing."

"This happened Friday, you say? When you came home from work? Had you had words that morning, sir?"

"No, nothing like that at all. We *never* argue. And I know she was happy, I'm not an insensitive brute. I don't know what to do."

"I see. So you've no picture. That will make it more difficult. But I'm sure there's a simple explanation for her disappearance. Can you describe Mrs Morris — she is your wife, I assume sir?"

"She's the other half of me, I'm incomplete without her."

"That's a nice thing to say about her, sir. Not many couples like that today, unfortunately. If there were, it would make my job a lot easier. So can you give me something to go on, Mr Morris? Height, build, appearance, what she was wearing last time you saw her, anything like that. Even the most trivial of pieces of information can help."

Charles spent the next hour telling the sergeant everything he could about Sophie, but he could tell the man wasn't really interested. He had put everything into this final hope, and now it seemed that he was going to be disappointed.

He drove back home, though he was in such a daze that he didn't know how he managed to get there without having an accident. He sat in the dining room as the light gradually faded away and reached for the whisky bottle.

#

It was Sunday evening; almost exactly forty-eight hours since he had returned home to find the house empty. Charles poured himself another whisky, and tried to make sense of recent events. He considered again the four possibilities he had half-mockingly come up with during his first, sleepless, night.

Having analysed them, in conjunction with the information he had gleaned over the weekend, he came to his conclusion. He had taken the *Holmesian* adage that once you've eliminated the impossible, whatever remains must be the truth, however unlikely it must be.

Charles relaxed for the first time all weekend, and smiled. Everything was clear. He poured another glass of whisky and took it with him as he climbed the stairs. Taking the key from his pocket, he unlocked the padlock leading to the attic, pulled the ladder down and climbed up. Turning the dim light on, he squinted against the gloom.

He walked to the far corner, opened the trunk, and took out a small suitcase. Then he switched the light off, climbed back down the ladder and went into the bedroom. Closing the curtains, he stood in front of the mirror and undressed. He opened the suitcase and took out a red dress, a pale green bra and a matching pair of pants. Slowly, he dressed himself, all the time checking the reflection in the mirror. Finally, he took a long blonde wig from the suitcase and expertly applied it to his balding pate.

Sophie stared back at him from the mirror, an impish smile on her face.

"What did you think you were doing?" he asked, angrily.

"Now, now," she replied, her voice as soft as a lamb's wool cardigan, "you broke the rules so I had to get away for a while."

"But I've been going frantic looking for you. I've called everybody in the book, but they denied ever having heard of you."

"Yes," she laughed, "that's because they *don't* know me. You've forgotten that nobody but you can *ever* see - or hear about - me. When you wanted to take me out for a meal, I had to stop you. They wouldn't understand here any more than they did in Aberdeen, Glasgow, Carlisle or Leek. Now give me the address book and tell me who you've contacted. I'll have to cross them out, you can't ever speak to them again. And, I'm afraid we're going to have to leave here, especially if you've alerted the police."

Charles turned away from the mirror. Sophie was right, of course. There was no option; they would have to move. He thought Kent would be nice at this time of year.

The Man in the Moon

Camulodunum, Britain, AD 92

"What are they, daddy?" asked five-year old Gaius, pointing towards the stars.

Lucius looked up, and wondered how to reply. He didn't want to tell the boy that he didn't know; that none of the tribe knew. "Well," he answered, "that is a big painting, like the cave paintings I've shown you. Only somebody has drawn on the sky instead of a cave wall. The bright lights are tiny holes. And see over there," he said, pointing at the moon, "there is a big white disk. Whoever does the painting keeps changing the picture, so that sometimes the disk is missing, and other times it is only half there. But today, it is there in full."

Gaius looked thoughtfully in the direction his father was pointing. "Daddy," he said, "it looks like a man's face. Does somebody live there?"

"No," laughed his father, "don't be silly. It's just a painting, that's all. Now come on inside, it will be cold soon." And Gaius followed his father back inside, casting one final look at the moon before returning to their home.

Middelburg, province of Zeeland, the Netherlands. December 1608

"What have you brought home, papa?" asked Johan.

"It's Mr. Lippershey's latest invention. He calls it 'an instrument for seeing things far away as if they are nearby'. Look through it and everything seems bigger."

"Oh, papa, that sounds *so* exciting. Please can I try it?"

"Patience, Johan," laughed Mr. De Bruin, "patience. It will be dark soon, then we can go outside and look at the moon and stars."

Ten-year old Johan could barely wait, and hardly thirty seconds passed between each anxious look outside the tiny window of the de Bruin's small cottage. Finally, he could wait no longer. "It *must* be dark enough by now. Please, mama, tell papa to let me try it."

"Alright, Johan, I will." Sanneke turned to her husband. "Pieter, take the boy out and show him that contraption, otherwise he'll never settle."

Pieter went outside, with Johan closely behind him. Excitedly, Johan put the device to his eye and looked up at the stars. Then, disappointedly, he said, "it doesn't do anything. The stars are still tiny."

"They are too far away, my son, but if you look towards the moon, that should appear to be larger."

Johan turned towards the western sky and looked through the scope again. "Yes, papa," he babbled excitedly, "it's *much* bigger. And there really *is* a man in the moon; he winked at me."

Pieter laughed again. "Is that right, son? Come on, it's getting cold. Let's go back inside and eat our supper. Besides, I promised Mr. Lippershey I would return it to him later this evening."

"Awww," said Johan, but he knew better than to disobey his father. He took a last glance over his shoulder at the moon, looking so small now without any magnification, and wondered whether the man in the moon *always* watched over them.

Apollo 8, Lunar Orbit, Christmas Eve 1968

The three-man crew looked out of the windows of the Command Module as the spacecraft began another orbit of the moon, this time less than a hundred kilometres from the lunar surface. "I guess that finally gives the lie to the *'man in the moon'* theory, Jim," said Frank Borman to James Lovell. "Now they'll have to accept it's just a rocky exterior."

"I don't know, Frank," interjected William Anders, "those wrinkly edges down there in the *Bay of Billows* sure looked like a big nose to me."

"Always the contrary one, aren't you Bill," said Lovell. "Anything to get your name noticed."

"Yea," piped in Frank, "just because the Lunar Module wasn't ready in time, you've nothing to do on the flight, so stop inventing things to make yourself important."

Bill jocularly threw a plate at Frank's head – a pointless gesture as it just floated serenely in the zero gravity environment. "That's it," he laughed, "you don't get your Christmas present now."

Bill took one final look out of the window as the spacecraft continued its high-speed orbit and – just for a second - could have sworn that the *nose* twitched.

Apollo 11, Lunar Orbit, July 22nd 1969

Neil Armstrong and Edwin 'Buzz' Aldrin settled themselves now they were back in the Command Module. "Whew, Mike," said Neil, "I'm glad to be safely back here. Let's be heading for home, shall we."

"Don't come the *it was horrible* tack with me, Neil," replied Mike Collins, winking through his visor at Buzz as he spoke, "we all know you're going to be the two everyone talks about, while I'll go down in history as the *third wheel*."

"Hey, Mike," said Neil, a serious tone entering his voice, "you know you're the most important of us all. Without you, we'd be stuck down there on the surface and would never see home again."

"I'm only yanking your chain," laughed Mike. "Go on then, tell me. What was it really like?"

"It was like we told everyone," said Buzz, "no more, no less."

"So you didn't make the man in the moon flinch when you jumped all over him then."

"Trust you to bring out the old fairytale. Come on, oughtn't you to be getting us out of orbit and homeward bound?" said Neil.

Mike accepted the light-hearted rebuttal and began the preparations for the return flight. He didn't say that – just for a second – it had looked as if the features on the surface of the moon had altered as the Lunar Module *Eagle* landed. But that was ridiculous. He returned to his seat and readied the engines for departure.

Kennedy Space Centre, Florida. July 21st 2011

As the crew relaxed in the buggy taking them back to the control centre, Chris Ferguson turned to his three companions. "That's it I guess," he said, "there won't be any more manned missions in my time."

"That's a bit negative, Chris," said Doug Hurley. "Just because the government has cut down on funding, it doesn't mean that private companies won't step in."

"Yes," echoed Sandra Magnus and Rex Walheim in unison. "After all," added Sandra, "the International Space Station is still out there. There's too much invested for them to leave it to go to ruin, isn't there?"

"You know," said Rex, "I can still remember how I felt back in the sixties when we first landed on the moon. I was only six, but it made such a huge impact on me. I wanted to become an astronaut and land on Mars. Who'd have thought that there would only be another five manned landings, and none since 1972?"

"Perhaps we didn't want to risk upsetting the man in the moon," joked Chris. "After all, how would you like it if bits of metal kept landing on you?"

"You shouldn't joke about these things," said Sandra, "there's a lot out there that we don't understand."

"See," shouted Doug, "I told you they should never have allowed women in space. They think *ET* is real!"

Sandra threw her notebook at Doug, and laughed as it bounced off his nose. "I take it *you* don't like things landing on you either," she said, and the four continued to trade badinages as their journey back to base continued. As they turned the last corner, Sandra looked up at the sky and wondered if man's last chance of meeting extra-terrestrial intelligence had ended.

The Moon, December 10th 2011

The man in the moon looked towards the blue planet; the one all the invasions had originated from. He had waited patiently for years for the intrusions to cease, but now his tolerance was at an end. It was bad enough that *they* had hurled their junk onto his features, even worse that they had actually deposited some of their living creatures to crawl all over his face and body. Thankfully, they hadn't done that for some time, but that hadn't stopped their latest invasion of space, and now he had decided that enough was enough.

He would have been happy to live peacefully side by side with them, but they obviously didn't want that. Now everything was in position; the eclipse had begun and it was time to put an end to this. He took one final look to make sure that all three

The Man in the Moon   110

heavenly bodies were lined up, then inhaled deeply. Puffing out his cheeks, to ensure maximum propulsion, he blew the planet out of its stable orbit and sent it hurtling headlong into the fiery sun.

- Camulodunum was the Roman name for Colchester. Hans Lippershey is accredited with the invention of the telescope in Holland in 1608. The unmanned spacecrafts Luna 2 (launched by Russia in 1959) and Ranger 4 (launched by the USA in 1962) destructively crashed onto the moon's surface. In later years, Japan's Hiten (in 1993), the European Space Agency's SMART-1 (in 2006), India's MIP in 2008 and China's Chang'e 1 (in 2009) also crash landed on the moon's surface. Apollo 8, crewed by Frank Borman, James Lovell and William Anders, was the first manned spacecraft to leave Earth's orbit, orbiting the moon on Christmas Eve 1968. Apollo 11 saw the first moon landings, with Neil Armstrong and Buzz Aldrin walking on the moon whilst Mike Collins piloted the Command Module. An additional five manned landings were made, the last being Apollo 17 in December 1972. In addition, a dozen unmanned spacecraft made soft landings. The 135th and final space shuttle mission, using the shuttle *Atlantis,* concluded on July 21st 2011 as the STS-135 touched down at Kennedy Space Centre, bringing to an end almost thirty years of space shuttle flights. The crew were Chris Ferguson, Doug Hurley, Sandra Magnus and Rex Walheim. The first lunar eclipse following the final shuttle flight will be on December 10th 2011. The nose of the 'man in the moon' is often perceived as the area called *Sinus Aestuum, The Bay of Billows*

Sisters

Beverley Morris peered through the curtains, as if the very act would suddenly make Kaye appear; it didn't, of course. She looked at her watch – an unnecessary action as she'd been staring at it constantly for the past forty minutes; it was 9:42 p.m. *Where is that girl?* she wondered.

Although barely twenty months separated the siblings, Beverley had always seen herself as more of Kaye's mother than her sister. Not through necessity, though; they had been brought up in a love-filled home and had both been given the start in life that most children would envy. Despite this, Beverley had always imagined herself as the sensible sister, especially after the car crash that killed their parents. Beverley grimaced at the thought of their parents. She'd hated the fact that they'd been named after two singing groups, even more so when she found out that the Kayes weren't even sisters, but now she missed them badly. So she'd promised herself she'd take on the role of parent to Kaye now they were gone. To be truthful, she knew she relished the role of overseer and protector of young Kaye. Now, at the age of 41, she was permanently typecast in the part.

Kaye, perhaps as a consequence of the somewhat stifling environment, thought Beverley grudgingly, rebelled, taking on the persona of a drama queen in defiance whenever Beverley tried to instil some structure into her life. Take tonight, for example.

"Now you be home by 9, young lady," was all that Beverley had said.

"9?" screeched Kaye. "I didn't come home at 9 when I *was* 9. I sure as hell aren't now I'm 39." And she'd stormed off, slamming the door behind her. If anybody ever dared to behave like that at the library, Beverley would have them banned for life. But Kaye was her sister; she couldn't ban her from her home.

Beverley looked at the watch again. 9:53. She took a sip of her tea, screwing up her face at the realisation that it had long since gone cold. What could she have done differently to stop Kaye from turning bad? She'd known all along that her sister would disobey her; the girl always did. Beverley hadn't even been able to enjoy the night's episode of *Coronation Street*, and she'd been so looking forward to finding out the ramifications from Ena Sharples' shouting match with Annie Walker in the snug at the end of last week's episode.

A noise outside caught her attention and she pressed her face against the window so she could see what was happening. It was Kaye, of course, staggering drunkenly along the path. The clock struck 10 p.m. as she heard the scratching of Kaye's key while her sister tried in vain to open the front door. Tutting loudly, Beverley marched towards the door and flung it open.

"What time do you call this? And just look at the state of you. You're an embarrassment, that's what you are. I don't know how you can live with yourself."

Kaye looked at Beverley, and for a second seemed about to say something, but then she thrust her hand over her mouth and ran upstairs. Beverley knew that there would be nothing to gain from talking to her tonight, but tomorrow – yes, tomorrow, then she'd take her to task.

#

Kaye sat on the edge of the bed, shivering as she tapped on her iPad. In part, she was shivering from the cold – winter really did seem to be setting in early this year - but only in part. She looked at the door and sighed. Beverley would no doubt be waiting outside, determined to start another row. She couldn't face that, not tonight. Kaye knew she'd put it off too long; it was time to do something about her sister.

#

Beverley was up at six the following morning. Although she wanted to charge in and berate Kaye, she stopped herself; that wouldn't be the sensible thing to do. No, she'd have some breakfast, and then, at a more reasonable hour, she'd demand answers.

Twenty minutes later, she was outside Kaye's room. Not surprisingly, her feckless sister had locked the door, but Beverley wasn't about to be stopped by something as trivial as that.

"I know you're awake. There's no point putting this off. We need to have a talk about your attitude, girl."

"Hmppph … gerraway …" came the muffled response.

Despite banging on the door for a good ten minutes, Kaye refused to come out, and Beverley decided she'd have to opt for different tactics. "Right," she shouted through the wooden panels, "we'll continue this tonight. But mark my words, girl, we *will* have this out."

#

When the front door slammed half an hour later, Kaye tentatively opened her door. She was almost certain her sister had gone to the library – where else could she go? - but she wouldn't put it past her to pretend to have left just to draw Kaye out; she hadn't, though, and Kaye almost felt disappointed. She knew she had to tackle the problem, but it was hard to find the courage. *Tonight*, she muttered, *I'll definitely sort things out tonight.*

#

The day passed in a daze for Beverley. She didn't even realise that a minor – a boy of no more than fourteen – had checked out a book containing pictures of human reproduction until he was out of the door clutching his prize in sweaty hands. That was what hurt most of all; she prided herself on her composure, and now that was at risk because of her out-of-control sister.

Five-thirty couldn't come quickly enough, and she almost ran the half mile home, even forgetting to bring home the filthy books that she had confiscated from the new delivery. That was another thing Kaye had to answer for; she'd been looking forward to reading them for weeks. *Well*, she muttered, *I have to make sure that they're suitable, don't I?*

As she reached the front door, Kaye was on the other side pulling it open. Before she could say anything, Beverley stopped her. "We need to talk, girl. This has

Sisters   113

been going on far too long, and I've decided there's only one thing for it. You're grounded. There, I've said it ..."

Beverley didn't get the chance to complete her sentence before Kaye pushed past her, not saying a word as she ran down the path. Beverley sat down in the armchair and sighed; this was going to be another night where she wouldn't be able to enjoy Coronation Street.

#

9:30 pm, and John Connors locked the front door of the supermarket. He looked at the five staff waiting outside and nodded; they could go now. One of them was already halfway to the street, not even stopping for a chat with the other girls. No need to ask who it was; Kaye. She was always late, and never stayed a moment longer than necessary. He'd tried to ignore it, considering the circumstances, but he knew he couldn't remain passive about this for much longer; the other staff were beginning to complain about the special treatment she was being given. They just didn't understand.

#

Beverley sat in the armchair facing the front door. She hadn't moved since Kaye had pushed past her so abruptly. She'd spent the last four hours going over her options. The girl simply refused to obey her. Grounding her should have taught her a lesson, but, instead of showing remorse for her outlandish behaviour, her conduct had been even more disgraceful. *That's the thanks I get for everything I've done for her,* she muttered, *to be shoved around like a rag doll. Well enough is enough.* Beverley had finally reached the harsh conclusion; she could no longer look after Kaye, and she'd have to have her taken into care.

Footsteps echoed down the path; they were slow, almost weary sounding. A glimmer of hope rose in Beverley's breast; perhaps she *was* feeling remorse. Then she heard the key scraping, trying to find the lock. *Drunk again,* she hissed.

#

Kaye's hands shook with cold as she tried to put the key in the lock. *No, not just cold,* she thought. *I have to do it now. Tonight's episode really was the final straw.*

She opened the door, and saw Beverley. She was sat in exactly the same place where Kaye had carefully placed her before hurrying off to work. Without her job, she didn't know how they'd cope, and although Mr Connors had been wonderful, making allowances for her situation, she knew that he couldn't protect her forever. She needed this job, otherwise there'd be no money coming into the house. Especially since the government had cut Beverley's disability allowance.

It was so unfair. Just because she was able to go out to the library each day – and Kaye was eternally thankful to the library staff for allowing her sister to sit inside in this cold weather – the officials deemed that she was capable for work. Their tests were meaningless. They had totally ignored the doctor's reports, confirming by second and third opinions that Beverley was delusional, had been ever since she had drunkenly caused the crash that killed her parents twenty years earlier, and would be until the day she died.

Kaye smiled at Beverley; a sad smile. Her sister didn't see the smile; she knew that. Beverley was already ranting on at her, eyes following a non-existent sister up the stairs, no doubt inventing another series of misdemeanours that she had done.

"I love you, sis, but I can't cope any more. I'm sorry, but it's for the best," she whispered as she picked up the phone and dialled.

"Hello? Is that social services? It's Kaye here, Kaye Morris.... Yes, it's about Beverley. You were right, her delusions *are* getting worse and I don't think it's safe for her to be left alone any more.... Yes, tomorrow morning will be fine."

Clear and Present Danger

Her stomach rumbled as she crouched outside the cottage; she hadn't eaten for what seemed an age, although in reality her last meal was probably less than twenty-four hours earlier. Desperation almost caused her to ignore caution and march in, irrespective of what – or who - she would find waiting for her. *Almost*. But not quite; she hadn't come this far to surrender her life so easily.

Was it only yesterday that she had fled, fear accompanying her every footstep as she ran through the forest, with her pursuers only a few feet away? They had decimated her village, and only the gods knew how she had managed to evade the slaughter and destruction meted out to all and sundry. She had only seen three of them, but that had been enough; *more* than enough.

Tears rolled down her cheeks as she recalled the look of horror on her mother's face when *they* discovered their hiding place under the loose floorboards. Their safe haven had been demolished within seconds, and her grief threatened to overwhelm her as she saw in her mind's eye the bloodied remains of what was once her parents and younger brother. She knew that the memory of the dead eyes of her dismembered sibling – how could it have happened to him? He was barely more than a baby – would haunt her for evermore. The image of his body with the bottom half of the face missing was engraved into her memory; it made her heave until her stomach hurt and bile lay in pools at her feet.

Panic and a natural instinct of self-preservation had acted to force her legs to carry her away from the scene of devastation, even though she wanted only to lie down and die alongside the remains of her family. It was only the nightmarish thought of the carrion feasting on what remained of her loved ones that kept her going, each step taking her further and further away from the only life she had ever known.

She hadn't stopped, not even for a brief respite, in more than sixteen hours, and her young body was at the very limits of exhaustion. It seemed that she had shaken her hunters off sometime during the night, but she'd heard all about them; the elders in the village constantly told her how dangerous they were. And they were clever, very clever; after all, hadn't they attacked them when everybody had told her that they *never* ventured into the village? If they were that devious, it would be child's play to make her think she had shaken them off. And so she had plodded on, somehow managing to force one weary foot in front of the other, barely even aware of the direction in which she was heading. It was only when she reached the cottage that her legs refused to take her past the gate, hence her current situation.

She had been there for almost half an hour, and the sun was moving towards the mid-morning position. Exhaustion vied with hunger to bring her to tears once more. She *had* to seek shelter and hope that there would be both food and rest available. She looked again at the cottage. There was no sign of anybody living there. If there were people inside, surely there would have been some activity by this time in the day? She didn't know anything about the occupants, of course, but if they chose to live in *their* territory, then that alone meant they were to be feared. Perhaps even more so. Something rubbed against her legs, and she leapt back in terror. It was a cat. But not a domesticated one, as the feral glare it turned on her bore witness. The emaciated animal hissed – a warning perhaps? – before slinking slowly away.

She returned her attentions to the cottage, and tried to peer through the single front window from her vantage point by the gate. Perhaps this was a sanctuary, and would provide safety. She had heard of such places, but had never seen one before. But what if she was wrong? Torn between the terror of being caught and the pangs of hunger that were doubling her up in agony, she shuffled slowly towards the rose-adorned door, swaying from side to side along the narrow path.

The door opened easily. Perhaps too easily. Could it be a trap? She waited outside for several minutes, listening intently for the slightest sound of activity inside, but she heard nothing. The only noise came from the pigeons watching her from the nearby trees; they seemed to be saying *"Choo...oose, choo...oose."* After waiting another five minutes, she made her choice, grasped her courage and marched in.

Golden light streamed in through the small quartered window-panes, illuminating a strange sight. A rectangular table filled most of the tiny room, with its three wooden chairs pushed back as if the occupants had departed in a hurry. The only other furnishing was a small cupboard on which half a dozen yellowing plates rested. The table appeared to be set for breakfast, and steam rose from three bowls containing a greyish substance. In front of each of the bowls was a brown wooden spoon, and to the left of each was a glass; two of the glasses were empty, the third was half full. A glowing cheroot nestled against the nosepiece of a pair of grubby spectacle lenses, sending a thin plume of smoke towards the door. A finger-length of ash had fallen onto the grubby tablecloth and it looked as if it would be joined by a second at any moment.

She remembered reading Conan Doyle's story about how the *Marie Celeste* was discovered abandoned in the Atlantic, with untouched breakfasts and warm cups of tea present on the cabin table. She had dismissed it as fiction, but now she wasn't so certain; after all, to her young mind, this seemed almost exactly the same. It was apparent that the residents of the cottage had left in a hurry; but it wasn't obvious what the cause of their sudden departure was. Perhaps living in the midst of the enemy hadn't been a wise choice after all? An icy tendril of fear threatened to constrict her chest and prevent her breathing, and she had to force herself to gulp in air that still retained a hint of smoke.

She reasoned that although she couldn't come up with an explanation for what had happened, there was sustenance on the table, and her needs outweighed her innate abhorrence of taking what didn't belong to her. Even so, she was still reluctant to eat their food, but there was the glass of water on the table. Surely taking that would do no harm? She took a sip from it. *Uggh* she spluttered, spitting the contents out over the dirty cloth. It wasn't water at all; it was a glass of lemonade. A glass of *flat* lemonade.

"Don't be stupid," she admonished herself. *"You have to drink something else you'll die. I know it doesn't taste nice, but you have no idea when another opportunity will come along."* And, forcing herself, she drained the glass, ignoring the unpleasant aftertaste it left in her mouth. She realised that she did feel a little better, but she was still weak. Her knees threatened to buckle as she leaned back from the table, and she knew she had to eat.

She took a bite from the first meal, but grimaced at the bitter taste of ash that had drifted onto the bowl from the nearby square-cut cigar. However hungry she was, she just *couldn't* eat that. The next one was little better, and she could only force one small mouthful down before her insides threatened to rebel and bring it all back; this was nothing like the rich smoky flavour she had always enjoyed when eating at the village barbecues. Without much confidence, she tried a mouthful from the farthest dish. This time there was no unpleasant taste; it must have been just far enough away to avoid contamination. The contents were little more than a thin gruel – less substantive than the meals she normally gave to the pigs – but it tasted like nectar. Without pausing for ceremony, she wolfed the contents down, idly thinking that nobody who had known her but twenty-four hours earlier would have thought her capable of such actions. And then she remembered; nobody who had known her twenty-four hours ago was still alive. She couldn't let herself think about the past any more.

She sighed, replete at last, and the warmth of the meal combined with the heat of the sun to accentuate the weariness in her body. Reason told her she should leave while she still could, but her legs refused to listen, carrying her instead towards the dining chairs. *"Just a couple of minutes, then I'll leave. I'll feel better for it."* She tried to convince herself, but deep inside, she knew she was wrong. She staggered, and a ridiculous memory of watching Bambi tottering on ice almost made her smile. As she tumbled towards the floor, she knocked aside two of the chairs before landing heavily across the smallest one; it broke apart under her meagre weight, and a wooden splinter bit deep into her side. The pain brought tears to her eyes and in an instant the warm feeling that the bowl of gruel had instilled in her dissipated.

The fall had knocked the wind from her, but had also caused her to regain some modicum of lucidity. What if somebody had heard her? She had already pushed her luck far too much as it was; to stay for even a second longer was just suicide. She stood, groggily, and stepped towards the front door. Then she stopped. What if the occupants were on their way back? Across the open fields, they'd be able to see her coming out of the front door even if they were a mile away. She couldn't risk that. There had to be a rear exit; that would be a little safer.

She walked towards the door at the far end of the dining room, and slowly pushed it open. A dark mustiness greeted her. She felt her way towards the covered window at the back, manoeuvring past rectangular objects. She drew the curtains back, but the window was barred and shuttered. There was no other way out of the cottage; she would have to leave through the front door after all.

The setback made her weep uncontrollably and she stood there for several minutes feeling sorry for herself, as she tried to dry her eyes on the sodden piece of cloth in her pocket. *"No. You have to stop it!"* she admonished herself. Wiping her nose across the back of her grubby sleeve, she turned towards the door leading to the dining room. The dim light that had entered was enough to show her that she was in a bedroom. The temptation to lie down and sleep was almost overpowering, but she resisted. Still unsteady on her feet, she banged into the first bed, jarring her shins on the long wooden legs. Biting her lip to avoid crying out, she stumbled forwards, working her way around the tiny bedroom. The mattress on the middle bed was soft and inviting but she forced herself to ignore it and inched slowly forwards.

She only had the smallest bed to pass now, but as she looked at it, noting the lure of the soft, welcoming mattress, all of her resolve disappeared. With a final wobble, she collapsed across it; she was asleep before she completed her fall.

#

She awoke in a panic. She could hear voices outside. Angry voices. She had been discovered. Desperately, she looked around for an escape; but she already knew that there was only one way out of the bedroom. The sunlight disappeared as a huge shape blocked the doorframe. Now she would suffer the same fate as her family. Goldilocks screamed.

So This Is Christmas

Friday December 23rd 2011 2:47 pm. A contracts office.

"Time to leave," says Tim. "And boy do I need a break. I haven't had a day off since September. Apart from the sick days, of course."

"Yea," replies Mick, "but those don't count, do they? I mean, we're all entitled to take *them*."

"We certainly are. Thirty days a year holiday is *nothing*. I still can't believe that the management have made us come in to work today."

"I know. It's shameful, Tim. When I went over to accounts for the drop-in drinks session this morning, they were saying exactly the same. Looks like Scrooge is still thriving in 2011."

"Only this one won't see any redemption, will he Mick? At least we're off now till the first week in January."

"Yep, and I think I might take a couple of sick days to start 2012 in the right frame of mind."

"Sounds good to me, Mick. I may just join you."

Saturday December 24th 2011 5:16 pm. A site manager's office.

Arnold looks at his computer screen as if by staring at it the figures will change; they don't, of course. "I know I've been putting it off," he mutters. "I didn't even make the spreadsheet until last week, hoping that things would improve." But they haven't; the damning evidence is there, in garish red.

It isn't the workers' fault. He can hear them on the shop floor, working steadily whilst talking about the upcoming three-day break, not realising that it will be much longer than that. No, those to blame are in the city, or in government; the ones who caused the crisis that resulted in a cut in demand for exports to such a crucial level that the company will have to go into liquidation at the end of the year.

Arnold rises from the desk and picks up the bundle of letters that he will hand out to the staff in the next ten minutes; the letters containing not the bonus they were anticipating, but the redundancy notices with effect from the first of the month.

Saturday December 24th 2011 10:27 pm. A nightclub.

"So Here It Is, Merry Christmas, Everybody's Having Fun," belts out across the dance floor, and, taking it as his cue, Guy sidles over to Mandy.

"I don't know about you, but I reckon we could have a lot more fun somewhere else," he says, slipping his right arm around her waist.

"Shouldn't you be saying that to your wife?" she replies, but the twinkle in her eyes shows that she is more than happy to be the recipient.

"You know that will never happen. She's perfectly content waiting at home with the kids, getting them ready for Santa to come. Well he isn't the only one who has designs on a stocking tonight," Guy replies, lowering his arm so he can feel the garter as he strokes Mandy's thigh.

"Come on then," she says, taking his left hand. "Let's go back to mine and I'll give you your present."

Saturday December 24th 2011 11:59 pm. A two-bedroomed semi.

Angela looks at the clock as it ticks over to midnight. Her fist is clamped over her mouth in an attempt to stifle her sobs; she can't let the children know how she feels. Oscar is too young to understand what has happened, but Chloe is only too aware. Angela can hear Chloe's heartrending cries, even louder now than they have been for the previous two nights.

It is all so senseless. One minute, they were looking forward to the first of two Christmases, one now, the other in February when John returned. The next, their lives were in tatters as they saw the news report; a soldier from *2nd Battalion The Rifles* had been killed in action in Afghanistan.

She is still ashamed of her reaction, when she prayed fervently that it would be somebody else, that some other family would be grieving this Christmas. But it wasn't to be, and the knock on the door cruelly confirmed that they were going to be alone, and not just at Christmas.

Sunday December 25th 2011 6:41 am. A detached house in the country.

"That's mine," screeches Abigail, tearing the present out of her sister's hands.

"No it's not, it's mine," yells Sophie, grabbing it back.

"Muuuum," whines Abigail.

"That's enough girls!" says their mother. "I told you, that pile of presents is for both of you. You have to share those. *Then* you can open your own sacks. Any more of this nonsense and I'll tell Santa not to bother coming next year."

"It's only rubbish anyway," mutters Abigail as Sophie rips the paper off and tosses the boxed doll onto the growing pile of opened presents.

Sunday December 25th 2011 7:36 am. A small terraced town centre house.

"I'm sorry, Natalie, but Father Christmas could only bring you one toy this year."

Mary looks sadly at her husband Paul as Natalie carefully unwraps the present to reveal a furry teddy bear. They couldn't really afford it, especially as Paul has been out of work since he was made redundant from his job at the council three months ago. They should have used the money to pay off some of the mortgage arrears, but they are growing so rapidly that the cost of a hundred bears wouldn't have made much impact on the deficit.

"It's perfect, mummy," squeals Natalie, clutching the bear tight to her chest. Mary forces herself to smile at her daughter; this will probably be their last Christmas in this house and she wants Natalie to enjoy it.

Sunday December 25th 2011 3:33 pm. A front room just after lunch.

Henrietta clears the plates away, piled high with uneaten sprouts and the remains of the turkey; *"Edward was right,"* she thinks, *"it was too big for the four of us. It will do for tomorrow, but after that – well, we don't want to be eating leftovers all holiday, do we?"*

Edward and the children are dozing in the armchairs, snoring loudly. They have slept through the Queen's Christmas broadcast, and even the advert with Roy Wood blaring out Wizzard's *"I Wish it Could Be Christmas Every Day"* isn't enough to rouse them from their replete slumber. Henrietta smiles; now wouldn't it be great if it *was* always Christmas?

Sunday December 25th 2011 6:17 pm. The Horn of Africa.

Abdiweli carries the small bundle towards the pit at the edge of the village. Although it had only been dug two days earlier, it is already brimming over with tiny emaciated bodies. He unwraps the cloth and gently places the almost-skeletal form of his daughter Kadija on top of the pile. It is just another day in the Somali desert.

All times. A manger adjoining an inn in Bethlehem.

The newborn baby boy looks up at the stars with timeless eyes that take in all the inequalities of the world. His parents try to comfort him but to no avail. Jesus weeps.

The Secret of Room 147

The letter arrived on my desk with the mid-morning mail, just as I was about to go to the weekly 10:30 a.m. staff meeting. I nearly left it, but something about the envelope intrigued me; I dread to think what the consequences would have been if I *hadn't* taken note of it.

Most of the correspondence that I received by mail came in standard manila envelopes, but this was an ordinary white one, with my name and address neatly written on the cover. The postmark was blurred – deliberately so? – which intrigued me even further. I looked at my watch: 10:28. The meeting could go ahead without me for once.

I slit the envelope open and removed a credit-card sized piece of plastic and a single piece of card; the plastic was completely unmarked, the card contained a photograph of a spread-eagled figure. I couldn't tell if it was a male or a female, as a book was covering the face. I turned the card over, and a chill went through me. The rear was blank, apart from a tiny drawing in the top-right hand corner of a perfectly-detailed black queen chess piece; underneath it was written in tiny letters *2 p.m.* So now I knew who had sent it; it was obvious, really. It had been exactly a year, and I knew that *something* was going to happen; but I hadn't expected this.

But knowing who had sent it didn't help; I still didn't know what the message meant. After spending half an hour trying to make sense of it all, I finally let my analytical mind take charge; that was who I was, after all, and as it had been sent to my place of work, it made sense that my professional skills would be required. I was certain that the envelope would contain everything I needed to solve the problem. I took a closer look at the photograph; it was obviously photo-shopped, so that was a start point. What was unusual about it?

There was nothing obvious to the naked eye, but perhaps it wasn't supposed to be viewed by normal means. I scanned the photograph into my laptop, then zoomed in to look at it. It became clear that the most unusual aspect of the picture was the book, which had been superimposed over the photograph of the body, so I concentrated on that aspect of the picture.

There was writing on the pages of the book, but as I zoomed in even closer, I realised that most of the characters were nothing but squiggles. But there were *some* legible characters dotted about over the two pages, and I jotted them down. The first page had nine letters – C, S. R, E, L, X, I, O, E; the second had five letters and three numbers: L, 6, E, O, 9, T, 2 and H. What were they supposed to mean?

I wasted the best part of an hour trying to unravel the letters – I was never any good at solving cryptic puzzles – before remembering that I could use the computer to try and solve them. I fed the letters in, those from the first page, then those from the second, and the anagram finder soon came up with two words – *Excelsior* and *Hotel*. There were three hotels of that name in the area, but the address of one of them contained the number 269 – the three digits written on the second page - and that was about an hour's drive away. Giving a garbled message to my PA, I ran to the car park and set off on the journey through the lunchtime traffic.

It was well after 1 pm by the time I'd parked on the hotel car park and made my way to reception. I don't know what I was expecting, but I was disappointed; there wasn't a message for me, and the hotel staff looked at me most suspiciously, so I left the lobby and stood outside the hotel again. Now what?

As I stood there, looking perplexed, an old gypsy woman walked across to me. "Flowers for your lady. Only £10 for a bunch." I turned away, but she wasn't to be put off. Because I couldn't concentrate while she was chattering away, I checked my wallet and thrust two £5 notes into her hand. "I need a £20 note," came the response, handing the fivers back to me. I almost decided to take her into the hotel and hand her over to the staff for causing a nuisance, but time was running out; it would be 2 pm soon, the deadline on the message. I took the only other note from my wallet, a twenty, and gave it to her.

Surprisingly, she handed me a large bunch of fresh flowers *and* a £10 note in change. What was that about? I looked up to ask the gypsy woman, but she had gone round the corner, and when I went after her, she was nowhere to be seen. I was still holding the flowers and the money, and was just about to put the note in my pocket when I noticed some numbers written on it; 7, 4 and 1.

I realised straight away that this *must* be the number of the room where I was supposed to be, in – I looked at my watch – 2 minutes time. I ran back into the hotel. It had three floors of rooms, so I was certain that the room I needed was on the first floor. I climbed the stairs, two at a time, and looked at the signs directing guests towards the various rooms; the highest room number was 160, so I wanted room 147.

I'd worked out that the plastic card in the envelope was a hotel room key, and I used it to enter the room just as the clock ticked over to 2 p.m. It took me but a second to weigh up the sight that met my eyes; on the bed lay a naked woman. Her arms and legs were handcuffed to the four bed posts, and a gag was in her mouth. She looked at me wide-eyed.

#

An hour and a half later, I unlocked her cuffs and removed the gag. Spitting to get the cotton out of her mouth, she said, "I knew my white knight would come to rescue his black queen."

"Yes," I replied, "but next year, why don't we just go out for a nice meal to celebrate our anniversary?"

Burnt

I tried to ignore what I was walking through; *"It's just warm sand between your toes, that's all,"* I muttered, hoping I could convince myself. I failed. I *knew* what – or should I say who – I was stepping on. I should have worn shoes, not sandals, but how was I to know that I'd shortly be treading through the crematorium's latest output when I'd headed outside that morning? I looked down at the remains; it was impossible to equate the debris with a person who had been so full of life just days earlier.

I wondered again how I could be in this predicament. It wouldn't have happened if *they* hadn't rearranged our meeting time at the last moment, leaving us waiting in the Florida heat for days on end. Or, perhaps more importantly, it wouldn't have happened if we hadn't been so foolish. I chastised myself for the thousandth time. I'd been in this business long enough to know that there were boundaries, but greed had taken over and we had trespassed onto their territory. For the sake of a few thousand dollars, we had demolished a scam worth millions that they had spent months setting up. Now it was time to pay the penalty, but at least we would be able to walk away once the debt was settled, free to start over.

But that freedom now seemed a distant possibility because of *her*. If *she* hadn't had a body to die for – literally in this case – *he* probably would be eating fried chicken and drinking beer while he watched the world passing by his waterfront café. She told me how she had been bored with the waiting, flirted with him to pass the time, gone back to his basement flat, and then allowed him to engage in his every fantasy. That's where it had all gone disastrously wrong. She'd bought ropes and handcuffs, and had secured him to indulge his wishes. But when it was her turn to be bound, he wanted more than control, and swallowed the key in front of her to show how she was lost. Then his heart gave way. I found them hours later, after she managed to get to her phone. It took two hacksaw blades to remove the cuffs, and we barely made our escape before his body was discovered.

That was three days ago. Three days in which the minutes passed inexorably slowly as the time for the rearranged meet approached. Tonight. Six o'clock. Dead. And the word was not chosen idly; if I didn't come up with the money, then *I'd* be dead. You didn't mess with these people, and I'd no intention of trying to con *them*. We both knew when not to play the sting.

She hadn't been with me long, but she had already learnt almost all there was to know about the game. She was still raw, that was true, but she had that look of innocence that made everybody believe anything she said. We made the perfect couple; everybody trusted an aging grandfather and his teenage granddaughter. We only targeted those who could afford it, and we never hurt anybody. I liked to think of us as modern day *Robin Hoods* – except for the bit about giving to the poor; that's how I'd been able to raise the cash.

I had the money with me, locked away in the safe I had bought. It would have taken four men to lift, so I knew that the money was secure from any double-cross. Besides, there was *honour amongst thieves* in our profession – they would allow me to operate *provided* I kept to my side of the bargain. Fifteen million dollars. It sounds a lot; it *is* a lot; but mere pebbles on the sand compared to the riches that are out there. It had taken me years to accumulate, but over half of it had come since she joined with me; I saw no reason why the next few years wouldn't recoup all of that sum and more.

And then I got her phone call, minutes after I'd stepped outside to have a cigarette. "It's the wrong key." Four words, that's all. I didn't know what she was talking about, so I told her to explain. "That man. You know, the one from the café. I told you he swallowed the key to the handcuffs. Well it wasn't that key after all - it's still in my bag. I tried to open the safe, just to check, and the key wouldn't fit. *He* ate the key to the safe by mistake."

It was ninety degrees outside, in the sweltering November heat of Miami, but cold fear gripped me. I *had* to make the payoff tonight, otherwise I'd be returning home in a body bag. Overhead, little fluffy clouds without a hint of grey in them encircled the yellow sun, which carved a cheery circle into the sky; people sprawled wherever they could, luxuriating in the warming rays, topping up their tans and doing anything to avoid going back inside. I *hated* this place. Give me the cold of New York any day; my kind of town, my kind of people.

"Leave it with me," I told her. "I'll find it. You just make sure nobody gets at the safe." Could *they* have set it all up? Was this part of a plan to con *us*? Suddenly, I wasn't that certain about there being any honour in this profession.

It took me an hour to find out where they had taken the old guy's body, and I flinched when I found out he was being cremated. But then I thought about it. There was still a chance. If he'd been buried – well, there was no way I'd have been able to dig him up and cut him open in broad daylight, was there?

I hired a car, drove to the crem, only to find he'd just gone down the long corridor, so I had to wait, kicking my sandaled heels, for the three hours until all was ready. I used the time to do some research. The key was most likely made from brass, or nickel-plated brass, with a melting-point of somewhere between 1700 and 2700 degrees F; the crematorium heat would be around 1600-2000. I had to hope the key would survive.

A couple of hundred dollars in the top pocket of the manager bought me ten minutes unrestricted access to the raked-out and pre-pulverised remains, with the gritty bits slipping between my toes and into my mind despite my pretence that it was just sand.

I found the key, still warm and still identifiable. I checked it thoroughly; it looked as if it *might* open the safe. It *had* to. I had an hour before the pay-off was due to be made. I could just make it. But I hadn't figured on the Miami rush hour traffic. It was forty minutes before I reached the hotel and charged into the room.

She should have been there, waiting for me. But the room was empty. All her clothes had gone. And then I saw it. The safe. Open. Empty. Apart from the hacksawed handcuffs. I must have been on autopilot as I took the key and slipped it into the lock on the cuffs. With a click, they sprung open.

It all became obvious. The master had become the pupil, and with a sudden insight I realised that she had violated our unbreakable principle; Maid Marion had become Bonnie Parker. I don't know how she forced him to eat the key, but I knew there was nothing accidental about his demise.

But that was nothing in comparison to what she had done to me. I, who had made a living out of conning the rich out of their enormous fortunes, without them even realising they'd been victims of crime, had become the prey. I had taught her too well, and it would be the last lesson I would ever teach.

The clock struck six and I knew that I'd had my fingers well and truly burnt.

Life on the Box

I sit back, mulling over what has just happened; I've read about this sort of thing, of course – who hasn't heard of Scrooge? – but I thought it only occurred in stories. But, they do say, life is often stranger than fiction.

#

It had been another tiring day at work, and all I wanted to do was vegetate in front of the television. I flicked through the channel TV Guide. BBC1 *Pointless*, BBC2 *Flog It*, ITV *The Chase*, another pointless game show, and as for Channel 4 - *Coach Trip* followed by *Come Dine With Me*, where the aim of both 'reality shows' was to put together a group of people from disparate backgrounds and watch each eat his or her own words with a great deal of indigestion. I suppose that classed as entertainment, but it didn't inspire me to renew my annual licence. Channel 5 was at least being serious, showing the news, but I wanted to be entertained, not see yet more doom and gloom.

I panned down to the next channel, but it wasn't one I was expecting; instead of ITV2, channel number 6, the listing was for 5.5, *Life on the Box*. I knew that additional Freeview channels were frequently coming on line, although I would have thought there were enough whole channel numbers available to avoid them having to use decimal points. The programme listed was *This is Your Life*, so I deemed it to be another one of those interminable reruns, but then curiosity took a hold. Was it one of the Michael Aspel shows, or perhaps one of the original Eamonn Andrews ones? Possibly one where the guest walked off? I remember footballer Danny Blanchflower and author Richard Gordon doing that, although I never actually saw those programmes. I clicked the channel on, hoping that one of those momentous events might be beamed into my front room this spring evening.

Initially, there wasn't an image, but a spot of light formed in the centre of the screen, before gradually spreading outwards until I could see the picture. I didn't see Eamonn Andrews, or Michael Aspel, or, indeed, anybody that I recognised. There were three people on screen, a man, a woman and a baby. The man wore a dark-grey suit, with a thin brown tie neatly positioned against his stiff white shirt, whereas the woman wore a patterned fawn knee length dress that fanned out behind the high-backed light brown armchair.

The room was very like the one I was currently in, although it had a very austere appearance and the furniture looked as if it came from the 1950s – a large wooden-housed wireless set perched atop the sideboard to the right of the room. A calendar hung on the wall behind the armchair, and I could just make out the year 1957 at the top of the twelve-month display. Neither of the adults spoke, even though I watched for several minutes. The woman leant on the back of the chair while the man smoked a cigarette. This was a very strange programme. I took a closer look at the couple; there was something familiar about them, but I couldn't work out what I'd seen them in before. That was happening to me with increasing regularity, and not just where people from television were concerned. I knew I wouldn't be able to concentrate on anything else until I remembered, so I put my fingers to my temples and forced myself to concentrate. What had they been in before?

The answer popped into my head, but it wasn't one that I was expecting; they looked familiar because they reminded me of the black and white photograph of my parents on their wedding day. I leant forward, peering to take a closer look. There was no mistake. It was them, and they were in this very room, and – as I was an only child and born that year – the baby would have been me. I didn't know how the television channel had managed to get hold of this film, or why they had thought it worthy of an airing, but it did explain the silence, as I knew that home movies from the 50s and 60s rarely had any sound.

As I watched, the picture faded, to be replaced seconds later by another scene. It was the same front room, but there were half a dozen people in it, all stood around sombre faced and looking uncomfortable. The figure standing by the fireplace, with long curly hair and wearing a wide-lapelled shirt and purple flared trousers, was unmistakeably me during my 'glamrock' phase. The sideboard was still there, but a transistor radio replaced the wireless from the previous scene. The calendar at the back of the room clearly showed June 1977, with a photograph of a windmill the picture for the month, but the armchair was exactly the same as the one from the 1950s, albeit looking threadbare and worn.

It didn't take me more than two seconds to realise that I was viewing the time directly after my parents' funeral – they died of natural causes within days of each other. I was twenty at the time, and the five other people in attendance were an aunt and uncle on my mother's side and two aunts and an uncle on my father's. They were the entire family, although we were never close, and I lost touch with them after the funeral; I think they resented the fact that the house was left to me and they didn't receive a penny from the small estate. There was some animosity, and I didn't helped by greedily refusing to allow them to take even the smallest of mementoes away with them. I realised that in the thirty-five years since that day, I had barely been in contact with them, and I had no idea whether or not they were still alive.

I made a decision there and then to go and search for them, but as I was rising from my armchair, the television screen flickered and a new scene displayed. A man was carrying a woman into the front room, and I gulped involuntarily as I remembered that day, almost thirty years earlier, when I had carried my new wife, Angela, over the threshold. I still had my wedding suit on, with bits of confetti in my hair and over my shoulders, whereas Angela was in her going away outfit, a wide-belted dress with Joan Collins-style padded shoulders. We were both laughing, happiness evident everywhere. I didn't need to see the calendar, though a quick glance brought confirmation that I was looking at July 1983, with a seafront view of Blackpool trams the picture for the month. There was a brand new armchair, much sleeker than its predecessor and with golden cushions to match the golden years ahead that we were anticipating.

The memories flooded back. All the plans that we had. Whatever went wrong? The world was ours, we were going to have such a good life together, with laughter the key part. Neither of us had siblings, and we vowed we wouldn't make the same mistake, talking of having three, four or even five children.

As I remembered our family plans, the picture changed again, and now there were three of us there: myself, Angela and baby Oliver. It had taken more than ten years before we'd been able to have a child – he'd be eighteen soon, and I made a mental note to make sure I was in touch to commemorate that special day. The room hadn't changed a great deal in the intervening years; our clothing was more suited for a couple in their late thirties than some of the flamboyant items I remembered us wearing in our early years together, and the transistor radio on the sideboard was now a quarter the size of its predecessor. A computer screen sat next to the radio, although I couldn't see the desktop it was attached to, as that was just out of sight over to the left. The calendar was open at a picture of trees for September 1994, an autumnal image of reds, golds, greens and yellows.

I looked at the screen again, and although I was smiling broadly as I sat in my armchair, Angela looked fraught as she tried to settle our young son. It was so obvious now, but strangely enough, I never noticed at the time.

The screen shifted again, and this time I was alone in the front room. There was no longer a radio on the sideboard, and a closed laptop had replaced the old desktop computer. My hair was greying and also beginning to thin. I knew *exactly* when it was; I didn't need to look at the calendar hanging on the wall. The date was carved indelibly on my heart. February 25th 2004. It was the day she left me, taking Oliver with her, citing irreconcilable differences. I should have gone after them. Maybe it wouldn't have done any good, but I should have made the effort. But I didn't. I remained, sat in my armchair, now more of a dirty yellow than gold, letting the world pass me by

The screen went black, and I waited for another scene to come, but nothing happened. And, I suppose, there was nothing more to show. I had lived the last eight years on autopilot, getting up, going to work, coming home, going to bed, then repeating the cycle the next day. No, I hadn't *lived* those eight years, I had existed for them. I looked around the room. The sideboard was bare – I hadn't used the computer in years – and there was no calendar hanging behind me; I didn't want any reminder of the years. Or I hadn't. I knew what I had to do. This was my chance to change things, just as Ebenezer Scrooge had in Dickens' timeless tale.

#

The screen flickers, slowly coming into sharp contrast once more. But this time, all it appears to be showing is a reflection of my front room as it is now; there I sit, facing the television, exactly as I am now. Except, when I lean forward and look closer, it isn't *exactly* the same. The 'me' on the television is sat back in the chair, glassy eyes wide open in the unmistakeable pose of death. I sit back with a start. This is what I have to change. I'll begin straight aw...

No Go

I checked my money; nowhere near enough. I'd have to trust to luck. Old snake-eyes would put me in jail, but that would be a relief; I'd miss payday, but the alternative was ruin almost everywhere. Around the corner, hotels stretched as far as I could see, havens for some, no-go areas for me. I reckoned I'd only a one in a dozen chance of surviving till I could collect my salary.

I checked the numbers and my worst fears were confirmed. Ten. I wouldn't be collecting £200 as I passed Go; I had landed on Mayfair and was bankrupt.

The Da Vinci Code

Let me start by thanking you for inviting me to address you this evening on the occasion of my eightieth birthday. I know that some of you believe I haven't achieved the heights which many of my more junior published colleagues have reached. I, on the other hand, believe that I have been fundamental in shaping the future of the world, as I hope will become apparent over the next few minutes.

During my life, I have witnessed many changes, more than any of you could possibly comprehend. In these days of 3D television and a digital world, you'll probably find it difficult to believe that my idea of relaxation half a century ago was listening to Jimmy Clitheroe on the radio. I note the blank faces and whispered cries of *Jimmy who?* – all confirming that I am, indeed, a man from a different time.

Time. That is the key word. *Time Travel* has been a popular subject in fiction for centuries. My colleagues will claim it belongs in fiction, as in fact it is an impossibility. But then they would, wouldn't they? I, on the other hand, know differently; I have spent the last sixty years striving to breach the barriers of time and tonight I am going to tell you that I have succeeded.

I can hear the sniggers and see the looks of disbelief. No, I am *not* senile; far from it. Perhaps I should make myself clear. I'm not talking about actual time travel, but of crossing the barriers of time. Nor am I suggesting we could ever cross over into the *future*; now that *would* be impossible. The future hasn't happened yet, so how could you go there? But the past – well, that's different. Don't misunderstand me, though. You can't choose any point in time; it isn't that simple.

Let me explain. Consider time as a river, seen from above, meandering and flowing inexorably along. Visualise the River Dee at nearby Wrexham; picture how it winds and bends. At certain points the left bank of the upward stream almost touches the right bank of the preceding downward flow. Under certain conditions – such as high water after a period of heavy rain – the two distinct stretches can almost become one, and it is possible to cross back over onto a previously traversed region of the river. Care needs to be taken - if you mistime the pass from one bank to another, leaping a fraction early or a fraction too late, you'll not reach your intended landing point.

As it is with the river, so it is with the past, with the conditions that equate to the high water mark being the use of depleted uranium – isotope 235 specifically; as you know, during the fission process, large amounts of heat energy are released, and these create the circumstances that allow specific points of the present and past to, shall we say, temporarily overlap, facilitating the crossover.

When I say *crossing over to the past*, I'm not suggesting a person could make that journey. That *would* be the stuff of science fiction, and could introduce the *grandfather paradox,* where an individual goes back in time and kills their grandfather before he met their grandmother, thus ensuring that the time traveller could never be born. That cannot happen. It is an indisputable fact that the crossover points on the tangential bends of the time river are never less than 150 years apart. Science has to obey the physical laws of the universe, and they preclude anything that only came into being after the event from existing in a previous time period.

Let me illustrate this with another example, ignoring the *150-year* rule for the moment. Imagine it is 1960 and you are at a crossover point that leads to 1936. You have a pocket full of old pennies, one each from the reigns of Queen Victoria, Edward VII, George V, George VI and Elizabeth II. If you try to throw those coins into the river of time, two of them – the ones for George VI and Elizabeth II – will not be able to make that journey, because those coins were not minted until *after* 1936.

Another favourite plotline in fiction is the so-called *butterfly effect*, where something from the present inadvertently kills a butterfly in the past and changes history so that instead of a race of humans we suddenly become a *Planet of the Apes* society where man is the pet and monkeys rule the world. In reality, though, many events have little or no impact at all, especially in the long term. Let me demonstrate this by using another metaphor. Imagine you are driving along a main road, immediately behind another car, when the traffic lights change. The other car goes through, you have to stop. You think that the simple fact that the lights changed has affected your journey permanently, and you'll never regain the time that has been lost. Then the lights turn to green, you set off again, and a mile and a half further down the road, you come to another set of lights; these are already on red, and the car that you'd been behind previously is stopped at them, so you are once again right behind the same vehicle. In other words, whether you were stopped at the first set of lights or not, your journey wasn't affected at all once you travelled on for a further few minutes.

That doesn't mean that the butterfly effect *can't* apply; on a different journey, you would *never* catch up to that car, as it would find every subsequent set of traffic lights on green while you found every subsequent set on red. So, in order to influence the past, the correct event has to be chosen; after all, the reason for reaching back in time is because you *want* to change something.

If you did effect such a change, what would that mean in real terms? Would everything suddenly change overnight? Would England suddenly become good at penalty shootouts? The truth is – nobody would know anything had changed, because nothing *would* have changed. The present where we decide to change the past is a *now* predicated upon the *then* that has already happened.

Consider another example. Suppose you decided to send something back to, say, the fifteenth century. It would have to be an authentic item from that era. You could get pieces of parchment that dated from that time, chemically treat them to remove any writings, and then scribe whatever message you wanted to send back using a crude version of the Greek and Roman inks in use during that century. You could create a combination using carbonised soot and water, both of which date back millennia. Even without the use of animal glue to bind it together, the resultant mixture would be sufficient to record a message.

Everybody is aware of the designs of Leonardo da Vinci in the fifteenth and sixteenth centuries – for example, the tank, the machine gun, the aeroplane and the hang-glider. How could a man renowned solely for his art suddenly come up with designs which wouldn't exist for several centuries? He couldn't. What he could do, though, was appreciate the drawings sent to him from the future and pass them off as his own. And that is *exactly* what happened. I sent a series of sketches back in time to da Vinci and he took those drawings, redrew them and passed them off as his own, resulting in many of the inventions and developments of the five hundred years since. He didn't get everything right - he misinterpreted the helicopter drawing I sent, his design having the propellers turning against the direction of the rotors, so it couldn't possibly work – but we already knew that, didn't we? And he also tried to invent things of his own, such as special shoes to allow man to walk on water. He was probably feeling inspired as a direct result of the sketches I sent him, but as he wasn't really an inventor, he was unsuccessful.

Don't even consider lecturing me about the consequences of what I did. I'm old. I no longer care what happens to me. Besides, there aren't any consequences, and never will be. I sent da Vinci those designs five hours ago, but the world has known that I did it for five centuries; our present only exists because I changed the past in order to create the future.

Lounge Lizard

By the time I finally reached the hotel I was almost exhausted, but the sight of the imposing building and the promise of its hidden delights acted as nourishment to my weary body. I had arrived by train but had chosen to walk from the station rather than take a taxi. It had been a considered decision, as I always endeavoured to make as little impression as possible each time I visited a new town; every taxi driver was a potential future witness. However, as it had taken me the best part of an hour to reach my destination, there were times during the trek when I would have gladly sacrificed my anonymity for the comfort of a bench seat and four wheels as offered by the landaus that patrolled the seafront; granted, that mode of transport might be little quicker than walking, but it would have been infinitely more relaxing. Tiredness alone wasn't the problem – if it were, I might perhaps have grumbled, but angry words would have been all there was to it. No, the main thing was my desperate need for nutrition. It had been far too long since my last meal, and I was regretting my decision to delay my departure home to take in this trip to the seaside. After all, what possible attraction could hundreds of illuminated bulbs really have for someone like me?

I hunched up, trying to protect myself against the wind and the rain. *Welcome to sunny Blackpool*, I told myself. This might be only what the locals termed *a summer shower* but I *hated* this country, with its persistently miserable weather. I didn't know why I'd stayed here for so long; I suppose if I was honest with myself, it was all down to pride. I had been bored and wanted to experience exciting new flavours, so had left Africa, believing that things had to be better elsewhere; when they clearly weren't, I should have accepted I'd made a mistake and returned home, but I was too pig-headed to do that.

Admittedly, I did arrive in England on what was a very pleasant summer's day, but that soon proved to be a false impression of the British weather. In the twelve and a half months since that afternoon, I doubt if the mercury ever came within twenty degrees of that initial chart-topping mark. I spent much of the last year in one dingy room or another, with the heating turned up to the maximum, trying to survive the cold that the English accepted as part of everyday life. Until finally, as another so-called summer neared its end, I decided enough was enough and it was time to go home. The only question was why had it taken me a year to come to that decision? And, continuing with the *being honest* part, I did know the reason; it was the people who made it bearable. They were unique, unlike any I had ever encountered before. Whether in the city or the country, by the sea or in the mountainous areas, the sight of young women, provocatively displaying flesh as they prepared to party, never failed to set my mouth watering. But, however much the populace might have been to my taste, the time had come to depart for warmer climes. *One more night*, I told myself. *Just one more night, and then you'll be on your way home, back to the desert and its comforting warmth*.

I pushed these thoughts to the back of my mind as I took in the impressive façade of *The Brightwater Hotel*. It looked more like a country estate than a hotel, with history seeping out of every window; it was as if I were stepping back into a different time period, more the beginning of the twentieth century than the twenty-first. I had never been here before, but from first impressions, it was already more than living up to its reputation; I know that the surroundings weren't really relevant as far as my purpose was concerned, but I still sensed that I was going to enjoy my stay here.

I stepped through the front door, and immediately revised my opinion. Inside, everything was twenty-first century, airy, bright and completely fit for purpose. It was totally unlike so many of the hotels I'd stayed in, anonymous clones of each other. This one oozed character. Whoever was responsible, they had done a good job here.

I headed towards the semi-circular reception desk, and then froze in mid-step. What was *he* doing here? I had specifically chosen this location for the solitude, and within thirty seconds I had seen somebody I knew; I didn't know him well, but he was an acquaintance. And an inconvenience. What was his name? Mark? Mike? Then I remembered; he was called Max. I was on the verge of panic; this would change everything. There was nothing I could do about it, though, and I grudgingly looked him in the face as he walked towards me. However, instead of greeting me, he walked straight past me, and as he came within range, I sensed my mistake. It *looked* like Max but it wasn't him; a blood relation, almost certainly, but – thankfully – not one that I had ever met.

I resumed my approach to the desk, thankful that my indecision hadn't drawn any attention to me, and introduced myself ready for the checking in process. I wondered what it would entail at this hotel. I saw from her name tag that the receptionist was called Fiona. She was a voluptuous blonde and I sensed she be eminently suitable, but I immediately choked off that line of thought; anonymity was the prime directive. She handed me a registration card.

"Just put your name and address on here please."

I began to fill in the information, smiling to myself as I signed it *Rex Green*. I truly felt like the king of my profession as I handed her the completed card. She glanced up at me, trying to pretend not to be interested but failing miserably. She couldn't help it; it was part of my animal magnetism, an appearance that I had laboured successfully to create for some considerable period. Few women could resist my film-star looks and herculean build, and – truth to tell – I didn't normally discourage them.

"It's just the one night, isn't it, Mr Green? Will you be dining in the restaurant?"

"No, I don't think so. I'll probably take something up to my room." I found it difficult to keep a smirk off my face as I spoke.

Fiona looked disappointed, as if her salary depended on her securing guests for the probably over-priced restaurant, before adding, "We offer a first rate room-service. The menu is in the room, on the small table by the bed."

"Thanks, I'll take a look at it. I'm sure I'll find something appetising," I concluded, preparing to leave for my room.

"Just a second and I'll call a porter to carry your case. Vlad, over here please."

"No, it's alright thanks, I can manage perfectly well myself." Vlad stopped in midstep and returned to the shadows, no doubt counting the cost of a missed gratuity. It wasn't that I didn't want to have to tip the porter, rather that he might question why he was carrying an empty case into my room. It would be different when I was leaving; I'd have no problem letting him bring my suitcase down then.

As I looked for the lift, I spotted a group of young women in the foyer. They were gathered round a table whilst drinking coffee, and they immediately caught my interest. Unobtrusively, I tuned in to their conversation; from the few words I picked up, I concluded they were in town for a wedding. One of the women stood slightly apart from the others; I almost gasped when I saw her. She was petite, barely more than five feet tall, I would say, and had flame-red hair. She wore a lilac flower-patterned dress that accentuated the curves that were in perfect proportion to her body, and her slender ankles were enclosed by three-inch-high cream shoes. I'd classed her as a woman, but she was barely more than a young girl in her late teens or very early twenties. She was *tasty* and smelt divine. I was salivating as I watched her; I imagined her sumptuous curves and knew I had to have her. From a dozen yards away, I flashed my most disarming smile towards her, gazed deeply into her eyes and – as always – it did the trick.

Without a word, she moved away from her companions – they were engrossed in a conversation about the wedding and didn't even notice she had left them – and followed me at a discreet pace. I checked constantly all the way to my room, but there weren't any cameras in the corridors; the only ones I'd seen were in the foyer, and I'd ensured that I was far enough ahead so as to not be in the same shot as her, so there would be nothing to connect us if the tapes were inspected at a later date. I closed the door behind us and we were alone.

She stood just inside the room, waiting for me to instruct her. This was my favourite part. I've seen snakes mesmerise their victims with a simple look; some combine the gaze with a swaying, hypnotic dance. Either way, look or glide, the end result is the same; the victim can do nothing about it. I didn't need to sway, as my piercing stare always produced the results; once I had attracted their attention with my smile, everything else would always fall into place. I suppose people might call it mind-control, or some other such mumbo-jumbo, but the scientific explanation is that if you look closely into my eyes, you will see that the green of the iris is in two distinct shades, and they interweave like snakes crawling through grass. The movement is constant, and has a deeply hypnotic effect, especially on young women. I don't know why that should be, and, frankly, I don't care. Young women are fine as far as I'm concerned. The effect is long lasting, so that even after only a few seconds of watching the swirling green patterns, the girl will be under my control for a while, irrespective of whether or not I continue to gaze into her eyes. It takes a different length of time with each victim, which I think is probably inversely linked to the person's IQ - the smarter the girl, the quicker the transition. However bright the girl is, after a period of between five and fifteen minutes the hypnosis wears off, leaving the victim totally paralysed for a further ten minutes until the blood begins to flow, gradually dissipating the effect; *if* they were able to survive a further ten minutes, of course.

This girl must have had a slightly above average intelligence, for she was barely malleable and not much more than five minutes had passed since I instigated eye contact. I preferred it that way, as it meant less work for me. I didn't need to speak; she sensed what was expected of her, and began to undress. As her outer garments were divested, I congratulated myself on making the perfect choice – she wasn't skinny, like a lot of these girls who try and be like supermodels, but neither was she running to fat. As I heard somebody say once, there was meat on them bones. Her ample breasts bounced like succulent chickens on a spit, and her firm thighs held promise of a feast of delights. I was almost drooling at the sight of her; she really was the perfect sight to set before a starving man.

Once she was completely naked, I glanced at the bed and she walked stiffly over before perching demurely on the edge, watching as I began to disrobe. It was such a relief to shed the accoutrements of twenty-first century life in England, and as I returned to my natural state, I stretched and relished my newfound freedom.

Her eyes appeared to have grown wider, reflecting the onset of panic, but I knew that was just an illusion; the state of paralysis had begun, and it was now impossible for her to contract a single muscle. I collected her discarded clothing and put every last piece in my suitcase, pausing to look at my reflection as I passed the full-length mirror; it barely contained my nine-foot frame, and I marvelled once again at how refreshing it was to see my green scales once more after a day of wearing the pink skin that I was forced to wear while I perused the community for my next meal.

The girl might not have been able to move, but now that the hypnosis had worn off, her senses were working overtime. If we were the same species, then I suppose they would be called pheromones; whatever, they had the same effect on me. This was my favourite part, when the victim was cognisant but powerless to resist me. In anticipation of the delights to come, I breathed in her fragrance as I opened my jaws, my ligaments stretching to their full extent until the opening was large enough to take the terrified girl. Slowly, savouring every moment, I approached my meal.

#

Replete, I lay back on the bed. If anybody were to come in now, they would find nothing amiss – apart, that is, from a scaly reptilian creature – as there was not a shred of evidence in view to suggest the girl had ever existed. I wondered how her absence at the wedding would be explained, and chided myself for the first signs of carelessness. Normally, I only chose people who were truly alone, but this one had such an aromatic scent that I had felt compelled to feast first, analyse afterwards.

I considered leaving the hotel, but quickly dispensed with that thought; I had paid for the night, so to leave early might bring me to people's attention, especially if a search were mounted for the missing girl. No, far better to stick to my plan and stay the night before returning home, to another town in the sun, with another hotel and another gourmet dining experience. Besides, I knew that I would benefit most from the meat in my stomach far better in my natural form, and if I were to revert too soon to the human image, I would doubtless need to feast again before the month was out.

Satisfied that – despite following my near-carnal urge – everything was as it should be, I lay back, slid my lids across my eyes and began to digest the still-wriggling human.

Sealed With A Kiss

It started with a kiss; that was the highpoint. Julian Winter never expected it to be the kiss of death for his aspirations. From that moment on, he was spiralling downwards towards his present position, waiting uncomfortably in this small anteroom. He was sandwiched between a well-built woman and a burly man, both of whom were overflowing onto his seat, forcing him to sit rigidly upright to ensure he maintained at least some aspect of personal space. He toyed with – and discarded – the idea of getting up and moving, deciding instead to let his thoughts roam back over the last few months. Back to when he met her.

#

It was Friday, and after a hard week both at work and home, he felt in need of liquid fortification before heading back to his family in the suburbs. Julian was a consultant for a large software company based in London, although he spent most of his time away from home on clients' premises. In the early days, his wife, Sandra, had objected to seeing so little of her husband, and when first Oliver and then Rose had been born, he had almost acquiesced to her wishes to find a more stable position; but the money was good, the trimmings better - he and the family could use the company's luxury penthouse flat in the city whenever they wanted to. That, allied to her love of fine food and quality wines, had eventually won Sandra over.

Sacrifices had to be made, though, and he had missed out on the formative years of his children; the school sports day fathers' race had yet to see him at the start line. Julian reluctantly accepted absenting himself from such events, consoling himself with the thought that he'd have ample opportunity in the years ahead to forge relationships with his offspring.

He'd missed a major event today, hence his mood and the need for alcohol. It was a school performance over which young Rose had been excited for weeks, as she had the role of one of the sheep in the farmhouse. Sandra had gone to watch, of course, but with the stringent rules forbidding video photography of school events, he would only be able to hear about his daughter's first acting role. He felt a little hurt that he'd not received a text telling him how the play had gone, and in a childish response he'd decided not to phone to ask, but to have a couple of slow drinks instead.

The bar was sparsely populated, perhaps surprisingly so for a Friday evening, and Julian found an unoccupied booth which allowed him the personal space that he so craved. He hadn't been to this establishment before, but he marked it down as one for the future; it wasn't often that one could find peace and quiet like this in the city. He was halfway through his second whisky when somebody sat in the seat across from him. Annoyed, he looked round – yes, there were still plenty of other available seats; why did they choose to sit here? He turned to face the newcomer, hoping that the glowering look he proffered would be sufficient to force them to move. When he saw his companion, though, he was no longer able to maintain his severe countenance.

"It's so nice to have a relaxing drink on a Friday evening, don't you agree?" She smiled warmly as she spoke.

On hearing her silky, seductive tone, Julian could only mutter in response, regressing to a young teenager who had just been addressed for the first time by the hottest girl in school. She didn't appear to notice, though, as she continued, "But I hate sitting alone, don't you? My name's Emma, by the way, I'm a contracts manager in the city. I've never been here before – is it always this quiet?"

Julian took her offered hand and gave her a warm handshake in return. Just the touch of her skin on his was sufficient to send anticipatory tingles up his arm and bring warmth to his entire body, but he'd managed to regain some of his composure now; years of being forced to think on his feet in meetings with clients had left him able to cope with the most arduous of situations. "Hi Emma, nice to meet you. Yes, it's nice to have company, someone you can wind down with. And no, I don't know if it's always like this – I've never been here before either. I'm a software consultant for a blue-chip computer company and I spend most of my time on clients' premises, so it's quite a high pressure environment. I'm sure your job is equally demanding, though."

"It can be, but it can also be quite dull. Not like yours, I'm sure – I know practically nothing about computers, I'm a real technophobe, but I'd be fascinated to hear about what you do."

Julian was happy to comply, as in the dozen or so years he'd known Sandra, she had never once taken an interest in his work. Normally, that was fine, as it was good to leave the concerns of the job outside the front door of his home, but there were occasions when it would have been nice to have somebody who could share his frustrations at the unreasonable demands of some of his clientele.

For the next hour, Julian proceeded to bare his soul to Emma, going far beyond work problems, and he didn't realise how long he'd been talking until he glanced at the clock at the back of the bar and noticed it was almost 7 pm. By now, the roads would be quiet, and he would have a straightforward journey home – he'd be back for half seven, plenty of time to have dinner before reading a bedtime story to the children. Rose would no doubt tell him excitedly about her acting debut. Only he didn't want to leave the ambience of the bar, or his companion. He'd been given an unlooked for and unexpected opportunity when Emma joined him at the table, and he wanted to try and take full advantage of it.

He tried to think of a plausible excuse for delaying his return home. Emma gave him the opportunity he was seeking for, as she said, "I suppose in your line of work, then, that you must be at the beck and call of your clientele, and if they want you to work into the night, you don't have any say in the matter? Even on a Friday..." Just in case he hadn't understood the hidden undertones, Emma leaned over and kissed him sensuously on the lips. With that kiss, Julian's fate was sealed.

Although he'd never done anything on impulse before – he was a planner, an organiser, and didn't like leaving things to fate or chance – he took out his mobile and rang his wife. "Hello darling, it's me. Sorry, I've only just finished work. I was called out to one of our Scottish clients urgently, and I didn't get here until after lunch. I'm going to get something to eat now, but it'll be too late to drive back home after my meal, so I'm going to find a place for the night and I'll come home in the morning..... Yes, dear, that's right ..... We'll still have most of the weekend, we can do something, the four of us. See you later, give my love to Oliver and Rose, and tell them I'll be home as soon as possible."

The deed done, Julian turned to look at Emma and smiled at her. "It's a good job she doesn't know it's a company rule that we never go to a client's site on a Friday afternoon. But she never did take any interest in my work."

#

Emma had found it difficult to keep the smirk of satisfaction from her face as she'd listened to Julian making the call to his wife. She'd thought from the second she spotted him from the bar that he would be an easy mark, and she anticipated a very profitable night in store. Men were so stupid! It was so easy to get them to forget all about their wedding vows with the lure of her tempting flesh, reel them in to her trap and then spring it – the threat of a visit to see the wife at home *always* produced results. And, as a consequence, Emma was now a very wealthy woman.

Having decided there was no need to rush off, they'd stayed and had a couple more drinks at the bar, leaving only as it began to get more crowded later on. Now, as they walked through the streets to his car, Emma began to put the next stage of the seduction into place. "My flat isn't too far from here, and it's very cosy at this time of year."

"Actually, I've got a better idea – that's if you don't mind?"

"That sounds intriguing – tell me about it." And, truth to tell, Emma really *was* intrigued. Most men were only too happy to take up her offer of a free bed, thinking they would save themselves the cost of an expensive hotel room in the city. It was only later that the truth of "there's no such thing as a free..." came back to haunt them.

"Well, it's like this. The company has a luxury penthouse flat, and – as a senior consultant – I have the use of it whenever I want. It's ideal for times when I've been working into the night and can't face the drive home; my wife doesn't like it if I get in late and disturb her," he added quietly. "It has a perfect view over the river. We could sip champagne while we talk if you like. Don't worry," he added quickly, thinking she might not like the idea of going to a strange man's flat, "I won't be offended if you'd prefer not to. I just thought ... well, it seems such an ideal setting ... but it doesn't matter ..."

"I think it's a *wonderful* idea. As you said, it sounds perfect. I'd love to see it."

"I'm so pleased. And don't worry, I'll make sure you get home – we have a fleet of cars and drivers, so you won't have to bother with a taxi."

"That sounds nice – as long as they come *after* breakfast."

Julian appeared to redden as she said this, and Emma almost felt sorry for him. He didn't seem like the usual men she picked up, men who were actively seeking extra marital relations. *They* really did deserve everything they received, whereas this one might just be a lonely man in need of a friend. But then she remembered his words to his wife, how easily the lies had tripped from his tongue, and any feelings of sympathy she might have had for him evaporated. *No,* she thought, *if anything he's worse than the rest; at least they are open and honest about their deceptions. He's trying to pretend he doesn't know what's going to happen when we both know full well what this is about.*

In a matter of minutes, the car pulled into an underground garage alongside the waterfront flats. Emma felt a shiver of fear just for a second. She was taking a bit of a risk. She'd never seen this man before, and it was highly unlikely that the few customers in the bar would remember seeing them together if anything were to happen. *Stop being stupid* she silently admonished herself, *you've done this dozens of times before. Just keep your wits about you and you'll come to no harm.*

Julian hadn't appeared to notice her change of mood, and he was still full of olde-worlde charm as he parked the car and then almost ran round to her side so he could open the door for her. Emma relaxed as she linked arms with him and walked back into the brightly lit streets as they continued towards the penthouse. She gasped as he opened the door and she saw the flat; he hadn't exaggerated in the slightest. Thick, pure-white carpeting covered the floors, and as she stepped onto it, she felt as if she were sinking deep into its warm embrace. Julian poured two glasses of champagne and handed one to Emma as she continued to take in her surroundings.

As she sipped from the long stemmed glass, she saw that the walls were covered with an eclectic range of paintings. She walked across to read the square metallic labels underneath them and saw the names of Constable and Pollock amongst others that she didn't recognise. Reproductions, presumably, but representing a touch of class.

All of this paled, though, as she stepped onto the balcony and looked across the illuminated river. With the lights twinkling on the dark water, and motor craft and launches gliding across the surface, it resembled a scene from a fairy tale. She turned to Julian, about to compliment him for his choice, but stopped open-mouthed as she saw the figure behind him. Noticing her look, Julian whirled round to face the woman who was staring at them, arms folded. "So, this is your Scottish client is it? Do you think I was born yesterday? You never go and visit clients on a Friday. It's a company rule and *everybody* knows it. You're a very bad actor, you know, you never fooled me for a second. As soon as you put the phone down, I took the children to mother's and made my way here. I'm only surprised that it took you so long to get here – but looking at the tart you've brought in, I'm not surprised you've taken your time. You know, I'm disappointed; I would have expected you to throw your marriage away on something a bit classier than *that*."

Julian could barely utter a word, stammering incoherently for a few moments before lowering his head and staring at his feet.

Emma loved every moment of it. Granted, she'd lost her opportunity of blackmailing this pathetic individual, but viewing his destruction like this was more than worth it. Usually, she wasn't there to witness the deserved suffering that her men received, and she relished each exquisite second. Eventually, though, as Julian appeared to sink further and further into the white pile carpet, she decided it was time to leave. There was still time to entrap another philandering husband this evening.

As she passed Julian, she stopped to give him a peck on the cheek and squeezed the front of his trousers. "Such a shame, darling, you'll never know what you've missed, and after your wife has finished with you, I doubt if you'll be getting any for a long time." And with a smirk, she sauntered towards the door. She never reached it, though.

"Oh, I don't think I'll miss anything at all. What do you think dear?" Gone was the hesitation, the nervousness of before. Instead, Emma heard a voice full of confidence. She turned and saw Julian and his wife, both looking at her with smirks on their faces.

"I agree, darling. You won't miss a thing. By the way, I locked the door after you two came in. There's no escape." She turned to face Emma. "We thought we'd play out a little scene for you, just to see how you enjoyed it. Convincing, isn't it? Mind you, Julian and I have performed it many, many times before, so we should be good at it by now. Isn't that right, darling?"

"Yes, quite right Sandra." He turned to his wife, then looked at Emma. "Of course, normally we plan it out well in advance, but tonight was such an unexpected opportunity. It's a pity you could only hear my half of the conversation. You would have enjoyed the excitement in Sandra's voice when she realised we'd be able to play tonight."

Emma tried to run to the door, but her legs wouldn't respond. She cast a questioning look towards Julian, and he looked at his watch. "Hmm, just over a minute. You know, Sandra, we'll really have to try and find something that works even faster."

"Oh, I don't think so dear, that would take all of the fun out of it. You don't know how much I enjoyed seeing her walking through the flat, sipping her drink, thinking she was in control, while I knew that in a few minutes she'd be dead. And then seeing the realisation on her face – look Julian, look at the horror in her eyes. This is why we do it, after all. It's not about money, it's not about sex – it's *power*." Sandra reached into her bag and pulled out a carving knife. "Now, dear, let's make a start. No need to wait until she's totally paralysed, that would take some of the fun away." Emma tried to scream, but her vocal cords were frozen and she couldn't utter a sound.

#

Two hours later, the bedroom resembled an abattoir. Plastic sheets covered the floor, bedding and furniture, but they couldn't prevent the blood from spraying over the walls. This was Sandra's province, though, and she attacked it with relish. By morning, nobody would even know anybody had been in the flat, let alone what had taken place. She turned to Julian, who was in the process of putting the body parts into a black bag. Once weighted down, the river alongside the flat provided an excellent way of disposing of unwanted carcasses.

"You did well, there dear. Did you see the look in her eyes when we started to cut into her? That's the beauty of using *Suxamethonium* – it paralyses but leaves the patient conscious."

"I think congratulations are due to you, Sandra, not me. You're the one who can keep the patient alive for such a long time. She was aware of what was happening until the end. It's just a pity the drug affects the tear ducts so quickly, I love to see them cry."

"Well perhaps we can find something different in future. By the way, when we get home, Oliver needs some help with his maths homework."

"I still don't see why they have to do homework at junior school. *I* never started until I was eleven."

"Oh, you old fuddy-duddy! That's the way it is now, they begin at seven, as soon as they've finished Key Stage 1. I do most of it, as you know, but I've never been good at sums and problems."

"Well, we can do it tomorrow afternoon when we get back. And you can tell me all about Rose's play this afternoon. You know, I don't mind missing it now, it's all worked out for the best. By the way, was your mother alright about taking them at such short notice?"

"Oh yes, no problem at all. It's a good job I called there, as I 'borrowed' her carving knife – I'd left home in such a hurry I'd forgotten to bring ours."

"I thought you'd bought a new one. *That's* why I didn't recognise it!"

"We will have to get … what's that?"

They turned to the front door, hearing the sound of a key in the lock. And they could hear voices, at least three different male ones, laughing and talking. Julian recognised the dulcet tones of his departmental manager, who was saying as he opened the door to let the group in, "...staff use it if they're working late. It avoids them having to make a long journey home as most live in the suburbs. But *nobody* works late on a Friday, so it's always free. I'll pick you up in the morning and we'll get a couple of rounds in – you'll love the course, it's ..... WHAT THE ..."

#

Julian Winter shifted on his bench seat. He couldn't think why they'd waited even this long, surely there could be no doubt about the verdict? He looked at the guards on either side of him. Not surprisingly, they refused to look at or speak to him. After what had emerged at the trial, he doubted if he'd live long in jail. *I guess I never will get to forge relationships with Oliver and Rose now*, he thought, as the door opened and the court bailiff spoke to the guard on his left.

Mway Madness

Marmalised mice, mutilated by the mammoth military machines moving at snail's pace as they straddle the middle lane, make a macabre mixture of meat and molten Macadam under the mighty midday sun.

Multiple pile-ups create mayhem. Motorists stare morbidly as mile-long near-motionless traffic meanders towards the Dartford Tunnel, like a burrowing mole. Millions of metallic motors glint in rear-view mirrors.

The magenta-faced machismo male thumps his horn, while the myopic map-reading mother with macular degeneration keeps mace in her handbag to ensure she isn't molested. Marie cranks up the volume, producing sound without musical melodies, maestros or madrigals; Mike's fingers fly across his mobile, texting messages to missing mates. The medicine-cabinet hasn't kept dad's migraine at bay.

Malfunctioning manifolds are the cause of myriad problems while manual transmissions give up the ghost. The only mystery is why anybody would holiday like this.

It's a miserable, manic, Mayday on the M25.

Voyage of the Damned

#

<u>April 15th 1912</u>

"Captain Smith."

The captain looked up from his meal, annoyed at yet another interruption. "Can't it wait man? Dinner will be over in another half hour." He turned back to his Waldorf pudding and took another mouthful.

The white-coated purser didn't leave, but fidgeted nervously, rocking from foot to foot. *It must be something very important for him to come and interrupt a meal at the captain's table,* thought Smith, and he rose after wiping his mouth on his napkin. "If you would all please excuse me for a moment. I have to deal with certain ship's matters." He followed the purser until they were out of earshot of the other passengers. "Now tell me. What is so important that it justifies such an interruption?" His voice was steady but firm. Captain Smith was a fair man, but he did not suffer fools gladly.

The purser cleared his throat noisily. "We have had more warnings about the ice drifts around the Grand Banks, sir."

"Is that all? How many voyages have you been on? Ice is common in these parts, and we follow standard practices. I ordered full-steam ahead and the ship will break through any of these objects."

"The lookout, sir..."

"What about the lookout. Out with it man. My pudding is getting cold."

"Yes sir. The lookout is concerned about the large number of ice floes in the vicinity. First Officer Murdoch has been informed, and he said that I should tell you as a precautionary matter."

"Which you have done now. I will continue with my dinner and appraise the situation afterwards. That will be all."

#

Three hours later, Captain Smith sought out Murdoch on the bridge. He liked him, and had complete trust in his abilities. "What's all this nonsense from the lookout, Bill?"

Murdoch turned around quickly, an element of surprise in his face as he had been intently concentrating and hadn't heard the approaching footsteps. "Captain!" he saluted.

"Forget the formality for now. Nobody else is within earshot."

"Yes, sir," he said, unable to drop years of rigorous formal training. "There have been several more reports about the ice, and we've just heard from one of the lookouts, Fleet. He says there's an iceberg directly ahead of us."

"And what are you doing about it?"

"I've ordered that the ship be steered around the obstacle and the engines have been put in reverse."

"That's quite rig…" The Captain paused. Murdoch's instruction was entirely the correct one, yet a sixth sense told him that it would lead to disaster. He knew Fleet – he had made it his business to learn about all nine hundred or so crew members – and the man wouldn't have raised the issue unless it was extraordinary in some way. "Countermand that order immediately. Continue full-steam ahead directly towards the iceberg. We're going to meet it head on."

"But Captain…"

"That's an order, First Officer."

#

Two days later, the *RMS Titanic* sailed into New York Harbour to be met by hordes of cheering Americans. Even in so short a time, news of the ship's victory over the elements had travelled via the wireless telegraph and with each retelling, it had grown to take on almost legendary status.

"The ship continually turned and rammed the icebergs head on. Hundreds of them," reported one *eye-witness* in the New York Post. Captain Smith ignored those reports. He knew the truth. Pure good fortune had seen them through. Had they followed the First Officer's instructions, he had little doubt that the unforgiving ice would have ripped holes in the starboard side below the waterline; then, it would have been a very different story. The press reported the Captain's declaration from five years earlier, when he said *he could not imagine any condition which would cause a ship to founder*. He didn't think, hand-on-heart, that he could make such a statement today. He disembarked to receive a hero's reception that he only partially felt he deserved.

#

June 24th 1914

The impressive hull of the *Titanic* dominated the skyline as the car carrying Franz and Sophie approached Cherbourg docks. It was a pleasant afternoon, and Franz was looking forward to a relaxing journey to America. The ocean liner was every bit as impressive as he had expected it to be, following the extensive coverage it had received in the newspapers after its maiden voyage just over two years earlier. The captain on that voyage, a man with the modest name of Edward Smith, was now known in all corners of the globe for his navigation of the liner directly through a huge ice flow, averting what could have been a disaster that people might have talked about for years. As it was, they would now talk about the heroism of the captain, who had received the honour of a knighthood for his actions. Everybody wanted to sail on what was once the world's largest - and still was the world's finest - liner and getting a berth on the ocean crossing was nigh-on impossible. Even *he* had been made to wait for two years, and he had begun to suspect that the entire episode had perhaps been fabricated by the *White Star Line* owners in order to ensure that every voyage was fully booked for years to come.

As they boarded and were shown to their Bridge deck cabin, he turned to his wife and asked, "How do you feel now about our change of plans? Isn't this the ultimate in elegance?"

"Yes, I do admit that perhaps you were correct after all. I feared that to cancel our visit to Sarajevo at such a late hour could have repercussions, but I do believe that this choice is the best in the long run."

"I trust to providence. To hear that a berth had become available was as if fate was telling us to take this voyage instead of trying to resolve the differences with the Kingdom. When we disembark, I will make myself known to President Wilson and, with his backing, I have no doubt that it will put an end to the underlying problems that could have dragged us into another conflict. Until then, though, let us relax and make full use of the luxuries that are on offer."

#

Once they had settled in, they took a stroll along the Bridge deck and visited the Café Parisien for a morning cup of coffee. Franz wondered how some of his countrymen might view such decadence, but concluded that they would undoubtedly enjoy it at least as much as he did.

The café was relatively quiet, but he noticed that a man over at the far side kept looking at him. Perhaps he had been recognised? Franz walked over to the man and asked, "Are these seats taken?" pointing to the unoccupied chairs at the table. He knew that his English was heavily accented, but he reasoned that it would be more likely to be understood than his native tongue.

The man answered and Franz could detect an Eastern European accent to his words. "No, they are empty. Please, join me."

Sophie walked across and Franz held the chair for her before sitting down and beginning to converse with his fellow traveller. "I find that the conditions on this ship are even more luxurious than I had been led to believe. I feel it will be with regret that we disembark when we reach New York."

"I agree with you, sir. Are you travelling on business?"

"Yes, I am. I hope to arrange a very important meeting whilst in America. How about you? Do you have business in the new world?"

"No, everything I intend to do is here on this ship. I do not plan to disembark at all."

"Would that the same luxury were available to me."

"Pardon me for saying, sir, but you look as if you are accustomed to amenities such as these at home."

"Yes, I suppose I am. Please call me Franz, by the way, and this is my wife, Sophie. We live a life of formality, but for a short while, it is pleasant to try and forget some of those burdens."

"I'm sure it is, Franz. You may call me Gavrilo."

"That isn't a name I'm familiar with. Do I detect an Eastern European influence in it?"

"You do. I am from Sarajevo."

"What a coincidence. We were bound for that very city when I learnt that a berth on this ship had become available, weren't we dear? Otherwise, we would be there at this very minute."

"Which all goes to show how small a world it is that we inhabit," answered Gavrilo.

"I have been waiting for almost two years for this sailing. Did you have to wait a long time to secure a berth?"

"Not as long as you did. I didn't know until a few days ago that I would be on this voyage. I managed to acquire a berth very late on. I agree that the ship is the height of luxury. Have you made use of the Turkish baths yet?"

"No, we have not yet acquainted ourselves with them. Indeed, we have yet to find our way around all of the decks."

"May I show you the way? The baths are on the Middle deck, alongside the swimming pool. It is a strange setup in a way, for the cabins on that deck are for the steerage passengers but the pool and baths are exclusively for the use of first class clientele such as ourselves. At this time of day, it is unlikely that we will come into contact with any of the lower orders."

Franz and Sophie followed Gavrilo along the deck and towards the first-class elevator. They stepped in and began their descent. "Yes," began Gavrilo, returning to the earlier discussion, "my business will be entirely concluded on this ship. In fact, within this very elevator. Had you gone to Sarajevo as planned, I would almost certainly never have had the opportunity." He drew a Nagant M1895 Revolver from his inside pocket and fired all seven shots into the chests of Franz and Sophie until there wasn't a shadow of doubt that they were dead.

#

November 11th 1918

It was a quarter before five in the morning at Le Francport in Compiègne. Soon, the railroad carriage would be full of officials from both sides of the conflict, but for now, Marshal Foch and Admiral Wemyss were the sole occupants. In a further six hours, the Great War would come to an end, thanks, in part to the policies proposed by President Wilson at the beginning of the year.

"It is such a pity that it has taken a further ten months for the President's proposals to find full agreement," said Foch. "How many more lives could have been saved had there not been such a delay?"

Wemyss nodded but said nothing.

"Is anything wrong, Admiral? You appear to be deep in thought. Have you considered something that could add further delay to this process?"

"No, Marshal, not at all. In fact, my mind was elsewhere, thinking back to before this all began."

"Ah, I understand how you feel. It will be good, no, to return to the days before the nations of the world were in conflict with each other."

"No, I didn't mean that. Of course, Marshal, it will be good to see an end to all of this misery. Many people think that when the treaty is signed, there will be both winners and losers. I see only losers. Nine million dead serve testament to that. I was thinking back, though, to a time before the Great War started. Just suppose, Marshal, that Sir Edward Smith hadn't made that judgment call on the Titanic's maiden voyage."

"Then thousands of people would have died at sea. Are you trying to say there should be even more deaths?"

"Not at all. My thinking is along the lines that if the Titanic had floundered on the ice, even at the cost of a thousand or more lives, it might still have been worthwhile. For then there would have been no Titanic for Archduke Franz Ferdinand and his wife to voyage on, and no opportunity for Gavrilo Princip to assassinate them in that damned elevator. Austria-Hungary would not have declared war on the Kingdom of Serbia and nine million people would still be alive."

Marshal Foch looked at Admiral Wemyss with distaste in his eyes. No further words were spoken as the rest of the signatories arrived, but Wemyss could not rid himself of that one thought: *Nine million lives had been lost because of that one damned voyage.*

- The RMS Titanic, the largest liner in the world at the time, sank on its maiden voyage when it was in collision with an iceberg and was holed below the waterline on the starboard side. The ship sank with the loss of more than 1,500 lives

- The Great War began on July 28th 1914 and lasted until the signing of the armistice on November 11th 1918 in Compiègne. The trigger for the war was the assassination of Archduke Franz Ferdinand of Austria, heir to the throne of Austria-Hungary, on June 28th 1914. The Archduke and his wife, Sophie, Duchess of Hohenberg, were shot dead in Sarajevo by Gavrilo Princip, a Bosnian Serb assassin.

The Ministry of Fire and Miracles

They must have been furious at the combination of events that led to their discovery. I can imagine the initial smirk on their faces as they placed the HQ slap in the centre of one of the busiest parts of London, knowing that none of the hundreds of people passing within inches of its entrance every minute would ever realise what lay just beyond the periphery of their vision. I had to admit, it was *almost* a mark of genius.

Except that they hadn't taken account of everything. Today, it was no longer hidden. From their point of view, it was just pure bad luck – the sunniest day of an otherwise ordinary year, coming directly after one of the heaviest thunderstorms in recent memory. Even then, that oughtn't to have been a problem, but the sunshine was to blame. It was the wrong sort of sunshine, at that awkward height that caused its glare to bounce off the glass-fronted buildings across the road and reveal the image in the pools of water that were on the verge of flowing through the grids into the dirt-clogged sewers. And, even then, most people wouldn't have thought anything of it; all they would have seen was a jumble of meaningless letters – *selcariM dna eriF fo yrtsiniM ehT*. I wasn't 'most people', though, as my brain seemed to be permanently in puzzle-solving mode. It made light work of those reflected backwards letters, and I knew that, at last, I had found the location of *The Ministry of Fire and Miracles*.

By rights, I should have called it in, but I also knew that this might be a once-in-a-lifetime opportunity. For all we knew, they might constantly relocate their headquarters; how would it look if I wasted time informing my superiors, only to find they had moved once the team arrived? Besides, I wanted the glory for myself; a coup like this would do wonders for my career progression. I knew that I was in the vicinity, and it took but moments to locate some shimmering brickwork that seemed a tad out of place. I pushed my way through the crowd of people, who were rushing past oblivious of the fact that what was happening could have been taken directly from the pages of a *Harry Potter* novel, until eventually I leant against the camouflaged entrance; a small increase of pressure caused a slight opening in the wall. Nobody on the street paid it even an instant's attention, so I figured that I, too, must be hidden along with the building. I pushed my way through the wall and stopped, mouth open.

Although the entrance had only been two feet wide at the most, forcing me to enter side-on, I now looked at a vast expanse of corridors and desks, seemingly going on for ever; now I knew how each companion must have felt the first time they entered the Tardis. Hundreds – no, thousands – of people were busy working away at their desks, and from the noise they were making, I felt it was a miracle in itself that nobody had ever heard them, even if they couldn't see them.

Initially, it didn't appear as if anybody had noticed me – hardly surprising, as I was but one in thousands – but I soon realised I was wrong. Marching resolutely towards me was a middle-aged woman wearing a severe blue suit. Trouble was etched all over her non-smiling face.

"What are you doing here?" she barked, grabbing me by the elbow and beginning to walk me back towards the entrance. I had to think quickly; it had taken me months to finally find this place, the last thing I needed was to be thrown out before I'd had chance to do anything.

Employing all the skills of my training, I turned my wiles on her, desperately hoping they would produce an intoxicating mix of flattery and concern. I took a glance at her name-badge – Emilia Johnson - smiled at her and said, "Why, I'm here to see *you* of course, Emilia." Lowering my voice conspiratorially, I said, "*They* sent me. They said they didn't think you were up to the rigours of the role, and, knowing your exemplary record, I was concerned. But I can see that they were mistaken – why, the way you intercepted me, it's obvious that you are *totally* on the ball. In fact, I wish we had people like you over at you-know-where," I added, lowering my voice again.

I paused. Would she buy it? For a moment, I thought not, but then she smiled and I knew the first hurdle had been cleared. I suppose it was because of their somewhat arrogant over-confidence – nobody, surely, could ever discover their hidden headquarters – that she was so easily swayed by my words; had she been in the slightest suspicious as to my origins, I doubt that I would have lasted another minute in the building.

As it was, though, I was now in control. "I thought *they* must have sent you," she said, "and I must admit to being a bit worried when I saw you, but you've put my mind at ease now. Is there anything you'd like to see while you're here?"

I had tremendous difficulty in preventing my jaw from dropping wide open as I digested what she had just said. I hadn't really had a plan at all; finding the entrance had come as such a surprise that I hadn't thought about what to do once inside. And then, when the officious-looking woman had approached me, self-preservation was my only goal. Now, though, I had been offered my life's ambition on the proverbial plate; and I wasn't going to waste that opportunity. "Well, as I'm here, why not? I had expected things to take considerably longer than this, so I do have some free time. My next appointment isn't for another," I added, pointedly looking at my watch, "three hours. I'll tell you what I really *would* like to see – the control centre. *Everybody* talks about it but I've never had the privilege before."

"Well of course you haven't. *Nobody* gets to visit there. I thought you would have known that."

My heart skipped a beat as she spoke; had I committed an enormous faux pas and blown my chances? "So it's true then? I always assumed it was just a story they were fobbing me off with because I've always worn my interest in this on my sleeve. You know, I've always had a few ideas of my own, and I think they could revolutionise things around here," I added in a conspiratorial low voice. "But, if those are the rules," I concluded, flashing her my most 'genuine' smile.

Once again, flattery opened the door for me – literally, this time. "Well, I'd say guidelines more than rules. *Rules* sounds so formal. And who knows, you could be just what we are looking for, and if we don't take this further, we'd never know, would we? I don't think a small visit would do any harm. Now which department is of most interest? Fire? Miracles? Or perhaps both?"

There wasn't even the slightest hesitation in my choice; we knew everything we needed to about fire, but we were still light-years behind them in the field of miracles. "Miracles. Oh yes, definitely miracles."

She smiled. "I thought so," she said, and she held out her hand to indicate the way we should go. I had to repress a smirk; this was so much easier than I had expected. I even began to wonder whether we had perhaps overestimated the ability of our foes; but I quickly rid myself of those thoughts. These people were still dangerous, even though I had seemingly infiltrated them with ease.

We walked through one endless corridor after another, and I began to feel the first element of concern. Would I be able to find my way out again afterwards? But then again, why not? Emilia had no idea I was with the enemy, so why shouldn't she see me safely out once my tour had been completed? Whether or not I would see what I needed to do in that time was another matter, but I would face that hurdle should it arise.

I lost count of how much time had passed, and I began to think I should have made my next 'appointment' for five or six hours on instead of just three, but just as the first flutterings of panic were rising, Emilia stopped in front of an imposing iron door. "Here we are," she said, again flashing me a warm smile as she took out of her pocket a large, brass key, "I hope you're ready for a life-changing experience."

"Oh yes, that I am," I answered as she unlocked the door and pushed it open. Despite its size and impression of great age, the door swung open smoothly and silently. I instinctively put my hand to my eyes as golden light filled my vision. Emilia laughed. "Don't worry," she said, "you'll soon get used to it."

She was right, for within seconds my vision cleared. The room of miracles was about a hundred metres long and ten metres across. Dozens of capsules lined each side of the room, as if providing a guard of honour. They were slightly larger than an average-sized man and set at intervals of five metres apart.

"This," said Emilia, "is the hub of the operation. You see, miracles don't happen just like that," she added, clicking her fingers. "They need a stimulus, and what better stimulus than the human brain? It has an infinite capacity for invention and creation, and we make full use of it – each capsule harnesses a small percentage of that capacity, and *that* is where the miracles come from."

I could barely conceal my excitement. This was everything I had hoped for. We had no idea what the source of their creation was; now, even if I saw no more, I would have vital information to report back. But I fully expected to see a lot more, as Emilia showed no signs of having completed her tour. "Would you like to take a closer look at our capsules? The technology is something to behold."

"Yes, that would be quite interesting," I said, trying to keep the mounting excitement out of my voice.

"I thought so," she said, leading the way to one of the capsules and turning the huge wheel on the front. "The units are hermetically sealed, naturally, and we use this wheel to ensure that the environmental settings remain at *exactly* the correct level."

"But if you're opening it, won't that mean .."

"Oh no, nothing like that. This unit is due for replacement anyway, so it doesn't matter in the slightest. In fact, what we're doing now will bring new vitality to the whole process."

She opened the door and, with a hiss, a cloudy stream of vapour poured out. There was a distinct drop in temperature, and I shivered.

Emilia laughed again. "Yes, it is a bit cold. But you'll soon get used to it. Here, take a closer look."

Eagerly, I stepped forward, then stopped, amazed at what I saw. Instead of space-age technology, the unit contained a wizened old man, who collapsed to the floor as the door opened as there was nothing there to hold him aloft. As he fell, a metal helmet that had been attached to his head fell away, leaving a mass of wires dangling down and reminding me of scenes in television science fiction programmes; except this was fact, not fiction.

"But he's ... he's .." I began to say.

"Ancient? Actually, he's probably younger than you, but the process does use them up so quickly. He wouldn't have lasted more than another day or two, and I was going to send for a replacement. Fortunately, Head Office seems to be ahead of the game for once."

I didn't understand what she meant – at least, not initially. Then I saw that there were several uniformed guards behind me, and I felt strong hands forcing me towards the cabinet as more hands removed the gasping form that was looking up at me with pleading eyes. The true horror of events finally reached my brain, as Emilia concluded the tour. "I almost feel sorry for you. When you joined the organisation, you must have been so excited that you'd been chosen ahead of thousands of applicants. Didn't you ever realise that all we wanted you for was your brain power? To be nurtured until head office sent you along as a replacement for one of our used-up units. You didn't realise that the key phrases you'd been provided with – here to see me, having three hours to spare, talking about rules and only wanting to see the miracles section – were designed to seal your fate. You can at least take consolation in the fact that you will be furthering the cause for the remaining few weeks of your existence," she concluded, as she forced the helmet over my forehead before the door closed to signal the end of my life.

Shipwreck

I awoke in a cold sweat; it had been the same dream again, for the fifteenth night in a row, and still I had no idea what it meant. This time, though, I was prepared. I reached for the notepad that I had placed on the bedside table specifically for this moment. I knew that I only had a few seconds before all recollection of the events I had just witnessed would become nothing but ethereal memories. I scribbled as quickly as I could, ignoring the bizarreness of the images while I noted the odd word before the final vestiges of the dream slipped away.

I recalled Eleanor, Lady of Wild Things, resplendent in her gossamer robes that were as pale as the lightest shade of white, as she rode along the beach on a nameless horse. She passed several knights, also wearing white, who were sitting in a circle chanting. At the centre of the circle stood their leader, Quinn, a man of great might. He was holding his sword pointing up toward the sky. The lady ignored him and rode on, crossing over a rickety wooden bridge separating the beach from the mainland. Down below her, the waters were in turmoil but she remained calm and serene. In the distance, I could see the moon as it rose, but it glowed a sickly red and emanated evil. Back on the beach, the men had formed themselves into three overlapping rings, like a human Venn diagram, with their mighty Lord at the intersection, looking extremely comfortable as he reclined on a mattress of leaves.

The images disappeared completely and I took a look at the notes I had made. I tried to convince myself that they meant nothing, as in the dream time, imagination was unfettered and given free rein, so whatever it conjured up could be viewed as nothing other than mere fantasy; I tried to tell myself that, but I'd been plagued by these episodes every night for more than a fortnight, and such a thing had never before happened to me in my long and illustrious life.

I dressed, breakfasted and readied myself for the big day. This was the last thing I wanted to do; even fully rested, it would have been an ordeal, but in my current state, it was becoming a nightmare. I might well be a best-selling novelist, but no amount of books sold could help me with this problem.

I came to an instant decision; I wouldn't go. Instead, I'd take the car and drive off somewhere – anywhere. As long as it was nowhere near the recording studios, it would do. I pointed my key fob at the car, but just as I was about to press it, a voice said, "There's no need to do that."

I whirled round; there was nobody else in the street. Who had said that? I shivered. *That's* what you get for having a restless night. I was hearing imaginary voices and was about to topple over the verge of insanity if I didn't get a grip on myself. I pointed the fob at the car again, and the same voice said, "I mean it. There's really no need."

Who was saying this? There was nobody about. The only living thing was a black cat, sitting on the fence separating my house from next door. And, as I looked at it, I heard the voice again, only this time I saw the cat's mouth move at the same time. "Yes, it's me. Who did you expect? It took you long enough to notice, though."

"What ..." I began. "Who ... what is this ..." I stopped. I was talking to a *cat*! And, even more bizarrely, it was talking back to me.

"Who am I? That doesn't matter. What am I? I suppose you could call me a guide, from the realm between heaven and earth. I've been sent to help you. Although," the cat added, and I'm sure that if a cat could laugh, then that was what it was doing, "why they should think somebody as famous as you should need help is beyond me. All those plots you come up with and you can't manage a simple list."

I looked at it blankly. "List? What list?"

"Come on, now," it said, exasperation in its catty voice. "Alright, let's look at it another way. What have you dreamt about recently?"

"How do you know I've been having dreams? No, forget that," I added hastily, still finding it ridiculous that I was conversing with a feline.

"The dreams, then. What have they been about?"

I gave in. With a sigh, I said, "okay then, you win. The dreams? I don't know. They're ephemeral, and the more I try and think about them, the further away they seem to be."

"Why do you think you've been having them?"

"How the hell should I know? Who are you anyway? Sigmund Freud reincarnated or something?"

"Freud?" said the cat, and I could hear the distaste in its voice. "*Hardly*. You know, I always thought writers were rather bright chaps, but now I've met you, I'm reassessing that impression. Okay then, we'll try a different tack. Have you anything on your mind at all. And remember, there's no point in being evasive – I *know*."

"If you already know, why are you asking then?" I asked, adding a sneer to my tone.

"Because you need to admit it to yourself. Go on, confess what you were about to do when I called out to you, and why."

I snapped. "Alright, then, know-it-all. I was about to go off and take a drive for the next couple of hours. I don't know where I planned to go, but that didn't matter. I just needed to be out of contact for a while, because I'm supposed to be a guest on *Desert Island Discs* today, but I haven't a clue as to which eight records to choose, and I haven't even begun to think about the book or the luxury item. Satisfied now?"

"The question is, are *you* satisfied? Are you sure you don't have the list? When you awoke from last night's dream..."

"That damned dream again? What is it with you and the dream?"

"When you awoke from last night's dream," it began again, more slowly this time, as if explaining something to a child, "tell me what you did. *Exactly*."

I thought for a minute. "I scribbled down the basics of it on a notepad. But they were just a few random words – all memory of the visions had faded away before I could make any sense of them."

"What did you do with the list?"

"It's here, in my shirt pocket," I replied, pulling out the torn-off sheet of paper. Funnily enough, I hadn't even realised I'd put it there until the cat asked to see it.

"Read it," said the cat. "Out loud."

Humouring the animal, I began to read. And as I read, a tingle flew down my spine. "*Lady Eleanor* of *Wild Thing*s, wearing *a whiter shade of pale* on *a horse with no name*. *Knights in white sat in* a circle around the *mighty Quinn*. Crosses *bridge over troubled waters*, in distance there's a *bad moon rising*. Knights worship *Lord of the Ring*s, reclines on *comfortable mattress*.

"And there," said the cat, satisfaction etched all over its features, "are your eight records, your book *and* your luxury item.'" It licked its paw and began to rub it in circular movements across its face, but I only barely noticed; I had a recording studio to get to.

#

Lady Eleanor – Lindisfarne 1971
Wild Thing – The Troggs 1966
A Whiter Shade of Pale – Procul Harum 1967
A Horse With No Name – America 1971
Nights in White Satin – Moody Blues 1967
The Mighty Quinn – Manfred Mann 1968
Bridge Over Troubled Water – Simon and Garfunkel 1970
Bad Moon Rising – Creedence Clearwater Revival 1969

Lord of the Rings by JRR Tolkien

Beyond the Veil

I stand outside the house, looking up at the slate-grey sky. It's almost the end of July in 2015 and there isn't even a pencil-thin sliver of blue to lift the spirits; there's only the promise of more rain to come. If it wasn't for my need to exercise every day to ensure my high blood pressure doesn't become a problem, I doubt if I would have ventured out today. Being a freelance writer, and working from home as I do, it is easy to let the entire day pass without once tearing myself away from my computer screen, especially as I have no living relatives to encourage me to keep to a healthy lifestyle. Despite the weather, I am far from the only person who has braved the elements, as people scuttle up and down the street, eager to get to wherever it is they are going before the next deluge begins. No, that isn't quite true. *One* person is looking at me, as I knew she would be. She's always there, looking at me with longing in her eyes.

#

I first met Cathy just over three months ago. She was walking in front of my house, skipping along just a few feet behind her parents, when she tripped and fell headlong towards the pavement. Reacting out of instinct, I threw out an arm and caught her, just inches before her knees would have made first bloody contact with the hard ground. She stared at me, a questioning look on her face, and then gasped.

"Are you alright, Cathy? What are you doing?" asked her mother, who had turned round in time to see her daughter sitting on the floor; she hadn't seen *how* she came to be there. "Come on, we'll be late, we don't have time for this."

Something about the tone of her mother's voice made me feel uneasy, and I eased myself off to the side in between my house and the one next door as Cathy said, "I tripped, mummy, but that man stopped me from hurting myself."

"What man?" asked her mother, and I could hear the suspicion and fear in her voice.

"Why, that man ther..." began Cathy, and then she stopped. "Oh! He's gone."

"Oh, *that* man," said Cathy's father, and he looked at her mother. Even from where I stood, hidden from their view, I could read her father's lips as he whispered to his wife: *Don't tell me she's started having imaginary friends again! That's what she did when she was five, but she's almost eleven now.* He looked at his daughter, sadness in his eyes. "Now, Cathy darling, you know that didn't happen, don't you? It *couldn't* have happened, could it?"

Cathy lowered her head and stared at the floor through watery eyes. "No, daddy, it couldn't," she said in a voice almost too quiet to hear.

I could have stepped out from the shadows and confirmed the truth of Cathy's story, but I didn't. I figured that it wouldn't have helped, and would probably have only made things worse. I could still hear the anxiety in her mother's voice, and the last thing I wanted to do was to fuel her imagination.

Cathy stood, shrugged her shoulders and the three of them set off down the road; within a few seconds, Cathy was skipping away as if her little fall had never even happened. I smiled wryly as I watched, thinking that I would probably never see any of them again. I was wrong.

#

It was about a week later that I encountered them again. It was another miserable grey day in late April and people were, as always, rushing about their business. Cathy and her parents were just outside my front gate, amongst dozens of others, and I didn't see them. But Cathy saw me. "Mummy," she shrieked. "There's the man who helped me when I fell. Look, he's standing over there by the front door. It really *did* happen. Perhaps he can..."

Her parents looked across in the direction where Cathy was excitedly pointing, and then her mother grabbed Cathy's hand and said, "I don't have time for this now. Come on, we'll be late." Her father grabbed his daughter's other hand and the three of them hurried away – or, to be more accurate, the parents hurried away, dragging an unwilling Cathy after them. She kept looking back, and I heard her trying to explain to her mother as they slowly disappeared from view. I couldn't understand what the problem was, but the disapproval in her mother's voice had been unmistakeable. What did she have against me? Couldn't a man go to a child's aid any more without people thinking he was a paedophile? I knew that, as an unmarried man in his late thirties, people could look at me accusingly, but I wasn't single for any perverse reasons; I was just a perfectionist, and had never found the right person to even get serious about, let alone want to marry.

I remember shrugging my shoulders. I couldn't be held responsible for prejudices that other people might have, and, although I felt a certain amount of sympathy for young Cathy, it was really none of my business. I walked off, head down to protect myself against the rain that had begun to fall.

#

Over the next few weeks, I saw Cathy and her parents on more than a dozen occasions. Each meeting had one common factor – the rain, or imminent promise of it. I felt it odd in a way that they only ever seemed to be outside my house on miserable days weather-wise, each of them heavily protected against the elements in long dark coats that covered them almost to ankle level. They didn't appear to be a fashion-conscious family, but, then again, their garments were eminently practical, so who was I to judge?

Cathy saw me on most of those occasions, and tried to get her parents attention, but they repeatedly ignored her. I became intrigued. Why weren't they prepared to listen to their daughter? Why didn't they even look across in my direction? I no longer bothered trying to conceal myself from their view, but they still acted as if I wasn't there. I almost began to get paranoid about the whole thing, and had to check my reflection in a shop doorway to make sure I wasn't invisible.

After this had happened on three consecutive days, I decided to do something about it. No longer bothered about whether or not this was any of my business, I followed the three of them as they made their way along the street. My first impulse was to run forward, tap the father on his shoulder and make him confront the fact that his daughter was telling the truth, but some instinct held me back. Instead, I fell in step behind them, walking soundlessly as I overheard the parents having a conversation.

"Thomas," began the mother, "we've been through this time and time again. Cathy has a very strange vivid imagination. She always did, even before ..."

"Yes, I know, Lucy, but she's *always* been a truthful girl. And she's so adamant. Perhaps it really did happen."

"But how could it have, Thomas? After all this time. You're only getting your hopes up, and I don't think I could face yet another disappointment."

"But it *did* happen, mummy. I promise it did," interrupted Cathy. "*And* I've seen him loads of times since, and I know he's seen me. Why won't you believe me?"

Lucy looked sadly at her daughter, but Thomas spoke with an element of hope-come-pleading in his voice. "If what she says is true, Lucy, then perhaps – somehow – he might be able to help us?"

"No, Thomas," she said, the sadness of her look now echoed in her voice, "nobody can help us, and even thinking that someone might will only lead to heartbreak when it doesn't happen. Don't you remember that night when Blackpool won the cup and Cathy said one of the celebrating fans had spoken to her? How disappointed we all were when we realised he had just had too much to drink and was talking to nobody at all?"

"Yes," said Thomas sadly, "you're right. I know that, I just hoped..." His voice trailed off as I stopped following them, puzzled.

What had Lucy just said ... *that night when Blackpool won the cup* ...? But that was sixty-two years ago. Impossible. Then I slapped my hand to my forehead. What a fool! It wasn't *the cup* at all, but another, more recent trophy – she must have meant when Blackpool won the play-off final to reach the Premier League. *That* was five years ago and Cathy would have been five or six then. Yes, it all made sense now.

I looked up just in time to see the family crossing the street and heading towards the cemetery. I hurried after them. Perhaps that was why they only came here on miserable days? If they were visiting a relative's grave, maybe they didn't feel it to be appropriate when the sun was shining.

I reached the cemetery gates and saw them hunched over a small headstone away to the right. Heavy rain was falling and large drops were running down my forehead and into my eyes. I paused for a moment to take out a tissue and try and wipe away the excess water. When my vision cleared, there was nobody by the headstone any more, and there was no sign of anybody other than me in the cemetery.

I turned to leave, deciding I was wet enough and should return home, when curiosity took hold of me. Whose grave had they stopped by? Who was it that demanded their attention on rainy days? I walked quickly across to where I had last seen them and looked at the plot. It was unkempt, which surprised me. I had assumed that this was where they came every time I saw them, but, if they did, surely they would have removed the overgrown weeds and cleaned up the fading lettering on the headstone? This must have been a one-off visit, for whatever reason. No sooner had I concluded that than I saw something that chilled me far more than any amount of rain could have done. I took a closer look and read out loud the simple inscription on the gravestone:

Thomas Manson born 15th September 1882, died 19th February 1920 and his wife Lucy born 21st February 1885, died 19th February 1920 and their daughter Catherine born 5th April 1910, died 19th February 1920.

Thomas. Lucy. Catherine – Cathy. They had died almost a century earlier. All on the same day. How much of a coincidence was it that the three I had followed had come here, to the grave of three people with the same first names? And then, as I thought about it, I realised that, yes, it was a coincidence, but probably nothing more than that. Curiosity may well have brought *my* Cathy's family here, after hearing about a tragedy that affected a different family with the same first names as their own. Possibly something from the local history sessions at the library? Yes, that would be it.

I left the cemetery and trudged slowly homewards, barely giving the matter another thought.

#

The next day dawned hot and sunny. With the new day, I thought afresh about what I had seen in the cemetery the previous day, and concluded that suggesting it was merely a coincidence didn't make sense. It was now early June, a couple of months since I had first seen the family, but I didn't expect to see them today. I waited about, though, for quite a long time, just in case my theory about them only being seen on dull days could be proved wrong, but I didn't see even a glimpse of them. Eventually, I decided I couldn't wait any more, and I walked briskly across to the library. I needed to be there for some local research for my latest article – the internet had been of great value, but I knew the librarian, Mrs. Andrews, and personal knowledge was always of much more interest than just regurgitating the dry facts from a cut-and-paste internet article.

She was as helpful as I had hoped she would be, and, as I was about to leave, I decided to ask her advice on the topic that was threatening to fill my mind at the expense of everything else.

"I just wondered if you might know anything about a tragedy that seems to have happened nearly a century ago?"

"How old do you think I am, you cheeky young thing," she said, making as if to cuff my ear, but with a glint in her eye that told me she hadn't really taken offence. "Go on, then, what do you want to know?"

I told her the details on the gravestone, nothing more, and said it was just an idea I had for an article. I also told her that I'd looked on the internet, but hadn't found anything that helped.

"It's probably there," she said, thoughtfully, "but perhaps not that easily found. Not all of the newspaper records will have been fully digitised, so a search for the terms might not bring anything up. We still have all of the newspapers on film, though, going back to the late nineteenth century. Come on, let's take a look shall we?"

We spent about three quarters of an hour searching through the reels until I found what I was looking for. When I did, I almost wished I hadn't. The headline for

Thursday March 4th 1920 read, *Tragedy for local family* and underneath was a brief coroner's report:

> A tragic occurrence wiped out a local family a fortnight ago. The coroner today concluded that the deaths of Thomas Manson, aged thirty-seven, his wife Lucy, aged thirty-four and their daughter Catherine, aged ten were due to misadventure. The family were found huddled together in their single-roomed abode at number seventeen Adelaide Street, Layton. They had died from asphyxiation. It appeared that, on a cold February evening, having run out of coal, they had tried to heat their home by burning wood from the rhododendron bushes that they dug up from the back garden. They died wearing their outside coats, presumably in an attempt to keep any warmth in, but they had covered over all of the gaps where air could enter the home and the smoke that the burning wood produced slowly choked them all to death. As they had no living relatives, the council have decided to inter their bodies in a single plot at Layton Cemetery.

Underneath this brief report was a small, grainy black-and-white photograph, but, despite its lack of clarity, there was no doubt in my mind whatsoever that I was looking at a picture of the Thomas, Lucy and Cathy who I had been seeing regularly over the last couple of months. Just in case I still had any doubts, I need only look again at the address where the tragedy occurred – 17 Adelaide Street. The same house that *I* now lived in. The same house where I saw them day after day.

I vaguely remember muttering a brief thank-you to Mrs. Andrews as she handed me a printout of the page and I left the library in a daze.

#

I have to admit, the whole episode shook me up. I had nobody to confide in – Mrs. Andrews was the only person who knew anything about it, and if I had told her the full story, she would probably have rang for the men in the white coats to take me away. My only option was to try and pretend nothing had happened. For a month, I altered my normal pattern of behaviour. No longer did I go outside for an exercising walk unless the sun was shining brightly; I did everything in my power to avoid the possibility of seeing *them* again.

It didn't help. If anything, I found myself thinking about them even more of the time. I wanted to tell somebody – anybody - about what I'd seen and what had happened, but I couldn't. Who would believe me? Hell, it was happening to me and *I* didn't believe me.

And then, last night, I recalled what Thomas had said the last time I saw them. *He might be able to help us.* Instead of helping them, I was shutting them out. Somehow, they had 'lived' the last ninety-five years in a kind of limbo existence, unable to move on, forever trapped until somebody could release them from their hell. Once before – and now I did believe it was when Blackpool won *the* cup back in 1953 – they thought they had found their salvation, only for their hopes to be dashed. No wonder they were afraid to get their hopes up. This time, though, was different. I really *had* seen them. I had held Cathy briefly, and she was made of flesh and bone, not ether. I didn't know *how* I could help; I didn't know *if* I could help. But I knew I had to try.

#

The longing in Cathy's eyes is almost heart-breaking. I see accusation there as well. As if she's asking me: *where have you been recently?* I cannot explain to her. I can, though, make myself known to her. And to Thomas and Lucy as well.

I walk over to her, pat her on the head, and she looks up at me, joy unbridled in her eyes. Her parents haven't seen me – yet; they do when I speak directly to them.

Thomas' reaction surprises me most of all; after all, he is the one who said I might be able to help them. He looks terrified. "You ... you can see me." It is both a question and an accusatory statement. Perhaps he thinks I should have acted sooner. Perhaps he is right.

Lucy, in contrast, seems to have taken everything in without overreacting. She allows herself a small glance at Cathy, almost an apologetic look, then turns to me. "So it's true. You *are* the one."

Suddenly, I don't know what to say. I had been so full of bravado when I decided to do this; I thought of the look on their faces when they realised that Cathy had been telling the truth all along. I hadn't thought of what would happen next. I lower my head. "I don't know," I mutter. "All I know is that I can see you and you are all real to me. I didn't find out about ... what happened, I mean ... until a few weeks ago."

"Is that why you stopped coming to see me?" asks Cathy. "You never missed a day, then you stopped altogether for nearly two weeks."

I stare at her. "Of course I missed some days. You weren't always there when I came out. And it's been a month, not a fortnight."

Cathy looks puzzled; her parents, too, look surprised. "Cathy told us she met you every day," says Thomas, who appears to have regained his composure.

"Not every day," I reply. "For instance, I've never seen you when it's sunny."

"But ... it's *never* sunny," says Lucy.

"Of course it ..." I begin. And slowly, it dawns on me; I only see them when it's gloomy because that is the world they now inhabit. "I don't know what to do now, though," I say, changing the topic of conversation. I look up at all three of them. "Do you?"

Three shakes of heads confirms the worst; I may have found them, communicated with them even, but I can't release them from their living – dying – hell. I can't help them.

"I'm sorry," I say, and Cathy begins to cry. I see moisture in the corner of Lucy's eyes as well. Thomas puts his arms round his wife and children. Filled with a mixture of grief and remorse, I step close and complete the group hug.

My head whirls, and I am alone, outside my front door. But it is very different to how it looked moments earlier. The house looks newer, as if only built within the last few years rather than a century ago. It is night; it is cold. July is *never* this cold. I breathe into my hands and white clouds of vapour spread outwards.

A kind of understanding reaches me on some level. Without pausing to think, I run down the path and kick the front door in. Cloying smoke, released from its confines, floods out into the night air, momentarily blinding me. As my hands automatically go to cover my eyes, I feel the presence of somebody forcing their way past the ruined door and out into the cold, brushing past me as they do. Before I can look to see who it is, everything begins to fade away.

#

I am rubbing my eyes and I feel the warmth of the afternoon on my skin. I look at my hands, as if expecting to see them black from smoke, but can't think why I should think that. I look up at the grey sky and wonder when – if ever – summer 2015 will actually begin.

"Typical," she says. My wife, Angela, closes the front door behind her as she and Cathy, our daughter, come out, arms laden with summer flowers.

"You've forgotten, haven't you daddy?" laughs Cathy. "We're going to the cemetery as it's the anniversary, and then we're going to granny and grandad's."

"Of course I haven't forgotten," I tell her, as it all comes back to me. We walk to the nearby cemetery and, as we have done every year since I met Angela, lay flowers on the family plot.

I smile as I read the inscriptions on the neatly-tended graves, both the originals and the obviously later additions:

Thomas Manson born 15ᵗʰ September 1882, died 28ᵗʰ October 1951
Lucy Manson, wife of Thomas, born 21ˢᵗ February 1885, died 4ᵗʰ January 1957
Catherine Manson-Stewart, daughter of Thomas and Lucy, born 5ᵗʰ April 1910, died 26ᵗʰ July 2001.
Bernard Stewart, husband of Catherine, son-in-law of Thomas and Lucy, born 23ʳᵈ December 1908, died 2ⁿᵈ May 2001.

Always in our thoughts, your loving family Irene, Christopher, Angela, James and Cathy.

"Come on, James" says Angela, taking my arm as I stare at the inscription as if seeing it for the first time, "we don't want to be late for mum and dad's, do we? What are you thinking about?"

"Oh, nothing much," I say, as I walk slowly away, recalling how much I enjoyed seeing Irene and Chris – I even feel of them as substitute parents, considering I barely remember my own. "You know," I add, nodding in the direction of the inscriptions on the gravestones, "I know I never met any of them, but I just had the strangest feeling that I knew them, that's all."

And, each of us taking one of Cathy's hands, we walk away from the cemetery.

Lifelong Learning

The letters, stamped with *Overdue* in red ink, were stacked up in a pile that grew higher with every passing day. Paul Clarke knew that he was slowly sinking, and that, however hard he tried, he couldn't find even the smallest of handholds that would give him some hope for rescue. To try and take his mind of all of his worries, he browsed through the special 'local education supplement' of the newspaper, wondering idly whether any of the forthcoming courses on offer would be for his subjects of interest - history, geography, a foreign language or art. He read for a few minutes, then sat up straight as one snippet caught his attention. Unlike the others, which all originated from either the University or the FE College, this one came from an institution he hadn't heard of before. The advert read:

Do you ever wish you'd paid more attention at school? Does the pace of modern life often pass you by?

Yes, Paul involuntarily responded out loud, glad that he lived alone and didn't have to explain himself to anybody else. He continued reading.

Why worry about everyday affairs when you could be expanding your knowledge base?

Why indeed, he thought. Would that it were so easy. He should really have stopped reading at that point, as avoidance of the problem is never a solution. But he didn't.

Our courses are specifically tailored to suit the individual's every need. Covering history, geography, languages and art, we have the perfect programme for you. We combine all four topics into a course that will be exactly what you are looking for. To apply, contact us at the email address detailed and the rest of your life will begin immediately.

He made a note of the email address, intending to get in touch the next morning. Then he thought again. It said *immediately,* so why not get in touch straight away? And so it began.

#

Barely had Paul pressed the 'send' button than he received a reply in his inbox. It contained a link to the enrolment page on the company's website as well as an attached 'terms and conditions' document that he browsed through quickly – it ran to more than forty pages in a Times New Roman 8 font. It appeared to be a very thorough paper, and even though it was only an electronic version, he could almost envisage the richly embossed heading that began:

Life's Ultimate University - Division of Lifelong Learning (DoLL)

... and followed with a tagline of:

"The Doll that takes away all your worries"

There followed a prospectus giving more detail of the course content. The history section promised to *give the student a clear insight into the life and times of*

England from the reign of William I through to that of Victoria. Paul particularly liked the fact that it put great emphasis on the statement *we won't bore you with having to remember legislative clauses; this course is all about conflict, intrigue and deception.*

He smiled as he read that; it was, as they had said in their advert, as if the course had been tailored specifically to *his* requirements, for he still recalled how boring it had been to try and learn parrot-fashion all the terms of the *Poor Law Amendment Act of 1834,* for example; the prospect of having to do that again had been the main reason he hadn't considered taking up the subject until now.

He carried on reading. The geography portion of the course also ticked all the right boxes, promising to concentrate on the local geography of the north-west of England. *That's much better than crop production along the banks of the Irrawaddy River* he thought, recalling another of his pet hates from school half a century earlier.

The languages section promised to make him proficient in French and German - the only two languages that he knew a sprinkling of words in - and the art prospectus extolled the virtues of sketching with charcoal and painting with watercolours - the two aspects of creativity that interested him most.

There was only one catch to all of this – how much was it going to cost? He was already deep in debt, so even a reduced pensioner rate was unaffordable. But he wanted to do it. He glanced at the bottom line, then stopped and reread it to make sure it really did say what he thought it said. It did. The course was being offered free of charge as it was an experimental one, but the offer was only valid until midnight on the 21st, at which point the full cost would apply. Paul didn't even look to see what that full cost was – he was too busy checking the time and noting that it was 23:45 on the 21st, meaning that unless he enrolled within the next fifteen minutes he would lose the opportunity of a lifetime. He didn't have any time to waste – as it was, he almost missed the deadline, due to a drop-out on his internet connection just as he clicked the *Enrol* button. Fortunately, the connection was re-established within seconds and his enrolment was sent moments before the new day dawned.

Within seconds, he received an email from the company. He assumed it would be an automated response to his application, but when he opened it, he found that it was addressed specifically to him and gave confirmation that he had been successfully enrolled on the course. *Wow!* he thought, *that's efficiency for you.* He carried on reading the email, and noted that it included the full course content, with links to the pages containing the specific lessons. He felt a touch of disappointment when he saw that each subject area only consisted of ten lessons, but that quickly passed. *It's free,* he thought, *so don't look a gift horse in the mouth.*

Although it was now a quarter of an hour past midnight, all tiredness had fled, and Paul immediately made a start on the first module. He had an important appointment at the bank after lunch, and knew that he probably wouldn't sleep for worrying about the outcome, so what better than to let his mind concentrate on something else?

He journeyed until 6 a.m. with the army of King Harold Godwinson, fresh from their triumph at the Battle of Stamford Bridge as they began their march southwards to take on Duke William II of Normandy at what would become known as the Battle of Hastings. Paul couldn't believe his luck. This was *exactly* the sort of thing he had been hoping to find on the course, and he felt as if he was with them every step of the way.

At the conclusion of this introductory module, Paul still felt fresh and dived straight into the next segment of the course, which was all to do with the physical geography of the Lake District. He spent until noon reading all about the Cumbrian Mountains, fell by fell, from formation to constitution, marvelling at the knowledge he was gleaning and wishing that school had been like this. All those times he had visited the Lakes at weekends without ever knowing anything about the landscape he was traversing. Scafell Pike would never again feel insignificant to him.

He was hungry now, and tiredness was beginning to set in, but he didn't want to stop. Besides, there was little point in going to bed now, when he had to be at the bank in three hours' time. The geography introduction had now concluded, but, almost without realising, Paul found himself spending three hours learning conversational French, and a further three hours inspecting German vocabulary. He glanced at the clock, vaguely recalling that he should have had an appointment with his bank manager that afternoon, yet he wasn't bothered. The University's claim had been true – the course *had* taken away his worries.

By now, he was tired, hungry and thirsty in equal amounts, but his curiosity overrode all of those mere physical desires. Before he knew it, he was embroiled in the techniques of sketching using charcoal pencils, and, three very messy hours later, he was setting the easel up as he prepared for an initial lesson in painting using watercolours.

Paul glanced at the clock. It was midnight. He had spent a full twenty-four hours on the four topics he had signed up to, but, instead of finally wending his way to bed via the kitchen, he clicked the link for lesson two and was once again with Harold's army as the march southwards continued. He could feel the agony of those soldiers, faced with a 270-mile trek not long after traveling the 200 miles from London to Yorkshire prior to their previous battle.

Sweat poured from his brow as their joint ordeal continued. The hours, like the miles, crawled slowly by, but, whereas Harold's army were able to rest at the conclusion of each day's march, Paul was denied even that, as from 6 a.m. he was once again exploring the Lake District, this time concentrating on the valleys of Eskdale and Ennerdale.

As noon approached and passed, he became embroiled in conversational French at the bakery, buying *pain et des gâteaux dans les boulangers*, and when he should have been enjoying his afternoon tea, he instead found himself conjugating the German verb 'to eat' essen – iche esse, du isst, er isst, wir essen, ihr esst, sie essen. He learnt about the past, present and future tenses, the conditional, imperative, perfect, pluperfect and imperfect – he covered everything, in fact, about eating except for the physical act.

His head throbbed agonisingly at the end of this session, but instead of pausing even momentarily for a break to get refreshments, the cruelty continued. For the past half dozen hours, he had been talking about food in different languages, now he was sketching it as his charcoal study was a plate of bread, cheese and grapes, items that took on full colour three hours later as the image was transferred onto canvas by the strokes of his paintbrush.

As a second midnight came and went, he was again on the march with Harold's army as the next series of lessons began. Paul knew that he had to stop, yet he couldn't. He recalled there being ten separate elements to each of the four modules; he had just commenced the third of them. He would be doing this for another week and more. Then what? After a week without food, drink or sleep, he wouldn't need any more lessons. He wouldn't need anything. As the University prospectus said, this really was lifelong learning.

Caught on the Boundary

Inspector Johnson scratched his head as he looked at the letter that Sergeant Moore held under his nose. "It was pushed under the door sometime last night," said the sergeant. "It's from him, isn't it?"

The inspector looked at the young sergeant, remembering those days long ago when he, too, had been brim-full of enthusiasm. Thirty-odd years on the force, the last several of which had been spent fruitlessly trying to catch the faceless criminal known as *The Phantom,* had served to dilute his passion for this job. All he wanted to do now was enjoy his forthcoming retirement, but he knew he wouldn't be able to rest if he hadn't apprehended his nemesis before he left the station for the final time.

He glanced at his reflection in the window of the office door, trying to convince himself that the glass exaggerated his heavily-jowelled features. He was almost sixty, and, unlike the sergeant in front of him, who was half his age and the epitome of strength and fitness, the inspector knew that brainpower, not brute strength, was now his only hope of catching criminals. He envied the young sergeant; he still had his career ahead of him, whereas the inspector's now all lay in the past. At one time he had scoffed at people who were said to be *married to the job*, but now he knew exactly how they felt; in a few days' time, this office and he would get their divorce, and then what would he do? He shuddered involuntarily at the thought, then realised that the sergeant was staring at him, waiting patiently for a response to his question.

"Oh yes, Frank, it's from him alright. I'd recognise that handwriting anywhere." He read the letter, out loud, as if giving voice to the words might make the meaning behind them clear:

Inspector Johnson – or perhaps I should call you Robert, as our careers have been so closely woven together over the years that I feel we are friends rather than colleagues.

Johnson snorted; the arrogance of the man. Friends? Never. Colleagues? They were on opposite sides of the law, whereas he made it sound as if they shared adjacent desks in a town centre office block. He continued reading.

As you know, I've been very successful in my business ...

Again, Johnson snorted. If success was counted by the number of banks you had robbed and how many lives you had ruined, then yes, he could consider himself successful. In the Inspector's book, though, he was nothing but a common criminal, a peddler of misery. The letter continued:

... and, as I understand that you will be leaving the force in a few days' time at the end of the tax year, I feel it is now time for me to retire as well. I have decided on the institution that will provide me with <u>my</u> pension and will give you the opportunity to end your days with one last success. My final task will commence at noon tomorrow – in the spirit of friendliness that permeates our working relationship, and, knowing how you are such an aficionado of our summer sport, I've decided to tell you where I will be at that time. Catch me if you can.

Johnson turned the paper over, and saw what appeared to be a random selection of words and phrases. As he looked at them, though, he could see that there *was* a pattern to them; all of them referenced a county cricket side, doubtless the reference to the summer sport that Johnson liked to enjoy during his spare moments. The list, which appeared to make no sense whatsoever, read:

Will I be the cause of chaos in Lancashire? To find me will you need a seer from Essex? Perhaps I'll meet my demise in Derbyshire? Unless, that is, I decide to nest in Kent. I've never been guilty of smoking in Nottinghamshire. Will you find all this to be tiresome in Somerset? What will be my ruses in Sussex? While you chase me through the markets of Northamptonshire, perhaps my progress will be impeded across Middlesex? I don't want my voice to sound croakier in Warwickshire, I'd much rather you heard my song in Glamorgan. Why not make a grab for my shirt in Yorkshire or my shorts in Leicestershire? Although it's early April, I think that by the time you catch me, there will be a frost in Gloucestershire and the air will be fresh across Worcestershire. You will need to be an early riser in Surrey to chase me across Hampshire, but not to worry – I will not be harmed in Durham.

Sergeant Moore was keen to impress Johnson with his detailed knowledge of *The Phantom*. "It's a classic case of misdirection. All of his crimes have taken place locally, otherwise we wouldn't have been on the case. That means we can ignore all the other places in that list. All we have to do is find out what 'Chaos in Lancashire' means and we've got him.

The sergeant looked pleased with himself, and Johnson didn't have the heart to tell him he was missing the point. *The Phantom* never did anything that didn't contain some sort of logic, however nonsensical it might appear to be initially. Which meant that there was a reason behind the entire message. The only problem was – Johnson didn't have a clue as to what that reason was.

#

He spent the rest of the day trying to make some sense out of the letter, but to no avail. Johnson didn't want to admit defeat, but knew he wasn't going to have the option; nobody would blame him, but the taint would always be there, however hard people tried to ignore it. He had fought *The Phantom* and *The Phantom* had won.

He went home late that evening in a dejected mood, knowing that in little over twelve hours' time, his humiliation would be complete. He tried to get some rest, hoping that the solution would 'magically' come to him overnight, but sleep eluded him. After tossing and turning for several hours, he flicked his bedside lamp on and took a sip of water. As he finished his drink, he looked at his notebook, which was open next to the lamp. He had been wrestling with the problem, writing down phrases from the letter, and, as he leant forward to replace the now-empty vessel, the light reflected through the bottom of the glass and caused some of the letters to leap out at him. The words *chaos* and *Lancashire* stood out especially, with the *o* of *chaos* enlarged by the magnifying effect of the glass. He stared at it for a moment, until his mind attained full clarity and he understood. He grabbed the notebook and looked at the other word pairs he had scribbled down. Yes. It was the same for all of them. And that meant ... he quickly put it all together, and then he smiled. He took another look at the clock; it was 5:17 a.m. He made a phone call and set things in motion. Then he turned the light off and settled down to sleep, confident that he would now be able to rest comfortably. It didn't bother him that somebody else would perform the actual arrest; all that mattered was that *he* had solved the puzzle and the chase was finally going to end. *At last*, he muttered, as he turned over and closed his eyes.

#

It was a little after noon on the Friday, and Sergeant Moore ignored protocol as, in his excitement, he flung open the door to Inspector Johnson's office. "They've got him, sir. He tried to rob the main Post Office in Ormskirk, just as you predicted. He made a run for it, but we nabbed him at Lydiate yards before he crossed the boundary into Merseyside. So it's our collar, not theirs. But how ...?"

He left the question hanging, such was his awe of the inspector's expertise in solving the puzzle. Johnson smiled inwardly. For a moment, he thought about saying nothing – thus increasing the mystique surrounding himself – but then he remembered again how he had once been like the young sergeant, and felt that he owed it to him to explain his deduction.

"Sit down, Frank," he said, pointing to the chair across from his desk. "There's no mystery about it, lad, just a bit of good old-fashioned deduction. *The Phantom* became over-confident, and when he tried to taunt me this one last time, it backfired on him. He told us *when* the crime was going to take place, and he told us *where* the crime was going to take place."

"But how did he sir?" asked the impatient sergeant.

"It was all in the letter he sent. The message was as clear as daylight – once I looked at it the correct way. Here's what he wrote," he continued, taking the letter from his top drawer and turning it over to the side where the seemingly-random phrases had been written. "Take another look at it. If you split it down into the counties and the specific word that is used to refer to them, you get a list of eighteen pairs, like this." The inspector picked up his notebook and wrote in it:

> *Chaos – Lancashire*
> *Seer – Essex*
> *Demise – Derbyshire*
> *Nest – Kent*
> *Smoking – Nottinghamshire*
> *Tiresome – Somerset*
> *Ruses – Sussex*
> *Markets – Northamptonshire*
> *Impeded – Middlesex*
> *Croakier – Warwickshire*
> *Song – Glamorgan*
> *Shirt – Yorkshire*
> *Shorts – Leicestershire*
> *Frost – Gloucestershire*
> *Fresh – Worcestershire*
> *Riser – Surrey*
> *Chase – Hampshire*
> *Harmed – Durham*

"I'll admit," he said, more in an effort to make the sergeant feel better about himself, "that it took me a while to spot it. In fact, I was almost too late. The facts are, though, that it had been staring me in the face throughout. I actually owe my success to doodling. I'd scrawled *chaos in Lancashire* on my pad, and was subconsciously playing with the letters when I realised that all but one of the letters in *chaos* was also in *Lancashire*, and it set me thinking of one of those old rhyme-puzzles I used to do when I was a child – you know, the ones that go something like:

> *My first is in bat, but not in cat.*
> *My second is in rat, but not in that.*

and so on."

"Yes," answered Sergeant Moore, "I know what you mean. I remember doing them as well."

"Good, that makes it easier to explain. So, having tried that idea with the word *chaos*, and found that the letter 'o' is the only one missing from *Lancashire*, I did the same with the next pair, and 'r' is the only letter in *seer* that isn't in *Essex*. Each pair of words follows the same pattern, with one letter present in the first word that doesn't belong in the county name, thus:

Cha**O**s

See**R**

De**M**ise

Ne**S**t

Smo**K**ing

T**I**resome

Ruses

Mar**K**ets

Im**P**eded

Cr**O**akier

Song

Shir**T**

Sh**O**rts

Frost

Fresh

R**I**ser

Chase

Harm**E**d

... spells out *Ormskirk Post Office*

"Now we had the place, and we already knew the time, so in the end, this last one turned out to be one of the easiest collars I've ever made. Besides, he said he was going to collect his pension, where else would he go other than a Post Office? And now," he concluded, rising as he spoke, "I can retire."

"What are you going to do now you've all this time to yourself?"

"If you'd asked me that yesterday, I honestly wouldn't have had a clue, but this case has reminded me of something I always said I would do, Frank. The cricket season is about to start and I plan to spend my days following Lancashire across the country. After this case, I think that somehow seems fitting. Don't you?"

When Saturday Comes

Monday

As usual, Jake was one of a handful of employees who were at their desks a few minutes earlier than the company required them to be; not because he was an especially conscientious worker, although he could always be relied on to give of his best, but because he wanted to make the most of every moment when he was in the same vicinity as Laura.

Jake had been employed at *City Insurers* for three years, and had worked his way up so that now he had some seniority in the loss adjustment section. Laura had joined the section only a few weeks earlier, but Jake had immediately become smitten with her. At twenty-five years of age, he'd had numerous relationships, but nobody had ever made him feel like Laura did; for the first time in his life, he began to loath weekends and long for Monday morning to arrive. Laura caught the bus to work, arriving fifteen minutes before the official start of the day, and Jake looked forward to the chat by the water cooler that the two of them had in those pre-work minutes.

"Mooning over her again, are you?" asked Dave, his closest friend.

Jake knew that the question expected no answer, as Dave continued. "This has gone on too long, mate. Just ask her out – go on, do it."

"I can't," replied Jake. "Anyway, she might already have a boyfriend."

"I doubt it mate – didn't you hear about Phil Brooks in accounts? He asked her out a fortnight ago, but she rejected him. You know what she said? She said he didn't meet her standards! Mind you, if he struck out, that means you've no chance."

"You don't know that. Perhaps she just didn't like Phil – could you blame her? He can be totally obnoxious with his *I'm god's gift to women* attitude. I'm nothing like him."

"No, you're nothing like him, that's a fact. At least he's had a girlfriend in the last few months, whereas you, you've done nothing but go all gooey-eyed about *her*. Blimey," he added under his breath, "I haven't had a decent Friday night out in *weeks*." Almost as an afterthought, he added, "I'll give you till lunchtime. If you haven't asked her out by then – well, *I'll* ask her out."

Jake looked at Dave, fear in his face. "I didn't even know you fancied her."

"I don't. She's not my type – a bit too cultural for my likes. But I'll ask her anyway if you don't do something about it."

"She might say no," said Jake, but there was a touch of desperation in his voice, and his feeling of unease deepened when Dave responded with *but she might say yes*.

The rest of the office staff had turned up while the discussion was taking place, and for the next couple of hours, work priorities were to the fore; Dave's threat, though, was always at the back of Jake's mind, and as the clock approached lunchtime, he knew that he had to make his move. He waited until Laura went to the water cooler and, trying to appear as casual as possible, he walked over to join her.

#

The water cooler had always been *their* place. On the day she started, Laura walked past Jake's desk as he was reading Pelé's autobiography. A few minutes later, they were both at the water cooler and Laura said, "I see you're reading *My Life and the Beautiful Game*. It's good, isn't it?"

"I've only just started it, but I'm enjoying it so far. Are you a football fan then?"

"No, not especially. I like reading autobiographies of famous people, past and present – not these *X-factor* winners who are five-minute wonders, but people who really do have something to tell the world about. I've just finished reading Laurence Olivier's *Confessions of an Actor* and am going to start on Ingmar Bergman's *The Magic Lantern* when I get home."

"Quite highbrow stuff, then."

"Not always," she'd laughed, "I've also read Ronald Reagan and Ice-T to balance things up a little."

That was how it began, and every day since then, they had chatted generally whenever they could; although the office rules were quite strict – staff were expected to be at their desks almost constantly during working hours – the few minutes before the start of day and lunchtime were their time, not the company's.

#

The topic of conversation today, though, was going to be different, and Jake was full of nerves as he looked at Laura and blurted out, "Do you want to come out with me sometime? On a date I mean."

Immediately, he wished the ground would open up and swallow him whole; what a *stupid* way to act. He wouldn't have been surprised if Laura had laughed at him; or walked off without speaking. But she didn't. She just smiled, but he detected sadness behind the look; as if something precious had been spoilt. Her answer, therefore, when it came a few moments later, surprised him even more. "Okay, Jake. I'll see you outside the ticket office at half two on Saturday afternoon." And then she walked back to her desk without bothering to get her water.

It was only when Jake returned to his desk – also without a cup of water – that he realised what she'd said; she'd told him the day, she'd told him the time, but she hadn't told him the place. The ticket office? What ticket office? The theatre? The cinema? The amusement park? The football ground? The railway station? It could have been a thousand and one places. He looked over at Laura, but she was engrossed in a book as she ate her sandwiches. He didn't want to walk over to her, as that would have been too obvious, so he emailed her instead: *Half two Saturday is great. By the way, which ticket office?*

Dave came over to Jake's desk seconds after he'd sent the email. "Right," he said, "I'm going to ask her as you've done nothing about it."

"I have done something about it. I've asked and she said yes – I'm seeing her on Saturday."

"Good on you mate," he said, slapping Jake on the back as if he'd just taken a hat-trick in a test match. "Come on, let's go to *The Lion* for a celebratory drink. Where are you going to take her?"

"Not sure yet, I'm waiting for..." At that instant, his computer beeped to let him know he had incoming mail. It was from Laura. He clicked to open it and read her reply.

Which ticket office? That's what you need to find out. Jake, I do like you and I look forward to our chats at work each day. Away from work, I like people who are cultural, athletic, and with an enquiring mind. If those descriptions fit you, then you'll work out where I'll be on Saturday. If you don't make it, then I'll know you're not the one for me.

Dave was peering over Jake's shoulder reading the message. "What the hell is that about?" he asked.

"Beats me," shrugged Jake. "Come on, let's go and get that pint."

#

Jake meant to speak to Laura about her reply that afternoon but, whenever he planned to go across to her desk, as if by magic two or three others also went over at the same time, and his courage diminished with each passing minute. Just as he was about to leave for home, he received another email. Making sure that Dave wasn't around – he felt that this was something he didn't want to share, even with his best friend – he clicked to read it. The message opened, but instead of there being an explanatory reply, there was just a short verse:

Where will I be? Well hear me at least -
This message comes straight from my heart
Your task rhymes with this – not north, south or east
Decipher it and you'll have your start

Jake saved the email, but there was a troubled look on his face as he left the office that night. He spent a considerable amount of the evening trying to work out what this was all about. The clue Laura had left him seemed straightforward enough. *Not north, south or east* – that had to mean west, then? *Your task rhymes with this* – in which case, that was probably *quest*? She *had* set him a quest of sorts, that was true, but why mention that now? It was hardly a clue. Was she making fun of him? Jake slept fitfully that night, and his dreams only served to increase his anxiety.

Tuesday

Jake was in work early as usual the next morning, and he walked directly over to Laura, not waiting to meet her at the water cooler. "I got your email, but I don't get it, if you know what I mean. What is it all about?"

"Oh Jake," she replied, and he could hear the disappointment in her voice, "I *told* you. It's all there – or, it will be."

"It will be? You mean there's more to come?"

"Yes. One a day till Friday. Of course, if you suss it out before then, all the better."

"You mean I just have to guess where you'll be and that'll be it?"

"No, Jake. Not *guess*. You need to know, and, believe me, if you work it out, you will know one hundred per cent. I suppose it was inevitable that our daily chats would progress to something more, but I've had work relationships before, and they've failed because we've not had anything in common away from the office. This time, before I start on one, I need to know it has a chance."

"But we get on so well together don't we? We don't talk about work at all."

"I know, and that's why I've faith that you'll work this one out and everything will be fine. I'm sorry to be so cryptic – it's just the way I am. Are you sure you still want to go out with me?"

"Yes, of course I am," he replied. "I'm intrigued now, that's all." Jake realised that he'd get nothing out of Laura by questioning her so he resigned himself to waiting for her next message.

Dave made a beeline for him when he returned to his desk. "So? Have you got it sussed now?"

"Yes, all sorted," lied Jake. Deep down, he dreaded it all going wrong, not least because he didn't feel he'd be able to face up to his friend's sympathy if everything went pear-shaped.

The rest of the day dragged, but shortly before five o'clock Laura's next email arrived. He opened it up and read the second clue:

> *If I told you no more, I would be remiss*
> *So search out what you're looking for*
> *Children often hide and then they do this*
> *Do I need to tell you any more?*

Hide and do this? *What you're looking for?* This time, it seemed clear that she was telling him to *seek*. *That helps a lot* he mumbled – *so far she's told me that it's a quest and I've to seek. I bloody well knew that anyway. Is she making fun of me?*

As he made his way home that evening, he had to fight down a small but growing feeling of resentment towards Laura and what she was putting him through.

Wednesday

By the following morning, Jake's anger had dissipated, and he tried to treat the day the same as any other. He met up with Laura as usual for their bi-daily chats at the cooler, and tried to appear as light-hearted as normal; in fact, outwardly he was behaving as if Monday's question had never been uttered, and, to her credit, Laura made no reference to the events of the previous days either.

As they laughed together, Jake almost convinced himself that nothing that had happened over the last two days had been real. Then the next email from Laura arrived as the day was drawing towards its close.

This one informs you about goods, dear and cheap -
As in stamp, sticker, marker or tag
It rhymes with the place where horses go to sleep
Or the brother of Cain, the old lag

Brother of Cain? Jake's biblical knowledge was rusty, at best, but he did remember the story of Cain and Abel. *Where horses go to sleep?* A stable? Rhyming with that and identifying products – that would make it *label*. So that meant *quest – seek – label* – his quest meant he had to seek a label? What label? He was even more confused now. Even though Laura had told him there were another two clues to come, he failed to see how two more words could suddenly make all of this into anything intelligible; but, mainly because he didn't have an alternative, he would give her the benefit of the doubt.

Thursday

Jake was finding it more and more difficult to act as if everything was normal, and he found that he wasn't looking forward to his lunchtime chat with Laura for once. He also snapped at Dave once or twice during the morning. After he did it again in the afternoon, Dave snapped back. "What the hell's up with you? I see you didn't have your little tête-à-tête at the water cooler this lunchtime - has she dumped you already? Not that I'd blame her – you've been a right moody sod just recently."

"No, it's nothing like that. Look, I've just got something on my mind – something at home. Sorry, mate, I know I shouldn't take it out on you. I'll be okay in a day or two." He didn't say any more, but, deep down, he thought *I hope I'll be okay in a day or two.*

The late-afternoon email arrived and Jake immediately put aside the claim he was looking at to see – hope – if the puzzle would now become any clearer. He read the cryptic message:

This one's quite different, so unlike the rest,
"It's a knockout" did many watchers vex -
The international version was by far the best
Just look at the word without the x

It took Jake some time to work out what Laura was getting at this time. He had a vague inkling that he'd heard of *It's A Knockout* as it had been mentioned in the news over a recent unsavoury court case, but he knew nothing about an international version of the show. He checked online and found there was one, *Jeux Sans Frontières* – the only word with a 'x' was *jeux*, so without the 'x' it would be the singular *jeu*. Which would now make *quest – seek – label – jeu*. Any thoughts that the message might mean something disappeared as he read it. Now he was convinced; she *was* making fun of him. He didn't even stay to finish off the claim he had been dealing with, but picked up his jacket and stormed off out of the office.

Friday

Jake didn't get to work early the next day; in fact, he turned in ten minutes late, and he made a point of not looking towards Laura at all that morning. He did notice her glancing across at him out of the corner of his eye, but he was able to ignore it as he was busy with a particularly complex insurance claim that looked like it could cost the company an awful lot of money *unless* he could in some way find that there was something fraudulent about it all.

When Saturday Comes

The morning was almost over by the time he reluctantly concluded that everything was above board, and he sent the report confirming the fact to his line manager. Almost immediately, he heard the tell-tale *bleep* indicating incoming mail, but he ignored it until late afternoon; even then, he only opened it by accident, thinking instead he was opening a work-related message from the accounts department. He had been determined not to read it, but curiosity won out.

I was hoping that you'd have come over to see me to tell me you knew where I'll be tomorrow. I'm still hoping you've solved it and are going to surprise me by meeting me there. Just in case, here's a final clue.

I know it might not make that much sense
Trust me, the language says it all
Don't think English - it'll only make you tense
Imagine, instead, you're Charles de Gaulle

I do hope I see you tomorrow, but, if not, can we go back to being water cooler friends?

Jake was intrigued, despite not wanting to be. The clue seemed straightforward enough – he knew that de Gaulle was a former President of France. He would therefore view the message differently. In French. So how could *quest – seek – label – jeu* be viewed in French? *Jeu* was easy; it was already a French word, which was why he had been so puzzled and angry the previous evening. So the message ended with *game*. But what about the rest of it?

He looked at it from the beginning, word by word. *Quest*? How was that French? Written differently, it would also be sounded differently as *qu'est* – or *what*. Next came *seek* – thinking in French, it wasn't a huge leap to get to *ce que*. *Label* posed more difficulties, but, as French nouns had a male of female gender, splitting it into its constituent syllables *la* and *bel* would result in *la belle*. Putting everything together, he now had *qu'est ce que la belle jeu*, which, from what he recalled, translated to *What is the beautiful game?*.

Jake smiled for the first time in days. He had read Pelé's autobiography about *the Beautiful Game* only a few weeks ago – that had been the first thing Laura had spoken to him about.

He walked over to her desk and smiled. "I'm not that great on my languages, but shouldn't it technically be the masculine form, *le beau jeu*, instead?"

"Yes," she smiled back, "I suppose it should, but as it was about my being there, I thought it warranted the feminine touch."

"It's almost time for home," Jake said. "A busy weekend ahead. I'll see you at the match then at half two tomorrow."

"I'm looking forward to it," she smiled back.

A Dream Come True

This story appeared in 'Eclipse - The Red Rose Book of Science Fiction and Fantasy', published by uclanpublishing in May 2016

\#

Qahmat squinted as the glare from Karvell's suns reflected off the rippling surface of the pond. He patted his saddlebag idly while applying slight pressure from his knees to steer his draygill towards the waterhole. The intelligent beast picked up the pace as it realised it would soon be able to sate its thirst. Dismounting, he looked across at the animal while it lowered its long neck towards the blue-green water. It was twice his size and could have crushed him in an instant, yet it possessed not a trace of malice and bore no resentment towards its master. Qahmat lowered his wiry frame to the ground and knelt to take his own fill of the tepid liquid. He grimaced at the feel of it in his mouth, then cupped his hands so he could splash water into his face, allowing it to trickle down his chin and through his long, pointed beard. He glanced up at the twin suns, Darya and Ventar, seeing them as malevolent gods, hurling their heat downwards towards the planet in order to taint the refreshing water. They certainly seemed to be in collusion, for it looked like they were touching each other; he didn't recall ever seeing them so close together before.

As he was well clear of the village now, he returned to his mount and opened the saddlebag, addressing the animal while he did so. "Well Wayfinder, I know there was nothing in here yesterday, but that's not the case today. Let's see what last night brought us shall we?"

This was always the best moment; the anticipation of what might be there – jewels, coins, objects of great value perhaps. And, as was often the case, anticipation was immediately followed by disappointment. "Nothing but rubbish," he almost spat, for the bag was empty apart from a badly worn red dress. "We won't be able to trade *that* for a single meal. We'll have to go back again tonight." He didn't know why he had only taken the dress – he never remembered once it was over. He reached up and patted Wayfinder's ursine head, as if apologising for preventing her, too, from having a night's rest.

Today was a bad day. On good days, when he opened the bags to see what was inside he found items of tremendous value. On good days he could live like a ruler for many rotations of Karvell's chief moon Jovar. On good days Wayfinder would be the best-kept draygill in the Kingdom. But a bad day meant little to eat and no time to rest. It meant returning again the next night and risking discovery. And now there had been two consecutive bad days. *That* had never happened before.

If only he could have some measure of control about what he put in the bag. But he couldn't. A dreamcatcher inhabited a different world when he worked and Qahmat was one of a dwindling number of exponents of the trade. Perhaps he might even be the last surviving one, for he'd never heard tell of another. Then again, dreamcatchers wouldn't advertise their presence, would they? "Imagine," he said, reaching up to stroke Wayfinder under her triple chin, "if they knew I was planning to slide into the recesses of their sleeping minds once again tonight in order to make reality out of their dreams. Do you think I'd still be welcome in their village? No, neither do I. If anybody *does* ever find out, then that will probably be the day you'll have a new master."

He took another look at the red dress. That was last night's reality. "What on Karvell must the winemaker have been dreaming of last night for *this* tattered cloth to be the only thing worth bringing back? It doesn't bear thinking about. I can understand an empty saddlebag – that does happen sometimes. But an old dress?" As always he remembered the instant when he first entered the vintner's dream but nothing more; the next thing he recalled was exiting the dream when consciousness returned to his own body, barely an instant before the winemaker awoke to the dawning of the new day. That instant was all that kept Qahmat alive, for it just gave him time enough to leave before he was discovered.

Qahmat had some sympathy for his victims. Although the items he stole from them appeared to be intangible elements from their dreams, everything he took away robbed them of some of their essence. The items in his saddlebag might represent wealth to the dreamcatcher, but they were indicative of lost physical wellbeing for the dreamer. After visiting one settlement his saddlebag had been brim-full of gold coin. He had revisited the village several moons later and seen the corpulent banker whose dreams had furnished him with such riches. The man was now little more than a mindless fool, drooling as he sat in the corner of the market, ignored by all who passed by him. Qahmat was the cause of the man's demise and *that* was why nobody could ever know what he did. So far, nobody had discovered his secret and Qahmat had lived comfortably throughout the thirty Daryan annular rotations since he had discovered his inborn talent at a very young age.

His original intention had been to ride on to the next village during the day but now he had to find somewhere to sleep instead. "Come on girl, we have to return," he said, mounting Wayfinder and heading towards the cave they had found the previous morning. "We'll sleep here again today and then we'll be fresh for another adventure tonight." Suddenly, he shivered. It was getting colder. How could that be, when both orbs were still high in the sky? During this Jovarian rotation, the days lasted twelve and a quarter chrons and barely half of one had passed since the vintner awoke.

Qahmat knew he could not be mistaken, for knowledge of time was innate to all dreamcatchers. Without knowing *exactly* how long the darkness would last, they could not hope to survive, for a dreamcatcher *had* to be out of the sleeping mind before its owner awoke. Every night as the final rays of Ventar sank below the horizon, all across Karvell the people would fall asleep and dream. Every morning as the first rays of Darya rose above the horizon, all across Karvell the people would wake up. Only the dreamcatchers were immune to this automatic response. Only the dreamcatchers didn't dream.

Legends told that the ancient gods were displeased with the heinous atrocities that occurred once darkness fell and they acted to prevent this by enforcing instantaneous sleep upon the populace. To punish the people for these crimes, dreamcatchers were created to invade their dreams, which were reputed to be bountiful. Qahmat doubted the truth of this latter claim, especially if the winemaker's red dress was the most opulent item in *his* dream.

He reined Wayfinder to a halt when they reached the cave. The entrance was partially obscured by wild reeds and he pushed through them to lead his mount inside. Before going in, he squinted up at the suns and saw a grey sliver obscuring part of Darya on the right-hand side. What could it be? It looked like a chunk had been bitten out of the sun. Qahmat shivered, but this time with terror, although he didn't know what he was in fear of.

He knew he should lie down to sleep – only dreamcatchers had the ability to sleep during the sunlit hours – but he couldn't. For three chrons, he watched the grey shadow creep further across the twin suns. More than half of the bright yellow disks were now obscured by what appeared to be a trio of overlapping circles resembling the three moons of Karvell.

"I really do need to rest," he said to Wayfinder, who was munching at the reeds at the mouth of the cave. "I almost believed Jovar, Pelo and Satar had risen, but everybody knows they can't reside in the heavens while Darya and Ventar hold audience. Come on," he added, leading the beast back inside, "else you'll have eaten away our only patch of cover."

#

He awoke from his dreamless sleep with a start. It seemed mere moments since he had laid down on the dried-mud floor, but he felt the chill of the night and saw the accompanying darkness through the gap between the tops of the reeds and the cave roof. His sense of time seemed to be awry, for he hadn't woken naturally when the last rays of Ventar disappeared. That concerned him. It *had* to be right once he was inside the dream. Qahmat put it down to a third consecutive night of having to enter dreams. Sleeping during the day might be something that only dreamcatchers could do, but the quality of daytime rest left much to be desired. He saddled Wayfinder, who also seemed only partially rested, and rode the short distance back to the village.

On arrival he was amazed to see dozens of people sleeping in the streets. He often saw a few stragglers who had been caught outside their homes as darkness fell, but this appeared to be the whole of the village. Although it was dark, Qahmat's vision was attuned to working without light and he soon spotted an ample-proportioned richly-dressed man who he remembered from the market the previous day. His stall sold the most expensive cuts of meat, with entire draygill carcases hanging from hooks embedded in its roof. Qahmat hoped his dreams, too, would be of the highest quality.

He dismounted, knelt and leant forward until his forehead was touching that of the sleeping man. He closed his eyes and focussed, feeling his consciousness sending out tendrils to link with the other's mind, interweaving with the thoughts and dreams of the host. And then he was inside, trailing the merchant as he walked through a courtyard. The stall-owner was dressed in cloth of the richest purple. Qahmat himself wore flowing robes of a gaudy yellow, with his battered saddlebag looking quite out of place over his shoulder. The courtyard was bathed in a gentle golden light and at the far end of it a dozen maidens skipped barefoot through the grass in a fantastic display of synchronisation and elegance. Qahmat realised he would not remember any of this once he was back in his own body and, not for the first time, he regretted that flaw in the makeup of a dreamcatcher.

The dancing maidens were all adorned with sparkling jewels of exquisite beauty and immense value. Qahmat congratulated himself for choosing this man for his victim. He strode forward and the maidens ceased their dance as they saw him. The merchant, who had been admiring the lithe forms of the women, looked round. There was an expression of confusion on the fat man's face. It was always the same; the look of disbelief once the intruder entered into the dream. Qahmat walked across to the first maiden and tore a glittering necklace from around her delicate bejewelled throat. She screamed and the merchant gallantly came to aid her, but it was a futile attempt at chivalry; in the dream world, nothing had any substance without the dreamcatcher's will and the merchant's flailing fist went through Qahmat as if he wasn't there.

He continued along the line, ignoring the objections and the pathetic attempts to stop him as insubstantial hands passed right through his body. Almost casually, he dropped his purloined loot into his saddlebag. He had already collected a fortune and there were still three more maidens in the line. He didn't have to stay all night in the dream world after all. He would leave once he had relieved the final maiden of her gems and then he wouldn't have to worry if his sense of timing really was off.

And then he had an uncomfortable feeling, as if the night was already over, even though it had only just begun. Light filled every corner of the courtyard. Not the calming, golden rays that had been there when he had entered, but harsh, bright, yellow light, starting as a thin slice and growing wider and brighter by the moment. Qahmat recoiled in horror. He knew what this meant. The merchant had opened his eyes to welcome in the daylight. But that was impossible, for less than a quarter of a chron had elapsed since he had left the cave. The night should not be over for another six and a half.

Impossible or not, it was happening. He watched through the merchant's eyes as the villagers rose from their uncomfortable sleeping positions on the ground. He glanced up at Darya and Ventar. The suns were bright, yet incomplete. This time the obstruction was to the left and appeared to have been inverted. He heard shouts through the merchant's ears, saw villagers rushing over and pulling an inert figure from off the top of the merchant. He saw the figure. He recognised its features. It was the face that stared back at him every time he looked in a pool of water. It was his own face, yet it was different. It exhibited no signs of life. Indeed, it contained no life, as its substance was elsewhere.

He had failed to get out in time and now he was trapped in the merchant's mind. Not forever. Far from it. He would be imprisoned there until all vestiges of the merchant's dream faded from his memory; and once that happened, he, too, would fade away into an eternity of nothingness. He saw the merchant looking across to where Wayfinder was tethered and Qahmat's final thought was to wonder whether his one friend in this world would be destined to be impaled upon a hook in the meat vendor's booth. And then, even that thought was gone.

Don't Quote Me

It was Nathan Walsh's first day at work. After three years at University, graduating with a first in English Literature, an accounts clerk for *Helping Hands*, a subsidiary of *J.B. Coates and Co.,* wasn't exactly what he had hoped for. However, at the end of the day, a job was a job, even if it was lowly-paid. At least, he told himself, it was a worthwhile position, for the company's role was to distribute the charitable elements of the government's lottery fund to some of the smaller 'worthy causes'.

He was a little nervous as he was introduced to his work colleagues. At twenty-one, he was the youngest of the group, and he sensed an element of resentment amongst some of them at his being there. The fact that he was tall, lanky and, some would say, a little geeky, all served to further erode the small amount of confidence he had brought with him. He wondered whether taking this job was such a good idea after all.

He sat at his desk and tried to make sense of the training guide that had been thrust under his nose by the office manager. He was one of six in the team, and, as the first addition to the group since its formation almost two years earlier, four of the other five were already making it obvious that he was very much the junior. *My degree's going to do me a lot of good here,* he thought, with a wry half-smile on his face.

"You haven't met *Miss Quotes* yet, have you?" asked Brad Fenton, who was in his mid-twenties and had long, straggly hair that couldn't have looked any worse if he *had* been dragged through a hedge backwards.

"No. Who is she?"

"Ignore them," said Sarah Vale, the only female in the office and also the only one who had shown him any warmth at all. "They're referring to Valerie Coates, our manager. She's the daughter of J.B." Sarah was a few months older than Nathan, with brunette hair cut in a pageboy style and a smile that would make any Monday morning feel better.

"We're doing him a favour," said Harry Lewis, who was neatly groomed and in his early thirties. He had the tendency to scratch at some imaginary stubble as he spoke, which meant it was difficult to concentrate on what he had to say.

"And how exactly does asking him that qualify as a 'favour'?" asked Sarah.

"Because he's an English graduate, isn't he? We wouldn't want him correcting her and getting fired on his first day, now, would we?"

"What are you talking about?" asked Nathan, noting that Sarah rolled her eyes in an exasperated manner.

"We call her *Miss Quotes*," said Trev Peterson, "because that's what she does." Trev was a year or two older than Nathan and wore a scruffy t-shirt and baggy trousers that revealed far more than they concealed. He had spent most of the first hour of the day attempting – unsuccessfully – to flirt with Sarah. "She thinks she's being clever," he continued, "but really, she just shows herself up to be a complete ignoramus. What was it last time?" he asked Greg.

Greg Higson was the eldest of the staff, closer to forty than thirty and with a bald patch that he tried, unsuccessfully, to mask in a manner reminiscent of the actor in the old *Hamlet* cigar adverts. Except, Nathan reckoned, there was not a single element of humour in this man, who had already pompously declared himself to be the 'office manager' even though everybody was supposedly on an equal footing. "It was that bit from Shakespeare," he said. "You know, *Hell Hath No Fury Like A Woman Scorned*. Except she said, *like a woman spurned*. Probably because that's what she's been all of her life," he added, "the old maid."

"It's not Shakespeare," said Nathan, noting that Sarah was also about to say something, "it's William Congreve. From *The Mourning Bride*. The original line was, *Heav'n has no Rage, like Love to Hatred turn'd, Nor Hell a Fury, like a Woman scorn'd.*"

"See what I mean?" said Harry. "There he goes, been here barely an hour, and he's contradicting his betters already. He'll be out of here by lunchtime. Two to one on. Any takers?"

"Why are you always so nasty to M... Valerie?" asked Sarah. "And why do you say that about her? You've no idea ..."

"Give it a rest," interrupted Harry. "Women sticking together," he added in a conspiratorial whisper. "One look at her and anybody can tell she hasn't had any in a long time – if ever."

"Not from a real man, but you know what I think about the pair ... shush! Here she comes now," said Greg.

Brad, Harry and Trev laughed. "Here's where she gives him the test," said Trev, looking over at Nathan.

"What test?"

"You'll find out," said Greg.

The woman walked over to Nathan's desk. She was tall, elegantly dressed, immaculately groomed, and appeared to be in her early thirties. If was only when she was close to his desk that he saw by looking at her hands and neck that she was probably closer to fifty. "You'll be Nathan, I assume. I'm Valerie Coates. Normally I would have interviewed you, but I was away on business, which is why you saw my father instead."

"Pleased to see you, Miss Qu ... Coates," said Nathan rising from his desk.

A cloud passed over her face as she said, "call me Valerie, not Miss ... Coates. We're on first name terms here at *Helping Hands*."

"Of course," said Nathan, "I'm sorry."

"Don't mention it. They tell me you're very bright. An English Lit graduate, I understand. This job must seem a little beneath your great expectations, wouldn't you say?

"No ... not at all. I'm ... very happy to be here."

"Well that's good to hear. At *Helping Hands*, I'm always on the lookout for people with talent and intelligence. I need somebody who can work alongside me finding new suitable recipients for the funds. It's an important job, and is well-paid too. So, I'll say to you what I said to these five here when we began. Come to me and explain why *you* should be elevated to the management team, and, if I agree with you, this time next week you'll be working with me and earning four times the salary you're currently receiving. Now, as Shakespeare said in *Macbeth*, 'Bubble, bubble, toil and trouble'. That means there's work to be done, so you'd best get to it."

Nathan hesitated a second before replying, trying not to look at the other four males in the office who were grinning inanely behind her back. "Of course, Miss ... Valerie. Though I don't see how I ..."

"Oh, I'm sure you'll know when." She turned on her heel and left the office.

Nathan looked at Sarah. "I see what they mean, now," he said. "But anybody could make that mistake."

"I'm not sure," she replied. "I think she's a lot cleverer than they make her out to be."

"Yeah, right," said Greg, "I suppose you women have to stick together, don't you?"

#

The day passed quickly for Nathan. He had brought sandwiches with him, and he ended up eating them at his desk while he tried to get to terms with the job. One of his duties was to read the application forms from the members of the public who were trying to get some of the lottery funding. Many of the tales were harrowing, and yet, he felt, they didn't quite ring true.

He looked up to see Valerie standing in front of him. He had been so engrossed that he hadn't heard her enter. Other than Sarah and himself, everybody had gone home.

"So how would you say your first day has gone?" she asked.

He thought for a second before replying. Did she really want to know, or was this just a standard 'I'm-asking-but-I-don't-really-care-what-you-say' type of question? He decided to trust his instincts and go for the first option. "I've enjoyed it, but I'm also a little disappointed. I thought it would be very fulfilling to organise the distribution of the funds to those in need, but some of the people who are claiming are beginning to annoy me. It's obvious that they're scroungers, out for whatever they can get. If it was up to me ..."

"Don't be so hasty, young Nathan. As Tolkien writes in *The Two Towers*, '*Be not too eager to deal out death in the name of justice, fearing for thy own safety. Even the wise cannot see all ends.*'" Remember that, Nathan before you're *too* eager to judge."

"Point taken! I'm sorry, and I will."

"Well don't stay too long. It'll all still be hear waiting in the morning. Good night, Nathan."

She turned to leave, but paused as she passed Sarah's desk. "What's wrong, dear?" she asked.

"It's these figures. I'm trying to sign off on the expenditure for last month before I leave, but I can't get them to tally. Damn things – they're impossible."

"Tut, dear! As Christie has Poirot say in *Murder on the Orient Express*, *'The impossible could not have happened, therefore the impossible must be possible in spite of one's appearances.'* Remember that, and I'm sure it will stand you in good stead. Now, like I told Nathan, get yourself home. I'm sure your mother will be pleased to see you."

"Yes, M ... Valerie. See you later."

Shortly afterwards, Nathan and Sarah left the office. For Nathan, it had been an interesting first day.

#

Tuesday dawned with no change in the office atmosphere. If anything, Nathan felt even more the outsider of the five males, but he had determined not to let it bother him. That resolution was put to the test, though, as the morning progressed.

"Have you got the answer, yet?" asked a mocking Greg.

"What do you reckon, Harry?" asked Trev. "Do you think she'll take him anyway?"

"I do," said Brad. "She's like that old biddy in that film who's into young lads."

"What film?" echoed Harry and Greg.

"He means *The Graduate*," said Trev. "After all, that's what this clever git is, isn't it? A graduate with a first. That's done you a lot of good, hasn't it," he added with a sneer, "an office *junior*."

Nathan ignored them and carried on with his work. He noticed that Sarah didn't join in either, but she often looked up with a face that mirrored his own feelings. If it hadn't been for her quiet, yet obvious support, he doubted he'd have lasted until lunchtime. She had a vase of flowers on her desk – carnations, he thought. She didn't have them yesterday. Perhaps, now that she was working with yet another male, she needed to have something around which had a more feminine touch.

Valerie came into the building at just before noon. Sarah had already told Nathan that she wasn't in every day, as her role involved going out to view prospective recipients of the funding. "Some weeks we don't see her in the office at all. She's making a special effort to be here as it's your first week."

A few minutes later, Valerie came in to see them. "How are things going? Any issues I need to know about?" There was a general mumbling, but nothing specific was said. She looked round at the half dozen desks, and her eyes had a sparkle in them that seemed to say, *I know exactly what's been going on.*

She walked over to Nathan's desk. "And how are things with you today? Hopefully a little more tolerant – at least towards our claimants?"

"Yes, I'm sorry, you were right. It isn't up to me to judge, is it? I understand that you spend a lot of your time vetting these people?"

"Yes, I do, Nathan, and I do have to exclude many on the grounds you raised yesterday. Those that come through to this office have passed my initial test, but I know I'm not perfect. Some miscreants could still slip through, so you were right in a way yesterday when you had your doubts. That's one reason why I need somebody working with me, as I told you."

"I'll bear that in mind, then."

"Yes, you do that. I don't enjoy having to turn people down when they apply for the funding, because I always wonder, what if I'm wrong? I'd rather let the one through who doesn't need it than prevent the one who does."

"It must be very hard, and also very worrying."

"It can be, Nathan, but I always console myself that right will always triumph in the end and that the miscreants will be found out. After all, you know what it says in the book of *Romans* – 'For the payment of sin is death'. That's all a bit maudlin for a Tuesday morning, though, isn't it? How are they all treating you?"

She looked at him with searching eyes, and he found himself breaking eye contact for fear she would see right into his soul. He also sensed a tension in the air around the office. "Very well. It must be strange for them having been together all this time and then having to babysit the 'new boy', but I've been given plenty to do and I feel that I'm coping fine."

"Yes, that was what I heard from Sarah last night. Good, then I'll leave you to get on with it."

As she was leaving, Valerie stopped to admire the vase of flowers on Sarah's desk. With an almost imperceptible glance across at Nathan while she spoke, she said, "They're beautiful, dear, just like you are. As Wordsworth said in *I Wandered Lonely As A Cloud*, 'all at once I saw a crowd, a host, of lovely daffodils'. Don't you agree?"

"Yes Valerie."

"It certainly brightens the place up. Well done," she said as she went out to return to her own office.

Almost immediately, Greg stormed up to Nathan's desk. "What the hell was all that about?"

"All what?"

"Don't play dumb with me. You telling Miss Quotes there that you've been given plenty to do. Are you saying we give you all the work and are doing nothing ourselves"

"Of course I wasn't. I was ..."

"'Cos that's how it sounded to us, didn't it lads?" He looked around and the other three grunted their agreement. "We're watching you, *graduate*. And as for you," he said as he walked past Sarah's desk, "get rid of them bloody flowers. They give me hay fever."

#

Once again, Nathan found himself working through his lunch break. The afternoon passed quickly as he dealt with a mounting pile of paperwork. Despite what Greg had said, Nathan did feel that he was doing the lions' share of the workload. Well, not perhaps just him, for Sarah seemed to have almost as many on-going cases as he did. It was the other four who had time to laugh and chat and go for a long afternoon coffee break once Valerie had left the building.

"It's way past five. Aren't you going home?"

Nathan looked up to find that once again, only he and Sarah remained in the office. This time, though, even Sarah was ready to leave, as she had closed down her desktop and was holding her coat. He also noted that the vase of flowers was no longer there. "I didn't realise the time. I just want to finish the paperwork for this case, as I don't want there to be any delay in their receiving the money. It's a very worthy cause – not that they aren't all worthy, I'm sure," he added quickly, but Sarah just smiled.

"Yes, I know what you mean. I don't like leaving things undone, either. It's a pity not everyone feels that way," she added meaningfully. "See you tomorrow then?" There was a slight question-mark in her voice at the end of the sentence, as if she'd read his thoughts earlier in the day.

"Of course," he replied, perhaps a little *too* eagerly. He liked her, but he didn't want to risk upsetting the only friend that he'd made here by saying or doing anything that she might deem to be inappropriate.

"Good. Don't stay too long. 'Night, Nathan."

As she left the office, Valerie walked in.

"I just came back because I'd left some papers on my desk. I'm surprised to find you still here." She turned to look at Sarah, who had reached the end of the corridor and the exit door. "I like to think that I'm quite the observant sort. I've seen the way you look at Sarah. Have you asked her out?"

"What? No, of course not. It wouldn't be right. We're work colleagues, that's all."

"Is that so? Remember, then, what Elizabeth said in Jane Austen's *Pride and Prejudice* – '*When a woman is partial to a man, and does not endeavour to conceal it, he must find it out.*' Take note of that, young Nathan."

She, too, turned and left, leaving Nathan with a bemused look on his face.

#

Nathan decided that he'd try and see things from the others' point of view. He was, after all, the newbie in the office, and they might perceive him as a threat to their own positions. Nobody had mentioned their qualifications for the role, but the fact that they had made a point of his being a graduate implied that they might not have attained the same level of education as he had. Maybe they considered that he felt that this job, and his co-workers, were beneath him. In truth, they wouldn't have been that far wrong at the beginning of the week.

He entered the office on Wednesday morning at ten to nine, but Sarah was the only one there. They smiled at each other, but he felt a little embarrassed. Perhaps it was because of what Valerie had said the previous evening. Were his feelings that obvious? Consequently, he sat at his desk and began working instead of going across and chatting with her, which was what he really wanted to do.

The other four arrived over the next twenty minutes. Although the office hours were nine to five, and he hadn't been told that there was any flexitime, perhaps those rules weren't cast in stone.

There was some general chat for the next half hour or so, but it didn't include him or Sarah. The other four were discussing the Champions League match the previous evening. Nathan would have gladly contributed, but he had a mounting pile of work and did not feel that it was right to do so given the circumstances.

The normal office procedure was that people had a coffee break as and when they felt like it. Sarah had brought him his coffee on the first morning, but since then, everybody tended to their own needs. At half ten, Nathan rose from his desk and said loudly, "I'm going to make myself a coffee now. Can I get anything for the rest of you?"

"Yes, please," said Sarah. "I take it white, no sugar."

He looked at Greg, expecting to take his order. He was not prepared for the response his offer received. "Are you trying to be clever, insinuating that we take too many breaks?"

"Not at all, I ..."

"You're saying that you think we spend too much time away from our desks, aren't you?" said Harry, and there was a murmur of agreement from the rest of the quartet.

"Look," said Nathan, trying to keep his temper. "It was a friendly gesture, that's all. If you want to make your own, that's fine by me. I'll just get ours," he said, looking towards Sarah. *So much for that attempt at bridge-building* he muttered under his breath as he walked to the kitchen.

It was quiet in the office when he returned. He soon worked out why. Valerie was in. *Great*, he thought, *she'll probably think I'm off having a break while everybody else is working hard.*

He went back to his desk and carried on with the checks he was making on the current claimant. It was a family-run company, *Vacations of a Lifetime*, that provided holidays for terminally-ill children, a definite worthy cause in his eyes. Perhaps it was because he was still inwardly seething about the coffee-break 'incident', or perhaps it was just one of those things, but after spending a full hour on the details, he signed them off without completing his usual final double-check, putting them in the tray awaiting Valerie's final signature.

She duly came back into their office shortly before noon, collecting the trays of completed applications from the six desks. He noticed that his tray was nowhere near as full as any of the others; only Sarah's was anywhere near as empty.

"What's this?" asked Valerie, handing the *Vacations of a Lifetime* paperwork back to him.

He looked at it, and immediately saw what she was querying. The figures on the final page summary sheet didn't add up. He had transcribed them incorrectly as his concentration had wavered.

"I don't know, it looks like ... Okay, I'm sorry. I didn't check this thoroughly and it's wrong. I haven't made a good start, have I?" He heard some barely-suppressed sniggers coming from Harry's desk.

"Everybody makes mistakes, Nathan. As Kipling said in *If*, *'If one can meet with Triumph and Disaster, and treat those two imposters just the same'*. You know what that means, don't you? Don't get too cocky when things go well, and don't take it too much to heart when they don't. Nobody's perfect – except for me," she added with a light-hearted laugh, trying to raise his spirits. It didn't totally work.

He took the papers back off her and began checking them again. This would be another day when he would be lunching at his desk.

As Valerie walked out, Sarah said, "How did you spot that error so quickly, Valerie? You didn't even seem to go through the figures thoroughly, yet you knew."

"Sarah, dear, as Shaw said in *You Never Can Tell*, *'My specialty is being right when young people are wrong'*. One day, you, too, might be like me."

"I think that's a long way off," she said.

#

In mid-afternoon, *after* making himself a drink, he walked across to Greg's desk.

"What is it?" he asked in a tone that suggested he didn't want the question answering.

"It's about when Valerie came in before to collect the finished papers. I saw that everybody had managed to get a lot more done than I did. I think I could do with a bit of help so I can work a bit better."

Greg looked at him, glaring as if he wasn't sure whether Nathan was being serious or not. "You don't need any help, you just need to get on with the job and stop making so many mistakes." Greg turned away, and Nathan noticed that his computer screen was displaying a *Mah Jong* game.

Nathan returned to his desk and continued with his workload which was becoming increasingly frustrating.

At half past four, Greg walked up to his desk, but instead of offering him any help, he plonked a dozen manila folders in front of him. "As you said, we've all done a load more than you. We don't like slackers in here, so get these finished before you go home tonight."

"That's not fair," said Sarah, from the other side of the office.

"Who runs this office? If I was you, I'd be concentrating on my own workload rather than anybody else's. Don't think we haven't noticed that your out-tray is almost as empty as his?"

"It's alright, Sarah," said Nathan, "I can do this. It'll be good experience," he added, thinking exactly the opposite.

He took the folders and began working through them, barely even noticing when Sarah said goodnight to him as she left. The other four had gone long before that. He had made a decision; today was going to be his last day working here. He liked Valerie, he definitely liked Sarah, but he couldn't stand any more of the frightful foursome.

It was sometime after seven p.m. when he heard the office door open and looked up to see Valerie standing there." Good gracious," she said, "don't you have a home to go to?"

"Yes, but I've too much to do, and I can't leave it till tomorrow." He didn't add that he wasn't going to be in tomorrow.

"Is that because you had to redo the paperwork for *Vacations of a Lifetime*?"

"Not really. That set me back a bit, yes, but I must admit I'm getting a little overwhelmed by it all. It's only my third day, but everything seems to come straight to me."

"As Scrooge says in Dickens' *A Christmas Carol*, *'why do spirits walk the earth, and why do they march to me?'* It's part of the job, young Nathan, and you need to get used to it. That's what separates the achievers from the likes of Greg and his cronies. I know it's only your third day, but I can spot potential when I see it. I hope I get to see it again tomorrow."

She knows, he thought. *Is she some sort of mind-reader?*

"If I were you, I'd leave that stack until tomorrow. Please, go home and get some rest. You've earned it."

#

Nathan did go back to work on Thursday morning. Despite his decision of the previous afternoon, what Valerie had said had made its impression on him. Even though she hadn't quoted Dickens correctly, the meaning had gotten through to him.

Sarah was already at her desk, even though it was a little before 8:45 a.m. She looked unhappy, almost as if she'd been crying, but her face lit up when he walked in. "Nathan!" she said. "I wasn't sure if you were coming in after yesterday."

"It was that obvious, was it?"

"You aren't very good at hiding your feelings," she answered, and he wondered if there was a hidden depth to that statement.

"The truth is," he answered, if it wasn't for Miss Coates – Valerie, I mean – I might not have come in. It's funny, it doesn't seem right calling her Valerie."

"I know *exactly* what you mean there. But what do you mean, what did she say that changed your mind?"

Nathan laughed. "It was actually another of her quotations – yes, she didn't quite get the words right, but the meaning was pretty clear, and that's what's important."

"Everybody else makes fun of her when she gets things wrong."

"I know, but I find it quite endearing. I'm amazed, actually, that she always seems to be able to find the right thing to say for each occasion, even if she does mix the odd word up."

"She's a very well-educated woman. If you get to know her, you'll find there's little that she doesn't know."

Nathan thought for several moments. "I can believe that," he said at last. "Which makes it all the more odd that she does make such silly mistakes. Like when she said *lovely daffodils*. That's one of the best known lines in literature. I'm sure that even the uneducated have heard it and know it's *golden daffodils*. Why would she get it so badly wrong?"

Sarah looked at him before replying. "She has to be aware," she said. "She must know that she's using the wrong quotes. She's not a Mrs. Malaprop."

"No, she certainly isn't, despite what the others think of her. In Sheridan's *The Rivals*, he made Mrs. Malaprop a figure of fun through her humorous misuse of words. She said things like *the very pine-apple of politeness* instead of *pinnacle*. Valerie uses a different, but plausible, word each time. No, I would never say that Valerie is anybody to laugh at, would you?"

"No, I wouldn't. Tell me, Nathan. With all her mistakes, does it mean you think less of her?"

"Not at all, Sarah. I actually like her and I'm beginning to think there's something to what you just said about her knowing what she's doing. I hadn't really considered that before."

He went to his desk and began working through the folders that he had left the previous evening. Nine o'clock came and went with still only the two of them in the office. Brad eventually rolled in shortly after twenty-past. His eyes were red, but, unlike Sarah's, Nathan was sure his were the result of plenty of alcohol and not enough sleep. Trev turned up twenty minutes later. Greg and Harry didn't show at all.

"Keep the noise down," said Trev some minutes later. Nathan shrugged his shoulders. He hadn't spoken at all; the objection appeared to be to do with how hard he was tapping his computer keypad.

At half ten, he went to make a coffee. Sarah followed him out almost immediately. "It's like this every Thursday," she said. "They go to the pub on a Wednesday, ostensibly to watch the football on the big screen, but they always get so drunk that at least one of them doesn't make it in the next day. Once, all four of them were no-shows. That was a good day," she added, with a fond reminiscence.

The door opened and Valerie walked in. "Would you like a coffee?" asked Nathan. "It's only instant, I'm afraid, but there's enough water in the kettle for three cups."

"That's very kind of you. Instant is fine. I take it black without sugar. I didn't come in for that though. I was a little concerned after our talk last night. I wanted to make sure everything was alright."

"I'll go back to my desk," said Sarah.

"No, please don't Sarah. This is just a friendly chat. Enjoy your break. You've worked hard enough for it, what with having to cover for the no-shows as well." She turned to Nathan again. "Have you found you've had to do a lot extra to cover for them? You did say you were a little overwhelmed yesterday evening."

He glanced at Sarah before replying; her face was expressionless. "No, not at all. I think we're all coping well. After all, that's why we have a team of workers, isn't it?"

"That's a good attitude to have for a junior. Remember, as Tennyson says in *The Charge of the Light Brigade*, *'Theirs not to make reply, theirs not to reason why, theirs but to do or die',* she added."

The kettle clicked off having reached boiling point. Nathan heaped a spoonful of the instant coffee into a clean mug and poured the water into the three cups, before handing Valerie her black coffee.

"That's a nice necklace, Valerie," said Sarah, noticing the sunlight glinting on it through the window.

"Why thank you Sarah. Why don't you ever wear any jewellery?"

"Oh, I could never afford something like that. I'll make do without."

"Oh, my, dear. Don't become, as Wilde remarked in *Lady Windermere's Fan*, *'a woman who knows the price of everything and the value of nothing'.*"

Sarah glanced at Nathan, looking somewhat abashed, as Valerie took her coffee and left them alone in the kitchen.

#

Trev didn't return after lunch, and with Brad even more of a liability than on a normal day, it was left to Nathan and Sarah to keep things going as best as they could.

They didn't even manage to get a coffee break during the afternoon. Brad lasted until quarter to four before going home, and neither Nathan nor Sarah felt comfortable about leaving so much paperwork incomplete. They worked on in silence for a long while until Sarah said, "Valerie likes us to be up to date at the end of each week. She doesn't think it's fair to the applicants to be kept waiting unnecessarily for another two days when we're not here to keep things ticking along."

"I'm with her on that," said Nathan, "although right now, I'm beginning to have second thoughts. Just look at that lot," he said, pointing to a pile of folders that they hadn't even started to process. "I don't see how we are we ever going to get those done by tomorrow night, and that's without any that come in tomorrow. They're all merging together and it's getting so I can hardly tell the wood from the trees, as the saying goes."

"Because, as Holmes says in Conan Doyle's *A Scandal in Bohemia*, that's because *'You look, but you do not observe'* – isn't that the case here?"

Neither of them had heard Valerie coming in. Nathan wondered just how long she had been there. Had she heard their conversation? Had he said anything that she might take offence to? He didn't think so, but he couldn't be sure. Besides, she might interpret even an innocent remark as something other than what was intended. She didn't, though, appear to be angry with them.

As if she had read his mind, she said, "I do appreciate the two of you staying on until now to help out, but it really is time to go home now, otherwise you'll be no more use to me tomorrow than those other four idiots were today. Anyway, Nathan, you're new here, so you wouldn't know that no applications come into the office on a Friday, specifically to make sure that everybody has a sporting chance of getting up to date before the weekend."

Nathan looked at the clock on his computer. It was ten minutes after eight. He hadn't realised that so much time had passed. His stomach rumbled loudly, as if to tell him that *it* knew all too well. "I think you're right," he said, shutting his computer down. "I'll see you both tomorrow."

#

Nathan had a lot to think about as he made his way home. He stopped off to buy fish and chips, as it was too late to start making himself something to eat, and the meal did refresh him somewhat. Despite once more being physically and emotionally drained after such a long day, he switched his PC on as soon as he had taken his coat off and, within minutes, started some searching. What Sarah had said made sense. There had to be a reason why Valerie was making such silly errors in the quotations she used.

He closed his eyes and tried to concentrate. He needed to know the exact wording Valerie had used on each occasion. He wished now that he'd taken more note at the time, but after half an hour, he thought he had them all. He checked again to see if he'd written them down in the order they were said. He thought he had, and he went back to his computer. After another half an hour, a smile lit his face up. Sarah was definitely a lot more than a pretty face. Without her – well, Valerie's quotation that afternoon might just as easily have gone, *'you hear but you don't listen.'*

He was about to switch his computer off when another thought struck him. He performed another series of searches and found even more revealing information. *Well*, he muttered, *You were wrong, Greg. Valerie may be many things, but she certainly isn't an old maid.* Now his curiosity was completely satisfied, he did switch his computer off and prepared to unwind for the remainder of the evening.

#

Nathan entered the office at shortly after half eight on the Friday morning. For once, he was looking forwards to the day.

Sarah arrived ten minutes later. "You look happy," she noted, seeing the beaming grin he aimed in her direction.

"I am, and it's all down to you," he replied, but even though she pressed him to explain, he wouldn't say any more, other than the cryptic, "I'll leave my explanations for Miss Coates. Err, have you any plans for the weekend?"

"Not really. I'm going to spend tonight with mum. I rarely get to see her at home during the week. I've nothing planned for the weekend, though. How about you?"

"I've nothing planned either," he said. He was on the verge of suggesting they spent their 'nothing planned' time together but desisted. *Let's see how today goes first*, he thought.

He wondered when he should go to see Valerie. Would she come in again and misquote another well-known saying? To date, she had been in each morning and each afternoon, but the 'message' she had given Sarah appeared to be complete, so did that mean that everything had been said by Thursday night? Was that why she told him no new applications arrived on a Friday? Or was he over-analysing everything? Suddenly, he no longer felt quite so confident.

His mood didn't improve as nine o'clock came and Greg rolled in. He took one look at all the unprocessed files and hit the roof. He stormed straight over to Nathan's desk and slammed a dozen new folders down. "So this is what you get up to when I'm not here to keep you in line is it? What the hell were you doing all day yesterday? On one long coffee break no doubt. Just you wait till Miss Quotes comes in – I'll fill her in on what a lazy bastard she's employed. One thing's for certain – you'll not be in here on Monday morning. If you want to get paid for the measly amount of work – and I use that word in its loosest sense – that you've done this week, then you'd better get your head down and deal with all these before you clear your desk and leave. And as for you," he said, directing his ire at Sarah, "we all know the only reason you're still here is because *she* fancies you, but when she tires of you, we'll make your life hell." He almost spat the last few words out before storming back to his desk.

Nathan looked over at Sarah, and noticed that her eyes were watering up. He half rose to go and put Greg in his place, but at that moment, Brad, Harry and Trev all walked in, with Valerie immediately behind them. Nathan sat down again as Valerie looked across at him, Greg and Sarah.

She walked over to Nathan and said, in a low voice, "You look annoyed. Is Greg giving you a hard time because you're the new boy?"

Nathan shifted uncomfortably as he said, "No, everything is fine."

"Really? Are you absolutely certain about that? You need to remember what the hero said to Mr Rochester in Charlotte Brontë's *Jane Eyre*, '*I don't think, sir, that you have a right to command, merely because you are older than I*".

"No, it's fine, honestly."

"If you say so," she said, moving off to have a quiet talk with Sarah. Nathan listened carefully in case she quoted something else, but she didn't, at least, not so that he could hear.

He spent the next hour working on the backlog, but shortly after ten, he went on to his web browser and checked on the *Jane Eyre* quotation. He had studied the book during a *Life Writing* module on his course, comparing a fictional autobiography with a real one, but he didn't know offhand if the quotation she had used was correct or not. He soon found that it wasn't.

Was that it then? It certainly all made sense now. Should he go and see her now? He considered it, but then looked at the work that was still piled high in his in-tray. What sort of example would he be setting if he put his own interests first? He decided he'd go and see her once he'd cleared everything.

#

It took him a lot longer than he had thought. After another hastily-eaten sandwich at his desk, and no coffee breaks, morning or afternoon, it was close to four p.m. by the time he started on his last file.

The three stooges all left on the stroke of four p.m., even though they each had unprocessed files on their desks. The fourth, Greg, swaggered over to Nathan's desk. "I've told Miss Quotes how much of a liability you've been, and she has assured me that you'll not be here next week. She'll be along to tell you personally shortly. So much for your expensive education – what good has it done you?" He didn't wait for an answer, and Nathan didn't offer to give him one. Instead, he continued looking at the last file, though his mind wasn't completely on it. Had he misjudged things? He didn't want to be working in this office another minute, yet he also didn't want his departure to be on the terms that Greg was crowing about.

He looked up at Sarah, but she had gone across to the other desks and was collecting the unprocessed files. Doubtless she had abandoned any plans for spending a cosy evening in with her mother.

He heard footsteps approaching down the corridor, and looked up to see Valerie walking towards him.

"So how would you say your first week has gone?" she asked.

He thought for a moment. "It's had its ups and downs. There's certainly been a lot to learn, but I think I've managed okay."

"There's always a lot to learn, but you should never stop asking questions. As Einstein is credited with saying, '*Learn from yesterday, live for now, hope for tomorrow.*' I hope that you take note of all that, I really do."

"I certainly intend to." He had already noted what she said and now he knew that everything was complete.

"I suppose you know that Greg has been to see me. He has complained about you in no uncertain terms ever since you started, but today he has almost demanded that I fire you. You do appreciate the position that puts me in, don't you?"

"Yes, I think I do. If you don't back the manager, you risk upsetting the whole balance of the office. It would make his position untenable. I, on the other hand, have only been here for a week, and can be fired without consequences. I would say, therefore, that it is almost guaranteed that I will not be in this office next week. I do, though, want to finish this last file tonight before I go. Would you allow me to do that?"

"Of course, Nathan," she said, softly. "I'll be in my office for another half hour if there's anything you'd like to say before you go."

As Valerie walked away, Sarah looked across at Nathan with sadness in her eyes. Nathan smiled at her, hoping to make her feel better, then set about completing the paperwork for the final funding application.

"All done," he said thirty minutes later, putting it in the out-tray. "Can I help you with yours?" he asked Sarah.

"No, I've nearly done," she answered in a voice with a hint of a quiver in it.

"Okay then, I'll be off. I'll just pop in and see Valerie before I leave," he said. As he walked past Sarah's desk, she looked up at him with such a sorrowful look that he instinctively leant over and kissed her on the forehead. "Don't worry, everything will turn out fine."

#

"Do you have a minute, Valerie?"

"Yes, of course. What do you want to say?"

"When I started on Monday, you mentioned about my working on the management team. In light of what you said to me a few minutes ago, does that still apply?"

"I don't know. You tell me, Nathan? Are you the right person for advancement?"

"I'm not that sure," said Nathan. "I do have what you're looking for, though."

"Explain."

"Well, you have been saying well-known quotes incorrectly all week. Some have been said directly to me, the rest to Sarah. You have a reputation for doing so, but nobody could make that many mistakes so consistently. I have noticed that the ones said to me are different when contrasted with the others you have used in the office."

"Go on, I'm listening."

Nathan heard a noise behind him. He turned to see Sarah standing in the doorway. She no longer looked sad, but she did look puzzled. Nathan swallowed hard and continued.

"If you take the quotes you said to Sarah and concentrate on the incorrect words used," – he glanced up at Valerie, hoping that he hadn't made a monumental mistake by approaching it this way - "then we have the extra word *one's* in *the impossible must be possible in spite of one's appearances*, the use of *lovely* instead of *golden* in *a host, of lovely daffodils, young* instead of *other* in *when young people are wrong* and finally *woman* instead of *man* in *a woman who knows the price of everything*. If you then take those four words, you get *one's lovely young woman*. I don't know, though, if that was directed at me or meant for yourself. After all, even though you perceived that I have feelings for your ... Sarah, I now know that you love her. And, I'm almost certain, that emotion is reciprocated in full."

He paused, wondering if he'd overstepped the mark, but neither Sarah nor Valerie said a word, so he carried on.

"The quotes said directly to me, though, were different, in two respects. Firstly, unlike those that you most likely pre-arranged with Sarah, these were completely spontaneous, as you said them all in response to something I said to you. That was very impressive. The other difference was that it wasn't the incorrect words that mattered this time, but the correct ones. So, in order, the *Macbeth* quote should begin '*double, double*' not '*bubble, bubble*'. It is 'fearing for *your* safety', not '*thy* safety', and it is 'the *wages* of sin', not 'the *payment* of sin'. Similarly, it is '*if* a woman is partial to a man', not '*when*', 'if *you* can meet with Triumph and Disaster', not '*one*' and, for the spirits, 'why do they *come* to me', not '*march* to me'. The next one is often misquoted by accident, but I'm sure you deliberately said 'theirs but to do *or* die' instead of 'theirs but to do *and* die'. Holmes said to Watson, 'you *see* but you do not observe', not 'you *look*' and it's 'you have a right to command *me*' - you missed the *me* out. Finally, Einstein reputedly said 'live for *today*', not 'live for *now*'. So, if you put all these words together, you get *Double double your wages if you come and see me today.* If I'm right, then that ties back to what you told me on Monday about my earning four times the salary."

Valerie rose from her chair and offered Nathan her hand. "Congratulations, you have a new job on Monday morning."

"I'd love to accept ... but I don't think I deserve the credit."

"Oh? And why is that?"

"Because I wouldn't have worked this out it wasn't for Sarah here," he said, pointing behind him. He heard a gasp from the direction of the door. "She put me in the right direction. By rights, she should get the promotion, not me. But then again, she's not ready yet, I take it."

"Sarah. Sarah Vale? *One's lovely young woman*. But why would you say she isn't ready?"

"Because I've been researching the Coates family, and you have a reputation for avoiding nepotism. All members of the family who work in the business start at the bottom. They have to prove themselves before they advance. Mind you, although I've only been here a week, I have to say that I think she has more than proved herself."

"You know," said Valerie, "it's one of those strange things, when a couple divorce, the woman often takes her maiden name back, while the children retain the husband's name. I, of course, couldn't wait to stop being Valerie Vale, but my daughter remained Sarah Vale because to change her name might have made things difficult for her at school. You are quite correct, she works in the office because that's what we have always done in my family – don't we darling?"

"Yes, mum, that's right."

"As you appear to have done your research, Nathan, you already know that every family member starts off at the bottom for two years so they can get a good understanding of people as well as the job. Sarah's apprenticeship is almost complete. She'll be joining our management team in a couple of weeks. You should know, by the way, that she didn't offer any helpful hints to the others – not that any of them have the capacity to understand anyway – so I guess she must like you as much as you like her." She smiled at her daughter. "In fact, I *know* she does. She told me as much at dinner on Monday, and she was quite distraught on Wednesday evening when I said I wasn't sure if you would be coming in any more. I trust her judgement, although I didn't really need it in the case of those other four wastrels. I doubt they'll be here that much longer anyway. Once you and Sarah have left the office environment, I doubt they'll be able to keep up with the requirements of the job."

"So do I," Nathan agreed.

"So, I'll see you on Monday in your new office, Nathan. Oh, and one last thing. Remember, our main role is to ensure this money is distributed fairly. I was more impressed by your willingness to finish off the outstanding application files than by your ability to work out my little tests. That shows that you have the right attitude for the role as well as the aptitude. As Orwell says in *Animal Farm*, - and I'm deliberately misquoting him here by substituting 'men' for 'animals' – *'All men are equal, but some men are more equal than others.'* Getting it right will be the hardest part of your new job. Oh, and I'd appreciate it if you *didn't* tell anybody that I can correctly quote from literature. After all, I have my reputation as Miss Quotes to live up to."

You're So Vain

It was the first day of September when he arrived in the Papenhoek district of Delft. After noting the smells from the canals that criss-crossed the city, he walked to the corner and the home of his friend and fellow artist. He looked up and saw him at work in the first-floor studio, which overlooked the street rather than the waterways. *Doubtless he's painting another of his cityscapes*, he muttered as he walked up to the door and knocked twice.

A woman opened it and looked at him with a mixture of surprise and happiness. "It is good to see you again, Catharina," he said.

"I forget my manners in my surprise to see *you*," she said. "Come on inside, I will call Johannes." She hurried off to inform her husband of their unexpected guest.

Moments later, the artist came downstairs. "My dear Rembrandt," he said, "I had heard you were in London."

"I was supposed to be, Johannes," he said to Vermeer, "but I decided against it."

"I thought you needed the money," interrupted Catharina, "and I am sure you would have received a pretty purse for portraying King Charles."

"Especially," added Vermeer, "as he was so disenchanted with the portrait that Wright produced for him last year."

"Yes, all of that is true," said Rembrandt, "but in the end I decided against going."

"Why is that, my friend," asked Vermeer, putting a consoling arm around his shoulder, "were the accommodations too costly?"

"No, not at all. I had already made arrangements with Thomas Farynor at a very reasonable rate. Instead, though I decided I needed to use the time for other things, and that is why I am here. I need a change of venue to regain my inspiration. I would like to make use of your studio for some days to paint a self-portrait."

"Another one? You already have close on a hundred," said Catharina.

"Yes, I do, but my last one was in 1663. It is almost the end of 1666 now and much has changed in these three years."

"You're so vain," said Vermeer, "preferring to paint yet *another* self-portrait rather than accept a commission from a King."

"An artist must follow his calling," replied Rembrandt.

#

For the next few days, Rembrandt secreted himself away in Vermeer's studio, working on his latest autobiographical work. Catharina and Johannes left him very much to himself during that time, only calling him to join them for mealtimes. After a week, he displayed the work-in-progress to Johannes. "I will call it *Self Portrait with Two Circles*," he said proudly. "Another day and it will be finished." He stepped back to get a better view of the image looking back at him from the canvas.

Vermeer nodded his approval. "I still maintain, though," he said, "that you should have accepted the commission from the English King." Then he added, "You have been up here a long time. Perhaps you should go out for a stroll?"

Rembrandt was about to reply when Catharina shouted up to the studio. "Johannes, come, you must look at this."

"What is it Catharina? I am busy."

"I know, but you need to see this."

He gave Rembrandt a puzzled look and left the studio to go back down the stairs. Catharina was standing by the door, holding a newspaper in her hand. She looked startled when she saw that Rembrandt had followed her husband down the stairs.

"I thought you would have stayed up there to finish your work," she said.

"Johannes thought it best that I have a break and take some of this mild September air," he replied, though his tone suggested he disagreed with Vermeer's recommendation.

Vermeer strode over to his wife and took the newspaper from her. "Why, it's just the weekly edition," he said. "What is special about that?"

"Weekly edition?" queried Rembrandt.

"Yes," answered his friend. "It is *De Oprechte Haerlemse Courant* – the weekly newspaper of Europe. I don't know why you needed me to ... oh," he said, tailing off. "Now I do."

"What is it?" Rembrandt walked over to take a look at what had clearly distressed the Vermeer's. He read the headline: *Fire sweeps through London*. Beneath, the text described a great blaze that began shortly after midnight the previous Sunday, September 2nd, and raged out of control for the next three days. "It began," all three read out loud together, "at the bakery of Thomas Farynor in Pudding Lane."

"Much of the city was destroyed. You could have been there," gasped Catharina.

"If not for your vanity about that self-portrait, you *would* have been there," added Vermeer. "In truth, that vanity probably saved your life. You should forget about a stroll and finish the painting."

"No," said Rembrandt, rubbing his chin in a thoughtful gesture, "I do not think so. I will leave it as it is, and it will remain as a reminder of how close my life was to being finished.

- The great Fire of London started at Thomas Farynor's bakery in Pudding Lane sometime after midnight on Sunday September 2nd 1666 and swept through Central London until Wednesday September 5th 1666. 70,000 of the 80,000 inhabitants lost their homes. The death toll is unknown – only six deaths were verified but many victims may have been cremated beyond recognition and poor and middle-class deaths were not recorded at that time.
- Charles II reigned from 29th May 1660 until February 6th 1685. His coronation was on April 23rd 1661. John Michael Wright painted his portrait in the robes of the order of the Garter sometime between 1660 and 1665
- Rembrandt Harmenszoon van Rijn (July 15th 1606 – October 4th 1669) was considered one of the greatest painters and printmakers in European art. His later years were marked by financial hardships. He painted self-portraits throughout his life, forming a unique and intimate biography – approximately fifty were paintings, thirty-two were etchings and seven were drawings. *Self Portrait with Two Circles* was an oil on canvas work estimated at 1665 / 1669 and remained unfinished when Rembrandt died
- Johannes Vermeer (October 31st 1632 – December 15th 1675) lived and painted in the Papenhoek district of Delft in the Netherlands with his wife Catharina. He painted his cityscapes from his first-floor studio
- *De Oprechte Haerlemsche Courant* was first published in 1656 and is the oldest newspaper still in existence. Originally entitled *Weeckelycke Courante van Europa* (Weekly Newspaper of Europe) and was renamed to *Oprechte* (genuine) to protect it from imitators in 1664

Rigid

"Why the hell do we have to come here?" muttered Brian under his breath as the queue for entry to the National Gallery crawled slowly towards the entrance.

"What did you say?" asked Diane, his long-suffering wife.

"I asked why we had to come here," he replied, in a voice loud enough to get heads turning in his direction.

"It won't be for long, dear," Diane replied. "This is a once in a lifetime experience. Normally, Rubens' art is displayed in numerous galleries all over the world. We'll *never* get to see his collection under one roof again."

"As if that would be a great loss," he muttered.

"We won't stay long, I promise. I just want to get a quick look, then we can get off to your football."

Brian said nothing for a few moments. He'd only agreed to let Diane come down to London with him as it was better than the alternative of having her sulk while he went off on another of his footballing jollies, as she called them. The woman had no idea. They weren't jollies, but a labour of love. For years, he had been travelling the length and breadth of the country visiting new grounds, methodically rating them on a scale he had devised that took into the account the quality and value of the pies, the availability of cask beer near the ground, ease of travel, reading material in the match programme and a host of other characteristics. Barnet's 'Hive' ground was the latest on his agenda, and he couldn't wait to get across there well in advance of the afternoon's game against Newport County. He looked at his watch. 10:05. A quick glance up and he counted two or three dozen people in front of them. At the rate the queue was moving, it would be another fifteen to twenty minutes before they were inside. Call it 10:30, he thought. He did a quick calculation of the journey ahead of them. A two-minute walk to Charing Cross, then the Bakerloo line to Baker Street – allow ten minutes for that journey - followed by the Jubilee Line to Canons Park – a good thirty-five minutes more - and a five minute walk to 'The Hive'. All in all, it would take them the best part of an hour to get there. The game kicked off at three, but he needed to be there by twelve at the latest. He had a rigid schedule to stick to, and he wasn't prepared to vary it just so *she* could see some paintings that were nearly four hundred years old.

"You can have half an hour," he snapped, chiding himself for being so soft with her. On reflection, it would have been far better to put up with her sulking for a few days. Diane just nodded her rueful acceptance; she knew how unbending her husband was when it came to any deviation from his pre-match ritual.

#

Shortly before half ten, they were inside the Gallery and Diane was hanging off every word of the well-groomed guide who was pointing out the various pieces in the collection. *A right nancy-boy* thought Brian. *You don't see his sort at the footie. Far too rough for the likes of him.*

"Isn't the brushwork magnificent?" asked Diane.

Brian looked at her in amazement. There was a sparkle in her eyes that he'd never seen before. At least, not in the last twenty years or so. Normally, she looked disinterested and downbeat. And now, just a few paintings had unveiled a different person. *Well I never,* he thought. He looked at the wall where her gaze was riveted. It featured four of Rubens' works: *Venus and Adonis*, *The Three Graces*; *The Judgment of Paris* and *The Hermit and the Sleeping Angelica*. If he'd been supping a pint of ale, as he would normally have been doing at this hour, he would have sprayed beer everywhere. All of the women in the paintings were nude. It was unnatural. It was unnerving. It was sick. "Bloody hell, woman," he said, "didn't he know how to paint clothes? All I can see is a wall full of fat-arsed women. It strikes me that this Rubens character was a bit of a pervert."

Gasps and cries of *shame* emanated from the watching crowd. He ignored them, while Diane buried her head in her hands.

The guide, looking distinctly uneasy, began speaking quickly. "Well, yes, art is very much in the eye of ... different people ... the brushwork is what helps distinguish ... perhaps if we move on," he said, in a more confident tone. "This next display contains a collection of the artist's works revolving around the *Perseus* story. Now the story of Perseus is very well known in Greek mythology. He was sent by Polydectes on a quest to kill the only mortal Gorgon, Medusa, who had snakes for hair and a gaze that turned anyone who looked at it to stone. Polydectes expected that Perseus would fall victim of Medusa's stony stare, but Perseus, viewing her reflected image in the polished shield that Athena had given him, beheaded the Gorgon, stowing her severed head in a knapsack that the Hesperides nymphs had provided. When he cut off her head, the winged horse Pegasus was released and carried Perseus on his homeward journey. On his way back, Perseus stopped in the land of Aethiopia. Andromeda, daughter of the King and Queen, was fastened naked to a rock ..." Brian snorted at the word *naked* but the guide either didn't hear him or ignored the interruption "... as an offering to the sea serpent Cetus to pacify the sea God Poseidon. Perseus slew Cetus and claimed Andromeda as his wife. Now, if you'll follow me, we can see the story as depicted by Rubens."

The guide led them into the next room and stopped in front of a painting depicting a naked woman with her hands above her head as she was chained to a rock. "This is a painting of Andromeda, and has been loaned to the exhibition from the Gemäldegalerie in Berlin. And here," he said, moving to the next one, "is *Perseus Freeing Andromeda* which the Prado Museum in Madrid has kindly provided. This piece was painted between 1639 and 1640." Brian stared at it. It was very like the one of Andromeda, with Perseus alongside her in the act of releasing her.

"Rubens depicted this scene several times," continued the guide as he pointed out two more canvases depicting Perseus, Andromeda and Pegasus, one from the Hermitage Museum in Saint Petersburg and a second that had come from Berlin.

"I'll bet he did," sneered Brian. "Anything to keep painting naked women."

"Shush," hissed Diane, clearly embarrassed by her husband. For a moment, Brian thought she must have sounded like one of the gorgon's snakes.

The guide ignored them as he walked to the far end of the display. "And finally in this section, we have *Medusa* from circa 1618, depicting the Gorgon's severed head. The Kunsthistorisches Museum in Vienna have kindly loaned this piece of art to us."

Brian walked forward to take a closer look. Of all the paintings that he had been subjected to, this one caught his attention. For one thing, it contained no nudity, and for another, it depicted the type of scene that interested him as opposed to the previous offerings, complete with their angelic beings. It showcased the horror on Medusa's face. As he looked, a feeling of unease crept over him. The painting no longer interested him. In fact, it repelled him, but he couldn't take his eyes of it. The Gorgon's eye drew him in, staring, so he thought, deep into his soul. He tried to draw away from the gaze, but was unable to. He vaguely heard shouts and screams – he thought he recognised his wife's voice amongst them – but gradually the noise faded away. He tried to move, but his body felt rigid, as if it didn't belong to him. His arms were by his side, hands upturned but he could no longer move his head to look at them. And then, all sensations left him as he became no different from any another exhibit at the Gallery.

Diane stared at her husband, as rigid now in death as he had been in life. As the screams intensified all around her, a smile played across her lips.

Heysel

The remainder of this collection consists of a variety of factual articles and poems

#

A few days after his untimely death, the Sunday Times of October 4th 1981 published a memorial to the great Liverpool football manager Bill Shankly, reprinting his famous quote, "Some people think football is a matter of life and death. I can assure them it is much more serious than that".

Wednesday, May 29th 1985, clear blue skies and the promise of another warm spring day to come. As I left home in the early hours on the first leg of my journey to Belgium, all of my thoughts were on whether or not Liverpool would be crowned European Champions for a fifth time by the end of the day. Little did I know that within twelve hours football would be an irrelevance and Shankly would have been shown to be so wrong.

I met up with fellow Koppite Kevin in Preston for the drive to the airport. Kevin wasn't the best driver in the world, and on more than one occasion we had narrow escapes as we drove to games. I recalled one time when he wanted to check the time on his new 'light-up' digital watch, and proceeded to take his hands off the wheel and his eyes off the road for a good ten seconds as he tried to illuminate the dial! To take my mind off his driving on this bright morning, my thoughts drifted back over the years leading me to this momentous day.

#

I suppose I was always destined to be a football fan, for at just eight weeks old I lay in my pram while my mother sat by the radio, listening anxiously as our hometown team Blackpool beat Bolton 4-3 to win the 1953 FA Cup Final. As the years passed, I moved away from the seaside and my loyalties switched to a different 'Pool, Liverpool. I became a member of the famous 'Kop Choir', and travelled far and wide to watch the side have unprecedented success at home and in Europe. I had seen them win the European Cup four times, and success this evening against the Italians of Juventus would enable Liverpool to keep the famous trophy – an honour only the mighty Real Madrid had previously attained.

To say I was a fan would only be half the story – in truth, I was an obsessive fanatic. Analysts would probably have a field day with me, claiming that I was using the game to hide behind instead of facing up to life. Perhaps they'd have a point there, for I certainly used to turn to football on the far-too-many occasions when my aspirations for a love life were foiled as a student. Whatever the reasons, I put my faith in football, the one constant in my life (at least between the months of August and May) and allowed it to dominate my decision-making processes.

When my only sister, Pat, announced that she was getting married in March 1972, I checked the fixture list and told her that I'd be at Anfield instead. So, while she was getting married to Phil in Blackpool, I was enjoying watching Liverpool trounce Newcastle 5-0 with barely a thought for the events taking place fifty miles away. I'm not sure if she ever forgave me or not – such is our family that any matters of import tend to be bottled up rather than discussed in the open – and the subject has never been raised in more than thirty years.

My own wedding, to Barbara, took place in June 1977, during the close season – another of Bill Shankly's famous quotes concerns the time he was reported to have taken his wife out to celebrate their wedding anniversary during the winter. He cut the reporter dead with words to the effect of, "Anniversary? It was her birthday – you don't think I'd get married during the football season do you?"

When Barbara took ill just a couple of years into our marriage, I took two days off work to look after her. However, she was no better by the Tuesday evening, and Liverpool were at home to Leeds later that night. I was desperate to see the game, for I was aiming to get to fifty Liverpool matches in a season for the first time, and I was going to be hard-pressed to achieve this goal as it was. Consequently, despite her heartrending pleas for me to stay home, my only concession was to arrange to get a lift to and from the game instead of travelling by coach, which would give me a couple more hours with her. Feeling satisfied with my clever solution, I went to the game, leaving her all alone and unwell for five long hours.

I was no different when the birth of my first child was due. I was facing another of my dilemmas as Liverpool were due to play West Ham at Wembley in the final of the Football League Cup on the second Saturday in March 1981, and although the baby had been expected to arrive ten days before this game, nothing had happened. On the Saturday morning, with Barbara still heavily pregnant, I set off for London with my pals, and eased my conscience by getting them to stop at Watford Gap services so I could ring home and check all was okay. It was, and Iain wasn't born until the following midweek – but what could I have done if Barbara had informed me that she'd just gone into labour when I phoned home?

In short, seeing Liverpool collect trophies was more important to me than attending to the needs of my family.

Alongside the successes, though, there was an undercurrent of fear surrounding football, with uncertainty every matchday as to whether or not you would return home unscathed while the violence at football matches escalated out of control. My worst experience had been at a Blackpool match way back in 1969, when a crash-helmeted Birmingham City supporter had head-butted me outside the ground, leaving my nose gushing blood for two full days. There had been many other nasty incidents over the years both at home and abroad, in the streets of towns and cities such as Derby, Burnley, Birmingham, Sheffield, Nottingham, Manchester, Leeds, Glasgow, London and Paris.

In May 1984, I had travelled to watch Liverpool defeat Roma on their home ground in Rome to win the European Cup for the fourth time, but my celebrations were tempered by the nightmare after-match scenes as Roma supporters ambushed the Liverpool contingent and hurled anything they could get their hands on at us. I spent what seemed like a lifetime dodging flying bricks as I ran back to the comparative safety of the coaches – others were less fortunate, with several Liverpool supporters being hospitalised with stab wounds and some were even hurled off the bridges into the River Tiber below.

#

These thoughts flashed through my mind as we journeyed towards Speke, and for all of the anticipation of another trophy, part of me was concerned for what might be about to happen on the streets of Brussels and inside the Heysel Stadium.

As we boarded our aircraft following a relatively quick check-in procedure, I noticed a youth taking photographs of the Liverpool fans. I wasn't to realise it at the time, but those pictures were to be in the morning papers following the events that were about to transpire. All of this was far from my mind, though, as our plane took off and I settled back to take in the full glory of the day.

It was a short flight to Brussels, but as we were about to land we had our first hint that things weren't well in the city. Our travel courier announced that due to outbreaks of trouble, we were going to be driven straight to the ground instead of the original plan of taking us to the city centre.

We streamed towards passport control and passed a planeload of Juventus supporters disembarking on an aisle parallel to ours but separated by a barrier of glass. All was good humoured as we exchanged chants and taunts with each other - we thought we were crazily dressed in our red outfits until we saw what some of the Italian fans were arrayed in, and we laughed at their eccentricities.

On arrival at the ground it was clear from the colours on show that the Liverpool contingent outnumbered our Italian counterparts by at least ten to one, hardly surprising as we learnt that the main Juventus support had been deposited in the centre of Brussels. We walked around the area and it was noticeable that almost every shop was selling small bottles of beer to the Liverpool fans as fast as they could – ultimately, they have to take some share of the blame for the subsequent trouble.

The weather was beautiful and hot, and just a short walk away was a small park by a fountain. It was full of Liverpool fans sunbathing. As we approached it, a car full of Italians had to stop for other traffic. It was immediately surrounded by Scousers, but again everything was very jovial with handshakes between the two nationalities the order of the day. Once in the park we found a patch of unoccupied grass and stretched out in the hot sun for the afternoon.

 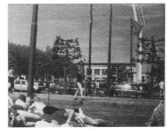

Every now and then we heard sirens as police cars raced through the streets, so obviously things weren't as calm as they looked from where we were. In addition, a lot of the empty beer bottles were being hurled into the road and smashed, leaving glass everywhere. Just before we were ready to leave the park, a young lad of about nine screamed in pain as he trod on a piece of glass, and suddenly blood was everywhere. It probably looked a lot worse than it actually was, but even so it put a sobering view on the afternoon.

A couple of hours before scheduled kick-off time, we made our way to the ground. Everything appeared at first to be well organised at the Liverpool end, with police blocking the small gaps in the wire-mesh fencing and checking tickets before allowing fans through. We did see one lad, though, trying to slide under the fencing to get through this first checkpoint, for, as usual, too few tickets had gone to the supporters of the two teams contesting the final.

We walked further towards the Juventus end and noticed how things were suddenly different. At first there were unguarded gaps between the fence, then there were tears and gaps in the fence and finally there was no fence at all by the time we reached their end of the ground. We walked past hundreds of Italians and started to walk back to our own end, but by now we were inside the fence without having undergone any ticket checks. Kevin and I had seats in section B on the far side of the stadium so we headed towards our turnstiles, but at first couldn't find our entrance - the way we thought led to it, past section Z, was a dead end. I was surprised, though, to see Juventus fans queuing there, for 'our' half of the ground.

We backtracked and finally found the correct entrance and went inside – the first thing I noticed with amazement was thousands of black and white Juventus colours on our end. It was apparent that we'd been given the rough edge of the ticket deal. The end to our right was completely filled with Juventus fans, as was three quarters of the stand I was in. The opposite stand was split about half and half, and 'our' terracing to my left was sectioned off, with the third of it nearest us filled of Juventus fans. Apparently, this section Z had been allocated to Belgians but almost all of the tickets found their way to Juventus supporters. The other two thirds of our terrace were packed solid with Liverpool fans, with only a flimsy-looking fence separating the groups. Kevin, seeing the Juventus supporters, said we were going to have to go through those Italians to get back to the coaches after the game, and he wasn't looking forward to it when – not if - we won.

By now there was just over an hour until kick-off. In section Z, a gap had formed between the massed Juventus fans and the hundred or so Liverpool fans who were in that same third of the terracing. The police led these Liverpool fans out of section Z and round to sections X and Y to try and maintain the segregation – the problem with this, though, was that sections X and Y were already full to capacity.

Kevin and I went to look for a match programme and some refreshments before returning to our seats. In the few minutes we'd been away, section Z had filled totally, and there were no gaps between the four thousand or so Italians and the few hundred Liverpool fans who were also inside that section, with ten thousand or more Liverpool supporters just on the other side of the fence in sections X and Y.

The trouble began with a fight involving three people near the front of section Z, two Liverpool supporters and an Italian. The Liverpool duo attacked the Italian, then ran off, but when they saw the Italians weren't giving chase, several more Liverpool fans came over and started another fight. In a matter of moments it escalated and about a dozen Liverpool fans rushed across at the massed Italians, kicking out at anybody and everybody in their way. The Italians retaliated this time, with about thirty or so of them rushing back at the Liverpool fans, who in turn responded with a charge comprising about fifty people. Kevin was saying they were crazy, and if they didn't stop they'd get us banned from Europe. After this latest assault, the Italians failed to fight back, choosing instead to cram themselves closer together as far away from the trouble as they could get.

All attention in the stadium was now on this trouble, with nobody watching the schoolboy match taking place on the pitch. The Liverpool fans were charging across now in greater numbers, and the Italians were retreating in panic. About half a dozen or so police, the only ones on duty in the ground, went into the no-mans land between the two factions, but a minute later, they ran out again, shaking their heads. Had there been adequate policing, the trouble could have ended there and then, but the Liverpool fans now knew they could get away with anything. They waded into the Italians again, battering them with fists, feet, flagpoles and any other objects they could lay their hands on. At the top of the terracing, any Italians now entering were set upon as soon as they came in. The flimsy fence between the sections had gone during the disturbance, and the Italians were crammed into one corner of section Z, trying desperately to clamber onto the pitch surround and safety. Unbelievably, the police were trying to force them back, even though it was clear that they were trying to escape to safety. The front of the terracing had been bedecked with Juventus flags and banners – now Scousers were tearing it down.

Meanwhile, at the other end the main Juventus support tore down the fencing separating them from the pitch and bombarded the police with missiles. The trouble at our end was worsening as Italians clambered desperately onto the pitch, climbing over fellow supporters in their panic. The fencing at the front had been flattened by the crush of people, and all the while the Liverpool fans were indiscriminately attacking anybody and everybody on the outside of the group, forcing the crowd further and further into a corner. Such was the crush that a wall at the side collapsed with a sickening thud, spewing fans everywhere.

The pitch was overflowing with escaping supporters, many of whom had been injured getting to safety. Surreally, some of them started kicking a football around, oblivious to what was going on behind them. Some Juventus fans noticed our small contingent, and after vainly trying to clamber up the stand to reach us, they attempted to get the other Italians in the stand to come and attack us. Kevin turned to me and said, "we're dead," and I couldn't disagree with him. For the first time, I was really worried. Thankfully, the Italians in the stand were as sickened by the violence as we were, and they had no wish to contribute to it.

I still didn't realise that this was far more serious than the usual trouble at games as I looked over at the mass of debris at the front of the terracing. People were still forcing their way out, and I noticed that there was what looked like a man's body on the ground, with everybody just trampling all over it. I shouted, "Hey, watch out" in shock, then realised that nobody could take any notice of me even if they'd wanted to.

It wasn't long after this that the last Italian was 'removed' from Z section. A Scottish Liverpool fan in our section was shouting at the Liverpool fans to 'get stuck in' even more to the Juventus fans, while another turned to me and asked, "How many are dead now?" I must have looked surprised, for he said, "What do you think they're carrying off on stretchers? There were twelve dead before".

Up until that moment, I had refused to acknowledge the seriousness of the riot. After all, it was only a football match, and fights at soccer grounds had been occurring for years now. But limp bodies were being carried on sections of broken fencing from the terracing and I suddenly had to believe that people had died. Odd skirmishes were occurring on the pitch now as injured Liverpool fans, being treated by ambulance staff, were attacked by revenge-seeking Italians. A cameraman came too close and was chased and kicked by the furious Juventus crowd. More police were on hand now and they moved the Juventus fans towards their end, where they congregated around the halfway line. One Liverpool fan was being carried on a stretcher towards the tunnel, but when he saw the hostile crowd waiting there he refused to go any further until police could restore some order, and even then he only just got inside unscathed.

At the Juventus end, their fans, with scarves covering their faces to avoid identification, battled in front of the terraces with the police, using missiles from the broken down fencing and shattered lumps of concrete. The police were totally passive during all of this, allowing them to do as they pleased. At one stage the mob ran all the way round the ground to the Liverpool end, hurling rocks into the ranks of the Liverpool fans in the sections V, W and X on the opposite side to me.

It was quieter now at our end, as if the enormity of what had been done began to sink into the heads of the Liverpool troublemakers. The stretchers were still carrying out lifeless bodies, and a steward indicated thirty were now dead. The tannoy, which had in vain been broadcasting appeals for the fighting to stop, now started reading out name after name, presumably from Italians trying to contact lost friends and relatives. I looked round at the numb faces around me. One woman who'd flown with us was crying her eyes out on a man's shoulder. I had removed my scarf and covered my red colours in shame - a small, but meaningful, gesture on my part.

It was now the scheduled kick-off time, but it was obvious that there was no chance of the game starting because the pitch was still full of people wandering aimlessly around. Liverpool's manager Joe Fagan had been out to try and stop the trouble, but he left in tears as he realised that his pleas were having no effect whatsoever.

Eventually, an hour after the trouble had started, armed police moved into the ground and formed line after line facing our fans, with mounted police supervising the operation. Once again, though, they demonstrated their total ineptitude, for rioting was still going on unabated at the Juventus end and no extra police had been moved in there.

An hour after the scheduled kick-off time, Liverpool captain Phil Neal made a tannoy announcement to the effect of, "Listen, we're sitting there waiting to play a game of football and we're sick and tired of what's going on. Behave and then we can get on with the match". He left the pitch to tremendous applause. The Juventus captain came out a minute later to make a similar appeal to their fans, and his worshipping followers, who seemed to have forgotten about what had happened, mobbed him.

At just after half-eight the teams took the pitch to an almighty cheer round the ground – it was as if nothing had happened. Both sets of players, though, were totally aware of what had gone on, and some of them, mainly Italians, had to be persuaded to play in the game.

You will have seen it at home on your television sets – and you probably thought that it was obscene to carry on with a game after what had happened, with fans singing and chanting as a meaningless football match took place. But you weren't there, were you – you only had to turn the channel over, or go into the kitchen and make a cup of tea, and you were back to normality. But we couldn't turn it off that easily – it was real. For my part, I was so relieved to have something else to think about that I cheered for that reason alone. I also knew that playing the match was the one thing that might defuse the situation, *providing* Juventus won - make no mistake, the behaviour of their supporters was the biggest problem now. The covering of their faces to avoid identification indicated that they were professionals in the violence stakes as against the English amateurs.

Thankfully, the football did appear to calm their supporters calmed down and although it was clear that it had been arranged for Juventus to win, as some small consolation for what their supporters had suffered, the fans didn't seem to care. I certainly didn't, and I was desperate for Liverpool *not* to score so that I could leave at the final whistle while the Juventus fans were still inside celebrating the trophy award. Kevin and I made our way to the exit and the second the final whistle blew we dashed out of the ground.

Outside, a solid line of police met us. Apparently on television it said they were going to be policing the route all of the way back to the coaches. This was a total fabrication, as the instant we turned the corner the line disappeared, and we didn't see another policeman all evening. We hurried through the unlit streets, which would have been full of Juventus fans from section Z had the match been trouble-free.

We heard some disturbances taking place, but ignored them and ran for the coaches, where we were able to relax a little. A girl sitting near said, "that's it, we're only in the UEFA Cup next year". I turned to her and said, "we'll be banned". There could be no doubt about that.

Back at the airport we saw Martin and Ron, two of the people we normally travelled to matches with. They didn't seem in the least bit concerned about what had happened - Ron, in fact, was getting irate with having to wait to board the planes and shouted, "Come on, the new season starts on August 17th!"

On the flight back we were all given cards to fill in with our names and addresses to hand into the police on our arrival in Liverpool, so that they'd have us in their records as 'safe'. While waiting to go through customs I listened as a family in front of me spoke with one of the police, who described what it had been like on the television. He confirmed that about forty had died with nearly five hundred injured. Scores of television crews were all around the airport, including some from Italy, stopping and interviewing odd people about the incidents. One fan, asked if he'd go to Europe again, replied, "No way", and I began to think about never going to an away game again, although at the time I still intended going back to Anfield. The interviewer then went up to another lad and asked him what he thought. "Great" was the reply, "I've had a fantastic time", and he walked on, leaving me feeling utterly disgusted.

I bought an early edition morning paper, read from the numerous pages detailing the horror and rang Barbara to let her know that we were safely back in England. She told me our next-door neighbour had offered her some sleeping pills so she could get some rest, but she'd refused, preferring to wait up for any phone calls. The phone had apparently been ringing all evening with anxious relatives wanting to know if I was alright, but obviously in those pre-mobile phone days, she couldn't tell them anything. I asked her to ring Kevin's parents to let them know we were back, and then we drove home from Liverpool.

I remember vividly getting in bed and squeezing Barbara tight, almost restricting her breathing – I just didn't want to let go of her at all. The next morning she was going to take Iain and Shelley for a walk in the park, leaving me in bed. Even though I'd only had a little sleep, I didn't want to be left on my own so I got up and went with them, lying down on the grass in the park in the hot sun – a macabre reminder of twenty-four hours earlier. But, after my worries that I'd never see my family again, I didn't want to be separated from them, and I began to reappraise just what the important things in life really were. Apparently I didn't shout at Iain and Shelley for days, whatever they did – and that, for me, was most unusual.

#

As the summer passed, I decided that I probably wouldn't be going back to watch football, whether at Liverpool or anywhere else - the Heysel tragedy had killed my love of the game. I finally made my decision when the phone rang a couple of days before the first fixture of the 1985-86 season. As I picked it up, I recognised Kevin's voice on the other end of the line:

"Hi, what time are you coming round on Saturday?"

It was the first time we'd spoken since the events of eleven weeks earlier, and yet he made no reference to them at all. I suppose that finally clinched matters for me, and I replied:

"I'm not going, Kev. I've been thinking about it over the summer, and I've decided I'm not ready to go back yet – perhaps later in the season, but not just now."

There was a pause for a couple of seconds, then:

"Yeah, I know what you mean. I cried when I saw the pictures on tele, and I wondered too. But not everyone feels that way – I spoke to Martin, and he almost seemed glad it had happened."

I don't know whether or not that last statement was true, but we ended our chat then with an implicit expectation that I'd get back in touch when I did decide to return, but that contact never happened – in fact I've only seen Kevin on a couple of brief occasions in two decades. He'd been affected by the Heysel disaster, but not enough to make him want to stop going to watch the game. For me, though, football was finished, at least for the immediate future.

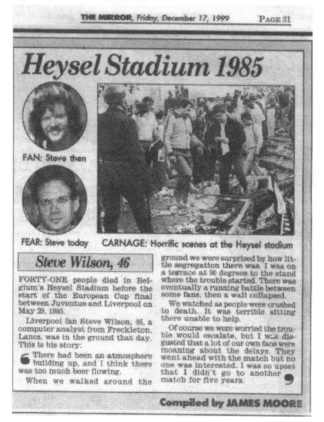

THE MIRROR, Friday, December 17, 1999   PAGE 31

Heysel Stadium 1985

FAN: Steve then

FEAR: Steve today   CARNAGE: Horrific scenes at the Heysel stadium

Steve Wilson, 46

FORTY-ONE people died in Belgium's Heysel Stadium before the start of the European Cup final between Juventus and Liverpool on May 29, 1985.

Liverpool fan Steve Wilson, 46, a computer analyst from Freckleton, Lancs, was in the ground that day. This is his story:

❝ There had been an atmosphere building up, and I think there was too much beer flowing.

When we walked around the ground we were surprised by how little segregation there was. I was on a terrace at 90 degrees to the stand where the trouble started. There was eventually a running battle between some fans, then a wall collapsed.

We watched as people were crushed to death. It was terrible sitting there unable to help.

Of course we were worried the trouble would escalate, but I was disgusted that a lot of our own fans were moaning about the delays. They went ahead with the match but no one was interested. I was so upset that I didn't go to another match for five years. ❞

Compiled by JAMES MOORE

The sun shone strongly that afternoon
as we lay in the park in the centre
of Brussels, our home for the day.

Preparing to celebrate the glory to come
when Juventus were vanquished -
Five-times 'Champions of Europe',
The world salutes Liverpool!

Three hours later, no more smiles.
Instead, tears and looks of horror.
On the terraces below, amongst the debris
of the crash barriers, lie the crushed bodies.

Who'd have thought their final breath
would come at a football match?

This is true tragedy,
Not a shootout defeat.
Shankly was wrong for once,
This was life and death.

May 29th 1985, Heysel Stadium, Brussels.
I mourn the death of my game.

In fact it took another tragedy – Hillsborough in 1989 – before I returned to a football ground. Almost a hundred Liverpool supporters were crushed to death at the FA Cup Semi-Final against Nottingham Forest and Iain and I joined the people of Liverpool as they proclaimed their grief by covering the Anfield pitch in a floral tribute to the victims of the disaster. I was saying goodbye to my own ghosts as I placed my scarf, hidden away in a cupboard for four years, on the pitch.

Many words of tribute have been written about Hillsborough, and I have penned my own contribution to this library. Anfield covered with tributes from the grieving supporters was reminiscent of McCrae's poem "In Flanders Fields", written after the 1915 battle at Ypres – when McCrae was there, the resilient red poppies were showing through, and I imagine it must have looked similarly impressive. My poem uses the format of McCrae's, and attempts to portray my thoughts about another senseless tragedy:

On Anfield's grass the flowers lie,
As does my scarf, once held so high
to show my faith; and on the Kop
the flags, hung on the fences, flop
Gently, amongst each grieving cry.

Tears for the lost - we watched them die
At Hillsborough, and wonder why?
My son and I, weeping non-stop,
On Anfield's grass.

They have a fight, we don't deny -
South Yorkshire police, they will belie
the facts; but truth will out to crop
the lies. Nana, mam and pop,
They won't forget; their tears will dry
on Anfield's grass.

If anything good can ever be said to have come out of tragedy, Hillsborough did serve as a turning point in football hooliganism, for although the problem didn't totally go away, things were never as bad as during those terrible days of the seventies and eighties

I took Iain to Anfield again on the first anniversary of Hillsborough, when the Football League computer had bizarrely decided that Liverpool would play host to Nottingham Forest – my first football match in almost five years, and in the years since then I have managed to visit more than two hundred and fifty grounds across Britain and Europe. But, whatever happens, I will never forget those scenes in Brussels all those years ago.

Glad All Over

Early in 2010, the *Sky Sports* website advertised their schedule of live matches until the end of the season, including *May 22nd Championship Play-Off Final – Blackpool v Cardiff*. As there were still several months and many matches before the competing teams would be known, this was obviously a mistake, but in that *stranger than fiction* way that often prevails, the two sides who progressed through the end of season Semi-Finals were, indeed, Blackpool and Cardiff City.

Blackpool reached their fifth play-off Final, a record, and they were also the first team to appear in play-off Finals in all three divisions. But, as the second smallest club in the Championship, the thought of Blackpool competing against the likes of Chelsea, Arsenal, Liverpool and Manchester United seemed ludicrous.

On the day the Wembley tickets went on sale, I queued for three hours to get three, one for myself and the others for my two sons. I had only been to a couple of Blackpool games all season, but my sons were season ticket holders, attending all home matches and over half of the away games - my last match had been four months earlier, when I had driven Iain and Craig through the ice and snow to see Blackpool play *at* Cardiff in January.

As I stood in the queue, I chatted with a supporter from St Annes, who had brought his dog with him. The long wait obviously proved too much for the animal, as just as I was about to enter the ticket office, it decided to relieve itself over my foot! I signed over almost £300 for three match and three coach tickets, before walking uncomfortably back to the car.

On the morning of the game, I set the alarm for half five, and Iain, Craig and I drove to Blackpool three quarters of an hour later. The tickets hadn't specified which coach we would be on, but with fifty coaches all due to leave at 8 am, we wanted to get to the ground as soon as possible as we anticipated that it might be problematic closer to the advertised departure time.

We arrived at Bloomfield Road before 7 am, and already hundreds of fans were boarding the coaches. It didn't seem as disorganised as I'd expected, though, and we managed to get three seats together on the back row of one that was almost full and seemed ready to depart. Just as I was thinking how easy it had been, we were all told we had to get off again – I still don't know why. It was even busier outside now, but after some to-ing and fro-ing, we managed to find another coach with spare seats. Iain and Craig sat together, I was on the row behind them, and after a short wait for the last couple of passengers, we were on our way at 7:40. I was fortunate enough to have the seat to myself, and was able to relax in some comfort as I settled down for the journey south.

We stopped after a couple of hours at Norton Canes services on the M6 toll road, and were met with the sight of thousands of Blackpool fans thronging every available space – there were so many coaches there, ours couldn't even reach a parking spot and had to stop by the grass verge. It seemed as if almost all of the near 40,000 travelling Blackpool fans had decided to stop for breakfast at the same time.

We set off again almost an hour later, but it was still surprisingly clear on the roads, and we arrived at Wembley before 1 pm. The coach park saw Blackpool fans and coaches outnumber those from Cardiff ten to one, although we knew that Cardiff would have at least as many supporters as us at the game. There was one unsavoury incident, when a partially-sighted Blackpool fan was struck a glancing blow by one of the coaches, and he tumbled to the ground, cutting his eye. However, after a few minutes and several helping hands, he was on his feet again, albeit a little unsteadily.

It was the hottest day of the year to date, and as big as contrast as you could possibly get from the game at Cardiff in freezing temperatures just over four months earlier. A Blackpool trumpeter played the national anthem, and Blackpool fans on the concourse joined in the rendition, as our protest at the officials' decision not to play the anthem prior to the game for fear of angering the Welsh supporters – it was noticeable that they were allowed to sing their anthem, *Men of Harlech* as part of their pre-match warm-up!

Before taking our seats, we bought exorbitantly overpriced drinks from the stadium outlets, but in that heat, we had little option. Our seats were perfectly positioned – at £64 a ticket, I expected nothing less – directly behind the goal, but we were sat in direct sunlight throughout the entire match. Blackpool began the brighter, but Cardiff exploited weaknesses in the Blackpool defence, with Chopra striking the post from close range. It was a lucky escape for Blackpool, but when Chopra had another chance, after eight minutes, he made amends for his earlier miss, shooting low beyond Gilks into the corner of the net.

Undeterred, Blackpool continued with their passing game, and kept play in the Welsh half of the pitch. Five minutes after the goal, we were awarded a free kick on the edge of the area when McPhail handled Vaughan's cross. Charlie Adam curled the ball beautifully over the Cardiff defensive wall and beyond Marshall for a stunning equalising goal that sent the 37,500 Blackpool fans wild – that goal alone justified the ticket price.

Blackpool continued to force Cardiff back, and Vaughan and Adam both struck shots just wide, but as the pitchside temperature reached 106.7 degrees, Cardiff went ahead again when Ledley beat the defence and slipped the ball beyond the advancing Gilks eight minutes before half time.

Rather than deterring Blackpool, the setback fortified the seasiders, and two minutes later, Gary Taylor-Fletcher struck a shot from the edge of the area that beat Marshall but came back off the post, before being scrambled behind. From the corner, 'Pool's decision to attack in numbers paid off as first Campbell, then Evatt, saw efforts blocked, but Taylor-Fletcher reacted quicker than the Cardiff defenders to nod the ball over the line from close range.

Cardiff were stunned by the Blackpool performance, and as the game entered first half stoppage time, DJ Campbell broke into the area, only for the ball to run free to Ormerod, who poked it under Marshall to put Blackpool ahead. There was still time for Cardiff to mount one more attack, and again the ball finished in the net, but thankfully, the linesman's raised flag curtailed the South Wales celebrations. The half time whistle blew shortly afterwards to bring to an end a truly magnificent half of entertainment.

Iain and Craig tried to buy some more bottled water at half time, but such was the queue they had to return to their seats empty handed, having missed the restart. The second half was just as open as the first, but whereas Blackpool had been totally dominant before the break, Cardiff pressed relentlessly throughout the second period. It was one of the most nerve-wracking times I can remember as I continually looked at the slowly-changing timer on the big screen. Chopra hit a shot against the bar, McCormack was narrowly wide with his efforts, and Gilks flapped and missed a couple of efforts, one bouncing inches the right side (for us) of the post,

Blackpool had chances of their own to seal the game, especially when Adam fired wide and Southern blazed an effort over the bar. The minutes passed interminably slowly, and an additional four were added for substitutions and injuries, prolonging the agony. As Cardiff committed everybody to attack, Burgess should have sealed the victory in injury time when through on goal, but he allowed the ball to run too far and Marshall pounced on it. Cardiff launched one final attack, but when the ball passed harmlessly through to Gilks, the referee blew the whistle one final time and the unbelievable had happened – Blackpool were in the Premier League!

The celebrations began in earnest, and there were tears mingled with joy for many of the Blackpool supporters. The fans' anthem, *Glad All Over*, played over the tannoy as the team celebrated in front of the legions of fans, followed by *We Are The Champions*, a fitting climax to a day few Blackpool fans thought they would ever see.

Eventually, after plenty of celebrating, we returned to our coach and the luxury of a cold drink before our journey home. The reality was now setting in – Blackpool would be richer by the tune of ninety million pounds over the next four years. But it wasn't about the money. Although it cost us £100 each for the day, the look of pure joy on the faces of Iain and Craig was priceless. And perhaps - as is supposedly the case if you get covered in bird droppings – a dog peeing on your foot might in future be seen as a good luck charm.

A Hitchhiker's Guide to the A47

Hitchhiking nowadays is as rare as a fulfilled promise from an election manifesto, yet in the early 1970s, it was just about the *only* way for a student to travel; on every motorway slip road, there would be several hitchhikers, individuals and couples, all waiting patiently for their turn as the traffic joining the motorway would invariably stop to offer a lift.

I was at college in Stafford in the early 1970s, and hitched my way around the country for the next few years, with the only time I had problems coming when I inadvertently stood at the southbound slip road once when I was heading north, resulting in an unnecessary extra thirty miles to my journey! But all the experiences I would have in future years could have been missed had I listened to reason and abandoned hitchhiking following my first experience waving my thumb.

It was the first week of 1972, and I followed Liverpool FC, travelling by train from Stafford to Liverpool for every home fixture. However, rail travel was costly, and made a big dent in my student grant, so I tended to avoid going to away matches until my flat mate Pete, a fellow football fan, suggested we hitch to games.

Liverpool were at Leicester the next day, a journey of a mere fifty miles, and Pete and I left our flat early on the Saturday morning, giving ourselves ample time to complete the journey prior to the 3 p.m. kick-off. Our selected route was via Lichfield, which really was where our problems began; had we chosen the motorways to cover part of the distance, we would have undoubtedly found more success. By 2 p.m., we were still more than thirty miles from Leicester, and had just decided to give up when a white van, packed with Liverpool supporters, passed us, then stopped; they had seen my scarf, and gave us a lift to the ground. They did seem surprised that we were trying to hitch, and couldn't understand why we hadn't tried to 'bunk' a rail journey, but, for all my faults, I wasn't into such activities.

We arrived at the ground seconds after kick-off, just in time to see Leicester score the only goal of a truly uninspiring game. At full time, Pete and I headed out of the ground and prepared for our journey back home. The lads who had given us a lift weren't going back northwards, so we had to rely on our thumbs once more.

I thought it would be much easier this time, as we headed for the busy A47, which we reached at about 5 pm. We had two choices, to stand there, thumbs outstretched, in the hope that somebody would stop, or to walk along, waving our thumbs at the traffic; we chose the latter, partially because it was too cold to stand as the temperatures dipped.

Hundreds of cars passed us; not a single one stopped. We had been walking for hours, covering several miles of the journey home, before we had some success; a double-decker bus pulled up, and we gratefully clambered aboard. Unfortunately, we had misinterpreted his actions; he wasn't offering two hitchers a lift, he had stopped 'on demand' to pick up two passengers. He dropped us off again a short while later, and we were made to pay for even that short journey, which cut deep into our tiny pile of coins.

We had one rest stop, for much needed food and drink in a roadside pub, before continuing our trek. Finally, at 1 a.m., and after eight hours and twenty-odd miles on the road, we were offered a lift into Lichfield.

Fortunately, once we had been given our first lift, it became much easier afterwards, and we arrived back at the flat at 3 a.m. I don't remember much about the latter part of the journey, but do know that my feet were a mass of blisters.

The experience would have been enough to put any sane person off hitchhiking for life, and had I been blessed with both money and sense, I would probably have never tried again; but I wasn't, so I did. Fortunately, I never had another experience like that, and I met some wonderful people over the years. Pete, however, wasn't as lucky; he hitched on his own to a night game at Cardiff and ended up sleeping rough in somebody's garden as he couldn't get a lift back.

Perhaps my problem wasn't the fact that I hitched to Leicester, but that I hitched to Leicester with Pete.

Vegetarian Rhapsody

Is this the real deal?
Did you check it at all?
Bought in a market -
No return if the fruit's too small.
Open your eyes,
And look at the size of these!
I don't like melon, caulie or aubergine,
So why'd you bring them home, in your bag?
You know they make me gag.
All that I can think is you did it on purpose, you're mean; so mean.

Edward,
Come and peel the spuds,
Put the saucepan on to boil, fill the fryer with fresh oil
Edward...what have you just done?
You've only gone and thrown the sprouts away!
Edward ohohohoh
You've just left the pots to dry,
If I wash them all up again tomorrow
Will you put the knives away when you peel the potatoes?

Come on, the kettle's boiled,
Steam rising to the roof, pour the tea and tell the truth,
Did you check the labels for gelatine?
For you know I can't eat anything like that.
Edward noooo,
Don't eat that pork pie!
I wonder if you've got any sense at all.

I see a figure that looks something like a man
Scaring me as I see that he's made from pancetta,
Covered all in bacon, and then I awaken – see
How my mind goes each time I doze,
I'm scared to close my eyes. I froze
From head to toes in repose – I see my foes!

I'm just a veggie, I cannot eat meat
She's just a veggie, she needs to have a treat
Spare ribs, rump steak, corned beef and pig's feet
Apples, pears, lettuce, beet, they are what I eat
Fish fingers, lamb, a slice of breaded ham
(I want cress!) *Beefburgers, oozing juice, such a mess!*
(Give me peas!) *Pork sausage! We will ignore your pleas*
(Artichoke) *Meat is not a joke*
(Runner bean) *Fatty cut or even lean*
(Celery) *Duck is right for me* (Cabbage leaf) Oh
No, no, no, it can't be so,
Oh Mr. Butcher, Mr. Farmer, Mr. Grocer, let me go
The abattoir has a banquet put aside for me, for meeeeeeeeeee!

Do you think you can force me to start eating meat?

Do you think if you nag me I'll admit defeat?
No, Edward, you've lost the battle Edward,
So go on, get out, its time you got right out of here.

Only veggies matter, kale and broccoli
Only veggies matter,
Only veggies matter to me …

Any way the plants grow...

My Favourite Sports

Ippons at judo and shooting the bullets,
Brazilian football, all flair and mullets
New balls and 'Hawkeye' and shots off the frame
These are a part of the Olympic Games.

Show jumping ponies and gymnasts with style,
Fencers, when beaten, who sit in denial
Cyclists with sideburns receiving acclaim
These are a part of the Olympic Games.

Girls in bikinis playing beach volleyball
Swimmers and rowers, each giving of their all
Seven young athletes, each holding the flame
These are a part of the Olympic Games.

When the boss shouts, when the tea's cold,
When all hope has gone,
Just switch on and view the
Games on the TV,
And this is only week one!

Winning Combination

From a single shaped reed straw, a length of bamboo
Or a feather of goose - even peacock will do -
Perhaps chalk or clay, maybe graphite or wax
Or a Parker or Biro, fresh from their packs.

Onto ancient cave walls or dried animal hide
Or possibly birch bark - that's for you to decide.
Reeds and papyrus in days of Ancient Greece
The Chinese brought paper, why not use a piece?

Ephemeral thoughts finally come in a flash -
You concentrate hard with a touch of panache -
Experience of life, remembering what's read
Seeking inspiration - it's all in your head.

Each, by itself, is vital, for sure
But when put together, the sum is far more;
Combined on a work-desk, where the magic lies,
Then on to the glory, the victory, the prize.

Fifteen to One

Numbers are everywhere in the modern-day world
Especially in sport, when the flags are unfurled.
Whether individual or team, the aim is to win
So from fifteen to one, let the countdown begin.

Ten years ago our fifteen ruled supreme -
With Jonny's late kick we were living the dream.
The Aussies were humbled, and on their own turf,
As Webb Ellis came home to the land of his birth.

On fourteen occasions a Brit's ruled the scene
From Hawthorn to Button, with nine in between
Overtaking at speed, changing tyres in a flash
For lap after lap before the victory dash.

At the thirteen-a-side game Australia are best
World Champions nine times as they thrashed all the rest
But they lost it in '08, to great rivals NZ
A defeat that the Kangaroos look back on with dread.

Great Britain and Europe master the small ball
As on a dozen occasions they've triumphed overall.
The 'Miracle of Medinah', close to Michigan's shore,
Was golf at its best, leaving us all wanting more.

It's almost half a century since that famous July day
When more than ninety thousand swarmed down Wembley Way.
"They think it's all over," the commentator said -
And it was for the Germans faced by eleven men in red.

From the green turf of Wembley to a green baize instead
And ten English winners who've potted the red
To become the World Champion, some time after time,
Three - all called Davis - amassing twenty-nine.

The next one is strange, as there are nine in an eight.
British success, after a near ninety year wait,
Came at Sydney 2000, when the eight with the oars
Plus the one doing the shouting led them home through the roars.

At London 2012, Britain's cyclists were best,
As they won eight gold medals, outsprinting the rest,
With Jason and Chris, and Laura as well,
Doing it twice, while the spectators did yell.

In Munich '72, he glided through the pool
On his way to seven golds, while the ladies did drool
Over the Hungarian Yank with the trademark moustache,
Smashing World Records during his victory dash.

The ice hockey six became legends one day,
At Lake Placid in '80. Unfancied USA
Beat the Soviets 4-3, and went on to the gold

And 'Miracle on Ice' was the story they told.

In five separate classes Britain ruled the waves
With 'Big Ben' the master and the rest all his slaves.
And who can forget our three blondes in a boat
In their strangely-named class? They get my vote.

On the track in Athens one Saturday night
Four British athletes knew they faced a tough fight.
The Americans, clear favourites, the best ever seen,
Were beaten when Lewis-Francis held off Maurice Greene.

Who would have thought we would watch horses dancing?
We did so at Greenwich, enjoying their prancing.
Laura, Carl and Charlotte were the heroes on the day
As yet another gold came Team GB's way.

More dancing, on ice this time, with classical tone,
As Ravel's Bolero showed their skills at full hone,
Giving Torvill and Dean a dozen perfect scores
Which three decades later still warrants applause.

For seventy-six years we'd been starved of success
In men's singles tennis - no more and no less -
Until Andy beat Novak under the lights of New York
To win the Grand Slam and put an end to the talk.

From fifteen-man teams to a man all alone -
The numbers don't matter if you're watching at home.
One becomes millions as we share, every day,
In the triumphs and failures that the games bring our way.

The numbers:

- 15 – England's Rugby Union fifteen defeat Australia 20-17 in the 2003 World Cup Final thanks to Jonny Wilkinson's extra-time drop goal. They brought home – the Webb Ellis trophy, named after William Webb Ellis, the Rugby School pupil accredited with inventing the game
- 14 – Great Britain has produced the Motor Racing World Champion on fourteen occasions:
- 13 – Australia's thirteen have won 9 out of 13 Rugby League World Cup tournaments, but they lost to New Zealand in the most recent final (2008)
- 12 - British and Europe have had twelve Ryder Cup victories, the latest (at Medinah in 2012) seeing them fight back from 4-10 down to win 14 ½ - 13 ½ .
- 11 - England's footballing eleven won the World Cup in 1966, defeating West Germany 4-2 in the Wembley final. Commentator Kenneth Wolstenholme uttered the immortal lines "Some people are on the pitch - they think it's all over – it is now" as Hurst scored the fourth goal in the final minute
- 10 - England have had ten World Snooker Champions, three of them named Davis, with Joe triumphing on fifteen occasions, Fred on eight and Steve on six.
- 9 – Great Britain's Men's coxed rowing team (eight rowers plus the coxswain) won gold at the Sydney Olympics in 2000, the first such triumph for more than eighty years.
- 8 – Team GB dominated the cycling at the 2012 London Olympics, winning eight gold medals (Hoy, Kenny and Trott each winning two).
- 7 – American swimmer Mark Spitz won 7 gold medals at the 1972 Munich Olympics, all in World Record times

- 6 – Later filmed as 'Miracle on Ice', the USA six defeated the mighty USSR 4-3 in the Ice Hockey at the 1980 Winter Olympics at Lake Placid, and consequently won the gold medal
- 5 – Great Britain has won Olympic sailing gold in five separate classes in the twenty-first century, as well as winning the most medals in each of the four games held. The winning crews in the Yngling class in 2004 and 2008 were nicknamed 'three blondes in a boat'
- 4 – Great Britain's 4 x 100 metre relay four (Jason Gardener, Darren Campbell, Marlon Devonish, Mark Lewis-Francis) won gold at the Athens Olympics in 2004 with a time of 38.07 seconds, GBs first such success in more than ninety years
- 3 - Team GB won gold in Equestrian Dressage at the London 2012 Olympics with their three-rider team (Carl Hester, riding Uthopia, Laura Bechtolsheimer riding Mistral Hojris and Charlotte Dujardin riding Valegro) scoring an overall average of 79.979 points
- 2 – Jayne Torvill and Christopher Dean won Ice Dancing gold at the 1984 Winter Olympics in Sarajevo, with their routine (set to Ravel's Bolero) earning them twelve perfect scores of 6 and another half dozen 5.9s
- 1 - Andy Murray won the 2012 US Open in New York, defeating Novak Djokovic in five sets – 7-6, 7-5, 2-6, 3-6, 6-2 - to become Britain's first male tennis Grand Slam winner for 76 years

Battling With Demons

It began late at night, as these things often do,
After a party at home, with a drink, perhaps two.
I rested my eyes - once everybody had gone -
While listening to a record from 1971,

And I was back at the County, it was a Thursday night
But the group in attendance gave me quite a fright,
For van Gogh's *Sunflowers* listened to Munch's *Scream*
As Rod Stewart's hit album accompanied the theme

Of fantastic fables told with incredible ease
While snow-covered padlocks embraced their keys
And communal reading glasses watched the story unfold
Occasionally shivering, although not from the cold

But in fear, at the battle, on a bridge made of jelly,
Where, dead, in the middle, with a sword through his belly
Lay a cocktail sausage – I didn't need telling twice;
I knew he'd been killed by the battling almond slice

That'd come onto the structure, all high and mighty,
When the pretty young girl opened the door in her nightie.
As the carnage continued I watched timepieces flee
From spot-changing leopards – they'd switched sides you see -

And then from above a booming voice spoke
But hardly had it started when I suddenly awoke.
I wanted to hear the message, but it was too late –
That's the price that I paid for having *one over the eight*.

Storyteller

Frodo the hobbit enjoyed life's simpler things –
Such as pipeweed, laughter and ale –
But when he became 'The Lord of the Rings'
He found the world would be lost - should he fail.
Through Mordor's barren lands he wearily went,
Many times on the verge of defeat,
Till right at the end, just as courage was spent,
Came victory; the quest was complete.

Gulliver's travels took him far off to sea
But the voyage didn't go as he'd thought
When shipwrecked on Lilliput, land of the tiny,
First as prisoner, then favourite at court.
A further adventure left him marooned
On Brobdingnag where he was the gnome,
Cared for by giants, lavishly festooned,
Till an eagle aided his return home.

Ebenezer Scrooge was a miserly sort,
With 'Bah humbug' his favourite oath,
Disdaining family without e'er a thought
When his nephew, Fred, plighted his troth.
But three ghostly spirits visited him one night
Causing the rebirth of the elderly miser
Who, when seeing what ultimately could be his plight
After this Christmas Carol, was wiser.

When Harry met Sally none could have guessed
That the two would ever be friends,
But over the years, Harry slowly redressed
His deficiencies while making amends
For his boorishness. But Sally now wanted more
Than did he, driving the couple apart
Until New Year's Eve, when she left the dance floor
And they embraced, giving the comedy its heart.

Less happy was Hamlet's eventual demise
When revenge he did seek for the death
Of his father, whose ghost demanded, with sighs,
That his uncle should take his last breath.
But Hamlet killed Polonius – an unmeant happ'ning
That led Ophelia to die of her grief -
And though Hamlet slew Claudius, bane of the king,
The tragedy was at the cost of his life.

Sharp-toothed Count Dracula came to this land
With a taste for the blood of young girls,
Resting all day in Transylvanian sand
While at night he tracked victims with swirls
That drew Harker's wife Mina under his spell
And led Lucy to go to her grave.

But trailing the monster to where he did dwell
Saw him overcome and Mina was saved.

Cinderella's step-family kept her in rags,
As a serving girl, down in the cold.
Banned from the ball by the mean old hags,
Till her Godmother she did behold.
Transformed in a flash, Cinders entranced the prince
Until midnight when the magic did end.
But he sought till he found her every day since,
And they wed, giving her riches to spend.

The quest, the voyage, tragedy, rebirth,
Comedy, monsters, rags to riches -
On paper or screen these tales showcase their worth,
Though every saga has its hitches.
We'd be so much the poorer without these main themes
To enchant us and maintain their hold
On our imaginations. Stories bring life to our dreams
And the tellers' write nuggets of gold.

Soundtrack of My Life

As far as music goes, I consider myself to be a late developer, and I was in my late teens in the early 70s before I really took an interest in the sounds that were gripping the nation. That's not to say that the era of The Beatles completely passed me by – although, due to sibling rivalry with my older sister, I actually preferred The Monkees at the time – and I, like millions of other people, was influenced by Procol Harum's *Whiter Shade of Pale* as the 60s drew to a close. This was the decade where everything seemed to change, with Sean Connery's James Bond one of the more iconic figures (although I always felt more of an affinity with Michael Caine's more down-to-earth spy Harry Palmer in *The Ipcress File*).

I went to college in Stafford in 1971 and shared a room with a lad who woke up to the Radio 1 Breakfast Show, thus introducing me to Noel Edmonds and the emergence of glamrock. A month after I started at the Polytechnic, Slade's *Coz I Luv You* reached number one in the charts and from that moment on, Slade were the number one band for me.

It wasn't all about glam, though. 1971 and early '72 saw the release of Melanie's *Brand New Key* and America's *Horse With No Name,* two songs that instantly transport me back to my flat in Stafford every time I hear them. I don't associate them with any major events, but I am back 'home' every time I listen to the opening notes.

Two of the biggest non-glamrock songs of 1972 were *Without You* by Harry Nilsson, and *American Pie* by Don McLean. *Without You* topped the charts, keeping McLean at the number two spot, although if they'd taken account of the number of times each record was played, it might have been different - I spent the evening of my nineteenth birthday with friends around the pub jukebox, and we played American Pie part 1, then part 2, then part 1 again and so on through the night. No doubt the regulars couldn't wait to see the back of our group that evening.

With less than half an hour to go before closing time, five of my friends decided to buy me a 'one for the road' drink. I might have been a student, one of the so-called brighter element back in the 70s, but that didn't mean I always acted sensibly. My five chosen drinks were a double rum, a double whisky, a double vodka, a double gin and a double Bacardi. Shortly afterwards, the effects of the alcohol hit me when I walked out into the March fresh air. We went back to the student flats, where one of my friends, Trevor, played his new LP, Lindisfarne's *Fog on the Tyne*. In my drunken state, I staggered into the record player, causing the stylus to jump across the record, scratching it. The next day, when I was sober and contrite, I bought Trevor a replacement copy of the album, and he let me have the scratched version. The upside of all this was that both *Fog on the Tyne* and Lindisfarne became firm favourites of mine, especially as the scratch on the record was barely noticeable – *and* it didn't affect the title track of the album.

During that first year at college, we had to attend a class called 'Liberal Studies', where we could choose from several options. None of them particularly appealed to me, but I chose classical music as the least unpleasant offering. For the sessions, we sat in armchairs and listened to whatever record the lecturer brought in that day. Despite the music often lulling me to a gentle sleep in my comfortable repose, I found myself fascinated by the notes and Shostakovich's *Leningrad Symphony* quickly became one of my favourite pieces. I also found that, 'old' or not, music was timeless, especially so when I took in Emerson, Lake and Palmer's latest album *Pictures at an Exhibition* so we could compare and contrast it with the original recording by Modest Mussorgsy.

My musical interest was, though, mainly glam, and Hawkwind had a big hit with *Silver Machine* in 1972. I was in a pub in Stafford one night with a fellow student and we started chatting with another lad we met in there. He wasn't a student but a local, but it turned out we had something in common – he had dated a girl called Karen Hemsworth who I had been at school with in Blackpool years earlier. Next thing I knew, we were getting into his car because Hawkwind were playing at Trentham Gardens in Stoke, fifteen miles away, and we decided we'd go along to see them, even though we didn't have tickets. All of us were drunk, and it didn't worry me that he was taking roundabouts at seventy mph – and anybody who knows Staffordshire knows that there are a *lot* of roundabouts along the A34. Of course, we didn't get to see Hawkwind – the concert had finished by the time we arrived, so our not having a ticket didn't come into the equation. That we didn't see the concert was no surprise; what was a surprise was that somehow we managed to complete the thirty mile round trip unscathed.

It would be fair to say that I didn't have much success romantically whilst at college, which was hardly a surprise as the computing course I was on was eighty per cent male dominated, and the other courses held at Stafford – Mechanical Engineering and Electrical Engineering – only had one female student between them. Consequently, when Karen Carpenter sang *Goodbye to Love* in the summer of 1972, I knew *exactly* what she meant.

Early in 1973, Sweet had a huge hit with *Blockbuster*. I was in my second year at the Polytechnic then, sharing a room with a youth from Birmingham, who kept trying to tell me what a blockbuster actually was – some sort of term used for a bus depot worker in Wolverhampton I think – I can't be any clearer than that because I found it so boring that my mind kept wandering whenever he explained it to me!

Later that year, I was watching *Top of the Pops* when a new (to me) group was introduced – Mud, singing *Crazy*. I was mesmerised, and they immediately became my second favourite band. Later, when the whole world latched on to them as *Tiger Feet* became their anthem, I felt both pleased to have found them 'first', but also jealous at now having to share them.

Slade were still my number one group, though, but when they released *Merry Christmas Everybody* in 1973, who would have thought it would still be getting air time forty-odd years later? It was a year later, in December 1974, that my main memory of it remains, when I was working at Guardian at Lytham. My diary entry for that night says it all:

Great night! It was the Christmas party at work at the Lantern in Lytham. I was with this married girl called Alwyn and I was dancing and necking with her most of the night. She's quite beautiful. We danced to Slade's "Merry Christmas Everybody" – and everybody in the room cheered when they announced the result of the League Cup replay - Chester 1 Newcastle 0

Slade, a beautiful girl, and football – what more could I ask for?

In many ways, that was the peak as far as my love of music went, even though a year later I was at the Guild Hall in Preston with my wife-to-be Barbara listening to Freddy Mercury and Queen performing *Bohemian Rhapsody* as glam began to fade into the background. However, brilliant as that performance was, for me, nothing will ever better those long-haired sequined glam groups from the early 1970s as they played the soundtrack of my life.

The Hunting by the Snark

"Are you sure this will work?" I asked of the crone
    As I placed the coins in her hand -
"I need her to love me, I can't be alone,
    I have to be wed - understand?"

"You must say it right," the old witch replied,
    "If you don't, chaos could ensue,
All of my spells are tested and tried,
    But take care what you say and you do."

So I sang every verse and chanted the rhymes
    On the common one dark winter's night,
But my tongue became twisted numerous times
    And that was the cause of my plight.

For instead of reciting the specific words -
    "Bring to me my true love in this arc," -
I became distracted by hovering birds,
    And said, "... my true love, this 'n arc."

With a flash and a bang that shattered the calm
    A shape formed in front of my eyes -
It was huge with two heads, six legs and one arm,
    And sharp teeth, all surrounded by flies.

I screamed and I ran as fast as I could,
    Desperate to get far away.
Branches assailed me as I sped through the wood,
    Praying for the onset of day.

I ran through the night for mile after mile -
    With the beast never that far behind.
My face was stretched taut, I grimaced a smile,
    I feared I was losing my mind.

Then finally I came to the end of the line,
    Denoting the end of my life.
But the Snark said, "I'm here as your Valentine,
    And mayhap I'll soon be your wife."

Thank-you for reading.

If you enjoyed this book, check out further publications by the same author at:

http://www.amazon.co.uk/Steve-Wilson/e/B00DHCTS5G

Printed in Great Britain
by Amazon

11679821R00136